Coming For You

Kristi Belcamino

Published by Kristi Belcamino, 2019.

COMING FOR YOU

First edition. February 26, 2019.

Written by Kristi Belcamino.

COMING FOR YOU

By Kristi Belcamino

• • • •

LETTER. UNSENT.

August 2019

To whomever did this to my bright, beautiful daughter:

This morning I went to see my dead baby.

I watched as they wheeled in the gurney. My baby was covered with a white sheet. The man in the suit and tie asked if I was ready. I said yes. But I wasn't ready. I will never be ready.

When they pulled back the sheet, I saw her face. It didn't look like she was sleeping. It didn't look like her at all. I could only see one side of her face clearly. The other half was wrong. It didn't make sense what I was looking at. Then they told me that, sorry, some animals had got to my baby and took part of her face. Her beautiful, sweet face.

This is what you have done.

I tried to go to her. They wouldn't let me. I fought, but they held me back. I could only look at her through the glass. I wanted to stroke her hair back from her forehead like I used to do when she was a little girl and was scared or had a fever. But they said I couldn't touch my own child.

What did you do to her? I need to know: Did she suffer? I need to know if it was quick or if you made her suffer. I need to know because it will determine how I make you pay.

Because you are going to pay. Wherever you are hiding, I will find you. And I will make you pay. I will not leave this earth before this happens. They only let me see her for a few seconds, but that bruise on her cheek is engraved on my memory. That tiny scratch on her forehead. That gaping hole where her dimple used to be ... I will remember every mark you left on her until the day I die. YOU did this.

This is what YOU have done.

This is why I'm coming for you.

CHAPTER 1

SOFIA

A*ugust 2019*
Minneapolis

Dan Williams arrived at the party late, armed with four bottles of Veuve Clicquot, a guilty grin, and a professed desire to get utterly shitfaced.

"Let's get this party started," he said sounding like a stoned surfer.

As usual, Dan looked disheveled, Sofia thought. His wire-rimmed glasses had slipped a little down his nose, sweat dripped from his temples, and tufts of his balding hair stuck up on the sides.

Sofia crossed the deck to give Dan a quick hug and grab one of the Champagne bottles out of his arms. "Everything okay?"

He shook his head. "I had a patient holed up with a gun. Wanted to kill his wife."

"For fuck's sake," Sofia said.

"All good," Dan said. "Had to call the police, though. Reason I'm late. Now, I have another patient in custody. That makes two."

"I'm so sorry, Dan."

"Goes with the territory. I went into marriage counseling thinking I wouldn't have to deal with this sort of thing, but ha ha. Joke's on me."

Dan's wife, Gretchen, who had been leaning against the deck rail, took a long pull off her beer and then wiped her mouth with the back of her hand. By Sofia's count, the petite woman had already polished off a six pack. Lately it had seemed like everything at Gretchen's Bible-thumping church was considered a sin *except* getting shitfaced.

"Come. Sit," Sofia tugged on Dan's hand, sensing trouble. "You must be starving. Cecile brought her famous flourless chocolate cake."

"Let me unload these bottles and I'll head over," Dan said, leaning over a large wooden tub full of ice.

Sofia gave Dan's arm a squeeze and headed back to hand her husband, Jason, a champagne bottle.

As Sofia walked past, Gretchen pushed herself away from the deck rail, lips pressed tightly together, and started Dan's way.

From behind, Gretchen's four-foot-nine-inch frame could be mistaken for a pre-adolescent boy. She had lanky blonde hair and wore tight Wrangler blue jeans, flip-flops, and a tank top without a bra as if to emphasize her lack of breasts.

She was physically the opposite of Sofia whose Italian roots manifested itself in dark eyes, black unruly hair, and a curvy body that edged toward pudgy if she wasn't careful. Her ancestry meant she was constantly vigilant in checking for the tiny moustache she'd once seen on her mother. She figured she'd spent more money waxing her various body parts than many women did on designer handbags.

Dan—who was still leaning down, poking in the ice— was the only one who didn't see his wife coming. Sofia found she was holding her breath, nervous about what Gretchen was going to do or say. It wouldn't be the first time Gretchen's temper had spoiled a get together lately. A few years ago, Gretchen had "found God" and been born again and now she was nearly unbearable.

Sofia considered herself a good Catholic, but the Basilica was a big city liberal church all about justice and taking care of the poor and accepting and welcoming everyone.

Gretchen's church was all about judging the fuck out of everyone and the fire and brimstone of hell if you strayed from what your Jaguar-driving pastor told you was right.

When she reached Dan, Gretchen jerked his arm and hissed, "You didn't answer your phone. Where were you?"

"Doing my job," he said, his face growing red.

Even across the deck with music playing, Sofia could hear every word.

Gretchen leaned in and examined Dan's clothes.

"That's not the shirt you had on this morning."

"I showered and changed before I came over here. I was sweating like a pig. I thought my patient was going to kill someone. It was an intense god damn night. Give me a break, Gretchen."

Uh oh, Sofia thought. *Thou shalt not take the Lord's name in vain.*

Gretchen closed her eyes as if she were exasperated and dealing with a difficult child.

When Dan looked up and saw everyone watching, a crimson flush crawled up his neck.

Thankfully, Jason chose that moment to work the cork on the champagne bottle and it popped loudly, startling everyone, prompting laughter and squealing as it went flying through the air.

In the chaos, Sofia saw Gretchen's face contort, but could no longer hear her words.

Sofia took another big slug of her Champagne even though she was already feeling quite buzzed.

The party was bittersweet. It marked the last weekend the three couples would have children at home. Next week, their three daughters would be away at college. They would officially be empty nesters. Sofia figured the only way to deal with it was how the friends dealt with most things—getting together to drink and eat. Over the years, the friends had made it through scary illnesses, marriage woes, money crises, Gretchen's river baptism at forty-seven-years old and more. They'd make it through sending their babies off to college, as well.

Out of all of them, this night was probably hardest on Dan, who was having a hard time accepting that his only child, Lily, was leaving home.

Sofia understood. She might have been the only one of their friends who did.

Jason's attitude about everything—including Kate going to college—could be summarized in his standard catchphrase. "The important thing is not to get too excited."

His calm, mellow, accepting nature was the perfect antidote to Sofia's fiery Italian temper and passion. They complemented each other well.

Even before she "turned it all over to God," Gretchen scoffed at her husband's anxiety and worries. She was the one, who when Lily was a baby, would wander off while Lily was wading in the shallow end at the lake when all the friends would hit the beach during the summer. More than once, Dan swooped in to rescue Lily from some impending disaster while Gretchen was distracted. No wonder he was an anxious wreck after eighteen years of that! It's a miracle that Lily survived her childhood, Sofia thought.

Sofia glanced over at her other friends. Cecile and Alex were French to the core and the epitome of European laid-back. You know? The kind who walk around naked in front of everyone. Who smoke weed in front of their kid. They had been eagerly awaiting Julia going away to college. It meant more time for them to indulge their hedonistic ways!

They hadn't batted an eye earlier this summer when Julia and her boyfriend had taken off to South America for a month after graduation. Julia had been gone two whole weeks without even being able to call home and when she did, she told a harrowing story about getting lost in the jungle and nearly starving to death. Cecile and Alex had recounted the story with delight and pride.

So, in the end, it was really only Sofia and Dan stressing out about their daughters going away to college. That's how it had been over the years. Dan and Sofia had bonded immediately as anxious parents, worried about their babies dying of SIDS. After all, didn't Cecile and Alex know that bumpers in cribs could kill little Julia!

And that you should never let a toddler walk around the house eating whole grapes! She would choke to death.

And yet somehow all three girls had survived and were heading off to college.

The six friends had known each other since Dan, Sofia, and Cecile had started Early Childhood Family Education classes when their girls were infants. It hadn't taken long for the three friends to socialize outside of class with their spouses. The daughters had become fast friends, as well.

Despite Gretchen's oddities, Sofia loved her clan of friends. Leaning over a platter of bruschetta, something caught Sofia's eye. For a split second, she thought she saw a ripple in the neighbor's curtain. On that side of the deck, the neighbor's house was alarmingly close. Unlike their own home, the neighbor's house was set back from the street. It was right next to the deck that stretched out from the house to the backyard fence at the end of their small lot.

It wasn't the first time Sofia suspected the neighbor of spying. Once she thought she saw a round white face watching her as she gardened. Another time, while she sat on the deck reading a book she got the feeling she was being watched. When she turned to look, a curtain had fallen closed. The worst was one night when Kate had a sleepover at a friend's house. Sofia and Jason took their drinks out on the deck to enjoy the summer night. The drink had led to more. At one point, Jason had lifted her dress and had her up against the railing making love to her. She leaned her head back and something caught her eye: some movement at the window behind her.

"Oh, my God. He's watching us." She'd tugged down her dress and ran inside.

Jason laughed it off, but the neighbor gave Sofia the creeps. They'd installed lattice fencing on the deck where it faced the neighbor's house, but if she looked closely, she could still see the neighbor's windows through the grape vines.

Tonight, with all her friends laughing and enjoying themselves, Sofia tried to let her irritation slide away. She wasn't going to let anything—not Gretchen's foul mood or the weird neighbor—spoil her party. She stared in the direction of the window, daring the neighbor to peek out again, but the curtain remained still.

Outside the beam from the lights on the deck, the yard and the rest of the neighbor's house dissolved into darkness. It was the night of the new moon and the black sky yawned above without end. Sofia thought a new moon in the sky was appropriate for the theme of the get together. A new life. A new start as empty nesters.

She felt Jason behind her before she saw him. She sank back into his body and closed her eyes. He wrapped his arms around her from behind, nuzzling his face into her hair and inhaling. With one last glance at the neighbor's house, Sofia tried to turn her full attention to her husband, but still felt dread slither across the back of her neck.

CHAPTER 2

SOFIA

August 2019
Minneapolis

Later, under the fairy lights illuminating the warm glow of friendship and alcohol and love on her friend's faces, Sofia's unease dissipated. It would be okay. They would adapt to being empty nesters just like parents around the world did every day. It would be a little quiet in the house, but Jason and Sofia would find plenty to do and say. She was still crazy about him.

It didn't hurt that Jason seemed even better looking the older he got. It was so unfair. He still had a full thick head of hair, even when some of their friends, like Dan, were balding. He was also fit from playing racquetball daily. But his best feature was his infectious smile.

Even after all these years together sometimes he would smile at Sofia, and, if he said so, she would willingly abandon all her earthly possessions to run away with him. Well, only if they took their daughter Kate with them, that is.

Sofia watched Cecile—dressed in white linen pants, a matching sleeveless top, and a massive beaded necklace she'd picked up on safari in the Serengeti—wend her way through the crowd, holding her glass of champagne high on her way over to Jason.

Just then Cecile's husband, Alex, appeared in front of Sofia, bobbing his Lenny Kravitz-style Afro as he sang along to a Nina Simone song. He flashed a smile as she danced with him, closing her eyes and savoring a slight breeze that swept across the deck. When the song ended, Alex gave Sofia a small kiss on the forehead. She leaned into it, closing her eyes for a second.

"Oh, Alex, what are we going to do without our babies?"

At that moment, her stomach grumbled loudly.

"We will all eat and drink and dance and make love," he said pulling back. "First, though, you need to eat."

"You're right," she said. She'd been so busy preparing for the party and making sure everyone had food once it started she'd hardly eaten anything herself. Very unlike her. And Alex was right about enjoying empty nest life. Once again, Sofia was grateful for his friendship. He and Cecile balanced out her neurotic side.

She poured glasses of champagne for her and one for Alex and walked to the middle of the deck, clearing her throat.

"Attention everyone. Please grab a glass and raise it to our bright, beautiful, brainy children who are flying free from our little nests to explore the wonders of the world."

She'd rehearsed the toast, but now as she said it, a lump of something stuck in her throat causing her to pause.

Dan raised his glass to his lips, but Sofia wasn't done yet. She swallowed hard and continued. "May God protect them and keep them safe and help them to find themselves and the life they dream of living. I also want you to raise your glass to yourself, parents and dear friends of mine. Over the years, we've all faced our own struggles and it hasn't been easy. I'm so grateful for your support and your friendship through the years."

Jason lifted his glass higher and solemnly said, "Hear, hear."

"So here is to you—to us—and to a job well done. Our job is over now. Our hearts are about to move away from home. Our biggest challenge now is to let them go."

More cheering and then Sofia raised her glass even higher. "Here's to us! We did it! *Salute*!"

The friends erupted in laughter and cheers. Sofia signaled to Jason. He leaned over and hit the play button on his old-school ghetto blaster. Kool & The Gang's "Celebration" blared and everyone began to dance, whooping, and holding champagne glasses high.

An hour later, when the music had grown mellow, Dan grabbed Sofia to dance. He pressed his cheek to hers as they swayed to U2's "With or Without You."

"God, I love this song," Sofia said softly.

Dan didn't answer. She felt something wet on her neck. She drew back. Dan's face was shiny with tears. He wiped at them furiously. "I'm sorry."

"Oh sweetie, it's okay. It's going to be okay. Truly it is. Lily is going to be just fine. She's a smart, responsible girl. She's a good kid, Dan. Both our girls are careful and safe. They'll be fine. Trust me."

"No, they won't," he sobbed the words. "I'm so sorry." He put his head in his hands. "Kate was such a good kid. I don't know what went wrong with Lily. I tried. I swear. I'm so sorry."

"Dan? What are you talking about?" Sofia glanced around, alarmed and realized that Gretchen had disappeared. "Did Gretchen go home?"

He rolled his eyes and took another big slug of his wine.

"You okay to drive?" Sofia searched his face.

He held up his wine glass. "This will be my last one."

"Good." Sofia wondered if he was so drunk he'd have to stay the night. There is no way she was letting him get behind the wheel right now. But then again, she wasn't the best judge at that moment. The alcohol had hit her so hard, Dan's face appeared double.

Dan stared for a second and then said, "I love her so god damn much, Sofia. Maybe too much."

For a second she wanted to playfully scold him for saying "god damn" but she saw he was more distraught than she'd ever seen him.

"Oh honey, it's going to be okay."

She patted him on the back. Sometimes, like right now, she felt like Dan's mother. Dan's first wife had committed suicide when Lily was only six months old. Dan still beat himself up for not recognizing her post-partum depression—and because he suspected Carla may have known he was having an affair. With Gretchen. By Lily's first birthday, Gretchen and Dan were married. This guilt and worry meant Dan hovered over Lily, obsessed with her safety and well-being. He was the only one of the friends who cried when they dropped the kids off on the first day of kindergarten.

Dan wiped away his tears. "I love her more than Gretchen. That's awful, isn't it? Are you supposed to love your kid more than your spouse?"

"Don't ever feel guilty about loving Lily." Sometimes Sofia wondered if she and Dan would've been more relaxed about parenting if they'd had more than one kid. It seemed that the more kids someone had, the more chill they were.

Sofia envied them so much it made her stomach hurt.

"It's all my fault." Dan was starting to mumble and he was slurring his words.

Sofia pulled back. He was drunker than she'd ever seen him before. "Dan. You're a great father. You've been there every minute of every day for Lily. Now, start on some water please."

Gently she removed the glass from his hand.

He looked down. "No. I've failed. As a father and human being. I've ruined her life. I've always expected too much of her. I never let her just be herself. I always pushed her so hard. It's all my fault."

Sofia frowned. "That's crazy. You've just had too much to drink."

Dan stared at her for a few seconds, as if trying to see through her. "I brought you a hostess gift. It's on the bookshelf."

"A book?" She was relieved he'd changed the subject from his self-immolation to something more normal. "Thank you."

"Was something I saw and thought of you."

• • • •

HOURS LATER, WHEN TO Sofia's immense delight, the police had come knocking asking them to turn the music down after a noise complaint by a neighbor—probably creepy dude next door—their friends kissed Jason and Sofia goodbye. After the front door closed, Sofia started to head toward the deck to clean up, but paused when she saw the book Dan had left for her on the living room bookshelf. It was facing out.

It was called "The Unofficial Empty Nest Guide: Enjoying your new life without children in the house."

The title blurred a little. My God, she was really drunk.

She was about to pick the book up when Jason grabbed her from behind.

"You smell good." His hands began to slowly move up her sides toward her breasts.

She closed her eyes for a second enjoying it, but then put her hands on his to stop.

"We better clean up outside. She gestured toward the mess of empty bottles and plates on the deck.

He began to kiss the back of her neck. "Let's leave that until tomorrow."

"Jason, there's food and everything ... the raccoons ..." His kisses were so distracting that her words trailed off.

Suddenly, she wanted him more than she ever had in her life. She loved Jason so much. Sure, she was drunk, but it was more than that.

Jason had *saved* her. Even though he didn't know it, he had saved her from her bloodstained past. He was so decent and good and wholesome that he countered all the ugliness she feared was inside her. She was her best self thanks to him. And the biggest gift of all? He'd given her Kate.

Bright, beautiful Kate. In Sofia's eyes, the most perfect creature on God's planet. Well, the reality was the past few months had been tough. But she also knew this was normal—for a teenager to seemingly reject her parents to assert her independence and ease the separation from them.

She forgot about Kate as Jason tugged the spaghetti straps off her shoulders and pulled her flimsy black sundress down to her waist. He moaned when he realized she was wearing nothing underneath. He turned her body around and his mouth found hers. After a few seconds, with one hand on her lower back, he guided her to their bedroom. With one kiss, she was completely under his spell and all her worries and concerns melted away. He'd always been the only one who could make her feel utterly safe.

CHAPTER 3

SOFIA

A*ugust 2019*
Minneapolis

Sofia tried to focus on the red hazy numbers on the bedside clock. 4:23 a.m. Her head was throbbing and her mouth felt like it was full of moths.

She needed water. Stat. She felt nauseous, too.

It had been years, possibly since college, since she'd let herself drink so much she was hung-over the next day. Now she remembered why.

Even so, her tender breasts and the sore spot between her legs reminded her that the night had been amazing. She hadn't had sex that great since before Kate was born. Maybe the night Kate was conceived.

Sofia's body had rejected the first three pregnancies. She'd given up by the time they moved into this house, a few years into their marriage. But something happened that first night. She and Jason had made love on a mattress thrown in the middle of the floor, beige boxes stacked in walls around them, and a low flying airplane rumbling the windows as they climaxed.

"Wow," Jason said, lying back. "That was intense. The whole house was shaking."

"I think that was a 747," Sofia said and lightly slapped his arm, laughing. "Do you think we'll get used to airplanes flying overhead all the time?"

"We're going to have to." Jason pulled her close and put her head on his chest, stroking her hair. "Don't you love our new house?"

Sofia answered by kissing his neck and chest, making her way down his body. "I do. We need to make sure we break it in properly, though. I'm not sure that was enough."

Jason groaned in agreement as her lips went lower.

That was the night they conceived Kate.

After she was born, it became harder to have marathon sex with a baby crying in the next room or a toddler who would stumble into their room after a nightmare or later, having a teenager on the other side of a thin wall.

Maybe this empty nest stuff wouldn't be so bad after all if they could do this every night. They'd been loud—extremely loud—and very rambunctious. At one point, after all the covers had been thrown off the bed, they'd not only knocked the light off the nightstand, but also sent a picture above the bed crashing to the floor behind the headboard.

Now, beside her, Jason slept so peacefully, so soundly. She reached over and gently brushed his hair back from his eyes. He made a happy sound and grinned in his sleep. She gave him a small kiss on his forehead and then leaned over, looking for the silky nightgown she'd thrown on the floor. The motion made her stomach heave. She paused a moment fighting down a wave of nausea.

After tugging on her nightgown, Sofia made her way toward the hall, which was dimly lit from the bathroom's nightlight. Walking made her stomach churn. She was going to barf. As she stumbled toward the bathroom, Sofia suddenly stopped stock-still.

Kate.

They'd fallen asleep around two and Kate hadn't been home yet. Had she even heard her daughter come home after that? Kate usually poked her head in their bedroom door and said, "I'm home, mama." Sofia usually mumbled a sleepy reply. But in all the years of Kate being old enough to go out on her own at night, Sofia had never once slept through her daughter coming home. Not once. Never.

Kate's bedroom door was ajar a few inches. Sofia pushed it all the way open. Kate's bed was made. And empty.

Before she could cry out for Jason, Sofia's turbulent stomach heaved and she rushed to the bathroom, throwing up a massive wave of liquid that barely made it into the toilet. After, spitting long streams of bile until her stomach had fully emptied itself, she rested her forehead on the cold tile wall and tried to calm the dark thoughts racing through her head.

Kate might have stayed over at Lily or Julia's house. The three girls had planned to meet up with other friends, too. Maybe they were there. Kate had probably texted and Sofia had slept right through it. Sofia had always told Kate if she were too tired to drive, she should stay over at a friend's house. Kate had done so before. She was a responsible kid and always texted to let Sofia know if she wasn't coming home. The text message had to be on her phone. Her phone was on the nightstand. She'd see the text in just a few seconds when she returned to the bedroom.

Sofia grabbed a washcloth and with trembling fingers quickly swiped at her face and then brushed her teeth halfheartedly, all the while telling herself to remain calm. There was a logical and good explanation for her daughter's empty bed. There had to be. She'd check her phone on the nightstand and the answer would be right there.

It's fine. Kate's fine. Even as she told herself this, waves of panic rolled off her.

As she walked back to her room, Sofia stopped at the long hall window and glanced out to make sure the old Volvo wasn't in the driveway and that Kate hadn't fallen asleep downstairs on the couch watching TV. But the driveway where Kate parked was empty. Across from it, Sofia saw movement in the neighbor's yard.

Over the years, Sofia had only seen him outside a few times. One year he came to the annual block party, but didn't stay long. He stooped to say hi to a six-year-old Kate. He smiled at her daughter and Sofia made her way over to talk to him. Another neighbor distracted her and by the time that conversation was done, he'd left.

If she'd been asked to describe him, Sofia wasn't sure she could. He was short, balding and had a round pale face. He looked like the average apple-shaped middle-aged man. Just someone who would blend into a crowd. One of the neighbors said he worked as a security guard at an old run down mall across town.

Now, in the dark, she watched his yard, eyes straining, wondering what had caught her peripheral vision. Then she saw it: a black and white cat. It emerged from the shadows, crouched and concentrating on some small unsuspecting prey.

Back in the bedroom, Jason's heavy breathing was comforting for a few seconds until Sofia lifted her phone and saw there weren't any text messages. She dialed Kate's number, glancing over at Jason. If Kate didn't answer, she'd wake him.

A shudder that was nearly a dry heave made her clamp a palm over her mouth. Her head was swimming in pain but her fear cut through all that when Kate's phone went directly to voice mail. Terror skittered through her. *Calm down. It's okay. She's fine. She's asleep at Lily's house. Her phone battery died.*

She took several deep breaths. If something bad had happened, say a car accident, the hospital or police would have contacted them by now. Everything was fine. Kate was going a little wild on her last weekend home. Maybe she'd even met a boy. Maybe she was asserting herself and hanging out with a boy in an apartment, drinking wine and listening to music by candlelight. Something that Sofia would have done at her age.

But Kate wasn't Sofia. Thank God. That's why Sofia had come to Minneapolis—to leave Sofia Castellucci behind. Not even Jason knew her real name.

Sofia had met Jason shortly after she'd fled Connecticut and settled into her classes at St. Thomas in Minnesota where not a single soul knew who she really was. The first thing she'd done when the scholarship money came through was pay for a legal name change.

As far as she was concerned Sofia Castellucci was dead. She'd introduced herself to Jason as Sofia Castle.

Now, in the dark bedroom with her head throbbing and her stomach's sour contents threatening to climb up her throat again, Sofia couldn't fight the voice that was always there, always lingering just below the surface. *Something is terribly wrong and you deserve it,* the voice said. *This is your fault.*

Shut up! She hissed the two words. Jason stirred and Sofia realized she had said them out loud.

Kate was just fine. Sofia knew she was silly to argue with the voice but still she did. *Kate's out being a typical teenager. She's not like me. She's good. She's wholesome.*

Staring at her cell phone, Sofia tried to calm herself down. As long as her daughter was safe, she'd deal with any other situation that had come up. As soon as she hung up, Sofia quickly texted Dan, Gretchen, Lily, Cecile, Alex, and Julia in a group message: "Is Kate at your house?"

Then she sent a text to Kate: "Where are you? It's four in the morning."

Staring at her phone, it remained blank and silent.

Panic welled up into her throat. She clutched at her stomach for a second, feeling as if she might have to vomit again. She reached over to wake Jason as she dialed 911.

CHAPTER 4

SOFIA

January 1980
Derby, Connecticut

"911." The voice on the other end seemed friendly, but Sofia was suddenly paralyzed, frozen. She'd done it. She'd dialed the cops.

"911. Please state your emergency."

"My name is Sofia Castellucci. I live at 1847 Old Springs Road."

A slight pause. "Hi, Sofia. How old are you, honey?"

"Ten." Sofia twirled the phone cord nervously, casting an anxious glance at the dark door to the basement. She'd run up the stairs and slammed it shut. It wouldn't lock from the outside, so she'd pushed a kitchen chair in front of it.

"Are you hurt, Sofia?"

Sofia shook her head no, but then realized the woman on the other end of the phone line couldn't see her. "No."

"Why are you calling 911, Sofia?" The dispatcher's voice sounded nice, but there was something else there, too. Like she was upset. Or worried.

"There's something in my basement. It has blood on it."

Another pause. "Did you tell your parents?"

"No."

Long silence. It sounded like mumbling on the other end.

"Sofia, can you go get your mom or dad and have them come to the phone?"

"They aren't here."

"It's one in the morning, sweetie. Where are they?" The dispatcher's voice sounded very concerned now.

"I don't know." Sofia looked over at the door again. Did the doorknob move? She was imagining things.

"Okay, I've got some nice police officers on their way over there to check on you and make sure everything is okay."

"I'm not supposed to call you."

"What?" The dispatcher sounded confused.

"My dad said we don't call the police. But Mr. Truso at school said if we were ever really scared or something really bad happened to call 911."

The dispatcher let out a long sigh. "You did good, honey. You did the right thing."

"Okay." But Sofia wasn't convinced.

"Sofia, are you still there?"

"Yes." She looked over to see that a knife was missing from the wooden block on the counter. The big one. The one her Dad used to chop onions and garlic and tomatoes for the Sunday sauce.

"What is it you think you found in the basement Sofia?"

Sofia scrunched her eyes closed before answering.

"A finger."

CHAPTER 5

SOFIA

A*ugust 2019*
Minneapolis

The thrum and rattle of a jetliner flying low above the South Minneapolis house was background noise to Sofia. She'd grown used to it over the years, but the two police officers exchanged glances. The roar had cut off the words of one officer completely.

Sofia perched on the edge of her black leather couch, folding and unfolding her hands on her lap. She stared at the two strangers on the loveseat across from her, trying not to barf all over the marble coffee table between them. Jason sat beside her, but he sat back against the cushions. It took all Sofia's willpower to sit still. Terror skittered through her, making her want to open her front door and run down the street screaming Kate's name.

One officer, a kid barely out of school with a military crew cut and a name she couldn't recall, cleared his throat as soon as the airplane's growling vibration grew distant. She squinted but couldn't read the little brass nameplate on his uniform.

He shot a glance at his partner, an older cop sitting with his arms crossed. The older officer gave the rookie a nod. "How has Kate been acting lately," the younger officer said. "Have things seemed normal?"

They were wasting time when they should be out trying to find Kate. "She's a teenager," Sofia said, her voice clipped and sharp. "I don't know what normal is anymore."

She turned to Jason. He was white faced. "She's been a little difficult lately."

The officer leaned forward. "Lately?"

Jason cleared his throat but didn't say anything.

Sofia's stomach heaved and she grimaced. The younger officer shot her a look. Finally, she spoke. "Well, she's been acting different for the past six months, I'd say."

Jason nodded.

"But," Sofia said, sitting up straighter. "She still has always followed our house rules. She calls when she's late. She doesn't just *not come home*."

Panic laced with rage and fear surged through her. *Quit wasting our fucking time and go find our daughter.* Her right knee bounced up and down uncontrollably. She noticed the older officer glance at it.

"Well, in most missing person cases..." Sofia tuned out the rest of what the officer said— "most missing person cases" didn't apply in this situation.

This was *Kate* who was missing.

Sofia could barely breathe. She was hyperventilating and dizzy and nauseous and wanted to run as hard as she could and not stop until she found Kate. At the same time, she felt glued to the couch. The older officer was staring at her. She tuned back in.

"What about 'find your phone?' Does she have that?"

"I don't know. I don't think so," Sofia said.

Jason shook his head. "I tried that. Nothing."

The cops exchanged another glance.

"If this is a missing person's case, we could get the FBI to track down her phone. They have a lot more ways to do that than we do. Why don't you give us Kate's number just in case?"

Sofia rattled off the phone number but then thought about what the officer had said "If" Kate was missing.

Right after Sofia had called 911, Lily had called, voice thick with sleep. Kate was not at her house. Lily said that the last time she'd seen Kate was at a Dinkytown bar called Lucky's.

"You guys were drinking? At a bar?" Sofia felt so stupid.

Lily said that she and Kate had gotten fake ID's a while ago "to have at college."

"This was the first time we used them, Mrs. Kennedy. I promise" Her voice rose. "Oh my God. Where is she? You swear she's not at home?"

"What about Julia?"

"She took off with Joseph early on in the night. I think they went to his place."

Sofia knew from Kate that Julia and Joseph were sexually active and that's why they often ditched their other friends—to go have sex.

Sofia had rushed off the phone to go dry heave in the bathroom saying she'd call Lily back.

Now, sitting in her living room, Sofia was infuriated at the police officer's insinuation that Kate was staying away from home on purpose.

"Her friends said she left the bar alone and now she's gone, not answering her phone, not with any of her friends. We've called them all." Sofia's voice rose in anger.

The older cop straightened up. "We're still not ruling out other scenarios right now, ma'am."

Jason, who was sitting beside her, squeezed her bouncing knee in warning, in a silent message. They needed these officers on their side, to help them find Kate. Sofia brushed his hand away.

She knew the only reason the police officers were even in her house right then was because Kate was still a minor—she didn't turn eighteen for two weeks.

"Something *is* wrong. There is no way she wouldn't come home. She's a very responsible teenager. She's never done anything like this before. You are wasting time asking all these questions when you need to be out looking for her. We *all* need to be out looking for her. Not sitting here doing nothing." Sofia's eyes bored into the younger officer, who looked just past her as he spoke.

"We're just trying to ascertain whether there is any chance she might have run away or fallen asleep somewhere."

"And we've gone over that," Jason said, scooting closer to the edge of the couch and draping his arm across Sofia's back. She squirmed out from under his arm. She couldn't stand to be touched right now.

The younger officer consulted his notepad, which, from where Sofia sat, seemed full of scribbles. "So, you were able to reach her friend, Lily, who said that your daughter ..." he paused flipping to the front of the notepad.

"Kate." Sofia grit her teeth.

"Right, that she was with your daughter Kate," he gave her a grateful smile. "At Lucky's in Dinkytown. Kate said she was going to the bathroom and never came back."

"Yes," Jason said.

Sofia was already dialing Lily.

"Lily, sweetie, I know we asked this already." Sofia eyed the officers, "But we have some police officers here now so I want to ask you again, do you have any idea where Kate might have gone after Lucky's?"

It was silent for a second.

"Lily, this is very important."

She heard the girl take a deep breath. "Maybe she walked to Ali's. They were ... kissing at his house earlier."

She heard Lily's fingers tapping on a keyboard.

"Walked? Ali? Where does he live?"

In the earlier call, Lily had said she'd driven them to the bar. Sofia's old Volvo was still parked in the driveway at Lily's house.

"In Dinkytown. Like, near the bar." Lily let out a loud sob. "Oh my God. I just messaged him. Ali says he hasn't seen Kate since before we went to the bar. Oh my God. Where is she? How could I have let her go off by herself? It's my fault. Oh my God, it's all my fault."

"Sssssh," Sofia said. "It's okay. We'll find her. I've got to go."

But even as she said it, she felt a flicker of anger at Lily, Kate's best friend since kindergarten. The two had always seemed like unlikely friends: While Kate was outgoing, independent, and confident, Lily was hesitant, needy, insecure.

Hanging up the phone, Sofia was flooded with guilt about her feelings toward Lily.

Although Sofia hated it, she knew that somewhere deep down inside she disdained people who were obviously so weak. It was a part of herself that she tried to deny, but sometimes, like right now, when she was hung over and scared shitless about her daughter, it was clear as day.

When Sofia was in first grade, she'd gotten in trouble for making fun of a boy who cried all the time over nothing. She told him the whole class was sick of him being "such a big baby" all the time. She'd had to go to the principal's office. When her father picked her up, she braced for his anger, but he took her out for ice cream.

"It's not your fault, Sofia," he said handing her a double-scoop of pistachio gelato. "We Castelluccis, we go after weakness like a heat-seeking missile. It's in our blood. We have no tolerance for the weak."

Now, in her living room, Sofia wondered if her dad had been right. Maybe she couldn't fight her DNA no matter how hard she tried.

The sun was rising to the east, coating the living room in a soft yellow glow that made Sofia scrunch her face in confusion. The light hurt her eyes. How could the sun be up like normal? How could her living room be so cheerful when her baby—her *life*—was missing?

Jason squeezed her leg again in warning. She wanted to punch him and scream *Quit Fucking Touching Me!* but instead gave him a look that made him draw back.

The police officer cleared his throat. He continued to ask questions. He wanted to know everything. Did Kate have any enemies? Good God, no. Where did she work? Until last week, the bookstore. Does she have a steady boyfriend? No. Is there a chance she was at a friend or family member's house?

"We don't have any other family."

It seemed the older officer shot her a look of pity. Sofia swallowed down her guilt. Her parents didn't count. Something in the back of her mind was clawing to get out and she wouldn't let it. She wouldn't allow herself to think of it. It was impossible. She concentrated on the police officer's questions.

Finally, they seemed to be done. The younger officer opened the front door.

"Wait," Sofia touched his sleeve. "What now?"

"We file a report and—" He shot a desperate look at the older cop.

"And we try to find her," the older cop said.

In other words, nothing.

CHAPTER 6

SOFIA

August 2019

Dinkytown, Minneapolis

Within ten minutes of the police leaving, Jason and Sofia were pulling out of their driveway heading toward Dinkytown, a commercial area in the middle of the University of Minnesota campus—some ten square blocks of small businesses, apartment buildings, bars and restaurants. Except for Lily and Julia who were also going to St. Thomas, many of Kate's friends were going to the U and had already moved into dorms and apartments in the area. The bookstore where Kate had worked for the past two years was on one corner. Like most of the businesses this morning, it was still closed.

The area was eerily deserted—normal for a summer Saturday morning in a college town before the students had returned. The only sign of life was the long line that wrapped around the corner from Al's Breakfast—the smallest restaurant in Dinkytown and maybe the state of Minnesota, a narrow strip of real estate with its counter seating only ten.

Through her blurry eyes, Sofia stared at the framed picture in her lap. She'd grabbed it off the mantle on their way out the door. She fought the urge to roll down the window and thrust Kate's eight-by-ten senior photo at pedestrians, asking if they'd seen her.

In the photo, Kate's long brown hair swooped to one side. She wore a vintage white blouse, all embroidery and lace. She had small pink lips but it was her huge brown eyes that drew people in—in the photo and in person. They'd always seemed abnormally large, like a doll and were framed by ridiculously long black lashes. Her long Italian nose and those riveting eyelashes were the only recognizable physical trait passed down from the Castellucci side. Thank God.

But the best part of her eyes was the joyous twinkle in them. Something Kate's Castellucci grandparents never had.

Sofia had always thought that Kate was fuller of life than anyone she'd ever met. It emanated off her in waves. Even as a baby, she'd been undeniably charismatic. She wasn't traditionally beautiful with that Italian Sofia Loren-type nose, but just like her father, Jason, something about Kate drew strangers to her wherever she went.

Maybe a little of the charisma that Sofia's father had. But nothing like Sofia's dour mother. Marie Therese Castellucci didn't attract people, she repelled them. Even her own daughter. Especially her own daughter. Again, thinking of her mother unleashed something menacing and primeval in Sofia's mind, something tucked back away in a dark corner. Something she wasn't willing to let into the light.

Sofia reached to roll down the window as they came across another pedestrian, this time a skinny young man in a green stocking cap and black tee shirt and jeans. The kind of boy Kate always pointed out was cute. Artistic looking. Boot wearing. Slightly emaciated.

Jason squeezed her knee. "As soon as we park, we'll ask every person we see if they recognize Kate."

He'd always been able to read her mind like that. Sofia had long ago stopped being surprised by it. He'd parallel parked in front of Lucky's before Sofia realized the place was dark inside. Closed.

Another wave of despair and dread washed over her.

The bar being closed suddenly seemed like the biggest obstacle to them finding Kate. Sofia felt like she was swimming underwater as her head swiveled, taking in the block around them. Even moving her head made her nauseous. She cracked the car door and spit bile onto the sidewalk. The look Jason gave her made her heart shrivel. She was hung-over on the worst day of their lives—the day their daughter hadn't come home.

They needed to find her. Every cell and nerve fiber yearned to hold Kate in her arms. When they found her, Sofia wouldn't ever let her go again. They had to find her.

Sofia wouldn't even allow herself to think beyond that.

CHAPTER 7

KATE

F*ive months earlier*
March 2019
Dinkytown, Minneapolis

I wasn't really paying attention until the boy was right in front of me.

Instead, I was concentrating on the big stack of books on the counter. I was rearranging them like the bookstore owner wanted—to showcase the week's bestsellers. It was busy work—I was looking for anything to keep me from thinking about my mom. If I thought about her, I would start screaming or crying or hit something. I hated her so much. Okay. I didn't *really really* hate her, but I'd never been so angry at her in my life. I thought she loved me, but really, she's been lying to me my whole life and keeping me from my family. My grandmother. Who was apparently alive despite my mom saying she was dead.

My entire childhood I was insanely jealous of the other kids who had grandparents. On grandparents' day at school, my mom didn't even try to find someone else to go. Sadie's grandparents were dead, too, but at least Sadie's mom had arranged for this grandma-like neighbor to go. My mom just shrugged when I complained about it.

Now I know why. She's a liar.

When I first saw the message on Facebook, I thought it was probably from some creepy old pervert pretending to be my long-lost grandma. Nobody I know ever gets on Facebook anymore. I don't even know why I checked it that day. I didn't want to believe her, but then she told me things about my mom that most people would never know.

Like how the burn scar on my mom's arm is from when she was trying to cook her own pancakes for breakfast when she was four. Or how she has this one mole on the back of her neck that you can only see when she puts her hair in a bun to take a shower.

What I can't understand, or forgive, is why my mother lied.

My grandma said that she'd explain soon enough. She told me not to trust my mom. She said that everything my mom says is a lie. She also told me not to say anything to my dad. Yet.

I'm so confused. Nothing seems real. Every day I come home and pretend I have a lot of homework, but instead, I go in my room and get in bed. I worry if I even look at my mom I'm going to scream. Sometimes when she's not paying attention, I've caught myself staring at her, wondering who the hell this lying woman really is and where did my real mom go?

I was so upset about my mom that I barely noticed the boy at the counter in front of me. When I looked up and saw him there, I jumped and he laughed. He stared at me with these black eyes and I couldn't look away. It was unnerving. For a second I didn't know what to say. And then when I did talk it was like I was ten again talking snotty to a cute boy.

"What?"

He laughed again. "Is that how you greet your customers?"

His accent was lilting and sounded sophisticated.

Before he opened his mouth, if you looked at him, with his short spiky dreads and baggy jeans, you'd think he was just some really cute thuggish boy from the north side. But when he spoke, he suddenly seemed like he should be on stage doing Shakespeare. It was unsettling. Who spoke that way?

I blushed. "Sorry. Can I help you?"

"Yes." He crunched an already wrinkled piece of paper he was holding. "I'm looking for 'The History of Herodotus.'"

"Oh." There you go, Kate, wow him with your scintillating response. "Actually, I'm not sure we carry that book but I can point you in the right direction, show you where it might be if we have it. It's nonfiction, right?"

I'd never heard of the book.

"Yes. There are actually a few books by him. They are called 'The Histories.' They are about the history, politics, cultures, and traditions of Greece and North Africa and Asia. There are nine books in the series."

"Oh." Again, brilliant answer, Kate. "I can see if we carry it." My tone was officious, businesslike to hide that I felt like an idiot. I started to come out from behind the counter.

"You don't have it on your computer?" He eyed the laptop on the counter.

I shook my head. It was the bane of my life. "The owner is a little old-fashioned. I've been trying to talk him into cataloging online, but it's a slow process. We order online, but we don't keep our inventory there yet. Kind of stupid, huh?"

He shrugged. He gave me this smile and I couldn't help but smile back.

I came out from behind the counter, self-consciously smoothing my skirt down as I stepped in front of him. "Follow me. I'll show you the nonfiction section and the area where it might be."

The old bookstore was a maze with one tiny room winding into another. And then there was the basement, which was more open, but still had lots of nooks and crannies. And had two creepy cats. And was haunted. And was where we were heading.

The cats were doing their usual freak show. Caterwauling and running around like banshees, hopping from old sofas to worn-out armchairs scattered around the basement of the store.

I usually tried to avoid the basement. It gave me the creeps. Today, I blamed the haunted part for the hairs on the back of my neck sticking straight up as I made my way down the stairs. It was that—not him being so close behind me.

We wove through the stacks to a back corner where I swung around to face him. "If we have it, it would be somewhere around here." I gestured to a small bookshelf.

He didn't say anything just stared at me. I held my breath, staring back. His eyes moved down to my mouth and he swallowed. It seemed impossible, but he was acting like he was nervous.

He cleared his throat. "Okay. Thanks," he finally said.

I turned to go and he said, "You're leaving?"

"Yes, I'm the only one here. I have to stay upstairs at the counter."

"Oh."

I waited.

"It's just kind of freaking creepy down here. It's like cold and shit and those cats are freaking me out."

"Yup." I said with a smile, tilting my head. "It's haunted."

His eyes grew wide. "Bloody hell?" His voice was incredulous and he quickly looked around. "Seriously, though." His voice wavered and a panic flitted across his face. "Can you just wait a second while I look?"

I was taken aback. He was six-feet-tall and looked like he could thump anyone who messed with him and, yet, he was frightened out of his wits.

I shrugged. "Okay. I'll probably hear the bell if someone comes in." It was a lie, but I wanted to stay close to this boy. For no good reason.

"I'll help you look." Kneeling, I scanned the bottom shelf. He knelt beside me, reading the titles quietly out loud. It took a while, but then I found it on the second shelf from the top. "*Voila*!"

I plucked it off the shelf and handed it to him, plopping it in his arms. It was heavy. I was rewarded a smile.

"Great. Let's get the hell out of here," he said and took off without waiting for me.

I followed him up the stairs this time, trying not to smile, but it was tough.

He was still at the bookstore an hour later, stretched out on one of our old beat-up leather chairs, concentrating on whatever he was reading.

For the rest of my shift, I mostly forgot he was even there as I went about my work. Every once in a while, I'd look over and watch him beneath my eyelashes. Watch how his brow furrowed for a few seconds and then he'd nod as if he just understood something.

It was cute.

When it was a few minutes after closing time, I cleared my throat until he looked up. Behind him through the window, I could see that the world outside was white with snow pummeling down.

He looked up as I reached for my coat.

"Oh." He sat up straighter. "Oh. What time do you close?" He seemed dazed, his finger holding his place in the book.

"Five minutes ago."

He scrambled up. "Oh dear, I'm sorry." He shrugged on his coat.

I laughed. Who said "oh, dear?" Nobody I knew. At least nobody under seventy.

I waited for him to bring the book up to the counter to buy, but he didn't, just held it dangling from his arm and then, seemingly reluctantly, set it on the coffee table.

It was a heavy book. And expensive. At least for our used bookstore. It probably cost twenty-five dollars or more. Maybe if he was a college kid, like I suspected, he couldn't afford it.

He opened the door and paused. A whoosh of cold air and small flakes of snow swooped inside. Then he turned. "See you next time?"

I didn't know what to say so I just smiled. I'm sure it looked like a grimace. So that wasn't awkward, was it? Totally. Cringy.

After I was sure he was gone, disappeared into the whiteness of the snowstorm, I picked up the book and put it behind the counter on a shelf where I kept my things.

I hoped the boy would come back for it. And I didn't know why.

Sure, his smile was nice. And he seemed smart. In addition, his accent proved he wasn't from around here.

All those things combined made him the most intriguing boy I'd ever met.

CHAPTER 8

SOFIA

August 2019
Dinkytown, Minneapolis

Standing on the sidewalk, Sofia clutched her cell phone, punching in Kate's number, praying that this time her daughter picked up instead of the voice mail message. It seemed as if she'd been dialing Kate's number every five minutes since four in the morning.

As her call went straight to voice mail, waves of panic threatened to overcome Sofia. She tried to breathe, slowly and deeply, but it wasn't working. She gave Jason a frantic look but he was busy on the phone. He'd told her they would search every inch of the neighborhood and he'd called reinforcements in to help.

Alex and Cecile were the first to arrive. Dan and Gretchen texted that they were on their way. Even though there was a spot down the block, Alex double-parked while Cecile climbed out. He was a Minneapolis city attorney so most of the time he thought he was exempt from city rules. Sofia always wondered if this irritated Cecile, who was also an attorney.

Looking impossibly chic in skinny jeans, heeled ankle boots, scarf, and a trench coat, Cecile rushed over to give Sofia a long hug. "Oh, darling, it's going to be okay. I called Julia. She and Joseph are on the way, but she is first blasting social media with Kate's picture asking if anyone saw her. She's worried sick. We all are."

For a second, everything went fuzzy for Sofia and then Cecile's concerned face came into focus before her.

"Sofia? You weren't answering and you were breathing really hard, looking right through me."

Sofia stared at her, blinking slowly. It couldn't be real. Kate was not missing. This was a mistake. Jason was over at the driver's side window of the couple's Range Rover speaking in a low voice to Alex.

Cecile put her arm around her as they walked, cooing in her ear. "We'll find her. It will be okay."

There was a reason Cecile was Sofia's best friend. She was optimistic and smart and cool-headed. Her presence was normally calming. But today it wasn't enough.

As they stood there, Dan and Gretchen pulled into a spot across the street. A sulky Lily climbed out of the backseat, wearing printed pajama pants, pink Crocs, and a baggy U of M sweatshirt. Her hair was in a messy bun and a sporty headband pushed back her bangs, revealing her birthmark, a smudge of red on top of her cheekbone. She stepped out and looked around as if she were lost. Dan struggled to get out from the passenger seat. He wore dark sunglasses and a wrinkled shirt that looked a lot like the one he'd worn the night before.

He wrapped Lily in a hug. She was swiping at tears and looking down and then shaking her head. Gretchen stood by herself, hands clasped on her cross necklace, eyes closed, lips moving, praying.

Julia and Joseph appeared from around a corner and Lily freed herself from Dan and ran toward them. The three teens grabbed each other in a tight hug.

Sofia watched, willing herself not to run over and shake Lily asking her where Kate was.

"I'm so sorry, Sofia," Dan mumbled as he and Gretchen walked up. Sofia couldn't see his eyes behind the dark glasses, but she knew they'd be bloodshot from crying and being hung over. Julia and Joseph and Lily trailed behind. Lily put her face in her hands weeping.

Gretchen looked at Sofia with wide eyes. "We need to create a missing page on Facebook. I can do that for you."

Sofia shot her a confused glance just as Jason cleared his throat. "Thanks for coming and helping. I think each couple should split off and search one of three directions."

He turned to the teens. "Why don't you hit every house or apartment where you guys have friends down here and ask about Kate. I've texted all of you a photo of Kate you can show people. Ask if anyone saw her last night or this morning."

The three teens took off down the sidewalk.

Gretchen was on her phone tapping "What should we call the Facebook page. Find Kate?"

Sofia looked at her in astonishment. "No!" She shouted it so loud everyone looked at her. She tried to regain her composure, but it was too late. "No. No. No. We're going to find her. She's around here somewhere. This is just some misunderstanding. There's not going to be any *god damn* missing page on Facebook."

Gretchen reeled back as if she'd been slapped.

"Okay. Here's the plan," Jason said, interrupting. He pointed out directions to the other two couples, indicating where they should search. Sofia looked at her husband as if they'd never met. Struck with pure terror, she was barely able to keep her knees from buckling. But here Jason was taking charge, sending people off in small search parties.

"Sofia and I are going to start in the alley behind here and then work our way toward the river."

The Mississippi River was only a few blocks away. In that direction, there was a steep cliff with the river one hundred feet below. It wasn't unusual for college kids to leave a bar drunk and later be found in the river. Sofia had always been astonished by how frequently it happened. She'd read a story like that in the newspaper at least once a year. It was always young college men. For a while, she had wondered if a serial killer was at work, but the medical examiner always ruled the deaths accidental.

There was no way that Kate would've wandered off toward the river drunk. She was too smart for that. Shaking those thoughts away, Sofia reached into her car and grabbed the photo of Kate off the front seat, clutching it in one hand and her cell phone in the other.

Dan and Gretchen headed in one direction while Cecile and Alex took off in another. Sofia followed Jason as he went to the end of the block and found the entrance to the alley.

He glanced at this watch. "The restaurant opens in twenty minutes. Let's take a look around and then head back this way to talk to the owners."

"Shouldn't the cops be doing this, too?" Sofia was biting back tears. "Why are we the only ones here?"

Jason sighed. "I'm sure they will do the same thing, but let's not wait around. I can't wait for them, can you?"

"No." Sofia said, hurrying to her husband's side.

He stopped and took her shoulders in his palms. "Sofia, we'll find her. I promise. We'll find her."

He took her hand and led her behind the restaurant. The alley was lined with trashcans. College students probably urinated and vomited out here with frequency, gauging by the smell.

When they reached the back door of the restaurant, it was open. Sofia gave Jason a wide-eyed look and they both stepped inside.

A man with a blue bandanna holding back his hair was mopping the floor of the kitchen. When Sofia rounded the counter, he screamed and thrust the mop end at her in fear. Sofia backed up.

"Holy mother of God! Could have warned me you were coming. Or said hey."

"I'm sorry," she said. "We're looking for our daughter. She was here last night."

Sofia held the picture in front of her, arms stretched out. The man squinted and leaned closer. Then suddenly, he drew back. Sofia watched his Adam's apple bob on his long neck.

She grabbed his arm. "You know her, don't you?" Her voice was shrill, a shriek she didn't recognize. "You saw her last night, didn't you?"

The man pulled away from her grip with a scowl.

"Didn't work last night, but yeah, I seen her around." The man looked away.

"Where did you see her? When did you see her? When was the last time you saw her? Was it last night? Did you see her after this place closed?" Sofia rattled off the questions.

He backed up and gave Sofia a look.

"Answer me." She minced her words, glaring at him.

Jason suddenly stepped in between them. "Sorry, man, we're just really worried about our daughter. This was the last place her friend saw her."

The man held up his hands, palms facing out. "It's cool. I get it."

"You seemed like you recognized my daughter?" Jason's voice was calm and soothing.

The man frowned for a second. "Yeah. Don't she work at that bookstore over on Fulton?"

"Yes," Jason said.

Sofia's hope deflated. He had seen Kate at work.

"Yeah. That's where I seen her. Took my grandson in for a comic book one day. I got a photographic memory. She was working there."

When he saw the look on Sofia's face, he shook his head "You'll find her. You know, teenagers. Maybe she's hiding out at grandma's house or something. My son did that once. Disappeared. Was with grandma. Says she's the only one who truly loved him and got him."

Sofia's face had grown cold at his words. It was if she felt the blood drain from her face. The man noticed and his eyes grew wide.

"Sorry. Just trying to help." His voice softened. "I'm sure she's fine."

"When does the manager get here?" Jason asked.

"Right when it opens."

"Do you have a phone number for him?"

"Nope. Got a key, come clean up before opening and that's about it."

"Okay. Thanks." Jason started to leave. Sofia stayed staring at the doorway leading to the restaurant.

"I'm going to go look in the bar," she said. "Maybe there's something— "

"Hey, you're not supposed to go in there."

Sofia kept walking.

The man hesitated, but then leaned over to hit a switch that turned on all the lights in the front room. "Hurry. It's my ass on the line. But I'll tell you, I just cleaned in there and I didn't see anything. Nobody left anything behind or nothing."

The place was nothing special. Typical college campus bar. Sticky and gritty even after just getting cleaned and permeated with the scent of pine cleaner. A long narrow bar against one wall, red booths against the other wall, small tables in between. TVs hanging from the ceiling. Sofia searched every booth, sticking her hand into the cushions, not sure what she was looking for. She looked on the floors under all the tables. There was nothing. Looking around wildly, she headed toward the bathrooms. Nothing.

Nothing that would tell her where Kate was.

Outside, Sofia walked over to a giant Dumpster. She gave Jason a look full of dread before standing on a wooden crate and pulling herself up to look inside. She took a long strip of cardboard and pushed the contents around. When she was done, she stepped down. Jason was crouched, his head in his hands. He stood and they continued.

Once they came out of the alley, Jason crossed the street to a group of young women, holding out his iPhone with a photo of Kate. Sofia could see heads shaking. She dialed Kate's number again. This time was told the voice mail was full. God damn it.

A young couple in jeans and flannel shirts turned onto the street, arms and hands and fingers intertwined. The girl gazed adoringly up at the taller boy.

"Excuse me? Have you seen my daughter?" Sofia thrust the photo at them.

At first the girl looked annoyed, but when she saw Sofia's face, she leaned down to peer at the photo. After a few seconds, she lifted her eyes and shook her head. The boy did the same. Sofia watched as they walked a little more and then stopped in the middle of the sidewalk to kiss.

Seeing the couple reminded Sofia of what Lily had said about some boy. She punched in another number and didn't wait for a sobbing Lily to answer.

"What's that boy's address? The one you mentioned? You said he lived close enough for Kate to walk to his house from the bar."

922 Oak Street. 922 Oak Street. 922 Oak Street. She repeated the address to Siri, who told her to walk southwest.

Jason didn't say a word, just followed her. A few blocks later they turned onto Oak Street. Sofia walked faster. She glanced at the houses, most with blinds still closed against the morning sun. 900. 903. 909. 913. 918.

There it was. 922.

CHAPTER 9

KATE

M*arch 2019*
Dinkytown, Minneapolis

He came in again tonight.

I tried to play it cool when he walked up, but I could feel my cheeks get hot.

Be cool. Hard to get. Like Lily and Julia said.

When I told Lily about the boy, she acted irritated. "Do you *always* have to have a boyfriend, Kate?" she'd said.

Which was stupid, since I broke up with Tom a month ago. I would never say anything but I think she's jealous. I still feel bad that I didn't know she had a crush on Tom until after we'd broken up. I would've never ever gone out with him if I knew she liked him. It's her fault for not telling me in the first place.

Maybe she's pissed because now that Julia also has a boyfriend, she'll feel like a third wheel or something if I have a boyfriend, too.

"I never said he was my boyfriend. Or even that I wanted him to be. All I said was he is cute."

She rolled her eyes, but said, "At least play a little hard to get this time."

Which sort of pissed me off, but she's right. I threw myself at Tom, but he dumped me after he realized I wasn't going to have sex with him. He was fun to date. A football player, easy on the eyes, popular and all that, but he was sort of boring. Although I would never tell my friends that. They thought we broke up because of the V issue.

Lily and I had a pact to remain virgins through high school. Julia had removed herself right out of that club during the summer between ninth and tenth grades when she went to France to visit her cousin and hooked up with her cousin's neighbor who was freaking twenty-seven-years-old.

Lily and I viewed her with both awe and fear.

Julia tossed her head. "Maybe Lily's right. Maybe you should be a little bit of a bitch. Joseph said that's what he first liked about me."

The truth was that all the guys liked Julia because she was cute and sexy and French. All she had to do was open her mouth and speak and her French accent had boys lined up to woo her.

Be a bitch. Play hard to get. Why couldn't I just be myself?

But tonight, I could tell right away when I saw his smile again that playing hard to get or being a bitch was going to be tough. But I'd do my best.

"Why aren't you out partying with everyone else?" I tried to sound bored.

He frowned.

I felt stupid. "You know. It's St. Patrick's Day. This place is dead. Everyone's out drinking green beer and singing Irish songs."

He laughed, but didn't offer any explanation.

We both stood there for a second. I started to feel my face grow hot, so I leaned down behind the counter, saying, "Hey, I saved that book for you."

I stayed crouched for an extra second, hoping I would get it together before I stood again. *This is not playing hard to get, Kate. Why did you tell him you saved that book? Like you've been thinking about him and stuff?*

"Really? That's totally cool. Thanks." His voice was muffled from my spot under the counter.

When I handed the book to him, he smiled. I smiled back. Damn it. I sucked at playing hard to get. We stood there grinning at each other like idiots for a few seconds and then he gestured over his shoulder at the leather armchair. "Is it cool if I park there again for a while tonight?"

I shrugged, trying to be the picture of nonchalance. "It's cool." I immediately hated myself for using the exact same word that he had: Cool. God. I was the opposite of cool.

He turned away. I didn't want him to leave yet.

"Hey," I said. "If you sign up for our mailing list we send out coupons twice a year for like ten bucks off. Sometimes that's a free book, you know." He turned back and I pushed the mailing list toward him.

It looked like he was about to shake his head, but then he said, "Sure. Okay." He leaned down and his forehead scrunched as if it took a lot of concentration to write his name and address. I pretended to be busy doing something else. He pushed the clipboard back to me and went to sit down. He slouched in the worn-out leather chair, legs stretched in front of him, face hidden by the big book resting on his chest. He stayed until closing, handing me the book with a smile before he left.

It was only after I could no longer see him walking down the sidewalk that I picked up the clipboard.

Ali Yassin, 922 Oak Street, Minneapolis, MN 55414.

CHAPTER 10

SOFIA

August 2019
Dinkytown

The small yellow house at 922 Oak Street had a crooked front porch sinking into the ground on one side. Two ripped rattan chairs sat among a few overturned milk crates, every flat surface covered with overflowing ashtrays and empty beer bottles. A doormat featured a faded imprint of the Vikings football team's purple and gold logo.

Sofia paused at the front door, closing her eyes. Please let Kate be inside. If she were asleep inside this house, all would be forgiven. Raising her fist, Sofia pounded.

And pounded again. Nothing.

Jason stepped in front of her and rapped his fist on the door. This time it opened. A tall boy with a smooth, toffee-colored chest stood there, yawning and scratching his bare abdomen. Dipping his head with its short, spiky dreadlocks, he plucked a pack of cigarettes from a table and scooted one out.

Sofia eyed his cigarette. She'd quit ten years ago but that didn't mean she didn't miss it every single god damn day.

The boy stood with his legs spread, cigarette dangling from his lips. He met Sofia's eyes as he lit it with a match. He didn't speak or take his eyes off her until he inhaled and then slowly exhaled above her head.

"You're Kate's mom." His accent surprised Sofia. She couldn't place it. "She looks a lot like you."

Sofia looked behind him into the dim room.

"That's why I'm here. Where is she?"

He narrowed his eyes and his head tilted.

"Kate?" she yelled it and the boy's eyes widened. She met his gaze. "Well, is she here?"

"Nah," the boy said, exhaling. They heard a muffled voice and then a kid with bleary eyes and a shaved head appeared. A sickly-sweet smell—like a combination of marijuana and patchouli—drifted out of the house.

"Is my daughter Kate here?" Sofia looked around the boy with the dreadlocks to ask the shaved head kid.

"No, man. Was here the other night, though. You remember, Ali?" He looked at the bare-chested boy.

"So, you're Ali?" Jason said, voice full of steel.

The boy with dreads nodded. "Lila tells me Kate didn't come home last night. The last time I talked to her was about eleven." He flicked his ash into an ashtray behind him.

Sofia shot him a glance full of dislike. "It's Lily, not Lila."

"Whatev," he said, exhaling. "I really don't know why you're here."

"This was one of the last places Kate was seen," Sofia said. "We are trying to find our daughter. She might have been headed here when she left the bar."

He looked away.

Reaching out for his arm, Sofia touched him and lowered her voice. He seemed like a bright kid. She'd appeal to his intelligence. "Please. We're worried sick. Please help us. When did you last see her?"

It seemed to soften him. "I told you. Listen, I'm sure she's fine. Here's the thing. She wanted to come over last night but I told her to wait until today. I didn't want to tell her that my ex-girlfriend was here. I didn't want to make her angry."

"Your ex-girlfriend?" Jason's voice was the nastiest that Sofia had ever heard.

The boy visibly cringed. "Listen, I really like Kate. It's not like that. I've been trying to break it off with Jenna for months. She won't take no for an answer. I was hoping last night I could convince her. I was going to tell her about seeing Kate now and hoped that would convince her we were really finished. Listen," he took a drag off his cigarette. "I know you're worried, but I'm sure she's fine, though. She's a smart girl."

Something about having a stranger tell her what Kate was like set Sofia off.

"I don't give a shit about any of this. Exactly what time was it when you talked to her?"

Ali narrowed his eyes. "I already told you—eleven. Jenna was coming over. I told Kate what was up. Told her she should stay with her friends until the situation with Jenna was resolved, you see."

Ali paused, taking his cigarette out of his mouth and examining the bright red cherry.

Finally, Sofia couldn't wait anymore. "And?"

"You haven't met Jenna. Things did not go well. We had a blowout fight, a big massive row. I felt bad and didn't want her to leave angry and drunk so I texted Kate and told her to hang tight. She called me back, pretty pissed off, could tell she was crying, but she seemed okay by the time we hung up. Like she'd calmed down."

"What time was this?" Jason said.

Ali squinted. "Maybe midnight?"

"You like to leave them waiting like that?" Jason's voice was sharp and he leaned in toward Ali.

Sofia gave Jason a look. It wouldn't do them any good to make an enemy of this boy right now. Not when he might know where Kate was.

"It's not like she was sitting somewhere all alone having a pity party. She was hanging out with her friends having fun."

"Keep going," Sofia said, putting her hand on Jason's arm. "What happened next?"

Ali shrugged. "That's it."

"What do you mean *that's it*?"

"That was the last time I talked to her."

"Bullshit." Jason sneered at him.

"Hey," Ali said. "I don't know what your problem is, man. I haven't seen or spoken to her since last night. When I called her it went straight to voice mail. That was it. I thought she was mad at me–and deservedly so—and had gone home. I called her this morning and it went straight to voice mail—again—so I figured she was still angry."

Sofia stared at the boy. "You don't seem very broken up by her being missing. You don't seem worried at all. Why is that?"

Ali eyed her. "Listen, Mrs. Kennedy, Kate isn't your little baby anymore. She could be asserting her independence. Maybe she didn't want to come home. Did you ever think of that?"

He raised an eyebrow when he was finished.

Sofia felt her mouth open in shock. *Cocky son-of-a-bitch*. Before she could process it, Jason took a swing at the boy, grazing his jaw and sending him reeling backward.

Ali came back swinging—one short, expert punch that caught Jason right in the jaw. Jason crumbled. Sofia dropped down to him, screaming. When she looked up, Ali was gone, the door shut tight.

"Oh no. Are you okay, Jason? I'll go get some ice. We should call the police and tell them he assaulted you."

Jason grimaced. "I'm pretty sure I threw the first punch."

Sofia bit her lower lip and helped Jason to his feet.

He put his arm around her. "I'm sorry. I know how much you hate violence," he said.

A twinge of guilt zipped through her. "Do you think she's inside somewhere?"

Jason shook his head. "No. Besides, we can't barge our way in, only the cops can do that."

"Where are the god damn cops, Jason? Where are they? Where is Kate? Where is our daughter?" She looked at him, feeling as if she was barely holding onto any self-control. "Where is she? Are we just running in circles?"

He stood in front of her and put his hands on her shoulders. "Keep it together. Be strong for Katie. We'll find her."

She stared over his shoulder. Across the street, a paved walking trail bordered by a small knee-high brick wall went on in both directions for as far as she could see. The tops of trees and thick bushes lined the wall. She knew the Mississippi River lay far below the foliage.

Without a word, she crossed the street without even looking for cars. Standing at the edge of the wall, she looked down upon a steep hillside so thick with trees and brush she could barely see the river below. Every once in a while, the wind parted the leaves and she caught a sparkle from the moving water some hundred feet below.

Did all those college boys who disappeared drunk from Dinkytown fall into the river somewhere around here? She couldn't think of any reason why they would climb the wall and go into the thick brush. Maybe other places on the walking trail had paths leading down to the muddy banks of the river.

Mesmerized, she didn't realize that a sound in the brush was getting closer until a giant wild turkey leaped out of the bushes near her onto the sidewalk.

She screamed.

Jason came running.

"What is it?"

She held one hand against her chest. She couldn't catch her breath. She gestured at the turkey, now walking on some nearby grass. Jason, who had been glancing from her to the steep hillside below, turned to look at the turkey.

"Oh."

CHAPTER 11

SOFIA

A*ugust 2019*
Dinkytown

They were nearly back at Lucky's when Sofia's phone rang.

"Hello?"

"Is this Sofia Kennedy?"

Sofia's heart stopped for a minute. Her face felt icy. "Yes, this is she."

"This is Detective Pete Marley. I'll be handling your daughter's missing persons' case."

A mixture of relief and despair filled her. Despair that he hadn't told her Kate had been found and relief that they were taking her daughter's disappearance seriously.

"Thank you, detective."

Jason eyed her. She nodded at him.

Down the street two squad cars pulled up in front of Lucky's. She began walking faster. Four uniformed officers stood outside the bar talking. Jason took off at a jog.

"We haven't ruled out a rebellious teen," The detective on the phone said. A long pause. "However, we are treating this as a missing persons case because of your daughter's age. We want to make sure she's not out there hurt or something. We had a case once of temporary amnesia where a girl about your daughter's age had hit her head and had some memory loss for about twelve hours. We've contacted all the hospitals and they haven't admitted your daughter, nor have they admitted any unknown young women." He cleared his throat before continuing. "In addition, we've contacted the coroner's offices in this county and the adjoining four. Nothing there and no unidentified cases."

Sofia started to see white. The detective was still talking. Jason had reached the officers who seemed to brush him aside before they went inside the bar.

"We're also looking at CCTC footage around the area. That might give us some clues as to where your daughter went ..."

Sofia noticed a camera on the building above them. She looked down the corner. Another one. Her heart raced. Cameras would show where Kate went, where she was.

"The cameras could show us the exact time that your daughter left, if anybody was with her, or anybody followed her."

Followed her. Sofia closed her eyes. "How soon are you looking at the video?"

He sighed. "It's going to take a while. Is there any place you can think of she might have gone? Another friend's house? A relative's house, maybe."

An image of Sofia's parents flitted across her memory.

Sofia shook it away. "No. But her friend said Kate might have gone to this boy's house, Ali's. He lives at 922 Oak Street. He says he didn't see her, but we couldn't look inside—"

"I see that in the notes here," The detective said something else that was drowned out by a group of kids walking by Lucky's. The first ones Sofia had seen that didn't have their faces buried in their phones. Jason stepped in front of them. They all talked excitedly as he held up the picture of Kate on his phone. Sofia was trying to listen to what the kids were saying at the same time she heard the detective say, "Mrs. Kennedy? What's all that noise? Are you at home?"

"No." Sofia said, distracted.

"I really think you should be at home in case Kate shows up there. I think—"

"Please call me when you find her." Sofia hit the disconnect button and reached Jason just as the kids were walking away. One boy cast a look back at Sofia with pity in his eyes.

She grabbed Jason's arm. He responded with a sad shake of his head.

"Oh." She said, biting back disappointment.

"What was that about?"

"They assigned a detective to find Kate. They're looking at camera footage of Kate leaving last night. They'll be able to tell if she got in a car or if someone followed her or ..." Sofia bit back tears.

Jason scrunched up his face. "We're going to find her. We'll get through this."

Sofia wanted desperately to believe him. But when she saw his eyes she knew even he didn't believe it. They stood watching police officers go in and out of Lucky's.

She walked over to where Gretchen stood by her SUV, looking at her cell phone. Lily was leaning against the building, eyes red, arms hugging her chest.

"Julia and Joseph drove over to the West Bank to see if Kate slept at Laura's house," Lily sad.

Who the fuck was Laura? Sofia didn't know all of Kate's friends. It hadn't been a problem until now.

When Sofia walked up, Gretchen turned. "I've been praying for her."

"Thank you so much," Sofia said and meant it. "Is there any chance you could go to my house in case Kate shows up there?" She wriggled her house key off her key chain and handed it over.

Wordlessly, Gretchen took the key and turned toward her daughter. "Lily!" The girl walked toward her mother with her head down.

"We'll bring Dan home ..." Sofia said, but Gretchen and Lily were already inside their car. Sofia watched Gretchen's face as she pulled away, lips set in a firm line. Lily was in the back seat. It looked like she was yanking small chunks of hair out. Her eyes were wild and her mouth moving somewhat spasmodically. It made Sofia pause.

Her heart went out to the girl, but only for a split second. *Why did you let Kate go off by herself?*

Dan came around the corner.

"Sorry," he said. "I got nothing."

"I asked Gretchen to wait at our house in case Kate comes home," Sofia said. "She took Lily with her. We'll give you a ride home."

"Oh, thank God," he said breathing out a big whoosh of air. "I didn't want Lily to come but I couldn't stop her. She's beating herself up over this. Letting Kate go off on her own."

"It's not her fault," Sofia said. But still, something deep inside her didn't one hundred percent believe that. Not right then. Maybe once they found Kate ...

"I'm going to go knock on doors on the next street over."

"Thanks, Dan." His face was red and he was huffing. He had a history of heart problems. "You doing okay?"

"God, I'm so hung over. I need coffee something fierce." He eyed a coffee shop down the street and patted his shirt pocket. "Damn, my wallet's in my car."

"Wait right here." Sofia had seen an ATM around the corner. She needed caffeine. Her headache seemed to be getting even worse and she needed to be sharp if she were going to help find Kate.

While Jason and Dan stopped some other students, Sofia walked to the ATM. Plugging in her card she tried not to look at the image of herself that came up on the small screen from the ATM camera. But for a second she allowed herself a small glance. She looked like a fucking bag lady. No wonder nobody would talk to her. They probably thought she was some crazy lady whose daughter was hiding from her or something. Like that boy said: maybe Kate didn't want to be found.

Even the girl behind the counter at the coffee shop gave Sofia a weird look. But Sofia held out the picture of Kate anyway. The girl shook her head and handed over two large dark roasts.

Walking back, clutching the coffees, Kate's picture, and her cell phone, Sofia started to panic. Desperation was clawing at her insides. She knew she was on the verge of hysteria. If she didn't hear from Kate soon, she was afraid she was going to either collapse in a heap in the gutter or run screaming down the street breaking every window she passed.

As soon as she rounded the corner, searching out Dan and Jason, she saw two police officers hurrying out of Lucky's toward their squad cars. Sofia reached Jason just in time to hear him ask, "Excuse me. What's happening? Did someone find my daughter?"

"Sorry sir. You're going to have to talk to the detectives." The officer's face was deadpan. The two squad cars pulled away. Each headed in separate directions.

"What's going on?" she asked Jason who shrugged and pinched the bridge of his nose. "Where's Dan?"

"He's using the bathroom inside Lucky's. He said he felt sick."

Heart pounding, Sofia grabbed her phone and punched in the numbers.

"Detective Marley."

"Has something happened? Have you found Kate? Everyone's leaving Lucky's."

"You're at the bar?" He sounded surprised.

Sofia heard some muffled words as if the detective were holding his palm over the phone.

"Mrs. Kennedy, I'm going to need to call you right back."

He disconnected. At the same moment, a black and white SUV with the words Minneapolis Police Department and K9 pulled up in front of Lucky's. The vehicle shook with movement and sharp barking grew louder as the officer in the passenger seat rolled down his window. Another uniformed officer came out of Lucky's and leaned in the window. They were more than ten feet away so she couldn't hear anything other than a murmur. She stared at his lips. His eyes were hidden behind dark glasses so she couldn't see his expression, whether it was serious or blasé.

The officer leaned in to look at something on the computer screen attached to the dashboard. He leaned his head back out of the window and the SUV pulled away from the curb.

But Sofia saw something on the officer's face. She rushed over, coffee splashing out the lids of the cups. "The cameras showed something, didn't they?"

The officer didn't answer.

"Didn't they?" She stared him down.

"Ma'am, you're going to have to talk to Detective Marley. He's on his way here right now. If you'll just step aside and wait over here . . ." Sofia was barely listening, her eyes trained on the back of the K9 vehicle that suddenly accelerated and rounded the corner.

She dropped the coffee cups on the ground and ran.

CHAPTER 12

KATE

March 2019
Dinkytown, Minneapolis

The third time he showed up, I handed him the book and decided to ask what his deal was.

"I was ... wondering ..." I began, but then I didn't know what to say.

"You're wondering why I don't just buy the book?"

I laughed in relief. "Yeah."

"It's complicated."

I raised an eyebrow.

"I can see you're skeptical."

I nodded.

"Let me buy you a cup of coffee after you get off and I'll explain."

A part of me deep inside sang with happiness, but then the enthusiasm evaporated. "I can't. I have to go home and study for finals. My mom's picking me up at closing because my car's in the shop."

"Ah, that's right. It's the end of the third quarter."

I tilted my head. "I'm still in high school." Might as well get it all out there.

"Really? You seem ... very mature."

I couldn't tell if that was a compliment or not.

"Do you go to the U?"

"I did," he said. "I'm working full time right now to save money to go back home."

"Home?"

"Somalia?"

"Oh," My mouth was wide. "Oh," I repeated like an idiot.

"Yeah." He looked grim.

"Wow."

"Yeah. It's pretty messed up over there right now. I left a few years ago because I was getting into some crazy shit and had to..." he paused and looked away. "...do some things I now regret doing, so I bailed. But there's been some new developments and I've got to go back."

"You have to?" I tried to make it a casual question but he grinned.

"Afraid so."

We stared at each other in silence for a few seconds and I finally got up the nerve to ask. "What was it like growing up there?"

He shrugged. "I don't know. Probably shitty. I didn't go back there until I was fifteen. I grew up mainly in Paris. My father's Somalian and my mother is French. She was a war correspondent and my father was a diplomat. You could imagine how that went."

"Was?"

"Both died. Bomb."

I sat there for a second, mouth open. "I'm sorry."

He looked down. "That's why I was sent to live with my grandmother in Paris. When she died, I was sent back to Somalia to live with my uncle. It was totally messed up. I was in a refugee camp for three years before I got to come over here."

"I'm sorry." I said again. I'd heard about those refugee camps.

"Was a long time ago."

Awkward silence.

"I love Paris. One of my best friends, Julia, is French. Well, she was born there and moved here as a baby, but she has spent nearly every summer over there with her grandparents. She even has a French accent." I was immediately embarrassed. I am the epitome of smooth sophisticated chic. The Midwest hick you see is a ruse. He says his parents are dead and I say I love Paris and my friend is French.

But he smiled. "I've got a brilliant idea. I'll buy you a cup of coffee after you get off work and drive you home. Your mother can stay warm at home and the caffeine will ensure you stay awake to study."

I shook my head. "I'm sorry. I just can't." It would involve too much explaining—to him and to my parents—and right then I wanted to avoid my lying mother as much as possible. Plus, I was really, really trying to play hard to get. For Lily's sake. She'd be proud of me. However, if he ever asked me again, I'd say yes for sure. But I'm sure he wouldn't.

I have to admit, though, for a second, I was tempted. I could call my mom and lie to her. She had no problem lying to me. Why was I expected to always tell the truth? No. I wouldn't lie to her, but I definitely wouldn't be sharing details about my life anymore. I would go off to college and only come home as little as possible. But I knew I was lying to myself. Even thinking about avoiding my mother brought tears to my eyes. I didn't want to admit it, but I loved my mom so much and her betrayal scared the shit out of me and hurt me in ways I didn't know existed. I knew my anger was the way I was dealing with it. I knew it was messed up. But I also didn't know what else to do.

The boy spoke, bringing me back to reality.

"We'll just have to do the coffee thing another time, right?

"Sure." I tried to hide my smile. I hoped Lily was right: that if a guy really liked me, he would keep asking even if I said no at first. "But wait. I don't get the story until then? That's not very fair."

He gave an exaggerated sigh.

"Fine. Here's the story anyway. I'll make it brief. I'm a minimalist. I don't own many things. I couldn't find this book at the library so I had to come here. I don't want to buy it because I'm already trying to get rid of all my stuff. I'm going back to Somalia in the fall. Everything I own needs to fit in a carry-on suitcase. And, besides, I enjoy reading here. My roommates aren't college students. They just like the college scene. They are partiers and they are up all night, every night. My flat smells like piss and beer and sounds like a bad 90s rock concert—all the time. This place, however, is heavenly. Quiet, warm, and everybody leaves me alone."

"Oh." I suddenly felt guilty for talking to him so much.

"No, not you. I just mean I can read in peace here. It's nice ..."

"Okay," I said. He turned to sit down and I tried to think of something to keep him talking. "There's a coffee maker in the back. I was going to start a pot. You want a cup?"

The smile lit up his face. "Yes."

"Great. It won't take long to brew. Be back in a sec."

For the next three hours, we both sat quietly doing our own thing. A few customers, all students came in, but not very many since it was finals week. I had my books splayed on the counter and was studying between customers. One reason I liked my job there so much. The owner didn't care if I did homework or studied during the slow times.

Tonight, when Ali stood to leave, he turned to me.

"I actually lied earlier," he said.

I had no idea what he was talking about.

"About why I haven't bought the book."

"What?"

"Well, I didn't lie—everything I told you was true. I *am* a minimalist. I *am* trying not to buy anything since I'm moving back to Somalia, but ..."

I arched an eyebrow.

"If I buy the book I have no excuse to keep coming here ... and seeing you."

His voice grew softer at the last three words. He looked away. I was pretty sure my jaw dropped down to my chest.

Just then there was a loud banging on the window right beside where we were standing.

A blonde girl with a red nose and angry scowl was using her fist against the glass to get our attention.

"Shit!" he said. He flushed as if he had been caught doing something illegal and I immediately realized the girl must be his girlfriend.

I turned. "You better go."

I know my voice was a little curt.

"It's not like that," he said. But I was already behind the counter, putting his book back on a shelf. I didn't stand up straight again until I heard the front door close.

When I looked outside again, they were gone.

It was stupid, but I felt a pang of disappointment. Hard to get?

CHAPTER 13

SOFIA

August 2019
Dinkytown, Minneapolis

Gripping Kate's photograph, Sofia ran, brushing past a few college students who gaped at her. Distant shouting behind her seemed surreal. Vaguely she could distinguish Jason calling her name.

At the corner, she caught a glimpse of the K9 SUV turning a few blocks ahead of her. The police vehicle was heading the way that she and Jason had already walked. Ahead of her, the SUV turned onto Oak Street, the street where that boy lived.

Sofia ran, gasping for breath, her sneakers slapping on the pavement, heart pounding in her throat. Kate. Kate. Kate. She needed to get to her daughter.

She'd neared Ali's street when her own car pulled in front of her, blocking her way. Jason rolled down the window. "Get in."

Ripping open the passenger door, she flung herself into the seat. Jason squealed away before she'd even closed the door.

His knuckles were white on the steering wheel and his jaw clenched, his focus on the road in front of them.

The police cars weren't parked in front of Ali's yellow house. They were parked across the street, where the road dead-ended at the high embankment above the river. Several squad cars were parked askew, at least a dozen officers were milling around, and a string of yellow crime scene tape blocked the road off from the bushes on the other side of the small wall above the river.

Jason slammed on the brakes and the car skidded to a stop with a loud screeching, scraping sound. Smoke enveloped them on both sides as they ripped open their doors and got out. For a second, Sofia tried to make sense of what she was seeing, frantically searching the crowd for Kate's dark head. When she turned to Jason and saw the look in his eyes, her heart stopped. She followed his gaze.

He was staring at a long vehicle pulling up on the other street, nosing close to the crime scene tape.

It was a black hearse with the word "Coroner" on the side.

Jason froze, his hand on his car door, but Sofia ran.

Her baby was there somewhere and she was going to go get her. And show them. They were wrong. They didn't need the coroner's van.

Kate. Kate. Kate. She mouthed the word over and over and rushed toward the crime scene tape. She smacked into two bodies. Two policemen grabbed her and held her arms. She arched her neck to see past them, eyes wide, screaming. "My baby. Where's my baby? Let me go!"

She punched and kicked at the two bodies. And then she remembered something she'd learned long ago in a self-defense class. She went limp. Slumping to the ground, she slid out of the police officer's grip. Before they had time to react, she'd crawled through a jumble of blue uniform legs and was on her feet running. She ducked under the police tape and had made it about five feet before another uniformed officer tackled her, sending her careening into the grass.

On her knees, Sofia tore at her hair, screaming, tears spurting out of her eyes. "My baby. She was going away to college this week. My baby. My baby. Oh God no! Noooooo!"

The two officers grabbed hold of her under her arms and dragged her back under the crime scene tape. She was too weak to resist. Her legs had turned to mush. Her heels trailed behind her, kicking up small tufts of grass.

They brought her to Jason, who grabbed her and held her, his eyes dead, his mouth ringed in white. As soon as the officers turned away, she struggled out of Jason's embrace and darted back toward the crime scene tape.

A flurry of bodies and voices shouting and she was down on the ground again.

"Listen, I don't want to have to do this," said one officer with sad eyes. "But we're going to have to put you in the back of a squad if you try to get past the tape again.

He held both her forearms and met her gaze. His eyes were large brown pools of compassion.

"We don't want anyone, not even me, behind that crime scene tape, because everything over there on that side is potential evidence."

Evidence. Sofia started to hyperventilate. "My baby's there, isn't she? They found her. It's a crime? That's why they're worried about evidence?"

The officer looked past her and said, "Ma'am, you have to leave."

"I know she's there. I know it. I need to see her." Sofia's voice was shrill. She darted a glance back at Jason who was sitting on the curb, his head in his hands.

"Do I have to put you in a squad car or will you go wait over there on your own? Detective Marley is on his way."

Sofia nodded, her lower lip trembling.

"There's a chaplain who just arrived. Would you like to go speak to him?"

The chaplain was crouched on the curb by Jason. The officer took her by the elbow and led her over to Jason. Both men stood and Jason wrapped her in his arms. She buried her face in his shirt for a few seconds but then lifted her head.

Looking over his shoulder in a daze, Sofia watched men in blue jumpsuits clipping ropes to special belts on their waist. Then the men climbed over the small brick wall and down into the bushes, the tops of their heads disappeared.

It was the same wall she'd looked over earlier when the wild turkey had startled her. Horror streaked through her. Kate had been down there the whole time. Maybe on the verge of death and if Sofia had crawled down there, maybe she could have saved her baby. The thought brought her to her knees. Or maybe they found Kate in the river below. Maybe Kate fell in and drowned like so many college boys had before her.

The next thing Sofia remembered was being put in the back of their car. Dan was there. He handed Jason some pills and Jason put them in her mouth and made her drink out of a water bottle. She swallowed, feeling the pills scrape her throat as they went down. She slumped back in her seat and closed her eyes.

And after a few seconds, blessed blackness and nothing.

CHAPTER 14

KATE

M*arch 2019*
Dinkytown

It was foolish, but all I could think about all week was working Monday again and hoping Ali would come in.

He had said he came to see me. But who was that girl?

He had also said, "It's not like that."

Well, what was it like?

Even if I didn't like the answer, I was going to ask.

He walked in with a sheepish grin and was holding something behind his back.

I tried not to, but I couldn't help but meet his smile.

Looking over his shoulder in exaggeration, I said, "You alone tonight?"

He closed his eyes for a brief second.

"She's my ex. We broke up a few weeks ago but it's been a messy break up. She's not accepting that it's over."

"That sounds like a nightmare."

He shrugged and looked away as if he were uncomfortable.

"It's not ideal," he said. "The shitty thing is I don't want to be a total dick. I don't want to tell her she can never call me or speak to me again, but I definitely don't want her showing up at my place like she did last week. My idiot roommate told her I was here at the bookstore."

Play it cool. Hard to get. I folded my arms across my chest.

"Did you tell her we barely know each other and that she has nothing to be jealous of?"

He swallowed and looked down without answering. Suddenly, I felt bad.

I reached down and brought out his book and placed it on the counter.

"By the way, this book is no longer for sale."

He looked up, surprised. "It's like a library book. You can come and read it anytime you want ... as long as I'm working. Because I bought it. It's my book."

He didn't say anything and for a second my heart seemed to stop. I'd blown it. So much for playing hard to get. I was about to turn away when his face broke into a wide grin and he laughed.

Looking down, he ran his finger across the book. "Your book?"

I nodded.

"So that means where you go, it could go, too?"

I raised an eyebrow. "Uh, yeah."

"So, if say one day I wanted to read the book back at my place. Maybe even in my bedroom ... you would have to come too?" he said. "So, I could read the book." He said hurriedly at the end.

At that point, my mouth had grown dry. My lips were parched and my face was on fire with heat. Hiding my embarrassment was not an option.

I opened my mouth to speak, but nothing came out.

He laughed again.

"Well, we can talk about that more. Why don't I sit over in this comfy chair and read for a while? But first why don't you tell me what you want to be when you grow up, Kate?"

I burst into laughter and suddenly the awkward tension was gone.

We spent the next two hours talking about our dreams and hopes for the future.

He wanted to go into civil engineering and take his skill set back to Somalia where he would devote his life to creating infrastructure that united people instead of divided them.

I told him I'd dreamed of being an occupational therapist. That I wanted to study medicine but didn't think I wanted to be a doctor.

By the time he picked up the book, it was time for me to close. He met my eyes and scooted it a little toward his book bag, raising his eyebrow. I shook my head slightly and put the book back under the counter.

"Can I walk you to your car?"

He waited until I locked up and then looked around. The street was empty.

"Where is your car?" he said.

"Next block over." The street was always crowded when I showed up and then deserted when I left.

"I don't like that," he said.

"Like what?"

"That you lock up by yourself and walk a block to get to your car at night."

I shrugged. "It's fine. This is the college district."

"That doesn't mean anything," he said. "Maybe I'll have to show up and walk you home every Monday night."

"Maybe," I said. My voice was nonchalant but my heart was pounding so loud I wondered if he could hear it.

When we got to my car, I unlocked it and turned to him. He tilted my chin up to his and when his lips kissed mine, I'd wished I'd let him grab the book and take me and it back to his place. But I pulled away.

"I better go."

He didn't protest, just smiled and kissed my cheek.

The tender gesture made me sink into his arms. But I forced myself to get into my car. He waited until I'd started the engine and turned on the lights and pulled out of the parking spot before he turned away. As he walked, he waved at me over his shoulder.

CHAPTER 15

SOFIA

August 2019
Minneapolis

In the dim light filtering in from her bedroom's closed curtains, Sofia could tell it was a beautiful sunny Minnesota day. It didn't seem right that the sun could be shining. Nothing made sense anymore. Not with her baby dead.

Her mouth felt like it was filled with dust, her tongue stuck to the roof of her mouth. She reached for the glass of water she usually kept on her nightstand. Fumbling, her hand knocked something over. She pulled herself up on her elbow and squinted. There were two bottles there, both apparently from Dan.

She eyed the first amber prescription bottle It had a small white label with the name of the drug written upon it: Lorazepam.

There was also a sheet of yellow notebook paper with a note from Dan: "Take Lorazepam for anxiety. Take a few drops of the Rohypnol in your water to help you sleep. Only start with a drop at a time, though. Can be dangerous. Picked up some when I was in Cuba. Used there for sleeping drug, but in very, very small doses. Call me if you need anything."

Sofia recognized the name. Rohypnol was the drug used for Roofies, that date rape drug. She hesitated, but only for a second. It was a little odd that Dan would be stashing illegal drugs, but then again, Dan was a little odd.

But he was trustworthy. Right now, she needed any help she could get. She was sure Dan got the drugs from a reputable source in Cuba. Probably another doctor.

Her hand was shaking as she unscrewed the cap on the Lorazepam.

She fished out a pill and swallowed it dry, then used the dropper to put two drops of the Rohypnol into her water and quickly gulped that down. Two drops wouldn't kill her, but would hopefully knock her out for a while. She lay back down, closing her eyes, waiting for the inertia to take over. For one half second, she wondered if it would kill her to dump the entire vial of Rohypnol into her water glass, but quickly shook the thought away.

She could never do that to Jason. He'd lost too much already. All that they had now was each other. His side of the bed was undisturbed. She had a vague memory of Jason stripping her clothes off and pulling her nightgown over her head before kissing her forehead. Before everything became fuzzy, she caught a glimpse of his silhouette in front of their window, shaking with sobs.

But it was more than sticking around for Jason. She had a job to do.

She had to find Kate's killer and make him pay.

Her mother's face appeared before her, an angry scowl marring her features. Sofia shooed her away. The drugs were kicking in and she felt a curtain of fatigue drop down on her.

The room had grown lighter when she was awoken by the softest squeak of the bedroom door. She quickly squeezed her eyes closed, hoping to shut out the world. The creak of the hardwood floors meant someone was in the room with her. But she didn't care. She kept her eyes shut. Now, the person was next to the bed.

A soft hand on her shoulder meant it wasn't Jason. She squinted and saw a shadowy figure before her. Cecile.

"Sofia, darling, the detectives are here. They need to speak to you and Jason."

Cecile gently pulled back the gray cotton duvet.

"Come on now, *ma cherie*, time to get up."

Struggling, Sofia pushed back her tangled covers. Her silk chemise was up around her waist. She tugged it down to her thighs, rolled over and tried to screw off the cap on the small amber prescription bottle.

Gently, Cecile took the bottle out of her hands. "I think you just had one when I got here earlier." Cecile had been here earlier?

Staring at the wall, Sofia sat still as Cecile rubbed her back in small comforting circles.

"You have time for a quick shower. You cannot go downstairs like this. You must look presentable so they will take you seriously."

"Where's Jason?" Sofia's voice was hoarse, croaky, from screaming.

Looking away, Cecile didn't answer. From the side, Sofia could see her friend closing her eyes as if she were trying not to cry.

After a second, Cecile said, "Come on, now. I will help you."

Sofia ignored her, leaning over and scooping up the first piece of fabric her fingers grazed upon. It wasn't until she pulled it on over her silk chemise that she realized it was a short dress she only wore around the house when all her other clothes were dirty. Looking down, she saw the cream-colored chemise hanging down past the dress about three inches.

In the bathroom, she brushed her teeth without looking in the mirror. On her way out of the bathroom, she caught a glimpse of herself: her hair a dark tangled mess and black smudges under her eyes.

In the living room, the curtains were pulled back and the light made it hard for her to see. Two figures sat on her leather couch. Jason sat in the love seat across from them. All three of them rose when she came in the room.

A lithe man in brown slacks and a striped shirt stood. He had a full head of hair and scar on his cheek that looked like a dimple.

"We've spoken on the phone. Detective Marley." He stuck out his hand. Squinting, Sofia took it.

Behind him, a woman moved forward and stuck out her hand. "Detective Suzette Johnson." Her handshake was a cruncher, but

Sofia met her eyes and squeezed back. There wasn't the slightest trace of smile on the detective's face. She was tall and thin, her steel blue eyes striking against her bronzed skin.

"I know this is difficult, but we need your help to investigate the homicide of your daughter," Detective Marley said as they all sat back down, Sofia sinking into a spot beside Jason. The word echoed in her brain. *Homicide. Homicide. Homicide.*

"We are going to need to ask you both some questions and take a look in your daughter's room. Probably will take some stuff back with us to see if we can get some idea what led to this."

All Sofia could focus on was "*Homicide. Of. Your. Daughter.*"

Detective Johnson leaned over and handed Sofia a slip of paper. "Could you please sign this? It gives us permission to search Kate's room."

While Sofia wasn't sure she was crazy about the detective's gruff manner, she appreciated that she said "Kate" and not "your daughter" like the other detective did.

Without reading it, keeping her eyes on the detectives, Sofia scribbled her name and handed the paper back.

"When do we get her?" Sofia asked, closing her eyes for a second.

"In a day or two," the male detective said, clearing his throat. Then the other detective, the woman named Johnson, turned toward Sofia.

"We just have a few quick questions. When was the last time you saw Kate?" The detective's blue eyes were a little disconcerting as if she could see straight through you. A notebook with a pen stuck through the coils sat on her knee, but she didn't pick it up.

Sofia shot a glance at Jason. He'd been the last one to see Kate. But he was staring off in a daze.

Sofia started. "I saw her about three yesterday. Or not yesterday. The day before" She stopped in horror. It hadn't only been yesterday. Kate had been dead for two days.

Jason reached over and patted Sofia's hand and she continued. "She'd just come back from the lake and took a quick shower and said she was going to her best friend Lily's house and then they were going out with some high school friends that night, saying goodbye before everyone went off to college."

The notebook sat untouched on the detective's lap.

Sofia looked at Jason. He was still open-mouthed staring at something near the window.

"Jason?"

He shook his head as if to clear his thoughts. "About five. She called because she'd gotten a flat tire on her way to dinner at Chino Latino. My office is close by there, so I stopped and helped her.

"How did she seem to both of you at the time?" The detective still wasn't taking notes.

Sofia raised an eyebrow. The detective clarified. "Was she agitated? Upset? Worried? Happy? What was her emotional and mental state? As far as you could tell?"

"When I saw her, she was really excited about going out that night," Sofia said and felt tears spurting from her eyes. "Excuse me." She held her fist to her mouth for a second before continuing. "She seemed to be in a good mood." *For the first time in months.*

"Same here," Jason said. "Katie was in a great mood. She thought it was hilarious that she'd gotten a flat. I didn't think it was quite as funny as she did. When I said this, she put her head on my shoulder and said, 'Sorry, daddy. I'm so lucky to have you come to my rescue.'" Jason's sob echoed throughout the room. "Why couldn't I have saved her? Your dad is supposed to always rescue you, protect you. I wasn't there for her. I wasn't there and I have to live with that for the rest of my life. I'm so sorry, Katie."

He jumped up and rushed from the room. Sofia stood as if to go after him, but the detective moved in front of her. "I know this is difficult, ma'am, but it is necessary if we're going to find the perpetrators."

Ma'am. So incredibly fucking impersonal. Apparently, this cop did this every fucking day. Let's find the perpetrators who MURDERED your daughter.

Sofia thought about pushing past her, but then saw Cecile had her arm around Jason in the sunroom, his head bowed in her lap, her hand stroking his back. Cecile caught Sofia's eyes and nodded toward the cops.

Sofia sank back down onto the leather cushion.

"What else do you need to know?" She shot a glance at the older detective. Fuck that other one.

"Is there anyone you can think of who might have wanted to hurt your daughter?" he said.

"No." Sofia spoke before he'd even finished the question.

"Does she have a boyfriend?"

Sofia slowly shook her head, but thought about the boy that Kate was kissing that night.

"No. I told you about that boy who lived right by where ..." *they found her.*

Detective Marley looked at his notes. "Ali Yassin. Yes, we have spoken to him."

"Spoken to him? Did you search his house?" Her voice was sharp.

The detectives exchanged a look.

"What if it's too late and he hid everything? All the evidence or something..." Sofia was wringing her hands in her lap.

For the first time, Detective Johnson showed a glimmer of warmth. She leaned over and grabbed Sofia's hands, pinning them down. "Honey, nobody will be able to hide anything from me. I promise you."

For some reason, Sofia believed her. And instantly forgave her for talking about *perpetrators* so coldly.

Just like when she was younger and had called 911, everyone was calling her "honey." Sofia felt a lump of something fleshy in her throat making it hard to breath or talk so she just nodded.

Detective Johnson asked a few more questions, about Kate's friends, her job, her goals, her hangouts, what she was wearing, her hobbies, where Jason worked, what work Sofia did, names of her clients, names of Jason's clients.

"We have the FBI trying to track her phone," Marley said. "I'm going to need to get information from you on her bank accounts and credit cards so we can trace those, see if any money was taken out of any accounts or if she spent any money after she left the bar."

"Okay," Sofia said in a meek voice.

Marley turned to the other detective. "Ready to search her room?"

At the doorway to Kate's room, Sofia paused. Her gaze focused on the little desk that Kate had used since she was a toddler. It was white and had small primrose flowers painted on the corners. Her laptop sat in the center of the desk. A small bookshelf above held Kate's most treasured objects. Sofia hadn't looked at it for months. She stared at the objects on the shelf, tears welling in her eyes.

There was Kate's worn stuffed rabbit; her favorite childhood book, a small slim yellow volume of Madeline in Paris, and a few other beloved objects. Kate had said she was leaving everything on the shelf when she went to college so she would know it was safe.

"Mrs. Kennedy?" It was the woman detective. "Do you mind waiting here? We'll keep you informed of anything we find or want to take down to the station."

Sinking back onto the couch downstairs, Sofia tried to imagine the detectives going through Kate's belongings. They would take all her journals. They might take the bound books on a shelf on her main bookcase—all containing poetry Kate had written over the years. She wrote her first poem when she was eight; something about the bald eagle she had seen flying over the skyscrapers of downtown Minneapolis. Her class had been on a field trip and was on the observation deck of the thirty-two-story Foshay Tower when an eagle had swooped by, making a lasting impression on Kate. Sofia squeezed her eyes shut tight trying to remember what the poem had said ... something about how the eagle had looked right at Kate as if giving her a message, an important message she didn't understand before it flew away.

A noise in the kitchen startled her out of her memory. Jason and Cecile scraping back bar stools. Cecile gestured for her to join them.

Jason's face was ravaged. Her happy-go-lucky husband was destroyed.

He started to say something, opening his mouth, but then clamped it shut and shook his head. Sofia stared in a daze past him to their backyard, the deck, where they had been laughing and drinking and celebrating while Kate was murdered.

She closed her eyes for a few seconds. She would never laugh again. Not laughter of joy. All the joy and light in her life was gone. Now and forever.

CHAPTER 16

KATE

April 2019

Dinkytown

Today, I lied to my mom about going to the Mall of America. I told her I wouldn't be home until very late as I was also going to catch a movie there with friends. I also lied to Lily, telling her I was going to be holed up studying. I had lied because a few weeks ago when I told Lily what had happened with the blond girl waiting for Ali, she had gotten a smug look on her face. I hadn't brought him up since.

Having lied to my mom and my best friend, I pointed my mom's old Volvo toward Dinkytown. I stopped by the bookstore for a few minutes first and then headed toward the river.

For some reason my heart was pounding when I stepped onto the porch of that yellow house. Had I got it all wrong? I checked the address I had copied down from our mailing list.

922 Oak Street. It was the right house.

It had been nearly a week since I saw him. What if he was back with his ex-girlfriend or what if I'd read him entirely wrong? I held the book in front of me as if it were precious and important and not just an excuse for me to be there. My heart pounded and my breath was coming fast and shallow. I couldn't remember the last time I'd been so nervous.

I knocked lightly, but the door immediately swung open.

When I saw the smile on his face, I knew I had gotten everything exactly right.

CHAPTER 17

SOFIA

August 2019
Minneapolis

People speaking in hushed tones solemnly filed into the Basilica of St. Mary's gloomy cavernous interior. Its darkness reflected the somber mood inside and the stormy skies outside. As Sofia stared at the heart of the altar—a fifty-foot-high baldachin perched on marble columns, adorned with gold-winged angels, and crowned with a blue-cloaked Virgin Mary—it began to glow.

The golden light spreading through the church as the lights were turned up, signaled that the funeral mass was about to begin.

Beneath the baldachin lay a white casket draped with silky cream fabric. The rest of the altar was covered in flowers of all colors. Kate's favorite flowers were wildflowers, a cacophony of mingling hues and sizes. Near the entryway, dozens of photographs of Kate were displayed on two wooden tables. Cecile had made a few giant collages on poster board that Sofia avoided when she had entered the church. She'd look at them later, at home, in private.

Pressing her fingers to her temples, Sofia fought back flashes of memory trying to surface of another casket. A tiny casket. People giving her askance glances. Her mother's vice-like grip on her wrist. No. No. It was an accident. The judge even said so.

Sofia shook off the dark shadows. The horror of this moment surpassed any previous nightmare she'd experienced. Deep in the pit of her stomach, a heavy shroud of blackness and gloom had dug its claws in, shifting and settling itself in for eternity. She knew it would never leave. It was a permanent occupant now.

When the funeral home director had recommended a closed casket, Sofia hadn't objected. That didn't matter. Very little mattered anymore. A gray suffocating fog enveloped her. She vaguely recalled making decisions about what Kate should wear – the lacey beige dress she'd worn to her graduation party.

The smell of incense drifted past and the words from the priest high on the pulpit became a dull murmur. His words didn't matter, either. Automatically, Sofia went through the motions of the mass, kneeling, sitting, standing, kneeling, sitting, making the sign of the cross, reciting the responses to the priest automatically, but her mind was not there.

She sat in the front pew, flanked by Jason and Dan. Cecile was on the other side of Jason, at the end of the pew, so she could get up and speak later. Sofia looked around for Lily and Julia, but couldn't find them or Gretchen. Maybe the girls were sitting with a cluster of teenagers a few rows back. That row of teens, a faceless mass of dark colors, were clutching each other and sobbing. Sofia couldn't look at them.

There were no family members. Jason's only living relative, his brother, made some excuse why he couldn't leave his family in Montana to attend the mass. That didn't matter either.

Their friends were their family.

Their blood relatives could not compare.

That's one reason Jason and Sofia had bonded in college—they were both orphans. Sofia had lied about it for so long, it seemed true now.

She was excruciatingly honest with Jason about everything—except the true details of her past. All he knew was that her parents had died and Aunt Rose had raised her. Sometimes when she remembered her past and examined her ability to lie about something so huge, it flattened her enough to send her to bed for a day or two. She blamed it on migraines. And when she came out of her self-imposed exile, she put on a happy face. Because ultimately, she knew that her entire world depended on living that lie.

Now, in the pew, Jason clutched her hand so tightly he left nail marks on her palms. She leaned her head on his shoulder and closed her eyes.

Sofia wondered if her life of lies had been worth it. She contemplated another alternate universe where she had told Jason the truth when they met. What would it have been like if she'd told Jason about the baby? And told him that her parents were alive—that her father was in prison for murder and her mother had abandoned her?

If she had told Jason, he probably wouldn't have married her and Kate would never have been born. You can't change your past.

As the priest droned on and the cantor led them in song, Sofia sank into herself, indulging in memories of Kate. Sinking into them fully. She began with the moment she realized she was pregnant.

It might seem crazy to many people, but that first night in their new home when she and Jason had made love on the mattress thrown on the floor, she curled up afterwards against his back and knew. Placing her hands on her belly, she had known she was pregnant.

It was her fresh start. Her chance to make up for everything. A baby would make everything right. She would be the best mother in the world. No harm would ever come to this child.

In her mind, she'd started making plans. No sushi. Cut out coffee and alcohol. Buy more pre-natal vitamins. She'd already had three miscarriages, she wasn't taking any chances. Until she held the baby in her arms, she wouldn't be able to relax. She knew the miscarriages were part of her punishment. But hadn't she been punished enough?

The church echoed with the sounds of singing as Sofia's inward focus moved to the soft hazy memories of Jason squeezing her hand tightly during ultrasounds, worried they would receive the news they had in the past—no heartbeat. Sofia was always a mess until she saw the tiny shrimp-like blob wriggling on the screen.

Her miscarriages had seemed a sign that she was unfit to be a mother and that the Castellucci bloodline should stop with her. Her Italian-American grandmother had instilled this superstitious nature into her, even though her Aunt Rose told her pay no mind to nana's mumblings about curses and *malocchio*—the evil eye.

Still, she had prayed the rosary every night during each of her pregnancies, praying that eventually Jason's wholesome Midwestern genes would cancel out the violent Castellucci DNA. They had to.

Holding baby Kate in her arms for the first time, tears spurted from Sofia's eyes, splashing Jason whose head was tilted against hers, looking down at their daughter. When she first held Kate, she let all her fears and superstitions go. This baby was blessed. She would be raised far away from Sofia's dark past on the East Coast.

Whatever had happened that night with her baby brother was an anomaly. She'd be so careful and attentive with this baby that no harm could ever come to her.

To ensure that, Sofia quit her job as a graphic designer. She wanted to always be within arm's reach of the infant. The crib stayed near Sofia's and Jason's bed until Kate turned one.

Now, in the church, with Kate's casket up on the altar, Sofia knew she had been a fool.

She stared at the statue of the Virgin Mary on the altar and soaked up images of Kate, clinging tight to them, terrified that the memories would one day fade. She vowed right then to remember them, to go over them again and again every night at bed. To never forget.

So many memories. So many firsts. She walked herself through them—First food. First word. First step. The pictures taken on their giant front porch on the first day of school every year. Gymnastics meets. Vacations to Mexico. Acceptance to St. Thomas. Senior prom. High school graduation. Shopping at Target for her dorm. The last time she saw Kate.

The last time she'd seen her daughter was uneventful.

And still it filled her with regret.

Sofia lifted her eyes to the casket.

How could she have possibly known when she'd breezily said goodbye to her daughter, not even looking up from paying bills—"Have a good night sweetheart. I love you. God bless you"—that it would be the last time?

Thank God Sofia had told her she loved her. That was her mantra. At least there was that. Every time they had parted—from the moment she stuck Kate on that bus in kindergarten—Sofia had ended her goodbyes with "I love you" and "God bless you."

Sofia was still rolling through her memories when she felt Dan trembling beside her. He was shaking with his tears. She looked over and his face was wet with them. He bowed his head in his hands. His shaking shook the entire pew. His face was scrunched up and he looked as if he had just been punched. He'd always treated Kate like she was his own daughter.

Sofia looked at Cecile, sitting next to Alex. Her eyes were red and puffy. She gave Sofia a pained smile.

Sofia avoided looking at Jason, afraid if she looked into his eyes, she would slide off the pew onto the floor and never get up again. The cantor had begun a heartbreaking rendition of Ava Maria. The altar became a blurry kaleidoscope of color as her vision filled with tears. She squeezed Jason's hand even tighter.

At the funeral home, when they had gone to pick up Kate and pick out her casket, Jason had briefly disappeared.

Sofia found him in a small chapel. Seeing her husband there, shoulders slumped, defeated like he'd never been before, sent an alien noise out of her—an anguished keening that was somewhere between a gasp and a sob. She knelt beside him, but he didn't look up, lost in his own hell.

That's what they didn't tell you—how solitary grief is. You can mourn the same person in the exact same amount and yet, you are on your own. Alone in your grief. For eternity.

CHAPTER 18

KATE

April 2019
Dinkytown

The smile Ali gave me when he answered the door made me want to melt into the front porch. Music poured out into the night air and I heard the low murmur of voices from inside.

"Hey," he said.

"Hey." I could feel my traitorous cheeks grow hot.

He stepped inside and pushed the door open as he did. "Want to come in?"

I shivered. I couldn't tell if it was from the sudden cool breeze coming off the Mississippi River or his heavy-lidded gaze.

"Sure." I stepped in.

The living room was entirely lit by candles. Mexican-style blankets hung on the windows instead of curtains. I noticed a guy slumped in a bean bag in a corner, smoking a joint. A few other people sat on a burnt orange couch. One guy sat on a light green armchair and two guys sat on the floor. It seemed as if everybody was smoking either weed or cigarettes. A massive poster of Bob Marley hung over the couch.

"This is Kate," Ali said it in a low voice. People nodded. Their faces were blurred in the dim light.

"Want something to drink?" he said. He stretched and his shirt came up as he scratched his bare belly. I could feel the heat on my cheeks spread. I followed him into the kitchen and he gestured toward some bottles on the counter.

"I can make you a drink? Or do you want a beer." Now he was leaning over searching inside the refrigerator.

"Beer is good."

I didn't really like beer. But I figured that would be easiest.

He opened a brown bottle and handed it to me.

As he did, his fingers brushed mine and then wove into my own. At the same time, his other hand reached around my waist. He pulled me close and then abruptly turned, holding onto my hand and pulling me with him.

We went down the hall—away from the living room. He ducked into a dark room, pulling me behind him and then closing the door, pressing me up against it. The room was dark except for a lava lamp. His face was lit red from the glow. He searched my eyes and when I smiled, he leaned down and kissed me.

We didn't come up for air for what seemed like forever. I'd been kissed before, but not like this. I was weak. My body felt like it was going to seep into the floor. He pulled me over to a small twin bed. We lay down and he traced his finger across my lips before he kissed me again, longer this time.

Finally, after it became clear that a decision had to be made, I told him. "I should probably go."

He seemed disoriented. I stood up and he pulled me back down. "It's late. Can you stay the night? I promise I won't pressure you to do anything. I'm a feminist."

I smiled in the dark.

"I promise. We'll just sleep." He yawned loudly. "See? I'm already asleep."

He did a loud fake snore that made me giggle.

I leaned over and grabbed my phone out of my bag.

I would text my mom and lie even more than I had already. I didn't feel an ounce of guilt about it. After learning that she lied to me my entire life about my grandmother being alive, I felt like I had carte blanche to lie to her a time or two. After all, I was almost eighteen and I could count the number of times I'd lied to her on one hand. And half of those times were when I was in elementary school.

My text said that I was staying at Julia's house— a safer bet than saying I was at Lily's. Even if my mom called and checked up on me in the morning, Alex and Cecile wouldn't remember whether I'd been there or not. Especially if they'd spent part of the night in the hot tub smoking weed and listening to music from the seventies. They were like the old-fashioned version of the people out in Ali's living room.

After I hit send, I settled into the crook of Ali's arm. He leaned down and kissed the top of my head gently and I couldn't wipe the smile off my face.

"Night."

"Night."

Sometime in the night I woke, disoriented. It took me a few seconds to remember I was at Ali's place. In his bed.

But I was alone.

I heard a voice from outside the closed bedroom door. Ali. He sounded angry. I slipped out of bed, holding my breath and trying not to make any noise as I crept to the door, straining to hear what he was saying.

As I got closer I could make out the words he was whispering.

"Jenna. I told you. No. I fell asleep. Listen, I've got to go. I don't have time for this. I'll call you tomorrow. Whatever. Later today then. I'm going to hang up now."

The door creaked a little and I raced across the room and jumped back into bed right before he opened the door. I heard him exhale loudly. A few seconds later, he was back in bed with me. I was tense, but tried to relax and breathe deeply as if I were sleeping.

He slipped his arm under my neck and around my shoulder so my head rested in the crook of his arm.

I felt both cherished and safe and suspicious as hell at the same time.

What was up with him and that girl? Was he still with her?

CHAPTER 19

SOFIA

August 2019
Golden Valley, Minnesota

At graveside, staring at the dark hole in the ground next to the gleaming casket, Sofia's grief was unseated by something darker, deeper, with shadowed wings.

Hatred.

The murderous black rage she managed to keep at bay most of her life was surfacing. *Stop! You are not like him. Stop!*

But then the unleashed anger—the capacity for violence embedded deep in her blood and DNA that she had fought against her entire life—overcame her. As she stared at the casket that contained her flesh and blood, she gave that deep-seated fury full rein. Just like she wrote in that letter: she would kill whomever did this to Kate. Without hesitation.

Staring at the grave, she clenched her fists together. Open. Closed. Open. Closed. Looking down at her hands, once smooth and pretty, she realized they were starting to look like her mother's hands: wrinkled, scattered with age spots, ugly. She stared down. No. She pushed down thoughts of her mother.

It was impossible.

But her mother's words had always haunted her: *You will pay.*

Her mother was a terrible parent, but a murderer? No.

She had said Sofia would pay. But Sofia hadn't believed her. And now she was paying with the one thing she had held most dear: her daughter's life.

If the person who did this to her daughter magically appeared before her right now, even if it were her own mother or father, Sofia would wrap her hands around the lying murderer's neck and crush the skin until she felt the spine crumble underneath. She would clench the neck as tight as she could, leaning and putting her entire body weight into it. She would not let go. Not if an army of men were trying to pull her off. She would hold on and tighten her grip. She would watch the murderer's eyes bulge until they became lifeless. And she would never—not for a second—regret it.

Jason nudged her. It was time to say goodbye. Everyone else had placed a flower on Kate's casket. It was her turn.

Clutching a single white daisy to her chest, Sofia slowly plodded toward the graveside, her legs feeling like tree stumps, her feet like anchors. She collapsed onto her knees in the dirt in front of the casket, unable to focus. She could feel the crowd part behind her, people leaving, giving her privacy. She knelt until her knees began to ache and the sun had fallen behind the trees. Jason cleared his throat behind her.

Leaning over, she kissed the cold metal and whispered. "Don't worry, Kate. I will find whoever did this and make them pay. I swear to you, baby. I will make them pay."

CHAPTER 20

SOFIA

February 1979
Derby, Connecticut

As soon as she heard her Aunt Rose's voice, nine-year-old Sofia leaped out of bed and rushed to the head of the stairs, but right when she was about to squeal with delight, she froze.

Looking down from the second-floor landing, Sofia saw her aunt, still wearing her coat and holding her purse, collapse into her mother's arms and burst into tears.

"I'm so sorry. I'm so sorry," her aunt said to Sophia's mother.

For a second, Sofia's heart clenched in fear. Her dad was dead.

But her mother laughed, startling Sofia.

"I'm surprised the old witch made it as long as she did."

It wasn't her dad. Then who?

"*Dio mio*!" Aunt Rose said, making the sign of the cross. "You shouldn't talk that way about the dead."

Sofia sank onto the top stair. Someone was dead and her mother was glad.

"That woman made my life hell. Even to the very end, she made sure to bitch about how awful her life had been and how her children had made it worse."

Aunt Rose had shed her coat and was now bustling about in the kitchen filling the coffee pot and wiping her eyes.

"I always liked her," she said quietly.

Sofia's mother pulled up a chair and lit a cigarette. This time she spoke in a low voice. "She was a good actress. She was nicer to strangers than she was to her own family."

They must be talking about the crabby old neighbor who lived across the street. Whenever her kids came to visit there was yelling and even once the sound of breaking glass. Sofia's mother used to roll her eyes and turn up the radio in the kitchen.

Rose hugged her mother again. "I know you had a difficult relationship. I think you are just in shock."

Sofia watched wide-eyed as her mother relaxed into the hug. Her mother who never hugged or kissed Sofia. Who swatted away her own husband's hugs and kisses. But then her mother pulled away abruptly.

"I'll get the biscotti for our coffee."

Sofia stayed quiet on the stairs, eavesdropping on her mother and aunt, pressing her forehead against the cold wood bannister.

The women smoked and sipped coffee and dipped biscotti into their cups.

After a while, Rose spoke. "Are you having a funeral?"

Her mother shrugged. "I suppose."

Sofia could think of no good reason why her mother would have a funeral for the neighbor. She didn't even like her.

Rose stubbed out her cigarette in Sofia's favorite ashtray, the ceramic rectangle one with the Eiffel Tower on it.

"Have you told Marco?"

"He won't care. He hated my mother more than I did."

It hit Sofia like a punch.

Grandma Malena was dead.

She burst into tears and hid her face in her nightgown to muffle the sound. Her sweet grandmother who had been in that care home for the past two years. Dead. It was the second person Sofia had known who died. The first was baby Angelo. The sweetest, happiest baby in the world. Sofia would never forgive herself for his death. Even though the judge had said it was an accident, her mother had told her the truth—it was Sofia's fault.

Now, below her, her mother said something that made her freeze.

"Maybe Sofia should go live with you like Marco said."

Sofia's face felt icy. Her father had wanted her to move in with Aunt Rose? Because of Angelo?

"You know I love Sofia like my own daughter," Rose said. "My door is always open."

Holding her breath, Sofia waited for her mother's response. She craned her neck to see. Rose was staring at her mother, but her mother was concentrating on rubbing a spot on their scratched table. Finally, she shrugged. "It's a little late for all that, isn't it? He's dead now."

"It was not the child's fault," Rose's voice was firm. But then she looked up, right at Sofia. For a moment, terror streaked through Sofia. Would her Aunt Rose say something, tattle on her for spying? But her aunt looked away as she spoke. "Sofia is always welcome in my home. That baby's death was not her fault." Her voice was firm.

The words made her cry even more. Tears streamed down her face and she held her breath waiting for her mother to say, "Yes. Sofia can live with you. Go get her right now."

Please. Please. Please. Sofia looked at the picture of Jesus with the flaming sacred heart on his chest. *Please. Please. Please.*

Then her mother spoke. "No. The girl is difficult. Maybe dangerous. They say it was an accident, but you didn't see her face when I found them. She is better off with me. I wouldn't burden you with her."

Sofia tried to remember that night. She'd pushed it down for so long. But now she strained, closing her eyes to remember.

She'd fallen asleep with Angelo in her arms. She'd heard him crying in the night and like, always, her mother had ignored his cries. Sofia had taken to getting up, warming the milk on the stove and feeding him herself in his nursery. She loved rocking him by the light of the nightlight, watching his rosebud lips drink and his eyes intently focused on her. It was the best thing in the world.

But that night, she'd fallen asleep in the rocking chair holding him.

Waking she'd seen her mother on the ground over Angelo's tiny body. Then her mother looked over at her with hate in her eyes. "You killed him?"

"What?" Sofia blinked and then horror shot through her. She threw herself on the floor by Angelo's body. His body was still. She put her head to his chest. Nothing. The worst pain she'd ever felt clutched her heart, wrapped in absolute terror. It couldn't be. She was still dreaming.

But soon the police were there, questioning her. It was only later that a judge determined that Angelo's death had been an accident. That she had accidentally dropped him out of the rocking chair.

"You were sleepwalking," her mother told her. "I heard you yell and when I came in, I found him like that. You were very angry. You fought me and hit me. You need to control your temper."

Sofia didn't understand how she could have slept through that. How something like that could've happened at all. If she'd been sleepwalking then how had she ended up back asleep sitting in the rocking chair?

Now, only a few years later, watching her mother and aunt, Sofia felt tears running down her face. She missed her little brother more than anything in the world. She would never have hurt him on purpose. Never. She would have killed herself if he could live.

Sofia didn't wait to hear anymore. If she couldn't move in with Aunt Rose, then nothing else that was said mattered. She stood and ran to her room, throwing herself on her bed and burying her face in her pillow. She sobbed for what seemed like hours until at one point, she realized instead of sadness, she felt anger. Fury. So much so that she pounded her fists into her pillow until her knuckles hurt.

CHAPTER 21

KATE

A*pril 2019*
Dinkytown

My so-called grandmother sent me another message on Facebook.

I was in my room when I saw her name pop up. I jumped up, ran, and closed my bedroom door, heart racing in my throat, before I read the message.

"I saw that you looked at my message. Why won't you answer?"

Because you told me not to trust my mom or dad and not to tell them you'd contacted me.

I guess I'd hoped it would all go away.

But it hadn't.

I swallowed hard and typed. "How do I know you're not some guy pretending to be my grandmother?"

I jumped when she wrote back. She was online right then.

"You know I already proved it with what I told you about your mother's scar and mole."

Of course, I knew she was right.

"Please give me your mailing address I want to send you a letter. I want to tell you about your family. Your grandfather. Me. Your great-grandparents. It's hard for me to get online. I can only check it once a week. I'd rather do it the old-fashioned way. Haha."

I was sure it wasn't true. She probably just wanted my home address. But the bait was irresistible: *"I want to tell you about your family."*

Quickly, I typed the address to the bookstore and then slammed my laptop shut.

I wanted so badly to learn about my grandparents and great-grandparents. I'd even thought about doing a DNA test secretly now that I knew my grandmother was alive. Who knew what other relatives were alive. My mom had claimed there was nobody. But, as I knew now, she'd lied.

Thinking of it made me both sick to my stomach and angry.

I couldn't understand why she'd lied to me my whole life. Did my dad know? Was he lying too? That idea was nearly incomprehensible. Most likely she'd lied to him, too. But why?

What secrets was she keeping? What could be so bad that she had to lie about whether her mother was alive?

CHAPTER 22

SOFIA

N*ovember 1981*
New Haven, Connecticut

Inside the cold conference room, eleven-year-old Sofia shivered. She'd wished she'd brought her sweatshirt.

The detective and district attorney were right outside the door. She could see them through the glass window. Every once in a while, they looked at her.

The room was empty save a few chairs and a big video camera on a tripod.

Sofia chewed on her fingernails; shifting restlessly on the uncomfortable orange plastic chair they had told her to sit on. She was in the middle of the room. The other chairs were behind the camera.

The door opened.

"Are you nervous, honey?" It was the social worker that had met with her that first night at the police station.

"I don't know."

"You're shivering." The woman with the tidy brown bun and gray suit turned to look at the thermostat control on the wall. "No wonder. It's like the arctic in here. I'll turn this up full blast."

She turned back to Sofia. "I have a really soft and warm cardigan in my bag. It's in the hall. Can I get that for you until it warms up?"

Sofia nodded. Her teeth were chattering.

The door opened and the woman slipped out. Nobody was in the hall right then. Sofia wondered what they would do if she just left. Without testifying against her dad. But then the thought of him free from jail sent shivers down her arms that had nothing to do with the room's temperature.

Her dad needed to be locked up. That's why she was doing this.

The dad she had loved was gone. In his place was a monster, a murderer, a person who killed people and cut off their fingers. He'd lied to her. Their entire life was a lie. She would never, ever forgive him.

The district attorney had told her that they would videotape her so she didn't have to go into the courtroom. He said he was worried about her safety because it was a "mob" trial.

"Sometimes people in organized crime aren't very nice to witnesses," he'd told her.

Her face would be in the dark on the video and her voice would be distorted while she testified. Everyone in the courtroom would watch her on a big screen while she was safe in another room. The district attorney had told her they could protect her—her and her mom. That she and her mother could even change their names and move far away. Later, he told her that her mother had refused the help. Sofia shrugged. She didn't tell him that she already had plans to move far away—without her mother. As soon as she was old enough, she'd move far away and never talk to her mother again.

Besides, she wasn't frightened of the "mob." She'd met the Giovanni Family. They liked her.

She was more afraid of her own mother and father.

Before the district attorney had picked her up that morning, she'd been in her room sick with anxiety and worry. When she noticed her mother standing in her doorway, watching her, she screamed and jumped.

Her mother didn't say a word. Simply stared at her with such hatred Sofia had never seen. Like Sofia was a bug that she wanted to step on. Usually, her mother simply ignored her, even scolded her without looking at her, like she was a nuisance and an embarrassment.

For most of her life, Sofia had simply tried to stay out of her mother's way.

When she saw how affectionate her friends' mothers were, Sofia pretended not to notice that her mother was a stranger who never hugged her. She hadn't abused her. She had just ignored her.

So, the attention right now was unnerving. It was as if her mother was seeing Sofia for the first time.

"You little bitch. You have no idea what you are about to do."

Sofia gaped at the name.

"You are ruining everything. You will pay for this. You think you are something special." Her mother spat, actually spat, on her pink-carpeted floor. "You are no saint. You are the same. You have your father's blood. You share his DNA. You have already proven that. He and you are the same. You punish him for providing for this family? Giving you this life? You could live like your cousin Tomas. How is his life? You like his life? Do you want to drop out of school to work so we can eat? That is what you are doing to our family. You mark my words. You will pay for this."

Sofia watched her mother in the mirror. Her mother's face was mottled with red. Her eyes were bulging. Her whole head was quaking with anger. A chill ran down Sofia's spine, but she remained motionless staring at her mother's reflection until a horn honked outside. The district attorney was there to pick her up.

Her mother's voice was low and deadly. "How soon you forget?"

Sofia closed her eyes for a second. And then her mother kept speaking. Sofia clapped her hands over her ears to drown out her mother's words.

But she couldn't stop the flood of memories. Angelo's body on the ground. The empty crib. Her mother's shouting and distorted face. The police.

"No!" She screamed, trying to drown out the memories. Opening her eyes, she rushed from the room, pushing by her mother's bulk straddling the doorway. Her mother hip checked her, slamming her into the wall, but Sofia only stumbled for a second and kept walking without looking back.

As she neared the stairs, she turned and met her mother's eyes. "You are the one who is going to pay. You and Daddy will pay for what you've done."

Her mother stood there, mouth agape. Without waiting for a response, Sofia stomped down the stairs and out the door, slamming it behind her.

Getting into the big sedan out front, her heart was pounding, but she felt free. She trusted the detective and the district attorney. They were the ones who told her what would happen. Not what her mother had said. They had told her that with her help, with her testimony, her father would never see the light of day again.

She was afraid of what he might do to her if he got out. But then she realized she probably needed to be more afraid of what her mother was going to do to her if he didn't.

But the thing Sofia was most afraid of was her mother being right—that whatever made her dad do those awful things was inside her, as well. It was her greatest fear—that she was like her father. She pushed back images of Angelo's motionless body. No. No. No. It was an accident.

With a loud bang, the door swung open hitting the wall opposite and the conference room filled with people. The social worker handed Sofia a soft sweater that smelled of perfume. Sofia quickly put it on.

"Sorry," the detective said. "Time to start."

Everyone settled into the chairs and grew silent. A spotlight behind Sofia was turned on. She could feel the heat on the back of her hair. A man she didn't recognize got behind the camera. "Okay. We're live in five. Five, four, three, two, one." He pointed at the district attorney.

She could barely make out the district attorney's face in the dim light, but focused on his eyes. "Thank you for being here today," he said. "I realize this is not easy, in fact, probably the most difficult thing you've ever had to do."

"Objection." At first Sofia was unsure where the voice had come from: a small speaker at the other end of the table.

"Overruled," said another voice.

"First, please state your name."

Sofia did.

"Could you please tell us what happened the night of May 15, 1980?"

Sofia nodded.

"You're going to have to answer verbally for the record," the district attorney said.

"Okay. Yes."

There was some mumbling and loud voices coming from the speaker.

"Objection. Your honor may we approach?"

"This better be good," a voice said.

"Your honor, we just received something we think you need to see."

"Relevance?" Sofia heard the sound of shuffling papers.

"We think introducing the juvenile record of the witness to the jury is relevant in order for them to fairly evaluate her testimony."

Sofia froze. The district attorney jumped up. Someone put a hand on his arm. He shot an alarmed look at Sofia. His eyes held a question. Sofia stared unable to look away. Unable to move or speak.

"Overruled. Juvenile records are sealed for a reason. I also don't appreciate this coming in at the last minute."

"But, your honor?"

"Sir, you are in danger of being held in contempt of court."

The district attorney sat back down. Sofia realized her entire body was shaking.

"Let's start when you woke up in the middle of the night."

Focusing on the district attorney and not the camera, Sofia recounted what she had seen that night.

"I woke up from a bad dream and went to my mom and dad's room. But it was empty. Then I heard the garage door closing. I looked outside and saw my dad's car driving down the driveway." She looked up at the district attorney not sure if she should continue. He nodded. "Sometimes he leaves at night. But I didn't know where my mom was. I looked in the kitchen. Then I thought maybe she was in the basement."

"Why did you look in the basement?"

"Because that's where the washing machine was and I thought maybe she was doing laundry."

"Did she often do laundry at night?"

"I don't know. Sometimes." Even in the dim light, she could see the district attorney giving the detective a look. Sometimes her mother burned things, awful-smelling clothes and who knew what else, in the basement furnace.

"So, you went to the basement. What did you first see when you went down there?"

"Blood." The district attorney shot another look at the detective.

"Where was the blood?"

"All over the floor. And the wall."

"What did you do?"

"I screamed."

"Then what?"

"I kept screaming for my mom." Sofia shifted. The warmth of the light on the back of her head was making her hair itch.

"Did she come?"

"No."

"What did you do then?"

"I looked in the closet."

The district attorney had lowered his head reading his notes. "There's a closet in the basement?"

"Yes."

"What's in the closet?"

"It's kind of a pantry. There's extra food and cleaning stuff."

"Okay. How come you looked there?"

"I dunno." Sofia shrugged. "To see if my mom was in there?"

"Was she?"

"No."

"Did she ever come when you screamed?"

"No."

During their first meeting, the district attorney had told Sofia that after she called 911, police had stopped her father's car near the border of New Jersey several hours later. He had a body in his plastic-lined trunk. The man had been stabbed. They found the knife in the trunk with him. It had her father's fingerprints on it. The district attorney also told her that the finger didn't belong to that body. It belonged to a woman who had disappeared the day before. Her body was never found.

When the police had stopped her father, her mother wasn't in the car.

It was only later—hours after she called 911—that her mother came home. In new clothes that Sofia had never seen before.

"What did you do then?"

"I went upstairs."

"But before that—what else did you see before you went upstairs?"

"Objection."

"Sustained."

"Did you see anything else that wasn't normal in the basement before you went upstairs?"

"Yes." At first, she'd thought it was a small animal. A mouse or something that maybe the cat had brought inside. But then she noticed the fingernail. It had pale pink sparkly polish. When she saw it, she'd leaned over and threw up, her vomit splashing all over the floor.

"What did you see?" She realized this was the second time the district attorney had asked this.

"A finger."

"Was it attached to a person?"

Sofia shook her head.

"Please answer verbally."

"No."

"Where was it?"

"On the floor of the closet."

"Is there a gap between the door of the closet and the basement floor?"

Sofia scrunched up her face for a second. "Yes."

"Is that gap big enough for the finger to fit under."

"Objection."

"Sustained."

She looked up and the district attorney made a gesture that she shouldn't answer.

"Did some of the blood also go in the closet?"

"Yes."

"Tell us about when you first noticed the finger."

"I just saw something pink."

"Did you touch it?"

"No." Sofia shrunk back in horror, making a face.

"What else was around the blood?"

"On the floor?"

"Yes, on the floor."

"A big bottle of bleach."

"Anything else."

"A mop."

"Did it look like someone had cleaned?"

"Objection."

"Overruled."

"No, it looked like someone was about to clean but ..."

"Objection."

"Sustained."

"Just one more question."

"What did you do after that, when you went upstairs?"

"Called the cops."

CHAPTER 23

KATE

A*pril 2019*
Minneapolis

My mom was in her element.

She loved nothing more than having people over and feeding them.

Every month, my parents and their friends took turns hosting a dinner party.

This month it was our turn. Lily and Julia's families were over.

My mom woke up early today to start the sauce on the stove. The homemade meatballs, Italian sausages and pork chops had been simmering in the sauce for hours by the time everyone arrived, laughing, and carrying bottles of wine and desserts.

As soon as they walked in, Julia, Lily and I headed to the basement. My room was small for the three of us so we headed downstairs to the family room where we either listened to music, watched a movie, or just gossiped.

We'd just settled into the worn leather couch when Julia, dressed in a long, flowered skirt and a tank top, reached into her canvas bag and brought out three airplane-size containers of rum.

I reached over to the small mini fridge and brought out three cans of cola.

Within a few minutes, we were buzzed and giggling, sharing stories and talking about cute boys.

"Speaking of ..." Julia said, sitting upright and jabbing me in the clavicle. "Your boy. Tell us more. Have you done it?"

"Oh, Julia!" Lily seemed really shocked. But I just giggled. Lily glared at me.

After sex ed class in eighth grade, Lily and I had made a pact to remain virgins until we got to college. It was too stressful to think about STDs and getting pregnant and getting serious like that. We'd hold our fingers up in a "V" sign for Virgin to remind ourselves of our pact.

Julia had thought we were absurd from the beginning.

"I'm losing it the first chance I have," she'd said.

And she pretty much did. She always spent her summers in France with her parents' extended families and she came back from the summer before ninth grade with tales of an older man who had taken her virginity and very nearly her heart. She cried about him for two months, and then started dating a senior at our school.

After a while, my mom shouted for us to come up for dinner.

When I walked in, I was grateful that my mom was such a good host. I loved the way our table looked with its brightly colored tablecloth and the dimmed lighting and flowers and candles everywhere. And the food smelled amazing.

My mom baked her own bread and the smell of it could make anyone swoon.

We took our places around the large wooden table and I felt warm and happy. It was probably the alcohol, but a feeling of such peace and joy overcame me that I thought for a second I might cry.

I smiled at my mother and father. I seriously had the best parents in the world. I didn't care what that crazy witch said, my mother was a really good person.

Watching her, I felt a surge of love. Her cheeks were pink like they got when she drank wine and her black eyes flashed in the candle light as she laughed.

Lily's dad, Dan, made a toast. He stood, his bald head reflecting the light of the dimmed chandelier. He was sweating a little, but that was just Dan. He was all man. Sweat and bald head and all.

"To lifelong friends. May we know them, love them, and never forget them."

"Hear hear!" Everyone raised their glasses. My mom had poured a few sips of wine into the glasses so Lily and Julia and I could participate.

After I downed mine, I set the glass down. Dan winked and poured a little of his wine in my glass. I looked around surprised but before I could do anything, Julia grabbed my glass and chugged it and then slammed the glass down on the table with a flourish.

We burst into laughter. Lily on the other side, just glared.

She never liked it when we got along too well with her dad. She was such a Daddy's girl.

But I couldn't blame her. Her mother was dead and Gretchen was off in la la land most of the time.

Speaking of Gretchen, she sat with her usual scowl. My dad, God bless him, had her engaged in conversation and actually managed to elicit a smile from her.

As we dug into our pasta, I felt a ripple of pride for my parents They were such great hosts. They made sure everyone had a good time. Even old Gretchen was now laughing.

Alex and Cecile were telling a story about how they got lost in Amsterdam after they smoked the local weed. My mom flashed a glance my way as if she were embarrassed that this had come up with us sitting there.

Lily and Julia and I exchanged looks. Did this mean we were considered adults? It was the first time they'd ever spoken like this in front of us.

My Dad arched an eyebrow and nodded his chin our way.

"*Mon dieu,*" Cecile said, noticing his look. "Is this inappropriate in front of the girls?"

My mom smiled. "I doubt it's anything they haven't heard before."

Dan spoke up. "As the resident psychologist, I don't think this conversation will do any permanent damage."

Everyone bust out laughing. Except Gretchen who rolled her eyes.

But I swear there was the slightest smile just under the surface of her serious expression.

After dinner, my parents grabbed their wine glasses and headed for the deck.

"Let's blow this joint," Julia said, grabbing her bag from the couch.

Our parents all smiled at us and told us to not stay out late, but we knew that on the nights of their dinner parties nobody paid attention to when we came home.

They usually fell into a deep sleep after a night of heavy food and alcohol.

In the car, Lily pointed at my necklace. She had a matching one at home.

"What should we get for our birthday this year?"

I shrugged. "We have some time."

In the flickering light from passing street lights, Lily's face looked odd. "Should we look at bracelets?"

"Yeah," I said. Every year we bought matching jewelry for our birthdays, which were only ten days apart. It had started when we were in first grade and Lily had given me a necklace that matched one she wore.

"Maybe I want a matching one too!" Julia said in a huff. She tapped her fingernails on the steering wheel as she drove.

I'd always wondered if she'd felt left out because of our birthday tradition.

"Yes!" I said. "It can be a birthday-slash-graduation-going-to-college gift we give each other."

"Deal!" Julia said, now smiling.

I noticed Lily didn't say anything

She'd always been a little jealous of Julia. Once she'd even said that she worried me and Julia would become best friends and ditch her. I'd told her she was silly.

CHAPTER 24

SOFIA

August 2019
Minneapolis

The next morning, Jason was dressed and ready to go to his job at the magazine. He leaned over the bed to kiss Sofia goodbye. Like everything was normal. She'd woken to his voice, low and comforting. Squinting, she tried to focus on his face. He had shaved but his eyes were bloodshot. His skin was gray. They'd both aged a decade in the past week.

As he pulled back from his kiss, she clutched at his arm. "Please don't go. It's Saturday."

He sank onto the bed, holding her hand tightly. "We talked about this last night, remember? We're on deadline for the January issue. I'm way behind. I have to go in today." He was patient with her, as he always had been.

Sofia remembered. He'd briefly mentioned it the night before.

Now, sitting on the edge of the bed, Jason was talking and she tried hard to tune in. Eventually she got the gist of what he was trying to tell her, the same thing he'd said last night: he needed to keep busy so he didn't let his thoughts and grief overcome him.

"Maybe that would help you, too," he said. His brow furrowed. "I worry about you being here alone all day."

Sofia had ignored all the emails from her graphic design clients, worried they'd be messages of condolence. She wasn't sure when she'd work again. If ever. She didn't care if they went into foreclosure and had to rent a studio apartment in a shitty part of town. None of that mattered anymore. All she wanted to do was find who killed Kate and make them pay.

Now, she realized that Jason was staring at her waiting. He had said something.

Sofia sat up. "I'll be fine. She tried to smile but it felt like a grimace. "I get it. Go to work. I'll be fine."

Relief flooded his face. "Are you sure?"

"Yes," Sofia smiled wanly as she said it, knowing her smile didn't reach her eyes. But Jason was willing to grasp at whatever assurance she offered, even if they both knew she was lying.

She took Jason's hand and broached the subject, carefully, delicately.

"Jas? Do you think they'll get the person who did this?"

He closed his eyes and shook his head. "I don't know."

"What if you found him first? What would you do?" She held her breath, waiting for his answer. Jason had always been the calm, cool, and collected one in their marriage. That's one reason she'd married him. He was her opposite. *Please tell me what to do. What I want to do is ... murder. Tell me the right thing to do.*

"How would I find him?"

"Just say you did." She watched him carefully.

He shot her a look with a question in it. "I'd hand him over to the police."

"Wouldn't you want to ... hurt him in some way?"

Jason shook his head, slowly, his tongue working the inside of his cheek. "Of course. But I wouldn't. It won't change a damn thing. It won't bring her back to us, Sof."

"But that person should be punished for what he did."

Jason stood, smoothing his palms down his pants, eyes blinking and darting this way and that, feet pointed toward the bedroom door. "It won't matter. None of it matters. If they find the guy or not. It doesn't change a god damn thing."

Now she was on her knees on the bed. "Our daughter's funeral was less than twenty-four hours ago and you're going to work? For fuck's sake, Jason."

But he was already gone. She heard the front door slam. He was pissed. She didn't care. So was she.

• • • •

FEELING A LITTLE WEAK, she ventured out of the bedroom and down to the main level, holding tight to the stairway bannister, not trusting her trembling legs. She caught a glimpse of herself in a mirror as she passed. Hair plastered to one side of her head and sticking up in tangles on the other. Cheek red and marked from the pillow. Her olive skin looked greenish, her normally berry colored lips a translucent whitish pink. And she smelled sour.

Downstairs, she peered in the refrigerator. It was full with a mishmash of covered dishes that people had brought by and Cecile had labeled in her neat handwriting. Lasagna. Tater tot hot dish. Lentil soup. Tuna noodle casserole.

She shoved them all aside and found what she was looking for – a plastic bottle of orange juice. She grabbed it and a hunk of gruyere cheese and slumped to the floor, her back against the cupboards and the refrigerator door still open as she bit hunks off the wedge of cheese and swallowed it down by chugging the orange juice, letting it dribble onto her silk cream nightgown.

A few minutes later she realized the refrigerator door was wide open and leaned over to kick it closed with her foot. She wasn't sure how much time passed before she finally pulled herself to a standing position and headed back upstairs. She crawled into bed with her laptop and cell phone and propped all the pillows against the headboard, making an impromptu command center.

Fingers trembling, she typed in her mother's name: Marie Therese Castellucci.

Nothing.

Of course, it wouldn't be that easy.

It had been years since that day she testified. The day her mother abandoned her. When the district attorney had brought Sofia home from the courthouse, the house had been empty, even of all Sofia's belongings—gone. Her mother had packed up the house and disappeared. After a few hours in a room at the county courthouse, Sofia's Aunt Rose came to pick her up.

Not once had Sofia tried to find her mother. Until now. If she were dead, it was possible there was an obituary out there somewhere.

Next, she logged onto several ancestry websites.

Nothing on the Castellucci family at all. Not a word. Not her mother. Not her father. Not her grandparents or even her Aunt Rose. Bizarre. It was as if they had never existed.

There was nothing on her father, either. No obituary. Nothing. But that didn't mean he wasn't dead. Maybe murderers serving life sentences didn't get obits.

After exhausting every avenue she could think of to find information about her parents or family online, Sofia realized she had one last option: calling the prison phone number.

Heart racing and her face icy, she typed in the name of the prison. Even seeing the name made her hands shake. Holding her cell phone, she stared at the number, willing herself to punch in the digits. She would have to call to find out if her father was still housed there. Or even if he were still alive.

She was shaking so badly she misdialed the first time, getting a disconnected number. The second time, she got an automated voice. When she finally got through to the operator, she was transferred and put on hold. Finally, after twenty minutes someone answered.

"Yes. Marco Castellucci is housed at this facility."

Hearing his name was like a small shock. She closed her eyes. He was alive. And he was still in prison.

"Ma'am?"

"Yes, I'm here. Thank you."

"Do you want me to transfer you to the line where you can request to speak to him?"

"No!" Sofia said quickly.

"I can give you that number for future reference so you don't have to go through the system again."

Sofia copied down the phone number on a scrap of paper, tucked it in her wallet, and hung up. It took her a few minutes to regain her composure. Images of her father and the baby and the finger intermingled.

Next, Sofia logged onto Instagram and created an account called CollegeCarla. Stupid name, but who cared. She found Kate's Instagram page and her heart nearly stopped beating.

The last picture Kate had posted had been the night she had died. It was a selfie with Lily. They were laughing and leaning into one another at the bar, two large mixed drinks in front of them. Sofia shook her head. She'd been so foolish. If she'd been monitoring Kate's social media activity, she might have realized her daughter was getting drunk that night of the empty nest party. She could have gone to pick her up instead of letting her walk out of the bar alone where she was ripe pickings for a monster to prey on.

Tracing her finger along Kate's face she knew she would give her own life for one more chance to touch that perfect skin.

Her daughter was wearing jeans with a white blouse and small gold cross necklace. Her arm holding the drink had a cuff bracelet Sofia had never seen before. Sofia bet that Lily had a matching one and that both girls had bought them to celebrate Lily's birthday last week.

With a jolt that made her gasp, Sofia realized that Kate's birthday was only a few days away. A birthday Kate would never celebrate. Her beautiful daughter would forever be seventeen.

A vise-like pain gripped her chest. She paused, closing her eyes and tried to calm herself. *Don't go there. Don't think about it. Concentrate on finding who killed Kate.*

After a few seconds, she opened her eyes and scrolled on.

The pictures Kate had posted were mainly selfies of her with her friends. A few pictures were of all the new items she'd bought for her dorm. She'd wanted a Parisian theme, so it meant a lot of black and white pictures of Paris and Eiffel Tower-themed sheets and a gray comforter. She'd hash tagged them #CityofLight.

Jason and Sofia had promised Kate a trip to Paris as her present when she graduated from college. Cecile had the whole trip practically planned already. Kate had never even left the United States. Now, she never would.

Sofia clasped her fist to her mouth. She had no more tears, just wracking tearless sobs that made it hard to breathe. Why had someone killed Kate? What had she ever done? She was innocent. She hadn't yet lived at all. Sofia would never see her daughter graduate from college, marry, have children, any of it. It wasn't fair. Why her? Why their family?

But she knew.

She knew why.

Sofia had spent her life expecting to someday suffer, not only for her father's sins, but for her own. But she never dreamed the wretchedness would come at her daughter's expense. Unless someone from her past had planned it that way.

She scrolled through Kate's followers, searching for Ali Yassin. She instantly followed him and then scrolled through his posts, hand shaking, waiting to see a picture of him and Kate.

She clicked the heart on several of Ali's pictures and then made a comment on one of them—a picture of him taken in July. He had baggy jeans and no shirt and his burnished bronze abdomen and chest, silky smooth and hairless, looked like it was straight out of a

1980s-designer underwear ad. Several girls had posted comments at the time, but now Sofia added her own: "Hawt!"

That ought to get his attention.

But he hadn't posted for weeks. His last picture had been with a blond girl. He had his arms around her and was smiling, but the smile didn't reach his eyes. She was gazing up at him adoringly. The about-to-be-dumped girlfriend? Facebook had tagged her. Jenna Carter. Sofia instantly tried to follow her, but her Instagram account was private. She sent a follow request anyway.

Within a few seconds, however, the girl approved CollegeCarla to follow her.

Sofia scrolled through Jenna Carter's photos, trying to match them with the night Kate was killed. Then she found them. Early on in the night Jenna had posted a selfie with Ali. She was glowing, but he was looking away. He didn't have his arm around her or anything. He looked uncomfortable and caught off guard.

Staring at the photo, Sofia's mind spun in endless circles. She examined the girl's haughty pose, hand on her hip. The slight snarl. She looked tough. What had Ali said? "You haven't met Jenna." What did this girl do when she found out Ali was seeing Kate? Was a girl like that capable of murder?

Hand shaking, Sofia scrolled to the next picture. It was three days after Kate's death. It showed Jenna on a Florida beach and said, "Enjoying the single life before I start school at St. Ben's."

St. Benedict's was up by St. Cloud, only two hours away from the Twin Cities.

Sofia looked at the girl, her head thrown back laughing, a drink in her hand. The other hand on her bare hip, above a red bikini. She either got over the break up pretty easily or had skipped town to avoid a murder rap.

Grabbing her cell phone, Sofia dialed Detective Marley. But the call went straight to voice mail.

"The boy's ex-girlfriend. Jenna Carter. He was dumping her for Kate that night. That's motive, right? Right?"

Realizing she was speaking to dead air, Sofia hung up.

After an hour spent trying to find anything she could on Jenna Carter, Sofia came up with the fact that the girl was from Blaine and was in her second year at St. Benedict's studying International finance and chemistry. She had been home in Blaine for the summer and now was in Florida with her parents, an annual vacation the family always took in August.

Still didn't make her innocent, Sofia thought.

She logged onto Instagram and left a comment on the beach photo: "Bet you miss that cute Somalian boy you were dating in Minneapolis, don't you? Wink. Wink."

It might be too much. She needed to beef up her Instagram page so it wasn't so suspicious. She Googled pictures and found a beautiful young woman who looked sort of like Kate—long brown hair, big brown eyes and pink lips—and used the photos as pretend selfies on CollegeCarla's Instagram. Once she posted a few of them, she went and followed every one of Kate's Instagram followers.

Then she checked to see if Jenna had commented.

She had.

"Did we meet at Ali's last week? Me and him are history. I can't be tied down at school. Too many cute boys at St. Ben's, ya know."

Sofia narrowed her eyes.

Was the girl playing some game?

If she was, she was in for a big surprise because now she was playing in the big leagues and had no idea what she'd gotten into.

"I hear you," Sofia typed. "Having a boyfriend is the dumbest thing we can do at this age. I'm totally a free agent. I break up with them, they don't break up with me."

Sofia waited for Jenna to respond, looking for a little arrow that showed there was a message. But there was nothing.

CHAPTER 25

KATE

April 2019

Dinkytown

Julia came to a screeching halt in front of a bar called Lucky's that wasn't far from where the bookstore was.

I raised an eyebrow as I looked at her.

Lily unbuckled and leaned into the front seat, her head between us.

"What's up, Jules?"

Julia was rummaging in her bag. Then she was shuffling what looked like business cards.

With a flourish, she handed Lily and I each a small identification card.

"Whaaaattt??!!" Lily and I both squealed examining our fake I.D.'s.

Julia had made us take photos at the drug store about a month ago. We'd told the clerk they were passport photos. I'd known Julia was trying to find someone to make fake I.D.'s, but I'd no idea she'd actually done it.

"Come on, bitches," she said. "Let's go order a drink."

CHAPTER 26

SOFIA

A*ugust 2019*
Minneapolis

Sofia was still in bed when Jason walked into the bedroom the next morning looking defeated.

"I know it's Sunday, but I'm going in to the magazine and I'm going to work late tonight. Deadline."

Sofia didn't answer, just nodded.

"You sure? I'll be home really late."

For the first time in their marriage Sofia wondered if he was lying about working late.

She'd never once doubted him. But everything had changed.

"I'll be fine." She watched his face carefully as she said it.

He didn't look guilty. He just looked wrecked.

"I'm sorry...," he trailed off. He was sorry for what? That their daughter was dead? That he was smothering his grief with work? That he was emotionally unavailable? Sorry for what?

"I know." Sofia stood, brushing her hair, something she forgot to do most mornings nowadays. Looking in the mirror at the dark circles under her eyes, Sofia estimated she'd aged ten years since they'd found Kate's body. She didn't care. None of it mattered. Watching Jason tuck in his shirt, Sofia was suddenly filled with jealousy. How great it would be to have a distraction, to be so busy she couldn't think about Kate. But it was impossible. Even if she had a demanding deadline she'd still be constantly distracted, figuring out how to hunt down Kate's killer.

Jason caught her watching. "You sure?"

She forced a smile and nodded. "I'll call Cecile and go out to eat."

Sofia realized it seemed weird to make plans like that. It was something she'd said and done a million times over the years and yet now it seemed like a massive betrayal of Kate. She should be spending every second searching for Kate's killer, not going out with her friend and eating.

Jason raked a hand through his hair and then bit his lip as if trying not to cry. His voice choked up. "Every time I walk past her room I want to die."

This time she did reach for him and they held each other for what felt like an eternity before he broke away.

As soon as she heard the front door close, Sofia grabbed her phone. When the detectives had left the other day, they'd carted a box of Kate's papers and journals, her laptop, and her iPad. They'd given Sofia a list of what they'd taken. It said "Evidence Sheet" at the top. Sofia hadn't wanted to look at it, just shoved it in her bag.

She hadn't heard from them. Maybe they'd found something. She punched in what had become a familiar number.

"Detective Marley."

"This is Sofia Kennedy—Kate's mom." She made a point to use her daughter's name. So far, Detective Marley had never said "Kate."

There was a long pause and she held her breath, closing her eyes tight, waiting.

"Yes, Mrs. Kennedy, I was going to call you later and see if I can have you come in again or if I can come over. I want to go over everyone who had contact with your daughter, everyone she knew."

"Okay. I'll get dressed."

Sofia was ready to race out the door when his next words deflated her:

"How about tomorrow at ten?"

• • • •

THE DOORBELL STARTLED Sofia out of a hazy, drug-induced nightmare where she was chasing a dark figure through shadowy streets.

Glancing at the clock, Sofia realized she'd been asleep for hours. It had grown dark outside.

After speaking to Marley, she'd taken a pill and drank some water with the Roofie drops and then collapsed on the couch. The drugs had made her brain fuzzy, hazy. She'd fallen asleep before she called Cecile.

Sofia sat up unsteadily, gripping the arm of the couch. "Coming. Just a second." Her voice cracked. For a split-second, hope filled her that it was the detectives and that they'd made an arrest. But when she pressed her eye to the peephole, she saw a cluster of teenage girls. Lily and Julia and Ava and Molly. Kate's closest friends. Their eyes were red and faces puffy from crying. Ava wiped tears away with her sleeve.

Sofia opened the door and gave a wan smile. "Come in, girls."

The girls trudged in, pausing at the entryway to kick off their Nikes and Adidas. Minnesota polite.

Sofia waved them on. "Don't worry about your shoes."

She gestured to the darkened living room. "Sit down. Can I get you something to drink? Some coffee or water or soda?" As she spoke, she flicked on the lights.

Lily and Ava sat on the loveseat, looking around as if they didn't know where to settle their gaze. Molly sat on the chair. Julia curled up on the couch beside Sofia.

"We wanted to come by before we left for school," Julia said, reaching for Sofia's hand.

It suddenly felt like a large stone had lodged itself in her chest. This weekend was supposed to be when she dropped off Kate at college. All the parents had planned on driving up together on Friday and spending the weekend. It had been delayed for Kate's funeral on Saturday. Now, only Gretchen was driving the two girls Monday morning.

Sofia sat on the couch, perched on the edge. Gently, she extracted her hand from Julia's giving her a sad smile. She pressed her lips tightly together before she spoke, trying to compose herself, fighting back tears. She had to be the adult here. "You girls meant so much to Kate. She really loved you."

Realizing she was talking about Kate in the past tense for the first time, Sofia cringed but then shook it off. She needed to be the strong one right then.

Nobody answered. Julia rubbed her back. It wasn't right that these girls were comforting her. They were the ones who needed comforting. She examined their pained faces.

Tears dripped down Lily's face. She wiped them off delicately with one finger. A large silver cuff on Lily's arm caught the light and Sofia stuck her fist to her mouth. It was the matching birthday cuff. She started to say something about it, but felt a giant lump lodge itself in her throat.

The girls all stared at her as she tried to regain her composure.

Finally, taking a deep breath, Sofia plastered a smile on her face. "Thank you so much for coming by." Her voice managed to sound normal, even though her heart hurt just looking at them.

They sat there in silence for a moment and then Lily burst into tears, burying her face in her hands.

"Lily!" Julia said, scolding her and rubbing Sofia's back even harder.

"I'm sorry," Lily said. "We said we weren't going to come over here and cry."

"It's okay to cry," Sofia said with meaning. "It really is. Please don't apologize for that."

"We wanted to come over and see if we could do anything, you know, anything to help. Anything you need, Mrs. Kennedy," Molly earnestly bobbed her head. "We want to do something."

Sofia looked at the girls. They must feel so scared and helpless. Sofia thought for a few seconds. When the detectives had searched Kate's room, she had realized that one day she was going to have to face dealing with her daughter's empty room. She didn't want to leave it untouched, as if it were a shrine. She couldn't do that. Walking by it every day and seeing it like it was when Kate was alive was too much. Maybe for some parents it was reassuring, but for Sofia it seemed like torture, like a stab to the heart every time she passed.

Although she didn't know if she could handle even saying the words, she took a deep breath. "I am going to need your help, girls."

All the girls looked up at her.

"But not today."

Ava nodded.

"It's going to be a really hard thing to do and that's one reason I need you guys to help me." She watched them. They were waiting eagerly. They really did want to do something. Maybe it would be best to do it sooner than later. But it was too soon. She thought about what Jason had said about walking by Kate's room.

"I'm going to need you guys to help me go through Kate's room. I don't want to do it. But I think I have to. I don't know if I can walk by her room every day with it ... the way it is. And I don't know what to do with it. If you want, you can sort through it ... maybe find some things you might want to keep. I'd like that." As soon as she said it, she realized it was true. "Kate loved you guys so much. She'd want you to have and enjoy her things. Her books. Even her clothes and jewelry."

It was barely a flicker, the smallest movement, but Sofia thought she saw Lily flinch. Maybe she was asking too much of them, maybe the task would be too painful, but when she looked at Lily again, the teen nodded.

"Mrs. Kennedy, you just tell us what you need and when. We'll be there," Julia said.

Sofia had been a little more forthcoming with the girls than she had planned, but she thought it was also good to not gloss over the pain. She wasn't going to collapse at their feet and beg them to let her hold them and stroke their hair since she couldn't hold her own daughter anymore, but she *could* share her pain. Let them know it was okay and healthy to grieve.

"Why don't we think about doing it during the Thanksgiving break, when you guys are home again?"

"That's when we'll do it," Julia said, standing.

Sofia stared at her. When had she become so mature, so poised, so wise? The other girls stood, as well.

Thanksgiving break would be perfect. That would give everyone some time. They needed to start their new lives at college. And seeing them this soon after Kate's death was harder than she had realized it would be. Sitting with them and seeing their bright faces with endless possibilities for the future was a brutal reminder of what Kate would never have.

Sofia stood. "Thank you for coming, girls."

Julia touched her arm on the way to the door, searching her eyes. "Are you sure there isn't anything else we can do?"

Sofia wrapped her in a hug and breathed the words into her hair. "Thank you. Thank you, dear Julia for being such a good friend to Kate. Your mother is so lucky—"

Her words trailed off. What was she going to say? Your mother is so lucky you are alive?

She pulled back and turned to the other girls. "Thank you. I think the best thing you can do is to remember our Kate and go on to enjoy your first year of college. Please do that. Don't feel guilty about it. It's what Kate would've wanted. I'm certain."

Lily looked down. Sofia knew she should go comfort her, but she just couldn't. Not right then. Someday, she would. She loved Lily. But there was that tiny lingering spark of something—anger or annoyance? Sofia knew it wasn't fair. Lily couldn't have prevented Kate's death. Maybe if she'd been with her, they both would've been killed. It wasn't Lily's fault. And one day she'd tell her that. Just not today.

A few seconds after she closed the door, someone knocked.

Lily was standing there alone.

"I know you said Thanksgiving, but can I please go see Kate's room now?"

Sofia smiled through her tears. "Of course, Lily. Go on up, sweetie."

"Thanks." Lily rushed by.

After several minutes waiting by the stairs, Sofia finally sat down. Part of her was tempted to call up to Lily or go see if she was okay, but she didn't have the energy. She was afraid of what she might find: maybe Lily sprawled on the floor weeping. Or staring catatonic at Kate's belongings.

Finally, after the other girls had honked the car horn, Lily came back down. Her hair was messed up and her nose and eyes were bright red. Sofia was glad she'd given her some privacy to grieve alone in Kate's room. Lily shuffled to the door without looking at Sofia. Opening it, she walked out, leaving the door wide open behind her.

Sofia stood in the doorway watching until their car drove away.

Back in the house, Sofia saw she'd missed about five calls from Jason and another call from Cecile. She punched in her friend's number and spoke before Cecile could.

"Julia just left. Cecile, she has turned out to be such an incredible young woman. She was comforting *me*. She is so poised and so wise. You've done an amazing job with her."

"Thank you." Cecile's voice was quiet. Then she cleared her throat. "Hey, listen. Jason called and said he was working late and you weren't answering your phone ... for some reason he thought we'd be together eating dinner or something?"

"Oh, yes. I'm sorry, I forgot. I think I'm going to go to bed now, but maybe tomorrow night we could get together?"

"Okay." Cecile's voice seemed hesitant and Sofia felt guilty.

"Talk to you tomorrow then." Sofia hung up before her friend could say more and collapsed onto the couch. Leaning over, she squeezed two drops from the vial on the end table into her water. Keeping her shit together in front of the teens had done her in. All the platitudes she had spewed, the happy face she had put on. It was too much. She had kept her shit together for those girls, but she was a fucking train wreck barely holding onto her own sanity. She felt so bad for all of them. And felt horrendous guilt that a small part of her blamed Lily for letting Kate go off on her own.

The drugs were starting to make her thoughts hazy. Whatever happened to girls' code? You never let your friend wander off at night alone, especially if she'd been drinking. Sofia's last thought as she drifted off to sleep was that Kate was dead because Lily let her go off on her own. Lily had always been a bit boy crazy. She'd probably wanted to stay behind and talk to some cute boy. And now Kate was dead because of it.

Sofia didn't know if she could ever forgive Lily for that.

It was standard girls' code to stick together. You never let a friend venture off into a dangerous situation. Not if you were a teen girl in today's world.

As Sofia's eyes grew heavy, she mumbled to herself with the past blending into the present. "You have to keep the code no matter what. Loyalty to your friends and family—nothing else matters."

Sofia knew this first hand.

CHAPTER 27

SOFIA

July 1988

Federal Correctional Institute, Danbury, Connecticut

The man on the other side of the Plexiglas window was shrunken and seemed frail. When he smiled, eighteen-year-old Sofia realized he was missing a tooth off to one side.

His smile left her cold.

She could tell he felt the chill—through the plastic between them and through the years—because his smile faded as he reached for the beige phone on the wall beside him.

Sofia sat still. Not moving. Not blinking.

This was the man she'd been afraid of the past eight years. This short, stooped man with gray hair and bad teeth. She was emboldened by the realization that he was nothing more than an old man who would spend the rest of his life behind bars. He couldn't hurt her anymore.

That's when she smiled back.

It wasn't a warm smile.

She carefully wiped off the phone and then put it to her ear. She didn't speak.

"Sofia, my *principessa*. You came to see your papa before you go off somewhere to college? Rosie, God bless her soul, told me you were accepted to about a dozen schools. You're a smart kid, aren't you?" He raised a bushy eyebrow and cocked his head. Something in his voice sent a tremor of fear through her. "You feel guilty for sending your old man up the river? You betray your own flesh and blood? The code of silence? *Omerta*? You broke it in a way I've never seen in all my years. And look at me now. Tell me you feel guilty?"

She didn't answer, but very slowly, nearly imperceptibly, shook her head, one eyebrow slightly raised.

"You betray, like a traitor, and you feel nothing?" He almost looked amused.

"Not a god damn thing." Her words were slow and measured.

He cocked an eyebrow at her. "You are not a little girl anymore are you?"

She shook her head again, eyes cold.

"Alas, that also means I may no longer be able to protect you."

"You never could. You never did."

"Ah. That is where you are wrong. Dead wrong. They wanted to teach you a lesson. Teach everyone a lesson about what happens to *traditori*." Traitors. His lip curled as he said the word. "The worst *traditori* are the ones who turn on their own *famiglia*. But I made sure you would not be hurt. It cost me a lot to stop them, Sofia. And I'm not talking about money only. The reason you are walking around today is only because of the respect The Family has for me."

Sofia stared past his shoulder. His words meant nothing to her. She had nothing to say.

"Because of me ..." He repeated, beating his chest.

She smiled. She was no longer afraid. Maybe that's why she had to come here today before she moved cross-country and left the Castellucci name behind forever. One last glimpse of her father. She needed to come and see him locked up. To see him where he belonged.

She stared at him. Her face a mask of indifference. She could tell it unnerved him and that made her feel powerful. He looked away and then cleared his throat.

"How is your mother?" As he asked, he gave Sofia a look she'd never seen before, a calculating, measured glance.

For a second, she was confused. He didn't know? Her mother hadn't told him about disappearing, abandoning her? Did that mean her mother had never come here to visit him? Then she realized none of it mattered.

She didn't care. Not anymore.

"I asked you a question." The same voice he used to command her around when she was little. Well, she wasn't little anymore.

She lifted her chin and met his eyes with her own steely gaze. "I have no mother. I have no father, *capisci*? I hope you both rot in hell."

"*Dio mio*!" His face grew red and he slapped a beefy fist onto the counter before him. The guard started his way but then he lowered his voice, leaning forward and glowering at Sofia through the glass. "What kind of monster have I fathered?"

That's when Sofia began to laugh. She laughed until she cried, tears streaming down her face, hanging up the phone, but still sitting there, unable to speak or stand, barely able to breathe through her laughter.

Her father watched her in horror, looking from side to side, as if worried other people were watching.

Finally, her tears and laughter finished, she stood and walked away without another glance at the withered old man on the other side of the glass.

CHAPTER 28

KATE

May 2019
Dinkytown

Dear Kate,

You are so beautiful.

I've watched you when you haven't known I was looking.

I know I'm not your type, but when I saw you looking sad and insecure the other day it prompted me to write this note. What I want more than anything is to beg you to run away with me.

You are everything a man could wish for in a woman.

I have to say, I've fallen madly in love with you.

But you don't even know I'm alive.

Your Secret Admirer

The note had thrown me off at first. I'd thought it was from Ali. He hadn't come to my work tonight, even though it was Monday. When I walked out to my car and saw the piece of white paper under my windshield wiper, of course I thought it was from him. It wasn't until I read some key phrases that I realized it was from someone else. And then the last bit: "You don't even know I'm alive."

I was reading the note sitting in the driver's seat of my car and I instantly locked all the doors, heart thudding, and searched my rearview mirror. I saw a figure coming closer—and fast—I gasped and fumbled for my keys.

And then the face was at my window.

Ali.

I rolled it down, tempted to drive away.

"I ran all the way here. I'm so sorry I'm late. I fell asleep." He was out of breath and didn't have a jacket on. He shivered. It was forty degrees.

"Do you want a ride back?"

He nodded fervently.

On the drive to his place, he explained that he'd helped a buddy move to St. Cloud over the weekend and they'd stayed up all night the night before partying. He drove home at three a.m. and then had to work for a few hours at the café where he waited tables. It ended up he didn't get to sleep until two in the afternoon. He had planned to wake in time to come see me at the bookstore, but had just now woken.

All I could think about was where he had been.

"St. Cloud, huh?" my voice was cold as I pulled in front of his house, keeping the engine running.

"I didn't go there because of that." His voice was quiet.

"But you saw her?"

He nodded. I didn't want it to hurt, but it did.

"I did see her, but I swear, it's over. I wasn't lying to you. We're just friends. If you could even call it that. She needs a friend right now. Her grandpa died and they were really close. She's taking his death very hard."

I didn't answer.

"I know none of that matters to you. Or to us. But what you need to know is that I really, really like you. And I promise I will never lie to you." He reached for my hand. "I promise."

I looked over at him, but the sincerity in his eyes wiped the scowl off my face. I exhaled loudly. Maybe I was a fool, but I believed him.

"Okay."

"Okay? Okay you believe me?"

I nodded.

His grin was brilliant in the dark car.

He grabbed my face and kissed me so long I lost track of time.

"My mom is waiting for me. We're going to catch up on Grey's Anatomy together."

He kissed my brow and then was gone.

It wasn't until I pulled away that I remembered the note.

CHAPTER 29

SOFIA

A*ugust 2019*
Minneapolis

"I can't." Jason's voice left little room for argument.

Sofia stood there with her mouth wide open.

"I thought your deadline was over." Her voice was emotionless, flat.

"It's not that."

She knew what it was.

"It's not like I *want* to go find out how our daughter died, Jason. It's not like something you can decide to do or not do," she said. "It's what you do as a parent. It's like changing your baby's diaper. Nobody wants to fucking change a diaper full of shit, but when you become a parent that's what you do."

"I can't." He repeated. He was deflated. A shell of a human. For a second, a pang of pity zipped through Sofia, but then it flipped to revulsion.

She wanted to scream at him to fucking act like a man.

But then she laughed.

"What?"

She shook her head. It wasn't even worth saying out loud. Act like a man? Men were weak. What he needed to do was act like a woman. A mother. Yes. That's it. Act like a goddamn mother! A mother would do anything for her child. Even in death.

Sofia stormed out of the room.

In her car, she grabbed her cell.

"Cecile? Remember you said if I needed anything? This is a big thing? Do you have any court cases this morning? Can you possibly skip out of the office for a few hours?"

• • • •

THE SOUTH MINNEAPOLIS Police Precinct station was in the same parking lot as the courthouse and jail. Anxiety trickled through Sofia. She hadn't stepped foot inside a courthouse since she testified against her father.

Cecile parked and turned the car off without saying a word.

They both stared out the window.

Sofia breathed in and out, counting to ten.

"Can you take notes?" Sofia said.

"Of course."

When Aunt Rose had cancer, the nurse had suggested that Sofia take notes during doctor's appointments. The nurse had said it was often difficult for a patient to absorb what was said because it was both overwhelming and disturbing.

In this case, Sofia figured she was just like the patient.

Detective Marley met them in the lobby of the police station.

Sofia introduced Cecile as her best friend. Marley didn't seem to think it was odd that Jason wasn't there. Or at least he didn't let on.

After introductions, Marley led them through a squad room with about twenty desks. Desks piled with papers and old cups of coffee. Sofia wondered why it was so quiet and deserted.

"Where is everyone?"

She was trying on normal. How she would have acted before. What she would have said before.

Detective Marley shot her a look.

"Johnson is still working your case with me, but I'll be your main contact."

"Oh." Sofia looked around. "No, I meant in here. Where are all the other police officers?"

"Right? This sure doesn't look like the police station in The Wire," Cecile said.

"Most people are out on the streets." Marley said, leaning down to swipe a handful of butterscotch candies from a bowl on the edge of one desk. "We only come back here to write reports and have roll call and meetings. Shit like that. Sorry. Excuse my language."

"I say 'shit' too. And sometimes even say 'fuck.'" Actually, it was her favorite word. She'd given up trying to stop using it years ago. Sofia tried to soften her words with a smile, but it felt like it was ripping her mouth at the sides, stretching some skin that was going to split in two.

Marley popped a butterscotch candy in his mouth and gave her what was probably a courtesy chuckle. He wove past a big stack of papers threatening to fall off the corner of one desk. "Watch yourself here. Since reports are such a pain, we try to avoid them as much as possible. Hence the empty room."

"Got it."

"Can I grab you ladies a coffee or water?" He spoke around the small yellow candy on his tongue.

"No. Thank you," Cecile said.

Sofia shook her head.

He held the door of a small conference room open. Once they sat down, he turned his chair to face Sofia, crunching the last bit of his candy into bits as he spoke. Cecile took out a sheet of paper and pen and placed them on the table with pen poised to write.

"We've received the results of the autopsy, as you know, and there's no easy way to say this, so I'm just going to be blunt—it looks like her official cause of death is suffocation, but that she also suffered an injury to the back of her head."

In her periphery vision, Sofia was distantly aware of Cecile scribbling on a piece of paper.

Sofia was stuck, her mind revolving around the word "suffocation." It seemed like a very intimate way to kill someone. Suffocating someone seemed to take a determination and strength and deep level of hatred. As a slightly claustrophobic person, Sofia had always thought not being able to breath, say from drowning, would possibly be one of the worst ways to go. She stared into space for a few seconds, focused on a beam of sunlight reflecting off a metal file cabinet. Vaguely, she was aware of Cecile clutching her hand. She didn't know if it was to comfort or be comforted.

The detective continued.

"We believe she might have already been unconscious when she was suffocated, so if it helps at all, her death was probably painless."

Probably. Even an unconscious person would struggle to breathe, wouldn't they?

"How could you know that?" Sofia shot the question at him, feeling guilty for directing her rage at him. Cecile's fingernails were digging into Sofia's palm. Her other hand was writing, making a slight scratching sound.

"I'm just reading what the forensic pathologist told me here. Maybe you might wanna speak to her?"

"I'm sorry, go on." Sofia felt bad. It wasn't his fault her daughter was killed in a horrific way by some monster. "Can you give me more details?" Sofia kept her voice steady.

"I can give you some information, but there are some things I need to keep to myself because they are things that only the perp would know."

He flipped through a file folder she hadn't noticed. He didn't look up as he spoke.

"Let's see here. She wasn't sexually assaulted, so that's good news."

"What the hell?" Sofia nearly stood up, upsetting a stack of papers on the corner of the conference room desk.

"Jesus Christ!" Cecile said with a screech, tossing the pen across the table.

"God, I'm sorry." Marley scrunched down on his knees picking up papers and retrieving Cecile's pen. Sofia glared at his neck until he looked up. When he did he blushed. "Damn it. I could've said that better."

"Yes, you could have." Sofia's voice shook with fury, but she sat back down.

He handed Cecile her pen, which she snatched out of his hand.

"Do you have any specific questions?" Marley said, his voice more subdued.

"That boy, Ali. And that girl, Jenna."

Marley blew out a big breath. "Yes. Got your message. We are confirming their alibis. Any other questions?"

"Are either one of them suspects?"

Detective Marley looked away before he spoke. His tongue was working the inside of his cheek. "We're looking into that right now. As I said, we are checking alibis."

"The bruise."

Cecile raised an eyebrow. Sofia nodded slightly.

Marley quickly flipped through the paperwork then looked up. "The bruise?"

"On her cheek."

"Aha," he said, looking down. "Let me check ... okay it says here, maybe received in an altercation before she lost consciousness."

Sofia sighed loudly and sat back closing her eyes. "She fought back?"

Cecile squeezed her hand tighter.

"It appears that way. A few of her nails were ripped off. Unfortunately, the forensic pathologist couldn't find anything, such as skin or DNA, under the nails. If there was a struggle, which it appears there was, it was brief."

"Oh."

Sofia tried hard not to imagine Kate's last moments, but found images popping into her head anyway. She shook them away.

Marley pushed over a piece of paper.

"It's a list of what we took from Kate's room. Also, a list of her personal effects. We're gonna have to keep all of it for now, you understand?"

Sofia tried to push away the images of Kate's last moments by concentrating on the sheet listing her personal effects. It was a short list. So very few items.

Cecile scooted closer and peered down at the list, her head close to Sofia's. Her hair smelled like grapes. Sofia read, the words blurring at first before she could focus.

1. Women's size small white button down blouse.

2. Juniors size 8 Anthropologie jeans.

3. Gold cross necklace on a 12-inch chain.

4. Brown leather Coach handbag with lipstick, compact mirror, powder.

5. Wallet with identification, $14 in one dollar bills, library card, and debit card.

6. Brown wedge sandals. Brand unknown.

7. Pink brand white underwear and bra.

She looked up at Marley. "That's it?"

"Afraid so."

It felt like cotton was stuffed in Sofia's throat. She wadded up the papers and stuck them in her purse. She couldn't let grief paralyze her. She needed to be strong so she could concentrate on finding who killed Kate.

Marley cleared his throat. "Just a few more questions. Can you think of anyone who might want to harm your family? Maybe not Kate in particular, but who might be after you or your husband?" He paused. "A work colleague? A friend of the family? An acquaintance from your daughter's school? Maybe a family member?"

You will pay for this. Her mother's words echoed in her head. For one split second, Sofia thought about telling Marley. But then she shook her head. Nobody knew her parents were alive. Nobody knew her real name was Sofia Castellucci.

"No. Nobody."

Marley turned to Cecile. She shook her head. "I can't think of anybody who didn't love the Kennedys."

Sofia smiled gratefully at her. But it was a lie. What about that creepy neighbor? He didn't like them. Or that one reader at the magazine who wrote Jason an angry email every week. It didn't matter what Jason wrote about, the man would write and disagree. But Jason covered business—tech—it's not like he wrote about politics or crime. How angry could that man be?

Marley looked down at his papers again. "And I know we went over this, but you and your husband were together the entire evening, correct?"

She looked at him sharply. "Yes." She spit out the word. "Jason was with me every second." Was he asking her this in front of Cecile in case it wasn't true?

"And you were there most of the night, as well, Ms. Moreau."

"Yes. We were there until two or three I think."

"Thank you," Marley said, relaxing into his chair. "We have to ask that. I'm sure you understand, Ms. Moreau.

"Mrs."

"Mrs. Moreau. You are on my list of interviews that I would like to do in this case. I was going to call you but it if would be more convenient we can just speak briefly for a few minutes now."

"That's fine." Cecile's voice was curt.

"Great," he said. "Let's finish this up first. Sofia, can you provide names and addresses of all your other family members?"

For a second Sofia was back in the prison looking at her father behind the thick glass.

"Mrs. Kennedy?" The detective looked concerned. "Other family members."

Sofia swallowed. "There's nobody."

He stared and she squirmed, shaking her head. "No, that's not quite right. Jason has a brother who lives in Montana. They barely talk."

"Is there some problem between them?" Marley said, his pen poised above a pad of paper.

"No, it's not like that. They are eight years apart and were never really close. After Jason's parents died, they pretty much only communicate through a Christmas card every year."

"And your parents?" Marley said.

She didn't hesitate. "Dead. When I was a child. Car crash."

"I'm sorry to hear that," he said.

Looking down, Sofia tried to look suitably sad.

"My Aunt Rose raised me, but she's passed now, as well."

"Rough break."

For a few seconds, it was silent. Sofia breathed deeply trying to calm herself without making it obvious. Marley looked off into space. The silence grew more uncomfortable.

"What about the CCTV footage? The cameras?" she said.

Marley cleared his throat and shuffled a few papers before looking up.

"We're still combing through it, working on some images near the bar. We did get a clip showing her closer to the crime scene. But it's just a snippet. But that reminds me, there is something I wanted to ask you—Do you know anyone who drives a dark SUV?"

"Did someone in a SUV follow her?"

"We're not sure. We did see a vehicle matching that description. We tried to enlarge the picture to see the license plates, but our technology can only go so far. We've sent the images along to another agency that might be able to pick some numbers and letters out."

Sofia searched her memory. Then it hit her. The neighbor drove a dark colored SUV. His was charcoal gray.

But so did thousands of other people who lived in Minneapolis.

Sofia bit the inside of her lip. "You were asking about anyone who might have wanted to harm Kate ... I don't know if he wanted to harm Kate, but if you want to know about people who seem a little suspicious or weird. Our neighbor."

"Oh god, he's an odd one," Cecile said.

Marley raised an eyebrow.

"It seems like our neighbor sometimes spies on us on our back deck ... I don't know if that means anything or not ...He drives a dark gray SUV."

Marley scribbled on his notepad. "Which house?"

"If you are facing our door, it's the one to the right. The brown one."

"Officers are canvassing your neighborhood today," he said. "I think we're done here unless you have more questions. I'll walk you out. You can wait in the lobby until I'm done speaking to Mrs. Moreau."

Cecile frowned. "Anything I would say to you I would say in front of Sofia." She crossed her arms over her chest.

"I understand. But it's standard investigative procedure to do our interviews separately."

Sofia patted Cecile's arm and stood. "It's fine. I'll wait in the lobby." She turned to Detective Marley. "I do have one more question. Is there anything I ... should be doing?"

He pressed his lips together tightly. "I think you need to concentrate on taking care of yourself and your husband. That's the best thing you can do right now. When we make an arrest, you are going to need all your strength to get through the trial. Some people think the arrest is the end, but in all honesty, it's the beginning. And it doesn't make it better. It's hard. Harder than you can imagine."

Sofia was nearly out the conference room door when the detective called her.

"Mrs. Kennedy?"

She turned.

"What is your maiden name?"

Sofia's heart beat double time. "Castle." She made a point to look him right in the eyes. He stared back, his glance unwavering.

"One more thing," he said, writing in his notebook without taking his eyes off her. "Where and when were your parents killed in that car crash?"

"Derby, Connecticut. 1982." Sofia said without a pause.

He gave a wide smile. "Great. Thank you."

CHAPTER 30

SOFIA

A*ugust 2019*
Minneapolis

"Let's go get drunk."

It was the first thing Cecile said when she joined Sofia waiting in the police station lobby.

"Hells to the yes," Sofia said. "But wait? Don't you have to go back to work?"

"Oh fuck 'em," Cecile said.

Once they had pulled out of the police station parking lot, Sofia got up the nerve to ask.

"What did Marley ask?"

"Oh, same stuff as he asked you probably," Cecile said lightly, but Sofia noticed her friend's knuckles grew white clutching the steering wheel.

"Did he ask about that time—you know? In the bar?"

"No. I don't think he knows and I sure didn't say anything."

"Thank you," Sofia felt the tension leave her body.

"It doesn't matter anyway," Cecile said. "It has nothing to do with this."

"Right."

Once when she was in college, Sofia had knocked a woman out in a bar. She'd only been dating Jason for a brief time. His band had been playing that night and his ex-girlfriend had shown up at the bar and provoked Sofia. Before she knew it, Sofia saw red and knocked the girl out. She'd been arrested, but Jason had convinced the girl and her parents not to press charges. After bailing her out of jail, he'd also told Sofia he loved her that night. It was the first time he'd said it and right then Sofia knew she'd marry him.

If he'd seen her violent genetic predisposition in action and still said he loved her, he was her salvation. She vowed then to never be violent again and up until now, had kept her word.

Soon, however, she'd unleash that violence. As soon as she found the person who'd taken Kate away from her. The bar fight was something she was deeply ashamed about. She kept it secret from everyone except Cecile and Jason.

"He also asked if he could question Julia. I said no fucking way," Cecile said. "My daughter is not getting dragged into a murder investigation."

As soon as the words left her mouth, Cecile must've realized how awful it sounded because she immediately apologized.

"I'm sorry. You know I'd do anything to help find Kate's killer, but Julia can't help and I just feel like it would make everything harder. But if you really need her to speak to him? I mean she already spoke to him that first day."

"No, it's fine."

"God, Sofia, I'm sorry."

Sofia opened her mouth to say "it's okay" or "I'll get used to it." But none of it was true so she didn't say anything.

CHAPTER 31

KATE

May 2019
Minneapolis

When I got to work today, there was a letter for me. There was no return address and the date stamp was from Florida. It took me a minute to remember my so-called grandmother has asked for this address. I waited until the manager left and ripped the envelope open. A piece of pink stationary fell out.

Dearest Kate,

Did you know your mother is a killer? Did she tell you how she killed her little brother, the sweet little soul? He was just an infant. She stole into his room and I found her there. He was dead. She has these fits. These uncontrolled fits of rage and violence.

Ask her. DO NOT tell her I told you. But ask her about Angelo. Ask her. See what she says. She will lie to you. Ask her and you will see I tell the truth.

I will be in touch. But DO NOT tell her I have told you. It would be dangerous for us both. She is a dangerous woman. Trust me on this one. I will tell you more later.

Your Grandmother

P.S. Make sure you close your curtains at night when you get undressed. Peeping Toms are everywhere.

I wadded the letter up in a ball in my fist. My knuckles were white. If I could smash my fist through the wall without damaging anything in the bookstore I would. I also didn't want to explain bloody knuckles to my mom and dad. But what could I do with this anger?

I don't know if I've ever felt this way in my life. I hate this woman.

This evil witch claiming to be my grandmother.

Unclenching my fist, I put the paper on the bookstore counter and smoothed it. I tucked it in my journal. I needed to save it. It could be evidence.

If this crazy lady ever said she was coming here, I would take her insane rambling to the police.

Because she was off her rocker. If I knew anything in my life, I knew that my mother would have never harmed a baby. I don't care if she was drugged and hypnotized or paid a million dollars, there is no way my mother could hurt someone like that.

My mom hated violence. She shuddered when she saw guys getting hit on TV in a football game. I begged her to play hockey, but she bribed me, promising me a trip to New York to see the Nutcracker if I'd do dance instead.

She abhorred violence in all forms. There is no way she'd hurt anyone else.

Especially not an innocent baby. I wouldn't ask her.

A tiny part of me wanted to know what my mother would do if I asked her about a baby named Angelo. But I wasn't ready to tell my mother about any of this yet because my so-called grandmother was clearly insane. And dangerous.

As I realized this, a chill ran down my back. She *was* dangerous. As soon as I'd thought it, I realized it was true.

For a second I was tempted to bring all her letters to my mom and dad, but I didn't want them to worry. She was already worried about me being away from home, freaking out about me going away to college. If she thought a loony old woman was after me, she might not let me go.

But if this old witch thought I was ever going to write back to her, or God forbid, meet her in person, she was delusional.

CHAPTER 32

SOFIA

A*ugust 2019*
Minneapolis

Lying in bed later that night, Sofia felt Jason turn away so that his back was facing her.

She replayed the day. Skipping over the autopsy results, she focused on Marley's questions afterward. What the fuck were those questions about her parents and maiden name? What was all that about? How did that have anything to do with Kate's death? Sofia pushed down the panic rising in her throat. But in the back of her mind a tiny part of her wondered if Kate's murder might very well mean that her past had caught up to her. She needed to face that and find out on her own. There was also something else on the periphery of her memory. Something to do with her mother. The harder she tried to grasp it, the more elusive it seemed.

Sofia let it go. For now. She needed to concentrate on one thing: finding the killer and quickly. Not only to avenge Kate's death, but to stop Marley from butting into something that was none of his business. She had no time to waste. She needed to find Kate's killer before Marley unearthed all her family's skeletons and destroyed what little life Sofia had left.

The next day when she awoke Jason was gone, already at work. It was nearly lunchtime.

In the shower, she once again replayed the conversation with Marley in her head.

The neighbor.

He drove a gray SUV. The same type of vehicle seen in surveillance video near Kate the night she was killed.

Sofia dressed and with wet hair and bare feet, stepped out her front door, walked down her steps, and peered over at the neighbor's front porch. Then, she quickly crossed the street and knocked on Mrs. Timmons door.

The elderly woman opened the door with a smile and wiped her hands off on her pants. "Hi, Sofia. I was just getting ready to go work the library sale. Are you ..." then she trailed off. "Oh my. I'm so sorry. I meant to say that I was heartbroken to hear about Kate. Just heartbroken."

Sofia nodded. She couldn't expect the rest of the world to stay on top of her life unraveling in the worst possible tragedy that could ever have happened.

"Thank you." Sofia glanced back across the street. The neighbor's house and front yard looked the same as it always did. Neat, but unlived in. He even had a yard service mow his lawn. He was never outside. That one time at the block party years ago was the only time Sofia had seen him. In fact, she realized she didn't even know his name.

"Mrs. Timmons. I got something in the mail that I think might belong to my neighbor in the brown house. What's his name, again?"

Her face squinted. "Oh, Lordy, I can't remember. Donny or something? Ronny? Something like that. He's an odd fellow. Keeps to himself."

"Yes." *Except when he's spying on me on my back deck.* "Has he always lived there?"

"I think so. He was living with his mom when we moved in around 1979. When his mother died, I think her name was Janelle but we called her Janie, well, when she died he stayed there. I don't know why a grown man would live with his mother, but what do I know?"

Mrs. Timmons cast a glance at her purse and a big bag of books on the couch nearby.

"I'm sorry," Sofia said. "You said you were on your way out. I'll check the name on the letter and slip it under his door."

"I'm really sorry about Kate. I brought over some Tater Tot Hotdish and your friend took it. I think you were sleeping. Don't worry about getting the casserole dish back to me. God knows, I have more than I need at this point in my life, but please let me know if there is anything else I can do."

"Thank you." Sofia turned to leave but then stopped. "Mrs. Timmons, did you see anything weird that night, the night that Kate died? Anything weird in the neighborhood?"

"Well, the police did come to your house, remember?"

Sofia blushed. "Yes, we were a little loud."

Mrs. Timmons patted her arm. "Don't worry. It was probably that grump Danielle Smith who lives down the way who called the police. Always complaining about the kids in the neighborhood. Such a crabby old lady."

Back in her house, Sofia tried to remember if she'd ever met the neighbor's mother, Janelle, called Janie.

And that's when she remembered what had been hovering at the corner of her mind: Her mother's nickname. Her father had always called her mother Nina. Not Marie. Sofia had wondered as a child why he had that nickname for her mother. It wasn't like it was a shortened version of Marie or Therese. She googled Nina Castellucci.

Nothing.

Then, with a jolt, an idea came to her. If her past had caught up with her, if they knew who she really was, they would also know about her name change. They would know she had changed her name to Sofia Castle. It would be just the sort of sick joke her mother would love: changing her name to the same name Sofia had adopted as her own.

She typed "Nina Castle" into the search window.

One hit.

It linked to a small art gallery owned by a Nina Castle. A tiny picture of the owner with her arm around an artist. Fear coursed through her. It was her mother. At first, she barely recognized her. Her mother was smiling. And her severe black hair was now a chic silver. But it was her.

After the terror at seeing her mother's face subsided, fury raced through Sofia. Her mother had been happy, living the good life running a fancy art gallery after abandoning her own daughter.

Fuck you, mother.

Sofia's hands were shaking as she picked up the phone.

"Echo Gallery." The woman sounded young.

Sofia was frozen, her vocal chords paralyzed for a second.

"Hello? May I help you?"

"Is Nina Castle there?" Sofia's heart was pounding so hard she worried the woman could hear it through the phone line.

"I'm sorry, Ms. Castle sold the gallery to us last year. She was in poor health. Is this a friend?"

Sofia swallowed. Get it together. "Do you happen to have a number for her?"

"No, I'm sorry. We haven't been able to find her. We actually owe her some money that we would like to forward to her. That's one reason I was asking if you were a friend. I can take your number if we do ever hear from her, but it's been about a year that we've been trying to find her without any luck."

Sofia didn't answer, just silently hung up and sat holding the phone for a few seconds staring at the picture of the woman whom she had once called Mama.

CHAPTER 33

KATE

J*une 2019*

Minneapolis

The light shimmering from the pool was blinding me.

I squinted at the shadow above me.

Lily.

She handed me a fizzy green drink.

"What is this?" I put my mouth on the straw.

She adjusted her bikini top and glanced at the house. "Shhh. It's a smoothie, but I added a little something-something from my parents' liquor cabinet."

"Oh my God." I sat up and sucked at the sweet and sour deliciousness. "You are awful. And the best friend a girl could have."

She plopped down on the lounge chair next to mine. "Right? Don't you forget it."

Lily had been different lately and I liked it. She was more adventuresome. Less shy and awkward. It was like she was channeling Jules or something. I liked it. I didn't have to spend all my time reassuring her about every little thing.

I turned over onto my stomach and put my head on my folded arms.

"Let me get your back. It's getting red." I felt Lily's fingers on my back, smoothing on sunscreen.

"Thanks, Lil."

"You're looking good, Kate. Did you lose weight?"

It was a weird, veiled, backhanded compliment. Typical Lily. I ignored the barb and said, "I don't know. I been working out, I guess."

I would never in a million years admit to her that I'd been losing weight in case I had a chance to have sex with Ali before I went off to college. I'd decided that if it was up to me, I'd lose my virginity to him before the end of summer.

He was the chosen one. It sounded so dramatic, but my mind was made up.

"You don't need to lose weight to impress any guys, you know," Lily sounded annoyed.

"I know."

Ali was a sore point between us. Lily had never met him but she'd already decided he wasn't good enough for me.

"We're going off to college soon anyway."

I sat up and found my sunglasses, pulling them on to cover my eyes. "I know."

I was glad that Julia wasn't there. She was so blasé and sophisticated about sex in a way that I simultaneously hated, admired, and was envious of her.

Lily reached over and patted my arm. Her eyes were unfocused and cheeks flushed. She'd probably downed one of the fizzy drinks inside before bringing us these. Along with being more assertive and confident, Lily had also been drinking a ton more ever since Julie had gotten us those fake I.D.s.

"There's lots of guys at college that you can date." Her words were slightly slurred. "Just make sure you're picky. Especially if you decide to end our pact." She held up her fingers in the "V" sign. "Be picky. P.I.C.K.Y."

I reached out and took her hand until she met my eyes.

"Lily. I will be." We stared at each other for a few seconds. I squeezed her hand. For a second I wanted to tell her that I'd decided. I'd decided that Ali was the one. But she wouldn't understand. So instead I smiled and said, "Promise me that you'll be picky, too."

"I will be." But she looked away. For a second I wondered if she was still a virgin. Nah. She would've told me.

Although I smiled back at her, I was a little sad.

Even though she seemed different lately, I was still wary to confide in her and tell her how I really felt about Ali.

Because even if I didn't want to admit it out loud, I'd fallen for Ali. And hard. He was all I thought about. He was all I wanted. I didn't know how I was going to say goodbye to him. My heart was breaking already thinking about it. And he didn't even know. That's why I had decided he would be the one. If I couldn't have him as a boyfriend, I would have him as my first lover. He would be that to me forever.

He was the one. I wanted him more than I'd wanted anyone ever.

I could tell he felt the same way. I wasn't even worried about Jenna. Not anymore.

I'd lose my virginity to him. He was sophisticated and smart and drop-dead gorgeous. He was the right one.

I wouldn't start college as a virgin, but as an experienced lover.

I'd looked it up online. Only twenty-five percent of college kids were virgins. Definitely the minority. Most girls lost their virginity at age 17.2. I was 17.9. But I also didn't necessarily care what the average age was. I just knew deep down inside that he was the one.

CHAPTER 34

SOFIA

August 2019

Minneapolis

Sofia clicked over to Kate's Instagram page.

Several people had left sad comments under the picture of Kate and Lily.

One girl, Lauren Mitchell, a name Sofia didn't recognize, said something interesting in a comment under the picture. "Do you think that creep upped his game?"

Rumors had been circulating the U of M campus for about six months about a guy who hung out at Lucky's raping women he met there. But nobody would come forward.

Another girl wrote. "I know who you are talking about. OMG! I saw him talking to Kate a few weeks before that."

Then, the first girl wrote, "Does anybody know if he was there the night she died?"

Heart pounding, Sofia immediately sent a follow request to the first girl, Lauren.

The request was accepted and Sofia shot her a direct message.

"I'm worried this guy was the same one who tried to grab me the other night. Can you tell me his name or what he looks like?"

She waited, pulse racing.

Then a message and link to a Facebook page popped up. The guy's name was Jake Walker. "I don't say his name publicly in case it's slander or whatever, but this is the guy."

Some young people *do* use Facebook.

"Oh. I guess it isn't the same guy. Thanks." Sofia wrote. Then at the last minute, wrote. "Stay safe."

She clicked on the link to Jake Walker's page. The first place she looked was his friends. Yep. He was friends with Kate. Her heart thudded.

Sofia spent the next hour scrolling through his posts.

She paused on one. He had posted an article from an obscure magazine she'd never heard of something called "Doing It." She clicked on it. It was about rough sex being confused with rape. Her throat grew dry.

But then she reminded herself: the coroner's office said that Kate *hadn't* been raped.

She lingered on Walker's page, eyes narrowed, looking at his face wondering if it was the face of a killer. On another post, a guy had posted a sexy picture of French actress Isabelle Huppert and said, "Since you dig Cougars."

He'd replied. "Like 'em young and old. Makes no difference to me."

Just then a message came across on her Instagram account. It was from Lauren.

"A friend warned me that Jake is going to Lucky's tonight."

Sofia quickly typed. "Thanks for the heads up."

Looking back at the Facebook page, she scrolled down a little further.

Then her heart stopped. There was a little icon of Kate's picture attached to a comment. "Sorry, but the Patriots wiped the floor with your Packers today."

"Them's fighting words," he wrote back. And then underneath, "I'll arm wrestle you tonight at Lucky's." The date was several weeks earlier.

Right below it was a photo. It was of her Kate. Sofia's hand reached for the screen wanting to touch her daughter's smiling face. Kate was standing with Jake. He had his arm slung over her shoulder. Sofia pressed her thumb over his face, pushing hard until the screen of her laptop bent back toward the table until it could go no further without breaking.

Standing suddenly, she slammed her laptop closed, feeling adrenaline rush through her. She needed to get out of the house. She clenched her fists and closed her eyes trying to calm herself.

Murderous desire raged through her. All her life Sofia had lived in fear that she would turn out like her father. That she had killer blood running through her veins.

And now, now that the worst thing possible had happened to her, she didn't know if she could fight it any longer. She dreamed about it. She thought about it most of her day. But she had to know who the killer was. Had to know without a doubt. When she imagined Kate's killer the face blurred, became hazy, morphing in and out as Jake, Ali, the neighbor.

She could see it vividly. She'd knock on a front door and when the killer—the blurred face murderer—answered, she'd fire a bullet right into his forehead. Jason kept a handgun and ammunition near the front door on the top shelf of the closet. She could put on gloves, get the gun down, load it ...

She shook the image away.

God help her. If she killed someone that meant she *was* just like her father. But a small voice inside her said *No, you're not. He's a monster. You are not.*

She was going crazy. She needed to talk to someone. Cecile had been so helpful in reassuring her about Jason, but even Cecile wouldn't understand this.

Sofia needed to talk to a professional. Someone who would stop her. Because more than anything, when she found out who the killer was for sure, she was afraid she wouldn't be able to stop herself.

CHAPTER 35

KATE

June 2019

Dinkytown

"Ooh la la," Julia said, holding up two tiny scraps of pink silk.

She'd taken me shopping at the Mall of America for lingerie.

I'd confided in her about my plan to lose my virginity to Ali.

She'd dubbed it Operation Get Busy in emails. I felt a little guilty going behind Lily's back, but I knew Lily would try to talk me out of it.

Calling it "getting busy" wasn't ideal. It stripped it of any romantic notions I had about the first time. But I wasn't going to argue with her. I was just grateful for her moral support.

And, honestly, was hoping she'd give me some tips for the first time, so it wasn't awful and awkward.

Julia was the perfect person to ask.

When we were in seventh grade, she'd demonstrated how to give a boy head on a banana. So far, I'd managed to avoid doing that in my previous hot-and-heavy petting sessions with boyfriends. But I figured if it came up, I'd know exactly what to do thanks to Julia.

"Try this one on," Julia said, tossing me a red corset.

"I thought you liked the pink?" I said, holding up the one in my hand.

"The pink is for later. Not your first time." She put her chin on her hand as if she were thinking and then her eyes grew wide.

"White," she said. "Virginal white silk."

"No way."

"Then black it is."

She held up a lacy black bra and underwear and I smiled.

"Hand it over."

I stared at myself in the dressing room mirror. Holy shit. I was a woman. A woman who was going to have sex. With a boy. Or a man. Was he eighteen? I couldn't remember. Right then, I could barely remember my own name.

"Let me see!" Julia knocked on the door.

"No," I said. I smiled into the mirror. "This one is perfect."

• • • •

I STOOD ON ALI'S FRONT porch in the navy wrap around mini dress Julia had found for me after we'd bought the lingerie.

"This shows off your gorgeous legs," she said as I examined myself in the mirror. "He can lift the skirt, easy access. And the top is wrap around so he can have his way up top, too. And *voila*, with a flick of his wrist he can pull the belt and the whole dress falls off your body. It is perfectly orchestrated for maximum seduction."

I tugged the dress down now as I waited for Ali to answer my knock. I was suddenly sick with nervousness.

All of Julia's advice on plenty of foreplay to ease the first time seemed ridiculous. It was going to hurt and be awful. I just knew it.

But even imagining Ali naked filled me with desire.

This was right.

And when he flung open the door and whistled, his eyes raking me over from my freshly washed hair to the "Fuck Me four-inch heels" Julia had loaned me, I knew that I was making the right decision.

"What's the occasion?" he asked. "If I would've known this was a formal affair, I'd would've made you something fancier for dinner. Right now, I just have rice and beans, wine, and chocolate dipped strawberries for dessert."

"That sounds perfect."

I should've known he would remark on my dress. I was more prone to wear cut off jean shorts and a tank top when I wasn't coming from work.

He stepped aside and let me enter. He held my hand leading me to the kitchen. Their small table was set and one red candle was lit, dripping wax onto the plate it rested on.

He poured me a glass of wine and handed it to me.

"Salut!" we said.

But he wasn't ready to let my outfit go. I guess it'd really thrown him off.

"Don't get me wrong, you look, you look amazing, but I feel a little underdressed. Is there some reason for the dress?"

I gave a slight shrug and tried to look seductive. It must've worked because his eyes widened.

"You said your roommate was out of town tonight?"

The slow grin he gave me made my heart beat double time.

He reached for a chocolate-covered strawberry and then lightly brushed it on my lips, saying, "In that case, let's start with dessert."

CHAPTER 36

SOFIA

August 2019

Minneapolis

Dan looked surprised to see her when she appeared in the doorway of his office.

Sofia was a little surprised, as well. She had pointed her car toward the Basilica intent on talking to Father Genovese, but at the last minute swerved and headed toward Dan's office. It was connected to his home but had a separate entryway on the side. There weren't any other cars in the long driveway, so she lightly knocked and opened his office door without waiting for an answer.

"We need to talk."

Dan closed his laptop and shuffled some papers before standing and coming around his desk to give her a hug. He pulled back and grasped her hands in his, searching her face.

His eyes were big and sad, like a basset hound's, with the whites showing.

He took her hand and pulled her down onto the love seat next to him. She could feel the heat off his thigh less than an inch from her bare leg. A thin trickle of perspiration dripped down from his temple.

Taking a deep breath, she turned to him, steeling herself. "I'm not here to cry on your shoulder as a friend. I'm here to get your advice as a therapist. I can make an appointment and go through the proper channels if you want me to...." She trailed off.

"You want to see me as a therapist?" He sounded surprised.

"Well, yeah," She shot him a frown. "What did you think? Why did you think I was here?"

He blushed and walked over to the credenza. He poured bourbon into two crystal glasses without saying a word. He handed Sofia one of the glasses and sat back down, tilting his own glass to his lips and draining it.

"Dan!" Sofia was a little shocked. It was only one in the afternoon.

"Only for really hard cases like this. I promise." He looked away. "Okay. I lied. Full disclosure. There might be a client or two I take a little nip with."

Sofia frowned.

About twelve years ago, when the kids were little, Dan had been pulled over and popped a .12 on his blood alcohol test. It cost him $10,000 and nearly cost his marriage. Gretchen had briefly left with Lily, moving in with her mother, but came back after a month, a born again Christian, seemingly full of forgiveness. Dan had later confessed to Sofia that when Gretchen came back she refused to have sex with him for two years.

"I'm not sure day drinking is a good idea for you, Dan."

"It's fine, Sofia. Really. It *is* past noon, after all."

Sofia pressed her lips together for a second but then tipped her own glass, downing it in one smooth motion. She smiled when she was done. "Ah. You're right. That's totally what I needed."

"That will be $450 for my session." Dan winked. "Hey, I'm craving a G&T now. Will you go grab the white knife, a cutting board, and some limes from the kitchen and I'll get the rest going?"

Why the hell not, Sofia thought. Whenever the six friends went on vacation, they always started happy hour at four with gin and tonics. It felt comforting and reassuring to drink G&Ts with Dan. In addition, the alcohol would make her brave, give her the courage to say what she had come to talk about.

After retrieving the items from the kitchen, Sofia set the cutting board on the buffet where there was already a bottle of tonic and began slicing the limes. Dan plopped ice in some tall glasses and measured out some gin in a tall shot glass.

"Do you always lubricate your clients so they talk more?" She was joking, but she looked at Dan waiting for him to answer. Despite his reassurances, she was worried he drank at work more than he let on.

"I admit, it does sometimes help rid people of inhibitions."

Once they were settled in, sitting down, sipping their drinks, Sofia grew somber and looked down at her lap. "There's so much you don't know."

"What?" Dan's forehead scrunched, but then he grew earnest. "I'm all ears, Sofia. There is nothing you could tell me that would make me think less of you. You are a wonderful, loving, kind, law-abiding, classy woman."

She gave a grateful smile. "I'm so lucky to have your friendship, and now, your confidence."

She suddenly felt too warm. The alcohol was hitting her hard.

"There's something about me nobody knows and it might have to do with Kate's murder."

For a brief second some strong emotion flitted across Dan's face that Sofia couldn't quite put her finger on. Glee? Relief? Excitement? For fuck's sake. Sofia frowned. This wasn't some fucking TV movie or true crime documentary like Dan loved to watch. This was her life. And her daughter's murder.

He saw her expression and sobered. He'd put on his clinical hat. Fine. That's why she was there.

"It's about my family. Where I come from. What my real last name is. Everything I've told you and Jason and all our friends is a lie. I come from the most depraved bloodline you can imagine."

Dan's eyes grew wider and he leaned forward. "What?" He stared at her. He tapped his pen hard and rhythmically on the side of the desk.

She inhaled sharply.

"My dad. His name is Marco Castellucci." She paused and waited for Dan to react.

He didn't disappoint. His eyes grew wide and he stood up from the desk, palms pressed down on the wood. "Holy mother of God."

"Yes." Sofia scowled.

He blew a big puff of air out and sat back down, shaking his head. "Wow. Sorry about that reaction. Some therapist I am. But shit, Sofia. Really?"

She pressed her lips tightly together. "I changed my name before I came to Minnesota to go to college."

"Okay. I can see why you lied and didn't want anyone to know who your family was. In my eyes, you are absolved. Anyone in your position would've done the same thing."

Sofia threw her shoulders back. "But that's not why I'm here."

Dan nodded slightly waiting for her to continue. She looked over his shoulder as she spoke. "I know I have killer blood in me. Now you know, too."

She looked at Dan. His face was expressionless. She continued.

"When my dad was arrested and convicted, I realized I was the daughter of a stone-cold killer. My mother had covered up for him for years. Lied for him. Probably even hid the bodies with him. The only decent thing my father ever did in his life was testifying that my mother knew nothing about his murders. But I knew differently. All those late-night forays to meet my dad, leaving me home alone. The clothes – and God knows what else – my mother burned in our furnace, saying they had lice or something. She knew. She fucking knew and went along with it. When I testified against my dad, she disappeared, abandoned me."

"That must have been very hard for you to realize that your mother had lied to you."

Sofia shot him a glance. "*This* is incredibly hard for me. This is the first time I've ever told a soul. Not even Jason."

"I've spent my entire life vowing to not be like him ... my father."

Dan held up one hand. "Question?"

"Okay."

"You say you never told Jason any of this?"

A wave of guilt swarmed over Sofia. She could feel her face grow warm. "Our marriage would be over. He'd never trust anything I said or did again. You know Jason. He's honest to a fault."

Despite Cecile's reassurances that Jason was a goner, Sofia knew that would change in a heartbeat if her husband discovered she'd been lying their whole life.

"Hmmm." Dan looked down and for a second Sofia thought she saw a smile on his face, but when he looked up again his eyes were sad. "You really have felt the desire to kill people? I mean in the past?"

Baby Angelo's face appeared like a punch to her solar plexus. She exhaled raggedly. "Dan, I'm terrified that I'm going to hurt someone."

They both sat silent for a few seconds.

"Dan, do you think that desire, or inclination to kill ... do you think that it's genetic?"

He nodded eagerly. "First, your desire to kill is somewhat normal considering your, er, circumstances."

"Really?" She felt both relief and horror. Relief that her urges were normal under the circumstances and horror that he acknowledged she truly had that desire.

"Really. But ... it's not completely out of the realm of possibility that there is some genetic aspect." He smiled, but it didn't quite reach his eyes and she noticed small droplets of perspiration forming at his temples. Was he afraid of her?

"I read an article in Discover a few years ago that said there was possibly some genetic connection between impulsive aggressive violence. In other words, a violent person can pass that gene to his or her children."

Sofia swallowed and nodded.

"At one point that genetic predisposition was a given, but most modern psychologists have discarded that line of thinking. I do think they are taking another look at it recently. Studying prison populations and so on. It opens up an interesting field of research. Opponents are worried that the government might someday do mandatory testing for this 'violence gene' and punish people who have never committed a violent act in his or her life.

"The study I read about said that there definitely is a violence gene, but it appears to only be in certain populations. Say, prisoners. So, I know you just told me your dad was in prison and was a violent man, but that doesn't make it a given that you've inherited this gene, Sofia."

Her heart sank.

Angelo.

A small ball of dread and despair was blooming inside her. She *was* genetically predisposed to kill. She had known this deep inside her entire life.

Dan, seeing the look on her face, jumped up and held out his hands. "Hey, hey. Sofia, I know what you're thinking. Don't do this to yourself. Don't go there. Because here is the thing. You can have that desire and not act on it."

"I want to act on it." She jutted her chin. "That's the problem, Dan. It's all I think about. I want whoever killed Kate dead. Dead in a terribly painful way. A lifetime in prison won't be enough. I don't think I can stop myself from acting on it. I'm sorry that you need to see this side of me, Dan."

He blew out a breath loudly and sank back into his chair. "It's just, well, it's quite a surprise, frankly. My sweet, mild-mannered Sofia with bloodlust. The woman who won't even watch boxing on

TV with us. You can see where I'm having a hard time with this. I'm trying to keep my therapist cap on, but good God, Sofia, I'm worried. I mean, the desire to kill is normal, in your case, possibly even inherited, but you have to realize you never ever have to act on it."

Sofia put her face in her hands. "I know. You must hate me. I'm a monster just like him." *My dad.*

"Oh no, Sofia, no."

"I spend every second I'm awake trying to find who did this to Kate, Dan. It's exhausting."

A slick sheen of sweat now coated Dan's brow. He was nervous around her. She scared him. She'd ruined everything. Now he knew *who* she really was and *what* she really was. She repulsed him. But when he met her eyes, instead of fear or distaste, his face held some other emotion. Sympathy? "Sofia. This *is* really unlike you. I can see why you came to me. Maybe I can help after all."

Head down, he scribbled something on a smaller pad of paper. "So, right now your neighbor is the main suspect?" He didn't look up, but his pen paused on the piece of paper, waiting for her answer.

"Honestly? I don't know."

Dan finished writing and looked up.

"But I'll find out. I swear I will find whoever did. I won't rest until Kate's killer is dead."

It felt so good just to say it out loud. To voice the thoughts and emotions she'd had bubbling inside her since they found Kate. The only time the thoughts had left her head had been the letter she had written to the unknown killer that she kept folded inside her wallet.

"Sofia." His voice was soft. His eyes had that hangdog puppy look. He sighed, ripped off the paper from the pad and wadded it up. He threw it in the trash and then leaned down. She heard him fiddling with keys and then he emerged with an entire drawer he put on top of his desk.

Sofia raised an eyebrow.

Dan held up his palm. "Sit tight. I'm getting some more pills for you."

"I still have some of the ones you gave me from Cuba. The bottle was full. And the Roofie stuff," she said. "God, I love that. Puts me right to sleep."

Dan eyed her. "I told you to be very careful with it, okay?"

"I am. Now, why do I need more drugs again?" She watched him lean down behind his desk.

"These are different. From Cuba, too." His voice was muffled.

Sofia craned her neck to see. "What are you doing? Are they in your shoes?"

"Secret compartment. Where I stash my Cuba drugs. Can't leave that shit laying around. Some of my patients would break into my office if they thought I had anything like this. Sick and sad, but true. Plus, it's against the law. See," his face popped up and he held out an amber bottle. "I break the law too. Every once in a while."

He handed her an amber bottle. She stared at it. She was buzzed before noon on bourbon and gin and now she was also becoming a druggie.

Dan pressed her fingers around the bottle. She opened her palm and peered at the bottle. One word was scrawled in blue ink: Clozapine. She could barely read the writing. "What is it exactly?"

"I think this might help. From what you've told me, I think you should try them. They'll help you not to obsess about ... killing ... him. It might stifle some of those urges. You don't have to stay on it forever, but it might do you some good to give it a shot." He enclosed her hand with his. "I hate seeing you like this. Promise me you'll start taking them immediately?"

Sofia closed her eyes. "Okay. Okay." She opened her eyes and stood, a few feet from Dan's face. "You don't think I'm crazy?"

He guffawed. "Of course not. And you know I know crazy, Sofia. You'll be just fine. Trust me."

For a second, she was tempted to hand the bottle back, but then a wave of fatigue hit her hard and she dropped it in her purse.

There was a loud bang above them. Sofia jumped.

"Is Gretchen home?"

Dan looked past her.

"Dan?"

He shook his head as if shaking off a bad memory. "It's Lily."

"She's not at school?"

"I had to go get her. She's having some problems."

"That's terrible. I'm so sorry."

He let out a big breath. "I didn't want to burden you with this on top of everything else, but she's having a hard time with Kate's death and all. I thought her going away and having a fresh start would help her forget—"

Another loud bang.

"What's she doing?"

"God only knows. She's depressed." He stood. "I better go check on her."

"Poor baby," Sofia said and stood to leave.

"I'm hoping to take her back to school next week. She just needed a break. Sitting alone in her room can't be helping. She needs to be busy, active."

Sofia nodded. She had her hand on the doorknob when she turned. "Dan ... you are the first person I've told any of this to in my entire life. Thank you. I really do feel a lot better knowing that you know. I just worry that Jason will leave me if he finds out what I'm really like. You accepting me and not thinking I'm a freak means the world to me. Thank you so much." She leaned over and pressed her face into his chest. He kissed the top of her head.

He pulled back and held up her chin and looked her right in the eyes. "Sofia, I promise you, your secret is safe with me. I'm here for you. I always will be. Call me anytime. You don't have to come to my office. I'll drop everything and come to your place, okay?"

"Thanks, Dan." Sofia bit back tears.

"And Sofia?"

"Yes."

"Start taking those pills I gave you. I promise it will help."

CHAPTER 37

KATE

July 2019

Minneapolis

"Oh. My. God," Lily said. "You lost your virginity to a boy your parents haven't even met. So much for making it special. You're full of shit, Kate."

"You don't understand."

We were in her room listening to a new Camila Cabello song.

"I understand. He used you. I'll be surprised if he ever calls you again. Well, he'll probably call— a booty call and that's it."

"You're wrong."

"Read this."

She threw a newspaper at me.

The top article was about a woman who had been raped on campus. Police were looking for a man: maybe Somalian, short dreads.

Sure, it fit Ali, but it could've fit a hundred other boys in that part of town. Minneapolis had one of the largest Somalian populations in the country.

Throwing the paper back, I said, "What are you trying to say, Lily?"

"I'm trying to say that the rape happened the night we saw him at the bar. After he stormed off. The rape happened a few blocks away."

My mouth hung open in shock. How dare she?

I'd felt the anger soar through me and felt my fingers clench into fists. I wanted to punch Lily. For the first time in our friendship I wanted to hurt her.

Instead I stormed out of her house. I saw her dad as I passed. He looked surprised and called my name, but I didn't stop until I was in my car and driving down the road.

Then I pulled over to the side and punched the steering wheel.

There was no way. Ali didn't have a violent or criminal bone in his body.

He was gentle and kind and I was half in love with him.

There. I'd admitted it. I was falling for him.

CHAPTER 38

SOFIA

A*ugust 2019*
Minneapolis

Instead of going home from Dan's, Sofia called Cecile.

"If Jason asks, you and I are driving to the casino. We are staying the night there at the hotel and gambling and drinking and having a good time."

Cecile didn't skip a beat. "Sure. Of course. That's my story and I'm sticking to it."

Sofia exhaled with relief.

"Thank you."

"Sofia? It's none of my business and you know I'm good to cover your ass, but do you need my help? You know I will be there for you. No matter what."

"I know," Sofia said. "Right now, this is what I need. I'll tell you more later."

"Okay." Cecile said right before Sofia hung up.

Until she knew for sure the neighbor did it, Sofia needed to eliminate other possible suspects. She texted Jason and told him she'd call him later tonight from the casino.

Within thirty minutes, she was in the department store bathroom stall changing into her new purchases: black leather pants, ankle boots, and a tight black tee-shirt that said Nirvana.

She applied the new burgundy lipstick and lined her dark eyes thickly with kohl before she stuffed her faded mom jeans and polo shirt in her shopping bags and headed toward the car.

She had a few more stops to make.

••••

OUTSIDE LUCKY'S SHE paused, steeling herself to go in. As she did, a couple about her age, came out. Stepping inside, she saw other patrons who looked older than college age and this reassured her. She didn't want to be too obvious.

Flashing the bartender a smile, she slid into her seat and ordered a rum and Coke on the rocks. A rowdy group of college guys had taken over a corner table within her eyesight. Surreptitiously she eyed them to see if any of them looked familiar. She caught her breath. There he was. Jake Walker. His hair was longer than the pictures on his Facebook profile and he had a five o'clock shadow, but it was him. She recognized the strong jawline and thick eyebrows over his crystal blue eyes.

She scowled, remembering the way his arm wrapped around her daughter, in a possessive manner. Sofia examined him. He looked like a dick in person, too. A predatory animal, just like she suspected. Sofia's resolve hardened. She would do whatever it took to find out who killed Kate. Sofia stared until he looked up. Then she smiled and looked away. After another round of this, his friends were nudging him. A few seconds later he was at her elbow.

"What are you drinking?" His voice wavered a bit and she saw him swallow.

In a split second, she discarded her previous plan to play hard to get. He was easy prey.

She turned her smile on him and tried to act shy. "Rum and Coke." She kept her voice low, so he had to lean in to hear.

He cleared his throat and gestured for the bartender. "Two rum and Cokes here." He tried to sound commanding, she could tell, but his voice betrayed him. He was nervous.

After the bartender brought their drinks, she turned to him and lifted her glass demurely. "Thank you."

"No problem." He slid onto the bar stool and downed his drink, signaling for another. "Keep 'em coming, buddy."

He turned to her. "That guy sucks. I mean, he didn't even ask if we wanted more. I swear this place has the worst service ever. Dude is totally not getting a tip from me."

She swallowed her retort and smiled, even though it felt like a sneer.

"I haven't seen you here before?" He tilted his head.

"I'm from Chicago. I just got in from the airport. I have a meeting on campus in the morning, but couldn't sleep and wanted a drink."

His eyebrow lifted.

"I'm staying over at the inn across the street." She gestured behind them. "I was feeling a little lonely."

He couldn't help it, it seemed: He bit the corner of his lip slightly and tried to hide a small grin, relaxing into his seat, and downing his second rum and Coke.

Hook. Line. Sinker.

If only he would go to the bathroom or leave his drink for a second.

"Would you mind doing me a favor?"

"Sure," he said, but seemed annoyed.

"Can you go check if there is a silver car outside? It's this weird ex-boyfriend. I doubt he's here but just in case he heard I was in town and followed me from the airport."

Puffing up his chest, he stood and walked to the window. Immediately Sofia realized it wouldn't give her enough time. She took her hand out of her purse and put the vial in the pocket of her jacket.

Besides there were too many eyes here.

"What's your name?" he said, throwing his shoulder's back. The alcohol had filled him with confidence.

"Kate." She watched him carefully between her lowered eyelashes.

For a split second, his forehead crinkled and then he shook his head.

"And yours?"

"Sorry." He stuck out his hand. "I'm Jake."

She took his hand. He didn't let hers go, rubbing her palm with his middle finger.

What the fuck? Was that supposed to turn her on? She fought her impulse to yank her hand away.

"Do you come here often?" She nodded toward the table where his friends were. "It seems like you know a lot of people."

He puffed up a little and ordered another drink. "Yeah. Those are my boys. We come here every once in a while. The food's good."

"Are you in school at the U?"

"Yep. Senior. Hospitality."

"Hospitality?" Sofia scrunched her face. Oh, his major.

"Cool." She leaned over and took another sip of her drink through the tiny straw. The two other drinks he'd ordered for her sat neglected.

He pointed at them. "Drink up. Those things are expensive."

Dumb *and* charming.

She downed the first drink and then the second two he'd ordered for her. She was feeling woozy, but pretended that the alcohol had hit her hard. She clutched his arm. "I'm sooo buzzed. Good thing I only have to walk across the street. Although that's starting to seem like a long way away right now ..." she purposely slurred her words.

His friends came by. "Dude, we're hitting the CC Club. You in?"

He made a face and jutted his chin at Sofia. "What do you think?"

The guy looked over at Sofia and smirked. "Right on. Catch you later, Romeo."

Sofia pretended not to hear. "I think I need to go lie down. I'm feeling really drunk."

He was off his stool in a second, helping her down.

She grabbed her purse. “Just give me a second.” She headed toward the bathroom before he could respond.

Locking the door, she blasted the cold and hot water taps and extracted a small bottle of ipecac syrup. She swallowed a few tablespoons and yanked her hair back into a ponytail. Within five minutes, she'd vomited not only her three drinks, but the bagel she'd had at the mall for dinner. She heard a knock.

“Just a minute.”

Quickly, she fixed her makeup, brushed her teeth and applied lipstick, taking her hair down and practicing her smile.

When she opened the door, Jake wasn't there.

Shit.

Then she saw him a few tables down talking to a cute brunette who didn't look old enough to drink. Obviously, Kate and Lily weren't the only ones who got away with fake IDs in this bar. When Jake saw her, he winked, leaned down and kissed the girl near her mouth and took his time making his way over to her.

“Sorry, that was my sister's friend.”

“Can you walk me across the street? I'm a little worried about that ex I was telling you about,” Sofia said, purposely slurring her words.

He touched her elbow and directed her to the door.

Outside, he wrapped his arm around her shoulders the same way he'd done in that picture with Kate.

The cold night air hit Sofia's face and suddenly she was stone cold sober. His arm around her neck hurt. For a split second, she wondered if she'd made a mistake. He wasn't much bigger than her, but the weight of his arm made her realize he could overpower her pretty easily. She'd have to play this right.

As soon as she thought this, she was shoved up against the brick wall of the building so hard her head hit and bounced off, making her see white for a few seconds. Jake had pressed his body up against hers, kissing her hard. His tongue thrust into her mouth and she tried to turn her head.

Just when she was about to knee him in the groin, he pulled away.

"Let's go to your room. I'm getting stage fright." He gestured to his groin and grabbed her arm, dragging her across the street to the side door of the inn.

At the door to the inn, he paused. "Where's your keycard? You know, your room key?"

She remained silent trying to stall. He yanked her arm again. "Where is it?"

Grabbing her bag, he dumped its contents on the sidewalk and began nudging them with his foot, keeping one hand on her arm as he looked down.

"What the fuck are these?" He nudged the handcuffs with his toe.

He looked at her with narrowed eyes? "Are you a cop?"

She didn't respond. His fingers pressed down hard into her wrist. "Are you?"

She cocked her head. "Why? Have you done something wrong? Something a cop might want to know about?"

There was no mistaking the guilt that flashed across his face. "No."

He leaned down and scooped the handcuffs up. They were lined in pink fur. He laughed. "You aren't a cop, are you?"

She smiled.

"This is a sex thing, isn't it?"

"That's right. Now if you're a good boy, I'll explain it all to you inside."

He stood. She kneeled and gathered up her things, shoving them in her bag. Relieved she'd put the vial in her pocket earlier. That was too close.

Once they were inside the room, he threw her on the bed.

She playfully pushed him off. "Hold on. I need a drink."

"Those things are expensive. The inn charges like ten bucks for those tiny bottles."

"It's on me, sailor."

"Right on!" He headed toward the mini bar. She put her hand on his arm.

"I used to tend bar. I'll handle it. Besides, I want to take a shower, freshen up. Will you go start the water while I mix our drinks?"

He looked confused.

She pulled him by the hands. "Over there. Go get the bathroom steamy for us. I've got plans."

He stood and stumbled toward the door as she unwrapped two plastic covered water glasses for their drinks.

Quickly, she dumped a big slug of Rohypnol into his drink. It seemed like too much. She swirled the liquid with her finger. She smelled the drink. It seemed normal. But shit, she had dumped so much in. More than she had intended. She didn't want to kill him—at least not yet—but she also needed it to work right away. Otherwise, she'd end up raped.

Stripping off her clothes, she slipped into the bathroom with both drinks.

His eyes bulged out when he saw her in the red bra and panties she'd picked up at the mall.

He grabbed at her boob, but she dodged his reach and stuck the drink in his hand. "This is the good stuff. Have a drink. Let's loosen up a little. We have all night, sailor. Try this and tell me what you think."

She was hoping to appeal to his snobbish side. It worked. He downed it. Perfect.

"Yeah, this is way better than that swill at the bar," he said.

She grabbed his hand and led him to the bed. He stumbled as he walked, cracking his knee against a dresser.

"God damn. I thought ... the shower?" he said. She put a palm to his chest and pushed and he fell back on the bed, laughing. "Okay. Okay. I get it."

She straddled him putting her mouth on his. She fought back a gag reflex. He repulsed her. His breath. His mouth. His smell. Every cell of his being.

But he was a means to an end.

The room was filling with warm steam.

"Let me go turn off the shower. It's getting hard to see your handsome face," she said, trying to get away, but he had her pinned.

"You're not going anywhere baby. I like how steamy it's getting in here."

Hang in there, Kennedy. His kisses were getting slower and sloppier as if the drug was starting to work. It had better. After a few horrific minutes of him groping and probing her with his fat fingers, he passed out. Thank fucking God.

She found the tote bag she'd hidden under the bed earlier when she'd checked in. She took out the lengths of rope and tied him securely to the legs of the bed so he was spread eagled. She placed the wrench on the nightstand and headed toward the bathroom.

The mirror was too steamed up for her to see her own reflection and she was glad. She was disgusted. She used the entire mini bottle of mouthwash on the counter, swishing it in her mouth over and over and spitting it out, trying to rid herself of his taste.

Her hands were shaking.

Steeling herself, she got dressed, pulled up a chair near the bed and waited in the dark.

When the green numerals on the clock struck midnight, Sofia closed her eyes and said a small prayer. When she was done, she walked over to the minibar, poured three of the bottles of alcohol into one large cup and raised it in the dark.

"Happy birthday, dear Kate." She downed the contents of the cup in one gulp and then leaned back.

• • • •

THE FIRST LIGHT OF dawn was seeping through the thick drapes by the time he woke.

Sofia took a sip of the coffee she'd made with the in-room coffeemaker. She'd texted Jason earlier saying she was sorry she had to be drunk with Cecile at a casino on Kate's birthday but that's how it was.

He'd replied that he understood and was shitfaced himself and going to bed.

Now, she felt a wave of guilt for lying, but it was what it was.

The boy in bed grumbled and tried to move, but his arms and legs were pinned. His eyes popped open in alarm.

"What the fuck?"

"Hey, sailor."

"What?" he arched his neck and saw he was bound. "This isn't cool. Let me go."

Sofia took another sip of coffee. She'd changed into a dress with stiletto heels. She clambered onto the bed above him, her legs straddling his waist, her heels digging into the mattress. "We're going to have a little talk first."

Crouching down on his chest, she put all her weight right about where she thought his lungs were and shoved the photo of Kate into his face. "What did you do to her?"

He scrunched his face violently. "What the fuck are you talking about?" He tried to turn his head away, but Sofia grabbed his chin with her fingernails and held it straight. "Look at her. Do you remember her?"

His eyes narrowed. "Yeah. I think so. She was that girl who died, right? Her picture's been in the paper."

Sofia slapped him so hard his head reeled to one side.

"Her name was Kate. You were friends with her, asshole. Today is her birthday and she's dead in the ground."

She held up her phone and showed him the picture of him with his arm around Kate.

Recognition dawned on his face. "Oh, the Pat's fan. Yeah, I remember her now."

"Did you hurt her?"

"What?" He genuinely seemed confused. "No. I never even touched her. We never even kissed. I wanted to, believe me. I wanted to get in her pants, but her friend told me she was a prude."

Sofia swallowed, trying not to show any emotion. "What friend?"

"That one she's always with. The one with that spot on her face."

Lily.

He chuckled. "Her friend sure wasn't a prude."

Sofia slapped him again. "Shut up. I ask questions. You answer."

"This is fucking crazy. This is some god damn fucked up mother fucking shit." His eyes were watering a little from the blow. "Isn't this like fucking illegal restraint or something?"

"No. You paid me to tie you up, sailor. Remember?"

"What?"

"It's right here on my phone." She hopped off him and held out her cell phone. It showed a text from his number to her. It said: "We agree, then? $400 bucks for you to tie me up and slap me around a little? Nothing that will leave a mark. And I need to be done by eight so I can get to class on time."

"What the fuck, you fucking crazy bitch."

"I actually usually charge much more than four hundred for what you wanted done, but I saw that was all you had in your wallet, so I agreed," Sofia flashed the money at him and plopped his empty wallet on his bare chest.

"You bitch."

He tried to spit at her. It came back down, and landed on his cheek, sliding down his face. She leaned over him, glaring.

"I'm going to ask you one more time: Did you hurt Kate?"

He shook his head.

"No. No fucking way. I never touched her." She took the wrench and put it between his bare legs, the cold metal against his shrunken penis making him jump. "I swear. I swear I never laid a hand on her."

"How do I know you're not lying?" She pushed the metal harder. He winced in pain.

"I swear, lady. I swear."

She moved the wrench. "You're lucky. When you were unconscious, I found some texts on your phone from the night she was killed. It looks like you were across town. It would've been pretty hard for you to make it over here to hurt her. I'm not saying you didn't, but it would've been tough."

He exhaled loudly. "See, I told you." He struggled to sit up. "So, are you gonna let me go now?"

She narrowed her eyes at him. "I don't know."

"What do you mean you don't know."

"You might not have hurt Kate, but it sounds like you haven't exactly been a gentleman to other young women you've met." She hit the wrench on her palm where it made a satisfying thud.

He winced and swallowed. The whites of his eyes showed as he looked to the side.

"So, the rumors are true." She stated it as a fact.

"I'm done with all that. I swear." He met her eyes.

She watched him, and nodded. "You better be. Next time, if there is a next time, there will be no warning. I'll come for you and you won't be walking out of the room when I'm done."

"I swear. I'm done with all that."

She leaned over and held his chin up, putting the water glass with bourbon up to his lips. "Drink this."

At first, he kept his lips shut tight.

She put the wrench back to his groin. "Do it. You'll be awake by check out time."

He sipped the alcohol, slowly, neck raised, draining the glass.

She leaned over again, watching his eyes grow heavy, and held out her cell phone in front of him, scrolling through a few photos she had taken in the night.

His eyes grew wide.

"If I hear a word of what happened here tonight ... one word, these pictures will be all over every piece of social media real estate in the universe."

When she heard him snoring, she undid his ties and put the "Do Not Disturb" sign on the door before she slipped away.

CHAPTER 39

SOFIA

August 2019
Minneapolis

Cecile rushed into the restaurant, shedding a sleek leather jacket and a filmy taupe silk scarf. She collapsed into the chair and slumped, her face turning somber.

"I'm so glad to see you. To get your call. I must admit I was a little worried last night, *mon chou*."

Sofia's French was rusty, but she was pretty sure her friend had just called her "my cabbage."

"It's a long story."

"I have time."

It was why Sofia had called Cecile and asked her to meet—to confess about the night before—but suddenly she questioned doing so.

"Don't you need to get ready for your trip?" Sofia said instead.

For the past year, Cecile and Alex had planned a month-long trip to Europe after Julia got settled in at college.

"The birth control trial just started. It will last about a week, I think. Then we leave."

"How's it going?"

"This trial. It's terrible and wonderful at the same time," Cecile said, her face glowing. "It's such a roller coaster. I swear I'm going to get those bastards. Ten thousand women have come forward with documentation that the implant has caused prolonged fevers, fatigue, and symptoms mimicking chronic fatigue syndrome." Cecile took a sip of her water. "And yet," she held up a finger. "And yet, they are denying it, saying these are common symptoms that women experience and can't be blamed on the birth control."

"Those sons-of-bitches."

Cecile flagged the waiter down. "Your finest burgundy, please. Anything that's about twenty dollars a glass."

Once he left, Sofia turned to Cecile. "He's going to bring you piss, you know?"

"As long as it has alcohol in it, I don't give a damn," Cecile smiled.

Cecile tapped her phone. "I'm going to win this case and as soon as the jury comes back with a verdict, Alex is waiting to book us tickets to Paris the first minute we can leave. We both need a break. We are going to stay in bed all day and sip wine and eat smelly cheese and baguettes. First, though, we'll drive down to St. Thomas and visit Julia. God, I miss that girl."

Her words hung in the air.

Sofia swallowed. Cecile blushed and reached for Sofia's hand.

"I'm so sorry."

Sofia tried on a wan smile. "Don't be. You don't have to censor your words with me."

But Sofia's heart sunk. She'd hoped to confide in Cecile. If anyone could understand what she'd done to that boy in the hotel room, it would be Cecile. But now she realized Cecile could not ever understand. Nobody could understand how she felt or why she did what she did the night before. They might pretend to, but unless they'd had a child brutally murdered, how could they?

Even Jason, her husband and Kate's father, wouldn't understand what drove her to do what she had done. Even he wouldn't understand the bloodlust that was driving her to hunt down Kate's killer and make him pay.

"Sofia?"

She realized that Cecile was staring at her, forehead crunched with worry.

"Sorry. I was lost in thought."

The waiter set down two wine glasses. Sofia grabbed hers and thrust it up in the air trying to wipe that concerned look off of her friend's face.

"Here's to sticking it to those bastards!" Sofia said it so loud people at other tables looked over.

But Cecile only laughed and raised her glass just as high, saying "Sticking it up their ass!"

They both burst into laughter. It felt good to laugh, but Sofia quickly stopped, taking a big gulp of wine.

• • • •

AFTER THEY HAD EACH finished a slice of the artisan bread in front of them, Cecile leaned forward searching Sofia's face.

"Darling, how are you? Do you want to tell me what was going on last night? Are you seeing someone? It's understandable after what you're going through."

Sofia couldn't speak for a few seconds. She pressed her lips tightly together.

"No. It's not like that." She reached for another slice out of the breadbasket.

It was obvious that Cecile felt sorry for her and more than anything Sofia didn't want pity. They'd never had that kind of friendship in the past. But she also had to face that everything, every single fucking interaction she had with anyone she had known *before* was now tainted with the looming knowledge that Sofia's daughter had been murdered. Not just died. Murdered. Taken by violence. By a madman. What had once been incomprehensible was now a major factor in every move, every thought, every breath.

The waiter brought their food, two bowls of linguine pasta with clams.

When he left, Sofia started twirling pasta onto her fork, not looking up as she said, "I saw Gretchen the other day."

"Oh God, what did *she* have to say?" Cecile said, taking a delicate sip of her wine.

Sofia wanted to spill it all, but something stopped her. She took a big bite of her pasta before answering. When she had chewed it until it dissolved, she answered. "I don't know. Nothing I guess. I still don't like her, of course, but now I sort of feel sorry for her. She's a basket case. I mean a total loon. It must be miserable to be her."

"You surely aren't serious?" Cecile's phone pinged. She looked down. "I have to run back to the courthouse." The waiter appeared at her side. "Check please."

She began fixing her lipstick in her compact mirror.

"Cecile?"

"Yes?"

"The detective investigating Kate's ... case ... is asking questions about my past and my parents and things that I don't really think have anything to do with it."

"Oh." Cecile snapped her compact shut. "I think that's good. That means they are being very thorough. They want to look into your past to see if anybody might have wanted to target Kate for any reason whatsoever. That bar arrest means nothing. Nothing, okay. Don't worry about it another minute."

Sofia stared off over her friend's shoulder. Cecile's words echoed in her head "*look into your past to see if anybody might have wanted to target Kate.*"

"Sofia? Sofia?"

She blinked.

"Where'd you go?" Cecile said. Sofia shook her head.

Just then the waiter dropped off the check. Sofia reached for her wallet, but Cecile waved her off. "My treat."

Cecile stood and shrugged on her jacket. Sofia looked helplessly at her nearly full plate of food.

"Stay. Please. Enjoy your lunch. Finish the wine. I'm sorry I have to run."

Sofia stood to give Cecile the requisite European kiss on both cheeks. When she drew back, Cecile's eyes were wet with tears. "I didn't want to upset you, but since you brought it up, Alex and I have been wondering if they've made any progress in Kate's case. I know an extraordinary prosecutor in the district attorney's office who would jump all over this case once they make an arrest. I've already mentioned it to him so he can be alert when it comes through his office. I hope that's okay."

Sofia looked away. She was afraid it would all show in her face—her murderous intent.

"Nothing yet." Her friend was the smartest person Sofia knew. She was also very intuitive. She would hear it in Sofia's voice so it was better to say nothing at all.

Cecile kissed her again on the cheek and then turned to leave. "Don't worry, they'll find him. And when they do, we'll make sure he will pay."

Sofia sat back down and watched her friend walk away before pouring herself another glass of wine and saying quietly to herself, "Yes. He will pay all right."

CHAPTER 40

SOFIA

August 2019
Minneapolis

Jason was working late again.

Sofia had fallen asleep on the couch when a thud outside the front door woke her.

She opened the door and glanced down at her feet. Half a dozen newspapers were scattered on her porch. She leaned down and scooped them up in her arms, holding them against her chest. They always went out the side door to where their cars were parked in the driveway.

That's when she noticed the boxes. They were boxes from St. Thomas. Kate had shipped a few boxes early. Most college kids did this, Sofia had learned. The college stored them until the students moved in. It was a very organized system.

And now, the university had shipped them back.

Seeing them made her stomach knot in pain.

Sofia threw the newspapers into the house and then pushed and shoved the two big cardboard boxes through the front door. They were heavy. Mostly loaded with new bedding she and Kate had picked out for the dorm and some winter sweaters and new clothes. She'd see if Lily or Kate's other friends wanted them. But not now. It hurt too much to remember how excited Kate had been to pack those boxes.

Trying not to sob, Sofia pushed the boxes against the wall near the door, grabbed the newspapers, and headed toward the kitchen. She put them on the kitchen table, unfurling them and putting them in order. It was time to read about Kate's murder. She'd put it off long enough. She'd avoided TV and radio, even her beloved Minnesota Public Radio since Kate's death.

It was time. Maybe the articles would hold some clues about the killer. Maybe some hot shot investigative reporter was on the case.

But first she needed another pill. Fishing for the bottle, she made sure it was the one for anxiety, not the new bottle of pills Dan had given her. She had no interest in squashing her murderous desires. Not yet anyway.

Once she felt the pill slide down her throat, she turned to the first newspaper. It was dated the day after Kate was found. For a few seconds, she stared, mesmerized by the picture of her beautiful daughter on the front page of the newspaper. Slowly, she dragged her eyes to the headline.

"Teen found dead in Dinkytown: police say homicide."

And a subhead: "Campus officials are on alert."

Sofia forced herself to read the article. It talked about how few details were known about the murder and that police were investigating. It talked about how Kate had been headed off to college. The reporter quoted Kate's drama teacher from De La Salle High School and a few classmates. Not Kate's true friends, though. Not Lily, Julia, Ava and Molly.

Sofia flipped to the next day. Still front page about Kate. The reporter had found someone at the bar that night. Jonathan Parker said that Kennedy had appeared "sober" when she left the bar that night.

That's not what Lily had said. Lily had said they had both been "pretty drunk."

"I don't think she'd been drinking at all," Parker said.

He also said that right before she left, she'd gotten into an argument with another girl sitting by her.

Lily.

"I noticed because she'd been pretty quiet up until then. Her friend had gone to the bathroom. I was going to go talk to her because she was super cute and she was all alone and looked kind of sad," Parker said. "But when I got there, her friend came back and they started to argue."

Parker said he didn't hear much what the fight was about but that she grabbed her bag and headed to the back door crying.

"She was obviously having a bad day."

Her friend yelled something after her and then ordered another drink, Parker said.

"I thought that was kind of cold. Your friend is crying and (stuff) and you just yell at her as she leaves. Not cool."

Parker, who said he's studying to be a civil engineer at the U of M, says he wishes he had gone after Kennedy when she walked out.

"Yeah, maybe if I'd actually followed her and checked on her nothing bad would've happened to her."

Sofia started to see white. Lily hadn't provided any of those details. She didn't say that she and Kate had an argument and that's why Kate walked out. She'd said that Kate went to the bathroom and never came back.

Sofia punched in Lily's cell number. It rang three times before Lily picked up.

"Yes?"

"It's Mrs. Kennedy." She would be gentle. The girl was struggling.

Silence.

"Lily, I just read an article in the paper that said you and Kate got in an argument before she left Lucky's."

More silence.

"Lily?"

Lily burst into tears. "I feel so bad. It's true. We did. I didn't want her to go to Ali's. He called and told her he wasn't able to meet her at the bar. Kate said she was going to go over there. I told her that was a mistake. She told me to go to hell. I tried to stop her. I even grabbed her arm and she tried to hit me away. I said, 'Fine. Go. You're a fool.'"

Sofia closed her eyes and waited a few seconds before answering. A small ugly part of her had blamed Lily for letting Kate walk out of that bar alone. But the girl was desperately hurting and Sofia's heart softened.

"Oh, Lily, I'm so sorry. You know it's not your fault what happened. You were only trying to stop her from ... from getting hurt."

"He was just going to use her." Lily sobbed the words.

"I know, sweetheart."

Lily's weeping turned into wailing.

"Shhhh, it's okay. I'm Kate's mother and so I think I know Kate pretty well and I'm going to tell you this. Listen up. I know this as sure as I know anything in this world. So, listen, Lily."

Lily quieted down a little until there was only sniffing.

"What I know, Lily, is that Kate loved you like a sister and nothing, nothing you could call her or say to her, especially words you said because you loved her, nothing you could say would change her love for you. Do you understand?"

Lily sniffed.

"Lily? Do you understand? Do you believe me?"

"Okay."

"You sound pretty upset, sweetie."

"Why? Because I want to die?"

Sofia's heart clenched. "Lily please don't say that. That's very serious. Saying something like that is very serious. Do you want to hurt yourself?"

Sniffing. "I don't really mean it."

Silence.

She didn't know if the teen was really suicidal, but she didn't want to take any chances. Lily shouldn't be alone.

"Hey, listen, is your Dad home?"

"Yes. He's downstairs." Sniff.

"Okay. Well, listen, do me a favor honey, go give him a message. Tell him to give me a call."

"Okay."

Sofia was about to hang up but didn't want to let Lily go yet. She waited a minute in the silence. "Okay, sweetie. Take care of yourself."

Sofia hung up and stared at the most recent newspaper. Articles about Kate's death no longer were front page news. Instead, the most recent article, which really had nothing new, was buried on an inside page. Every day that passed was taking them further away from finding Kate's killer.

CHAPTER 41

SOFIA

August 2019
Minneapolis

The phone startled Sofia.

"Sofia." It was Dan on the phone. "Lily told me to call you."

"How's Lily? She seemed pretty upset."

"She's okay." His voice was subdued. "Can you meet me for lunch?"

"Of course." Sofia sat up straight.

"One o'clock at Casa Blanca for tapas?"

"See you there." Sofia sniffed under her arms. She smelled like death. Upstairs, she stripped off her clothes as she walked from the landing to the bathroom until she was in front of Kate's room naked. She pulled Kate's door closed. As it made a loud click, she sank to the floor in front of the door on her hands and knees, sobbing, her hair hanging down around her face. After about five minutes, she wiped her tears and snot off on her bare arm.

Stepping into the shower, she turned the dial as hot as she could stand it, welcoming the stinging needlelike feeling of the near scalding water pounding onto her back and into her scalp.

Leaning against the tiled shower wall, she let the water pour off her head into a white-hot curtain in front of her face. Her knees were weak. She couldn't remember the last time she'd had more than a few crackers and cheese to eat. The thought of having tapas at Casa Blanca, one of her favorite restaurants, made her nauseous. But she had to eat. She had to stay strong to complete her plan.

After her shower, she gathered her hair back in a long ponytail and headed for her closet. She reached for a casual black linen dress with a scooped neckline, a tight waist and a straight skirt to the knee.

She slipped on tan sandals, swiped on a slick of red lipstick. Grabbing her bag, she fished out her car keys.

Pulling into a vacant spot along Central Avenue, she glanced at the clock in her car. Only five minutes late. Pretty damn good considering.

Dan rose to kiss her cheek. She sank into her chair, suddenly tired. Grief was exhausting.

"I've ordered a tapas platter and two beers," he said, reaching over to pat her hand. She clocked the three empty beer bottles already by his plate. He'd gotten here early. Maybe even called from here.

"Thanks. I just can't think," she put her head in her hands. "I'm supposed to be out finding Kate's killer and it's all I can do to get through the day. And then I'm out having lunch with friends and getting drunk instead of hunting down the monster who killed my daughter."

It all came out in one big breath and Sofia widened her eyes in surprise at her own outburst.

"I know." Dan's voice was quiet. The waitress appeared at her elbow and set down their beers and some plates and napkins.

"What's up with the neighbor?" Dan peered at her over his glass.

"I don't know. The detectives say everybody is a suspect at this point."

Dan grabbed his beer and downed it in one long motion, wiping his chin delicately with a napkin when he was done. "You know, getting drunk seems like the most reasonable option to me." He signaled for another beer.

For the first time since she walked in, Sofia took a good look at Dan. He had deep circles under his eyes and sallow skin. He didn't look healthy. She thought about the heart attack he'd had three years ago.

"You feeling okay, Dan?"

He shrugged.

"How's Lily? I'm worried about her. She said something about wanting to die. That worries me, Dan."

For a second, something flashed across Dan's face. Something she couldn't interpret. But it was gone before she could grasp it.

"I'm watching her closely. I think she's going to take the whole semester off."

"I'm so sorry."

He pressed his lips together. "Any closer to finding Kate's killer?" He didn't look at her as he spoke. She ignored his question, staring at how the armpits of his shirt were dark with perspiration.

"What's going on, Dan?"

He shook his head and sighed. "It's Gretchen. She's convinced I'm having an affair. I'm worried she's not mentally stable. Her jealousy – she's always been bad, but now it's really dangerous. She's gotten violent with me. She actually swung at me. Got me right smack in the jaw. It didn't really hurt, but I'm worried. I honestly think she might hurt someone. She's a little delusional. Imagining things that aren't true. She keeps saying I'm going to hell and if she doesn't work hard to get me to confess my sins, she'll go to hell with me."

Sofia didn't know what to say. She couldn't tell Dan that Gretchen was a psycho bitch and they'd always known that.

He blew out a burst of air. "Will you please let me know if she says anything weird to you? She's got some odd ideas in her head right now. I'm worried she's trying to sabotage my friendship with other women. God knows how far she'll stoop to do that."

Sofia rested her chin on her fist, staring at Dan. "What do you mean?"

"She thinks I'm screwing around."

"Really?"

"God knows when I'd even have time to have an affair—too much work. I can barely give enough of myself to Gretchen and Lily and my patients. I wouldn't have time to have an affair."

"No kidding. It'd be too much work, right?" Sofia laughed but then quickly sobered thinking of Jason working late.

"I feel awful even complaining to you about my own problems," Dan said. "But you're one of my best friends and I just needed to talk to somebody. That's part of the problem. She doesn't want me to talk to anyone. She'd probably freak out if she knew we were having lunch."

Sofia tossed her head. "Now, that's ridiculous."

Dan was quiet and looked down. "Her church says that a man who is married should never be alone with a woman besides his wife."

"What?" Sofia peered at him until he looked up at her.

"I know. It doesn't even matter. I'm not even close to your league. You're the New York Yankees and I'm the Little League team at the corner park. You're perfect. Kate was just like you, too. Beautiful. Classy. Intelligent. The freaking Kennedy family. Even your last name is like royalty. Not basket cases like us Williams. Lily is such a mess. And I know it's all my fault. God forgive me."

"Oh, fuck, Dan, now you're being absurd." Sofia shook her head and took another swig of beer.

"Plus, you're not the cheating kind, anyway," he added.

A flush of guilt raced through her. Her teeth had been brushed a dozen times in the past few days trying to get the taste of that boy off her lips.

Dan went on. "It's okay. I've always known that the really pretty girls—women—were out of my league. I've always been a nerdy guy who was awkward around girls. My whole life. I'm used to it now and accepted it. Now I'm a nerdy, chubby, balding guy. That's why I was so shocked when Gretchen asked me out."

"Hold the phone," Sofia held up a palm. "Gretchen asked *you* out?"

"I know, hard to believe, right?"

"I don't mean that, silly. I mean I didn't know she was the ... aggressor. I mean, it makes sense and all with her personality, but it seems like since I've known her she's been born again and adultery is such a big sin in her eyes, I just didn't know." Sofia chewed on her lip for a second. "Did she know you were married?"

"Yeah, we met at some fundraiser for the psych department at the U and she cornered me and asked me out. I told her I was married. I'm not proud of it, but by the end of the night, she was sucking me off in the backseat and telling me she wanted me to get her pregnant."

Sofia held her palm out. "Holy shit, Dan, too much information."

Dan blushed. "Sorry. But what's a guy going to do when a woman with the body of a sixteen-year-old wants you like that and your own wife hasn't had sex with you for a year? Carla stopped having sex with me the second she found out she was pregnant."

Sofia sighed. She didn't know what to say.

"Now, even though Gretchen seduced *me*, she holds that against me every second of every day, saying I cheated on Carla with her, so what's to stop me from screwing anything that walks?"

Again, Sofia was speechless. As he spoke, Dan held his hand up to signal he wanted another drink, but knocked over one of the empty bottles by his plate. It crashed loudly onto the floor, but didn't break.

"I'm driving you home," Sofia said, trying to hide her concern.

"Deal." Dan cleared his throat. "Um, Sofia. I swung by your house the other night. Your car was in the driveway but you didn't answer the door."

Her blood ran cold. “Oh yeah?” She tried to keep her voice steady. “What night was that?”

“Two nights ago. You know the day you came to see me in my office.”

The night Jason worked until 2 a.m. or the night she was in the hotel with that boy?

Sofia took a slug off her beer to avoid his eyes. She realized she was buzzed, too. Nobody would be driving for a while.

“I knocked and knocked but you must have been totally passed out. I told you to be extremely careful with the Rohypnol. It can be deadly.”

“I am careful. Only two drops at a time.” For a split second, she considered telling him what she had done, where she had been.

“I almost called 911.” He gave her a look that she couldn’t read. It made her squirm. Did he know? He *almost* called 911. But he didn’t. In her buzzed state of mind, Sofia mulled this over and then let it go.

She smiled, even though it felt like her face was a plastic mask. “I must have been in a really deep sleep.”

He nodded, but she could tell by the way he was watching her he didn’t buy it.

“Do you like being married to Gretchen?” Sofia tried to change the subject.

He shrugged. “Sometimes. I don’t know. It doesn’t matter. I can’t get a divorce. Even if I wanted one. I’m a marriage counselor for Christ’s sake, how would that look to my patients? A divorced counselor giving them advice? The only thing they would accept is if I were a widower. Then they’d all feel sorry for me.” He took another swig of beer. “What a joke. And besides, a divorce would destroy Lily. She would hate me forever if I ever left Gretchen. As far as Lily is concerned Gretchen is, and always will be, her mother.”

Sofia sucked on her bottom lip for a second. She had to admit that Gretchen *was* a good mother to Lily. She took another sip of her beer. Her head buzzed. They'd have to call an Uber to get home.

"Enough about me," Dan said, leaning forward and taking Sofia's hands. "How are you? Do the police think this guy, this neighbor, did it for sure? Are they going to charge him so we can finally end this and all relax?"

Sofia shook her head, irritated. "I don't know." She closed her eyes for a second. "Oh God, Dan. I know it's not true, but I can't help but believe that some of this pain, maybe the tiniest smidgen of it, will go away if the person who did this to Kate dies a terrible death."

There she said it. She looked up at Dan with eyes flashing. Dan was silent for a few seconds. They stared at one another. Finally, Dan looked out the window and sighed. "You're not taking those pills, are you?"

CHAPTER 42

SOFIA

August 2019
Minneapolis

"Hi honey."

Cecile's voice had something odd in it. Sofia couldn't figure out what it was.

"What's up?" Sofia didn't have the energy for niceties.

"Tomorrow is Gourmet Grub Night."

Sofia closed her eyes and rubbed them. "Our turn to host, right?"

"I was thinking, maybe I could host this month ... if you still were up for it."

There, she'd said it, Sofia thought. That's really what the call was about: whether the monthly dinner ritual was going to continue now that Sofia and Jason's daughter had been murdered in cold blood.

She felt the fury rise in her, but quickly tamped it down. Cecile was her friend. She was genuinely concerned. Sofia and Jason couldn't give up their entire lives, ditch their social life and become hermits, now could they? That's what she wanted to do, but she also knew that it would destroy them even further.

"I think it would be good to get together with everyone," Sofia finally said. "We'll host."

"You sure?"

"Yes." As she said it, Sofia realized it was true. For most of her life, cooking had been a form of therapy—feeding people she cared about was in her DNA.

Cecile cleared her throat. "It will just be the adults anyway."

Sofia closed her eyes. In other words, the lack of Kate's presence wouldn't be as obvious. What the fuck? Was this how every interaction between Sofia and her friends would go forever and ever?

She changed the subject. "I've been eyeing this new recipe for Cornish hen."

"Yum." Cecile's voice was falsely bright.

Sofia had lied. She hadn't even thought about cooking for the past month. Not since the morning of the empty nest party and then it had only been appetizers. She hadn't had an appetite for weeks. How could she eat when her baby's body was decomposing in the ground?

Just thinking that made Sofia slump to the floor, still clutching the phone. She could not go there. Could not. Could not think about where Kate was. It was too much.

"See you Friday." She hung up without saying goodbye.

CHAPTER 43

SOFIA

August 2019

Minneapolis

The next morning, while Jason was still sleeping, Sofia hid downstairs, logging onto her fake Instagram account, looking for anything new. Idly she scrolled through the feed.

Then she saw a picture Ali had posted and froze, the hairs on her neck tingling. It showed him hugging some other guys. He was in Somalia. He had left the country. No wonder she hadn't seen anyone at his house the other day. Fleeing the country was an obvious huge fucking red flag.

She punched in Detective Marley's number. "Ali Yassin is gone. He left the country."

"It's five in the morning, Mrs. Kennedy."

"For god's sake call me Sofia. And I don't care what time it is. What if he left because he killed her, because he's guilty?"

"He had an alibi."

"Yeah, by his girlfriend who used him as her alibi, as well."

Silence.

"Is he cleared?"

Marley gave a long sigh. "No. Not completely."

"What about the girl? Or his roommate?"

"Why don't you come in later and we'll chat. I wanted to ask you some questions anyway about some leads that have come in."

"Leads? What about my neighbor?"

"Meet me at the station at nine." He hung up.

Sofia sensed rather than saw Jason behind her.

"What's going on?" he said, his voice thick with sleep.

"Nothing," she closed the laptop hoping he hadn't seen the screen. "Detective Marley wants us to come in at nine to discuss some leads."

He didn't answer.

"Jason?"

"Are there any leads?"

Sofia blinked.

Jason sighed and ran a hand through his hair.

"You don't want to come?"

"Do you want me to? I was going to get dressed and go to the grocery store to get what we need for the dinner."

The dinner. Her heart skipped a beat. It was tomorrow. Jason was going to the grocery store instead of helping her find their daughter's killer. Jesus Christ.

Sofia wanted to scream, *Of course, I god damn want you to.*

But then she realized it might be better if Jason stayed far away from any knowledge of Kate's killer. It was better he didn't know. That way he would never be accused of helping Sofia.

She stood and walked over to him, brushing his bangs back from his forehead and leaning in to kiss his cheek. "If it's anything important, I'll bring you up to speed."

She worked her jaw, thinking. Coming up with a plan. Suddenly, she noticed the silence. She looked up. Jason was watching her. She'd nearly forgotten he was there.

• • • •

DETECTIVE MARLEY WOULD have made a terrible poker player.

The first thing he asked after Sofia settled into her chair at the police station, was what she knew about the manager at the bookstore where Kate had worked.

Her eyes grew wide. "Is he a suspect? That mousy little man?"

He shook his head. "Mrs. Kennedy."

"Sofia."

"Sofia, everybody is a suspect until they are not."

She chewed on that for a second.

"Am I?"

He shot her an amused look. "No."

"Is Jason?"

"Nope."

"Who else is cleared that we know."

"Frankly, nobody else is 'cleared' if that's what you mean."

"The neighbor?" She gave him an exasperated look. "Is he still a suspect?"

"He's a person of interest. But so are a lot of other people."

"Like Ali?"

"Maybe." He shrugged.

Sofia leaned forward and caught a whiff of cigarette smoke. She couldn't believe she'd never smelled it before. "So, how could you let him leave the country?"

"Let him?"

"Yes. Let him."

"With all due respect, you've been watching too many episodes of Law & Order."

Sofia felt the rage boil up inside. "With all due respect, fuck you."

He stood and put his hands out. "Hey, hey, hey, I'm sorry. That was uncalled for. But you can't roll in here telling me how to do my job. I've been busting my ass to find who did this to your daughter." He paced. "My kids are angry because I've missed every swim meet, every gymnastics match. My wife is on the brink of divorcing me because I've missed every dinner and every teenage hormonal melt down that she's had to deal with solo for the past three weeks. You've got to let me do my job."

Sofia watched him with eyes wide. And then guilt swarmed over her. He settled back into his chair. "Again, I apologize for patronizing you, but you have to understand the only person—besides your husband—who cares more about making an arrest in this case than you—is me."

Sofia chewed on her lip. "Then why do you call it "this case" and why do you refuse to say Kate's name most of the time. Your words make me wonder how invested you are in solving my daughter's murder."

"Aha. I get it now." He raked a hand through his hair. "It's like this. I'm the father of two girls. Seeing a girl a few years older than them murdered is a punch to the gut for me. I know your daughter's name. I know more about her than you'd ever dream. That's my whole life right now. I'm so immersed in your daughter and her life and her death that I'm neglecting my own life. Some cases fuck with me, pardon my French, more than others, and this one, a girl a few years older than my two, well, Sofia, this one fucks with me royally. So, if you think I don't give a shit, based on a few words I use, you are dead wrong."

Sofia had been listening carefully. When he was finished, she stood, pressed her lips together tightly, and nodded. "Okay."

He cleared his throat and waited until she met his eyes.

"By the way, for some reason, I can't find anything in the papers about your parents being killed."

Sofia felt her core grow cold. *Keep it together*.

She cocked her head. "Really? That's odd. But things weren't really online back then." She put a confused look on her face. "I was pretty young but you'd have thought it would've been a big deal at the time."

It seemed like he looked at her for an extra-long second, but then he stood.

Driving away, Sofia knew she was right to want to find Kate's killer herself. Her father was wrong about 99.9 percent of the things he'd taught her, but surprisingly, on this one thing—we don't call the cops, we handle it ourselves—he'd been right.

Marley was playing a game. He knew she had lied about her name and her past. Did that mean he knew about Angelo? She needed to find out who killed Kate before Marley found out who Sofia really was and what she was capable of doing.

CHAPTER 44

SOFIA

J*uly 1988*

Derby, Connecticut

Aunt Rose was dead.

Of breast cancer at thirty-five-years old.

Sofia was overcome with grief. The kind-hearted, loving, affectionate woman had been the mother Sofia had never had.

Now, without her, Sofia was bereft. She was all alone in the world.

After the graveside service, Sofia refused a ride from the priest and walked home in the gray dusk

She walked on the shoulder of the dimly lit and deserted road, not caring, not seeing.

It took her a few minutes to realize a large dark car had been driving behind her. Something in the back of her mind told her she should run, but she didn't have the energy to act. Or care.

She didn't look over when she heard the slight whirring sound of a window rolling down.

"You know, the next town isn't for another ten miles."

She shrugged, not looking over at the voice.

"Why don't you let me give you a ride?" The voice seemed normal. But then again who knew what a serial killer's voice sounded like. Nobody usually lived to tell.

As she walked, she was tempted to sneak a sideways glance at the person talking, but decided to keep her gaze straight ahead.

"Come on, don't be stubborn."

Again, she ignored him.

"It's getting cold out. I bet you'd rather be in the car with me having a drink to warm your belly."

She paused. Yes. That's what she wanted. A drink.

The car ground to a halt in the gravel. That's when she realized it was a limousine. A guy jumped out of the driver's seat and held the back door open for her.

She crawled in and only then saw the man who had been speaking.

He looked vaguely familiar. She didn't really care who he was, as she gratefully accepted the crystal glass he handed her.

She gulped it down and asked for another.

Later, after he took her to his Tribeca loft and took her virginity, she got up and stared in the bathroom mirror while he snored in the other room.

For a second she considered rifling through his wallet and leaving, but then felt such an overwhelming sense of weariness that she crawled back into the big soft bed next to the man. She'd ask for his help in the morning.

Despite being old and fat, he was incredibly kind. He made sure that she was comfortable when he made love to her, asking her frequently throughout if she was okay. When he'd finished, he'd kissed her forehead and said quietly, "Thank you."

He wanted to take her shopping and out to breakfast the next morning, he said.

She watched it all as if she were outside of her body looking down. Nothing touched her.

Now, she curled up beside his big warm body. In the morning, she'd ask him for help to get to Minnesota. She didn't have money for an airplane ticket. Rose had planned on cashing out some stocks or something to help pay her way to college. Once she got there, everything was taken care of by scholarship, but she needed money for the travel.

As she fell asleep, Sofia knew that this man would help her.

The morning light coming in the window was bright. It was past breakfast. They'd slept until lunch.

She rolled over to wake the man. He was stiff and cold.

She opened her mouth to scream but then wild-eyed, realized she'd killed him. Somehow, in some way, she'd killed him in her sleep. Like Angelo.

Grabbing her clothes, she dressed and fled the apartment, but not before taking a cloth and wiping her fingerprints off everything she remembered touching and withdrawing all the cash from his wallet. In the hallway, she paused and then headed for the back stairs that led to the alley instead of the street.

Back in her apartment, she was nearly catatonic. She lay, curled up in the fetal position in bed for two days straight, only lifting her head to sip out of a glass of water a few times a day.

On the third day, she got up, showered and dressed. She had a plan.

She'd leave on Thursday. First, she'd go see her father in prison. For the first time. And then she'd leave.

And never come back.

She saw the newspaper article after she'd bought her ticket to Minnesota under the name Sofia Castle.

A prominent Wall Street stock broker had been found dead in his bed. Coroner's officials say autopsy revealed he'd died of a massive heart attack.

CHAPTER 45

SOFIA

September 2019
Minneapolis

Sofia was up early.

She was serving Cornish Game Hens stuffed with Minnesota's famous wild rice and pecans. She also would serve braised greens with chunks of roasted sweet potatoes. Along with a good bread, good wine, and local ice cream for dessert, she'd make everyone happy.

But even staying busy in the kitchen couldn't fight off the dread that had been growing in her gut ever since Cecile reminded her about dinner night.

By the time Jason came downstairs bleary-eyed heading toward the coffee pot like a heat-seeking missile, she was ready to crawl back in bed again and not get up until the next day.

The thought of all her friends at her house for Gourmet Grub night was overwhelming. Even thinking of preparing "six" hens of the customary "nine" she would usually serve sent a stab of pain to her heart. Even if Kate had been alive and away at college, it would've still been strange to have the dinner party without her and the other teens.

After handing Jason a cup of coffee, Sofia turned to him. "I'm beat. I got up too early. I'm going to go back to bed for a while."

"Good idea," he said, leaning in and kissing her forehead. "Go rest."

Upstairs, Sofia set her alarm and grabbed some pills.

When she woke at five thirty, the house was quiet.

Downstairs she found a note from Jason. He was at the gym.

She put the hens in the oven and glanced at the clock.

Her friends weren't arriving until seven. She eyed the bar cart in the corner. The bottles of vodka, whiskey, tequila, and gin tempted her. Jason was at the gym.

Ignoring the siren call of the alcohol, she set the table. Then she placed the three bottles of red wine in strategic spots on the table. Again, the bar cart beckoned.

What the hell? She needed something to take the edge off. Turning to the refrigerator, she searched for limes. Damn. None. No tonic, either. So much for a gin and tonic.

They hadn't yet opened that bottle of tequila Dan had brought from Mexico.

She eyed the clock. Jason would be home any minute. For some reason, she felt like she needed to hide her early drinking. Tequila would fit the bill.

It would pack a punch and she'd be done with it and go hop in the shower to get ready for their guests.

• • • •

WHEN JASON SHOWED UP a half hour later she was sitting on the floor, holding the bottle and singing along to the tinny music piping out of her phone. It was Ariana Grande. The first concert she'd taken Kate to. They'd had so much fun.

Jason didn't notice her at first. She was slumped in the corner near the bar cart.

"'lo." She gestured with the tequila bottle in a half-hearted wave.

He was leaning into the refrigerator and he jumped smacking his head.

"You scared the shit out of me." Holding his head, he walked over.

"Sofia?"

"Sorry. I just was going to have one drink."

He looked at the time. "People will be here in less than thirty minutes."

She smiled. "It's all ready to go. We just need to grab everything out of the fridge and oven."

But he didn't seem convinced. "Yeah, but you should probably take a shower and get dressed, right." He leaned down and offered her his hand She pulled herself up with a grunt. A wave of vertigo made her lose her balance and she fell into his arms.

"You going to be okay going upstairs by yourself?"

He was being so sweet. She saluted him. "Yep. I'm good, captain."

But he didn't seem convinced. He eyed her warily. "I'll start some coffee and bring it up to you while you dress."

"You know that's an old wives' tale," she said, pausing at the foot of the stairs.

"What?"

"That coffee sobers you up."

He didn't respond.

• • • •

WHEN SHE CAME DOWNSTAIRS again, she saw Jason at the bar cart fixing drinks for their friends. He smiled and it seemed he was relieved she was up and about.

After kisses were exchanged all the way around without any raised eyebrows or comments about hitting the booze early, the couples stood around the large kitchen counter and nibbled on almonds and cheese before heading to the table.

Up until that point, the conversation had flowed nice and easy, but as soon as they sat down at the big table—the time when they normally would call the teenagers up to join them—it grew silent. Sofia wanted to scream.

The empty chairs were blaringly conspicuous. Sofia couldn't help it, her eyes kept darting to the seat where Kate usually sat. All the food had been placed on the table on platters. Jason rubbed Sofia's arm.

As the seconds passed awkwardly, until finally Alex said loudly, "May I offer anyone a Cornish hen? They look delicious."

He lifted the platter, serving Cecile on one side and Gretchen on the other before he took his own and handed the platter to Dan.

Gretchen didn't seem interested in the food on her plate. Instead, she filled her wine glass, downed it, and filled it again before chugging it and wincing.

She mumbled something under her breath and Dan leaned over saying something in her ear that made her scowl.

When she tried to pour a third glass, he put his hand on hers.

"What?" Gretchen said, glaring at everyone else. "It's okay for Sofia to be drunk, but I have to stay sober?"

Cecile arched an eyebrow.

"No, really," Gretchen said, her eyes going from face to face. "She's the only one allowed to drink too much? She's the only one whose life is so fucked up that she has to drown her sorrows in booze?"

"Gretchen!" Dan looked horrified. His face had turned white and perspiration was dripping from his brow.

Jason started to say something, but Cecile put her hand up.

"Allow me," she said. "As a matter of fact, Gretchen, you are exactly right. She is allowed to drink a little much if she so chooses. She is in a safe place, among friends. At least I'm sure that's what she believes. Or rather, what she believed."

Gretchen made a face. "A safe place? A safe place? You mean a place for your husband to find new playmates! That's what this place is. Not fucking safe at all."

"Gretchen!" Dan stood up, his face bright red. "You're drunk. You're talking nonsense and you've gone too far this time. Get your stuff. We're leaving."

Gretchen stood as well, flung her napkin down on the table, snatched up a bottle of wine and turned on her heel.

Dan turned toward the others. "Oh my God. Oh my God. I'm so terribly sorry. I think her medication is off. She needs help. I'm so sorry."

He looked like he was about to cry as he scurried after Gretchen.

Nobody said a word until the front door slammed.

"Jesus," Cecile said. "What the fuck is wrong with that woman?"

Sofia pushed away her plate and put her arms on the table and then buried her face in her arms. She surprised herself with the ferocity of the loud, wracking sobs emerging from her mouth.

Jason smoothed her hair and made soothing sounds, but when Sofia lifted her head, she saw his eyes looked wild and haunted.

Cecile sat as still as a statue with tears streaming down her face watching her friends.

Alex reached for her hand. "Maybe we should go?" His voice was low.

Jason looked up, staring into space. A mask of fury passed over him. His jaw clenched. His neck grew red and he grabbed an unopened wine bottle and chucked it across the room. It exploded blood red wine all over the orange wall with a loud crash. The one love seat pressed against the wall was streaked with red.

Sofia looked up in astonishment, eyes wide. Jason gave her a blank look.

She stood then and everyone held their breath.

Reaching over, Sofia plucked another bottle of wine off the table and without a word, slung it underhanded as if she were throwing a softball pitch. The bottle shattered with a resounding crack. Cecile looked around and not seeing another bottle, headed toward Sofia's wine rack on the wall. She grabbed a bottle and lobbed it to Jason who easily caught it and in one fluid motion hurled it against the wall.

Then Cecile walked over with her own wine bottle and pitched it over her head. It smacked against the wall at the same time Sofia screamed. It was a long, seemingly endless scream that continued even after she collapsed in a heap on the floor. Jason kneeled down and wrapped her in his arms, burying his face in her hair.

CHAPTER 46

SOFIA

September 2019
Minneapolis

It was the warmest September the state had seen in more than a decade.

People were swimming and kayaking in the lake. In the ninety-degree heat wave, winter seemed far away. Golfers flocked to the lush green courses and confused flowers still sporadically bloomed.

When Dan called, Sofia had been lacing up her running shoes.

"Will you please meet with me? I feel just awful about the dinner.

"I'm going running." Her voice was cold. She knew Dan wasn't responsible for Gretchen's behavior, but a small part of her blamed him for bringing that evil woman into her home.

"I'll come too. You say the word. I'll meet you anywhere"

"Lake Harriet."

She hung up.

It had been exactly a month since Sofia had buried her daughter. She hadn't found Kate's killer yet. The detectives were at a loss.

Ali's alibi seemed to stick. But there was still the troubling fact that he'd fled the country. More than once, Sofia had looked at flights to Somalia.

The neighbor had put his house up for sale.

When Sofia saw the for sale sign she had called Marley. He said the neighbor was holed up in some cabin in Wisconsin. Marley said not to worry, they were still keeping tabs on him.

Sofia knew she should hunt the man down and confront him, but she was exhausted. It took all her energy just to make it from the time she woke up until she could crawl into bed at night.

Plus, she didn't know for sure it *was* the neighbor.

Marley had said again that nobody was officially "cleared" except her and Jason.

Sofia still checked Instagram several times a day, hoping that she'd see a post that Ali had returned. Every day she paced, trying to think of something that would help her find Kate's killer. Sometimes she'd sneak off during the afternoon and park outside Lucky's. Other times, she'd park across the street from Ali's house, keeping one eye on the closed curtains and the other on the paved path near where Kate's body was found.

One day last week she'd mustered up the energy to go to Kate's grave. She had laid down in the fresh dirt and cried and told her daughter she still hadn't given up on finding the killer. But deep down inside, she was worried she was lying. That she might never find Kate's killer. She would die without avenging her daughter's death. The thought was unbearable.

Jason was working twelve-hour days and most often fell asleep on the couch in the living room.

Now, she gave her laces a firm tug. It was time. Running had been her therapy for years and when she woke up this morning feeling the anxiety stifling her, rising up in her throat, making it hard to breath, she almost automatically reached for her yoga pants and a snug tee-shirt. Other than shoes, she didn't believe in having special gear to run in.

Now, as she walked around Lake Harriett with Dan, they had to step aside for all the other people out jogging, walking, and pushing strollers. The lake was smooth and reflected the green trees. Above, giant puffy white clouds floated past in the cobalt sky.

For a few seconds, Sofia was overcome—and immediately ashamed—by the beauty of a world that could still look like this without Kate in it.

They were nearly halfway around the lake before Dan spoke.

"First, can you ever forgive me for Gretchen's behavior?"

Sofia exhaled and all her resentment went with it.

"You aren't responsible for her," she said.

"Oh thank God you feel that way."

A crease still furrowed his brow.

"What's up, Dan. Spill it."

"I'm worried," he said, huffing a little. Sofia had kept up a brisk pace. Since she couldn't run with Dan along, she walked as fast as she could.

"About?" she said without looking over at Dan, who was at her right elbow.

"Gretchen."

Sofia didn't answer.

"I mean that behavior you saw. It's getting worse. And I'm leaving town, to Chicago. I'm worried about leaving her and Lily home. But I have to go. I'm a featured speaker. I've already cashed the damn check. It's my annual conference where I get to talk about all those nerdy psychiatry theories that bore the rest of you."

Sofia nodded.

"I'm afraid she'll do something rash while I'm gone."

"Lily?" Sofia remembered Lily saying she wanted to die.

"No. Gretchen."

Sofia stopped, leaning down to massage her calf, which had a slightly knotted muscle. When she looked up, Dan's face was scrunched. Sweat was pouring down his temples. He shot her a sideways glance.

"You think she might try to hurt herself?" Sofia was never the kind to pull punches or beat around the bush.

He pressed his lips tightly together. "I don't know. Maybe. Or do or say something crazy."

"Like what?"

He ran a hand over his near balding pate. "God, I don't know." His eyes looked past her to the lake as a bright red kayak floated past. "She's been talking nonsense the past few weeks. Just like at your house. Accusing me of some outlandish things. She's even questioned whether she's done something or not."

"Like what?"

"The other night she came home and was hysterical. She said she wasn't sure but she thought she'd hit a deer. We went out to look at the car but there wasn't any dent and no fur or blood or anything. She says she can't remember if she did or not."

"Was she drunk?"

"No, nothing like that," Dan said looking down at the walking path. "And we got her meds straightened out. It's something else. It's an OCD thing. Sometimes with those obsessive thoughts we can't tell what we've done or what we haven't done."

Sofia bit her lip and didn't say anything.

"She spent all night on her knees praying for forgiveness for something she didn't even do."

"Good God."

Dan closed his eyes. "It's been hell at our house lately."

There was nothing to say to that. Her entire existence had been hell since the day she woke up and Kate's bedroom was empty.

Dan stopped and put his hands on his knees.

"Dan?"

He looked up and his eyes looked pained. "I think I want out."

"Of your marriage?"

He nodded.

"I thought you couldn't do that. Didn't you say it would destroy Lily?"

"You're right," he shook his head. "I don't know what to do. Everything is so screwed up."

Sofia didn't know how to answer that. She figured her life would be fucked from here on out, until the day she died. At least his only daughter was still walking the earth.

"How's Lily?"

"She lies in bed and stares at the wall all day. I keep trying to get her to get up and do something. I'm so worried about her and this thing with Gretchen is making it worse. Lily's not dumb. She senses the tension. I also think she's afraid. That whomever did this to Kate is still out there." Dan looked away. "Are you still intent on ... hurting the person who did this?"

Sofia stared at the big white clouds above the green trees. "Yes."

As they walked, Sofia decided she would call Lily. Maybe the girl needed an ear. Someone outside her feuding parents.

"Maybe I can talk to her," Sofia said.

"That's probably not a good idea," Dan said.

Sofia scrunched her face. That didn't make sense. She'd call Lily if Dan liked it or not. Just because he was a therapist didn't mean he was the perfect parent.

A group of runners came up on them just then. Sofia grabbed Dan and pulled him off the path to a bench. "Sit. You're pale. You look ill. Are you okay?"

He guffawed. "You're worried I'm having a heart attack?"

"Maybe." She looked past him at the lake.

"Trust me. It's not that. I'm just out of shape." He put his hands on his hips. "I guess I'm asking a favor. Will you call me if she contacts you? If she says anything weird or crazy?"

"Why would she call me?"

"I don't know." He looked away for a second and then turned back, meeting Sofia's eyes.

"That's not true. I do know. I'm just embarrassed to tell you."

"Spill it, Dan."

"Remember how I said that Gretchen thought I was having an affair? Well, I was embarrassed so I left an important part out—she thinks I'm in love with Cecile. That's why she said that at your house."

"What?" *Cecile?* Crazy. But in the back of her mind she felt a little guilty judging Gretchen.

"That's ridiculous," she said.

"You know Gretchen—she's jealous of every single woman I talk to—my friends, my patients, the little old neighbor lady—you name it. Now her focus is on Cecile. Don't worry, she's jealous of you, too. She's made cracks that I spend too much time with you, consoling you. She said that you should be over it by now."

Sofia's eyes flashed with anger. "What the fuck?"

Dan reached out and tried to touch Sofia's arm. "I know," he said. "It's irrational. That's what I mean. Promise you'll call me immediately if she tries to get in touch with you?"

"Fine." Sofia glared off into the distance. Every nerve vibrated with anger. It was like the fury was shooting off her in waves. How dare Gretchen suggest she get over her daughter's murder?

Dan dipped his head to look her in the face. "Oh, Sofia. I'm sorry if I upset you. You have too much to deal with already. I should have never turned to you."

"That's not it." She balled her hands into fists.

He sighed, blowing the air out in a big puff. "You never took those pills I gave you?"

"Yes, I did."

"I'm not talking about the ones I gave you that first night. I mean the second bottle."

Sofia wished everyone would just leave her the fuck alone.

"Listen, Dan, you don't look so hot. Why don't you turn around, head back to your car and I'll squeeze in a run? I think I need to burn off this anger before I punch someone."

He looked abashed. "I'm sorry. I needed you to know. I needed to warn you."

Sofia took off at a run without looking back.

CHAPTER 47

SOFIA

September 2019
Minneapolis

Lily seemed nervous.

She walked around Sofia's house as if she had never seen it, trailing her fingers along the couch, pausing at the family pictures on the living room mantle. She seemed dazed, almost drugged. Her eyes glassy and pupils dilated.

It broke Sofia's heart to see Lily act like a stranger in her home. Lily had spent so much time at Sofia's house that when the girls were little, Sofia would call them to do chores like they were sisters.

"Kate? Lily? Come empty the dishwasher!"

She'd always considered Lily one of her own. It had taken a month, but her heart had finally softened toward the girl. She'd finally forgiven her for letting Kate go off on her own. It was time. Sofia had always known that it wasn't Lily's fault. But up until now, it hurt too much to forgive. Now she was ready.

After hearing Dan's concerns about Lily, she'd called and invited her to lunch.

But as soon as Lily agreed, Sofia worried about her true intentions for having Lily over. She really did want to cheer the girl up and have a chance to let go of her resentment, but in the back of her mind, she knew there was another motive.

She craved Lily's presence in an unhealthy way. Sofia wanted a teenage girl in the house. Nobody could ever replace Kate, but just for one afternoon, Sofia wanted the house full of conversation and laughter instead of her and Jason sitting sullenly in silence.

She couldn't have Kate, but Lily had always been so much a part of Kate's childhood that in some ways it would feel a tiny bit like having Kate back. And hopefully she could help Lily in some small way.

But now Sofia worried she'd done the wrong thing. Lily seemed disoriented and on the verge of tears. Sofia walked up and put her arm around the girl's shoulder. It felt frail, as if she had melted away the past few weeks.

"Hope you're hungry, sweetie, I made your favorite: spaghetti and meatballs."

Lily turned to her. "The family one, right?"

When the girls were little, they'd beg for the Family Sauce. It was the one that took all day to cook. It involved sixteen meatballs, twelve spicy Italian sausages and eight browned pork chops simmered in the sauce until the meat fell off the bone.

Because it was so labor intensive, Sofia only made it twice a year. Usually one of the times was on Lily's birthday and the other time was on New Year's Day. Kate didn't really care about the Family Sauce. For her, the regular spaghetti and meatballs her family ate every Sunday was fine. But Lily loved the Family Sauce and would often ask Sofia to make it as a birthday treat.

"Oh yeah, baby. No scrimping when it comes to my Lily."

Lily didn't smile.

Sofia's voice was as chipper as she could make it. She could think of no better way to love on Lily than make her favorite dinner and have them watch a chick flick on TV afterward.

After she ladled out the spaghetti and sat down, she glanced over and saw Lily was sobbing, her face red and wet with tears.

"Oh Lily, honey." Sofia jumped up to hug her. "It's okay, sweetie. It's okay."

"I don't deserve this. I don't deserve for you to treat me like this. To act like nothing happened." Lily's voice was thick with tears.

"Oh honey. It's not your fault. You didn't know that Kate leaving on her own was dangerous. You didn't know something bad would happen. Please don't blame yourself."

Lily drew back and her face was suddenly white. She looked terrified.

"But I do. Because it's my fault. You can tell me it's not as much as you want, but it is. And I have to live with that until the day I die."

Sofia stood there, speechless. She wanted to comfort Lily so badly, but she didn't know what to say. It was only now that she had let go of the idea herself that maybe, just maybe, Lily could have prevented Kate's murder.

Lily obviously hadn't let that idea go yet.

"Lily?" Sofia's voice was pleading. "Please. Please forgive yourself for me?"

"No. I will never ever forgive myself." Lily's face was red. She was heading toward the door, grabbing her bag off the couch.

Suddenly Sofia doubted her own motives. Maybe this was wrong. Maybe it was too soon. Hadn't she wanted Lily over to eat and watch movies because she was lonely for her own daughter? Now, she'd made things worse for Lily. She ran to the door and grabbed Lily's arm.

"I'm so sorry. This was a bad idea. It's too soon. I hope someday we can do something like this. I really do. I'm so sorry you are hurting this badly. I promise you it will get better."

As she said the words, Sofia wondered if she were lying.

Lily jerked away violently and threw open the front door. Right before she stepped out, she turned to Sofia.

"It will never, ever get better." Her face was red and her eyes blazed. "Don't you understand? Don't you get it?"

She spit the words out and ran away.

Sofia stood frozen, listening to the sound of Lily's vehicle squealing out of the driveway and down the road.

CHAPTER 48

KATE

July 2019

Dinkytown

Each time a letter from my so-called grandmother came to me at the bookstore, I furtively tucked it into my bag. I think I was up to four now. The other employee, an old guy with thick glasses, raised his eyebrow but didn't say a word.

Today there was another letter. I grabbed it and walked past the front desk toward the back of the store. I was twenty minutes early to work.

"Just wanted to get some reading in before my shift." Which was the lamest excuse ever. We totally had permission to sit and read all we wanted while we worked as long as our tasks were done and no customers needed our attention. The main reason I'd taken the job.

Finally, today, I decided it was high time I read them. I curled up in the arm chair at the back of the bookstore and took the stack out of my bag.

I re-arranged them by date. The one postmarked the oldest first.

I ripped open the first envelope and pulled out the pink pages.

The words were printed in blue ink.

"Thank you for responding to my message on Facebook and for giving me your address. I bet you thought I was dead. But that's because, as I told you, your mother is a liar. She has lied to you about everything."

My stomach clenched in pain, but I couldn't stop reading.

"I thought it was fair that you know your mother is not who she seems. She destroyed our family. She killed her brother. She testified against your grandfather. He was a loyal family man. He has spent his life in prison because of your mother's lies. Think about that. I will tell you more in the next letter. – Your grandmother. PS DO NOT TELL YOUR MOTHER."

The next letter was dated a few weeks later. It was only a few lines and wasn't signed, but the handwriting was the same.

"Kate. You know your mother is a bad person? You must have so many questions about her now that you are finding out the truth. I think we should talk more. But in person. I will be in touch. DO NOT TELL YOUR MOTHER."

I quickly grabbed the next letter. Was my so-called grandmother going to show up here at the bookstore? My heart raced as I ripped open the letter and read.

"I wanted to come meet you. But I am not well. I will be in touch. Just remember your mother is a liar. She is a horrible, evil person! DO NOT TELL YOUR MOTHER. PS Close your window when you get dressed. You never know what the neighbors can see."

The woman was deranged.

But still. It made me feel like throwing up.

It was a terrible, dark secret that I didn't want to keep, but I couldn't exactly go to my mom and say, "I thought your mom was dead!"

Even though the woman was crazy, I couldn't deny that she was right about one thing: my mom had lied to me.

CHAPTER 49

SOFIA

October 2019

Minneapolis

Gretchen didn't seem surprised to see Sofia at her door.

Sofia had waited until Dan left town. That way her anger had somewhat subsided and she could talk to Gretchen without Dan knowing.

"Come in." Gretchen's voice was dull, devoid of any emotion. She wore baggie sweatpants, a tiny camisole top and bare feet. Her hair was greasy and she had an angry rash of acne on her chin. She led Sofia into the kitchen without a word. Opening a mahogany cupboard door, she got down two coffee mugs.

"Is Lily home?" Sofia asked. She was hoping the girl was gone, like Dan had said.

"No, she's at my mother's house."

Handing her a mug of coffee, Gretchen sat down at the kitchen table. Sofia sat across from her.

Gretchen closed her eyes and took a sip of her coffee before answering. "Dan doesn't love me anymore, does he?"

Sofia was annoyed, but tried to hide it. "What are you talking about?"

Gretchen slammed her mug down onto the table. "Come on, Sofia. You can tell me. I'm not going to do anything about it. I just need to know."

Sofia shifted uncomfortably in the kitchen chair. "I have no idea where you came up with that one."

"He's been different lately."

At first Sofia was irritated, but then she softened remembering she'd said much the same thing to Cecile recently about Jason.

"At first, I thought maybe he was still grieving for Kate." She gave Sofia a look. "She's our daughter's best friend. We've both known her since she was a baby for Christ's sakes. But, my God, he needs to move on."

Sofia's vision blurred. Any sympathy she had for Gretchen was gone. She began to see white around the edges. She almost got up and walked out. Her hands gripped the strap of her handbag under the table, her hands curling around so her nails dug into her palms. She'd stay a few more minutes and see what else the crazy woman had to say.

Gretchen was angry and was growing angrier. Drawing in a deep breath, Gretchen continued in a calmer voice. "So, like I said, at first I thought that was it—Kate's death combined with Lily being away at college. But Lily's back now and it's still like a graveyard around here."

Sofia stared. A strange taste filled her mouth, but she swallowed it, feeling the muscle in her jaw tighten.

Gretchen tugged at her hair, pushing it back behind her ears. "I thought maybe that was it. But then I found something." She stood. "I'll be right back."

In the silence of the kitchen, with only the hum of the refrigerator, Sofia felt the urge to scream.

Dan was right. Gretchen was a loose cannon. And now Sofia was her captive audience. A few seconds later, Gretchen appeared, clutching a piece of paper.

"I found this." She thrust it toward Sofia. It was the bottom half of a small lined piece of paper. The page contained a smeared blue mess. It had clearly been crumpled and smoothed out again.

It took Sofia a few minutes to decipher the handwriting.

"I don't think I can live anymore without you knowing how I feel about you. I know it will never amount to anything, but I need you to know. I've imagined kissing you so many times. I know it's wrong and would hurt so many people, but I can't help but think when you look at me sometimes, you feel the same way. I know you are too beautiful for me, but I can't help the way I feel. It's a sin, I know. Gretchen would say I'd go to hell for feeling this way about you, but I'm willing to take that risk. I've tried to deny my feelings for years. Every time our families are together, it eats me up inside to not tell you how I feel. You deserve to know. Remember last winter when we all went to Mexico, and you and I were alone in the pool that one time? The way you looked at me. I could tell you felt something too. Please tell me you feel the same way? We could run away to Paris and you could show me around ..."

That was all she could read. The rest of the page was wet, smeared, and soiled.

Sofia's heart was thumping. It seemed so loud she worried that Gretchen could hear it.

"It's to Cecile." Gretchen's voice was dull.

"Where did you find this?" Sofia held it out, realizing her hand was shaking.

"In the trash. I don't know why but something made me look. He'd ripped this out of his journal before he left for Chicago. I don't know why."

"How do you know when he threw it away?"

"Because our cleaning lady comes on Thursdays and empties the kitchen trash when she does. He left early Thursday morning. But Janice called me about nine and said she wasn't feeling good, so I did the cleaning."

Gretchen shot a sideways look that Sofia couldn't interpret.

Sofia didn't know what to say. She was still surprised by what she had read. Dan was right—Gretchen *did* think he was having an affair with Cecile. She'd always thought Gretchen was crazy to suspect Dan of cheating. Dan wasn't a Don Juan. He wasn't someone that women swooned over.

Gretchen stared at her. Sofia had to say something. "Well, he obviously didn't give it to her," she said.

"That doesn't matter, does it? The Bible says when we lust after another person we are committing adultery." Gretchen put her head in her hands and then looked back up. "I'm going to my mother's house. Lily and I are going to stay there for a week. I'm going to show Dan what it's like to come home to an empty house every day. No wife. No daughter. I want him to see what it's like without me. He'll be shocked when he comes home from Chicago and I'm not here. I won't be mean about it. I'll tell him I just wanted to spend time with my mother. But he'll know. He'll miss me. He'll see."

Sofia handed the page back to Gretchen who wadded it up and tossed it toward the big silver garbage can. It bounced off the can and landed on the floor just outside the kitchen.

"I'm sorry. I can't explain it ... but well, it reads like an unrequited love letter," Sofia said. "Besides, Cecile's in that huge trial. She barely has time to sleep. There's no way she'd have time for an affair."

Gretchen's hair hung down around her face as she peered inside her coffee mug. "I'm not saying Dan is having an affair. I'm saying that he's in love with someone else. That is adultery. In God's eyes that is a sin."

Sofia didn't say what she really thought—Cecile wouldn't give Dan the time of day romantically. And writing a love letter was a far cry from fucking someone else. Gretchen looked at Sofia, her eyes narrowed.

"I know what you're thinking. You're thinking that she would never have sex with Dan." She slammed her mug down on the table. "But the point is that he's in love with her. My husband is in love with someone else. He's not perfect. God knows he's not perfect, but I love him. When he had that heart attack a few years ago, I wanted to die. Without him, I would be all alone in the world. Adultery is a sin, but he could go to confession. He could ask forgiveness from God. God is his judge. Not me.

"He's the only one who understands me. He gets me." She threw up her hands. "He knows that I'm a sinner and he still loves me. And believe me, am I ever a sinner. The worst of the worst. He knows all my sins. I guess that makes us perfect for each other. Do you know what it's like to have a man who knows all your dirty secrets and protects you and loves you back anyway?"

She shot a glance at Sofia.

"Nah, you and Jason are perfect. Have the perfect life."

That's when Sofia started laughing. She laughed until tears were spurting out her eyes. Finally, she spoke. When she did, her voice was like steel, her eyes trained on Gretchen.

"If you only knew. You have no clue, Gretchen. And I'm not even talking about the simple fact that my only child was murdered and that some monster is still out there walking around free."

Gretchen stood up so fast her chair tipped over. "I think you need to leave. I need to go lie down and then pack for my mama's house."

"Why don't you just ask Dan about it? Why don't you talk about it with him?"

Gretchen shook her head so hard her hair whipped back and forth across her face.

For a few seconds the two women stared at each other. Gretchen stumbled toward her bedroom and slammed the door.

On her way out, Sofia scooped up the wadded paper. She'd give it to Dan later and ask him why he lied to her. Or maybe she wouldn't.

Her rage toward Gretchen had dissipated. She no longer wanted to punch her every time Gretchen opened her mouth. Her disgust had morphed into pity. The woman was really and truly sick.

There was nothing else she could say.

CHAPTER 50

SOFIA

December 1975
Derby, Connecticut

Sofia was bored.

She sat swinging her legs in the chair in the exam room. She was five and her feet didn't reach down to the floor. Not quite yet. She stretched, but it made her nearly fall off the chair.

Her mother was up on the exam table, pulling at her hair and mumbling. She'd been sick for the past two months and told Sofia she thought she was dying or had some bad disease or something. She'd spent most days in bed. Sofia had started making her own breakfast and then even attempting to make eggs and toast for her father who always seemed both grateful and annoyed by her efforts.

When she came home from kindergarten in the afternoons, her mother would be back to normal, except she would mumble something about her entire body hurting.

As much as she feared her mother, Sofia was terrified that she was going to die.

When her mother talked to the doctor about all the things that were wrong, Sofia had wanted to plug her ears, but instead she sat there singing a song in her head, trying to drown out her mother's words.

After poking at her mom for a few minutes, the doctor left the room. Her mother had seemed to forget that Sofia was there. Her mother was saying something Sofia couldn't hear.

There was a knock on the door and the doctor walked in.

The doctor was smiling. Sofia felt happy. Her mother wasn't going to die.

"I have good news, Mrs. Castellucci. You're not sick. You're pregnant." The doctor looked at Sofia. "You're going to be a big sister."

Sofia clapped her hands in excitement. Sofia had wanted a little brother or sister forever. It was the best news.

But her mother didn't seem happy.

And didn't say a word. The doctor looked worried. "I'm sorry. That wasn't my place," the doctor said. "I'll give you a few minutes to digest the news. The nurse will be in to check you out. If you have any other questions she can get me."

Sofia turned to her mother.

"Mama?"

Her mother pushed herself off the exam table and jerked her top over her head and then tugged on her pants.

Sofia was confused. "Mama?"

"It can't be. Impossible." Her mother muttered.

Biting her lip, Sofia didn't say a word. Her mother was unpredictable, like a volcano.

Her mother drove them straight home, walked into her bedroom and closed the door. It was time for dinner and her mom stayed in her room. Sofia watched the clock. Her dad was supposed to be home. When her stomach started to hurt, she snuck into the kitchen and grabbed some crackers, keeping one eye on her mother's bedroom door the entire time. There was no sound.

Later, when her dad came home, Sofia was huddled in bed under her blankets. She clapped her hands over her ears to drown out the angry and raised voices coming from her parents' bedroom.

The next morning when Sofia woke and stumbled to the breakfast table, her mother pushed a plate of eggs in front of her and said with a smile, "Sofia, aren't you excited to be a big sister?"

Sofia looked at her mother wide-eyed and open-mouthed. She shot a glance at her father. He had paused, waiting for her answer. Swallowing, Sofia forced a smile and shoved more eggs into her mouth.

CHAPTER 51

SOFIA

October 2019
Minneapolis

Simply being in the lobby of the medical clinic made Sofia's skin crawl.

She hated hospitals and doctors. But she was religious about her annual exam after her Aunt Rose died of cancer at thirty-five. And today was the day.

The form the clerk handed her asked about current medications.

Sofia dug in her giant bag. The prescription bottles Dan had given her were rolling around. She was almost out of her pills for anxiety, but still hadn't taken any of the other pills he'd given her. She didn't want to tamp down the murderous rage she felt. Although with time, she could feel it lessening in intensity. She wrote the names of the two medications down on the form.

Lorazepam and Clozapine. She didn't write down the Rohypnol. She glanced down at her phone. It had beeped a few seconds ago. There was a message from Cecile. She'd won the case and she and Alex were on a plane to Paris. For a second, Sofia dreamed about buying a one-way ticket to a faraway land and leaving everything behind. Even Jason, she thought guiltily.

When the nurse called her name, Sofia muted her phone. In the exam room, the nurse asked Sofia the normal questions. But this time she seemed to focus overly long on Sofia's alcohol use. Something Sofia said triggered a more involved discussion of her drinking habits. Then the nurse asked about abuse and depression. Again, something Sofia said triggered a longer questionnaire about her depression symptoms.

For a second Sofia wanted to tell the nurse—of course I'm drinking too much and depressed, my only child was murdered for God's sakes.

But she didn't.

She'd talk to her doctor about it. Someone she'd known for more than a decade. This nurse? She'd never seen her before. It was none of her god damn business why Sofia was depressed and drinking more than normal.

After she changed into the flimsy paper gown and covered her thighs with an equally flimsy piece of paper, the doctor came in. Dr. Patel was holding a clipboard and looked suitably sympathetic. She must know.

"Hi, Sofia, I was heartbroken to hear about your daughter. I saw it in the newspapers."

"Thank you."

The doctor looked at Sofia. "I'm not too concerned about your drinking and depression, right this minute. However, you should keep an eye on it. But there is something else I want to talk to you about. Would you mind having a seat over here and we'll do the exam in a few minutes?"

Sofia awkwardly hopped down from the exam table and sat in the plastic chair near the computer.

"Like I said, I'm not overly concerned about your depression and drinking right now. This would be a normal reaction, in my opinion. In your answers about depression, you don't actually qualify as a depressed person. I think this is all part of the grieving process. However, I would suggest you consider talking to a therapist about some of these feelings. It can only help."

Sofia nodded. She *had* talked to Dan.

"And the drinking? I guess I'm going to worry more if it continues. That amount of alcohol is not good for women our age. And the long-term effects could be dangerous. I'd recommend you really try to cut back. If you have difficulty, we can look at other avenues to help you stop. Plus, the medications you are on—alcohol is going to make them more potent." Dr. Patel paused and peered over her glasses at Sofia. "That's actually what I need to talk to you about—the medications you've listed here."

Sofia lifted an eyebrow.

"Sofia, who prescribed these two medications together?"

"A friend." What did that matter? And he didn't exactly *prescribe* them.

"A friend?"

"He's a therapist. I actually went to him to talk about some of my feelings."

Dr. Patel took off her glasses and rubbed her temple.

"I'm glad you're seeking therapy, but I recommend you don't let him prescribe you any medications. We've known each other long enough, Sofia, that if you simply want to call or message me and tell me you are depressed or suffering from anxiety or even have a bad cold, I probably would prescribe something over the phone without an office visit. These are unusual circumstances and so I think we can make some exceptions to avoid an office visit. Will you promise me you'll do that from now on? Call me?"

Sofia wondered what the big deal was.

"I don't understand," she said.

The doctor paused, biting her lip as if trying to decide what to say and then her fingers were a flurry on the keyboard. Sofia waited with an eyebrow raised.

"Do you have the medications with you?"

Sofia extracted the bottles. Dr. Patel looked at the computer screen. Then she sighed.

"Did he say where he got these? They look like contraband."

"No." Sofia wasn't going to get Dan in trouble.

"I'm going to print something out for you. It's a few pages from the Jefferson Journal of Psychiatry. I'll be right back."

As soon as the door closed, Sofia scooted around to look at the monitor of the computer but it was already on some funky screen-saver that was making her dizzy. Looking over her shoulder, she touched the mouse, but a login box appeared. Damn.

She'd find out what the doctor was so uptight about soon enough.

Dr. Patel returned and handed Sofia a sheet of paper.

"You obviously haven't taken these together—or else if you have, you haven't taken the prescribed dosage on the bottles. I'd say you've been extremely lucky."

"What?"

"Those two drugs at the prescribed dosage have been known to cause a fatal interaction."

"I don't understand." Sofia glanced at the sheet in her hands.

The headline read, "Sudden Cardiac Death with Clozapine and Lorazepam Combination." It went on to talk about a thirty-year-old man found dead in his apartment from sudden cardiac death due to the combined drugs.

"I know this man is your friend," Dr. Patel shook her head. "But I'm wondering where he got his medical degree."

Sofia's forehead scrunched.

"Whatever you do, don't take those medications together any more, please. I can renew your prescription for one of them, but please go through me for these things. As I said, we can talk over the phone and get something prescribed for you." She gave Sofia's hand a squeeze.

"Okay?"

Sofia nodded.

"Now let's get this exam done and get you out of here so you can get dressed and warm up again, your hands are like ice."

Sofia hopped back up on the exam table. Her hands were trembling and her arms and legs were covered with gooseflesh. But it wasn't from the chill in the air. Her thoughts were all over the place. But she didn't say a word.

• • • •

AFTER THE EXAM, SITTING in her car at a red light, Sofia rewound every conversation she'd had with Dan since Kate died, every meeting, every look. How many times had he urged her to take the new medication he'd given her? At least a few. He'd been so adamant about her taking the drugs he'd given her.

It was impossible that Dan would want to hurt her. She was losing it. He had no reason to hurt her. But then again, it wasn't like Dan to be careless when it came to medications.

Sofia pulled over to the side of the road near a park full of kids. She rested her forehead on the steering wheel. All these conversations with Dan came back. He'd acted odd so many times since Kate's death.

Kate's death.

Suddenly, it was hard for Sofia to breath. The sounds of children squealing and laughing seemed surreal. Her hearing was going goofy. The children's voices were alternating between loud and soft.

Dan would never hurt her, would he? He was always trying to help her. He'd given her that medication to quell her murderous impulses. As she remembered more odd looks, incidents, comments, a feeling of dread spread through her.

Every time she talked about murdering Kate's killer, he'd seemed so nervous, sweat pouring off him.

She replayed more comments that had struck her as odd at the time, but that she had pushed to the back of her mind. The comments that had set off small alarms she'd ignored: that creepy remark about Gretchen having the body of a sixteen-year-old girl. And that love letter Gretchen had showed her. Sofia fumbled in her bag. It was still there, wadded up in a ball. She spread it out on the steering wheel and re-read it: "I know it's wrong and would hurt so many people" and "our families" and last winter in Mexico.

Good God. Distantly, she stared at the kids in the park.

He'd also showed up late for the empty nest party in clothes he hadn't had on earlier in the day. What time was that? The party hadn't started until later because Cecile and Alex had a law firm dinner to attend first. What time *had* Dan arrived? Before or after Kate's death?

Sofia's face flushed hot. She began to hyperventilate. It couldn't be possible. No way. Maybe in her depression and quest to find Kate's killer, she'd become paranoid and delusional.

But she couldn't ignore it. She had to know.

Sofia started her car and whipped a U-turn, tires squealing as she changed direction.

CHAPTER 52

KATE

July 2019

Dinkytown

Making love to Ali was the best decision I'd made in my life.

He was sweet and careful, making sure we used protection, and was concerned about me the entire time. He kept asking me if I was okay and if it hurt and didn't seem to care at all about his own pleasure.

"I just want it to be good for you," he said. "I'm honored you chose me for your first time."

I had to confess to him about the whole "V" thing when he saw the look of terror on my face when he asked if I wanted to put it on.

From that point on, we went in reverse. Slow. Slow. Slow.

Until I thought I would die if we didn't have sex. And even then, he made me wait a little. "It's going to hurt some."

"I know."

And it did. I buried my face in his shoulder and bit my lip.

He pulled back immediately. "Are you okay? Should I stop?"

"No."

In the end, it wasn't spectacular, but it was sweet.

And while it was painful, I didn't regret a second.

After we both took a quick shower, he dressed me in a long tee-shirt and tucked me under the crook of his arm in bed, kissing my brow until I fell asleep.

But I couldn't explain any of this to Lily.

She just wouldn't understand. Worse. It might make her jealous and feel bad.

But I did tell Julia and then immediately felt guilty. I needed to tell Lily asap before she found out Julia knew.

I came over to Lily's tonight specifically to spill the beans, but she wasn't there.

Her dad answered the door.

"Kate?" He seemed flustered and looked behind him.

"Is something wrong?" I said.

He shook his head, "No. No. It's just that Lily and Gretchen went to a movie."

"Oh."

He must have seen the disappointment in my voice.

"Come in. They should be home soon."

"Okay." I didn't really want to, but it would seem rude to refuse.

After we settled into the living room with sodas, he leaned forward. "Is something wrong?"

His kind tone and concern made me want to cry.

I'd been keeping the stuff about my grandma in and suddenly had to say something. I took a deep breath and told him about my grandmother contacting me. It all came out in a big, rush.

"And I thought she was dead. But she's been alive this whole time."

He sat back. He didn't hide his surprise.

"You didn't know?" I said.

He shook his head.

I burst into tears. "My mom lied to you. She lied to my dad. She lied to me. She lied to everyone."

He jumped up and wrapped me in his arms and I sobbed into his shirt, wiping snot and tears everywhere.

Finally, he drew away and handed me a box of tissue.

"Sit," he said.

I did.

"Listen to me and listen carefully," he said. "I guarantee you that your mother had a good reason for not telling you. We don't know what that reason is, but I know your mother and she's only always had your best interest at heart. You have to believe me when I say this. Okay?

I didn't answer.

"Okay?"

I nodded, but grabbed my bag.

"Tell Lily I'll call her tomorrow."

I rushed out. I believed him. But it still didn't answer one big question: Why had my mother lied?

CHAPTER 53

SOFIA

October 2019
Minneapolis

Sofia had just turned onto Gretchen and Dan's street when her phone vibrated in her lap. She'd forgotten that she'd turned it to silent. She looked down. It was Detective Marley.

"Hello?"

"Where are you?"

"Driving."

"Pull over."

She veered onto the shoulder, hands shaking.

"You stopped?"

"Yes." Sofia closed her eyes for a second. Was Jason hurt?

"We're charging Ronald Derry with Kate's murder."

"The neighbor?" Her head began to hurt. A sharp pain above her left eyebrow.

"I wanted to tell you before you saw it on the news. We're holding a press conference here in ten minutes. At the station." He sounded out of breath.

"I don't understand." She opened her eyes but everything was blurry.

"I'm sorry. It must seem sudden. I tried to reach you earlier. We've already delayed it once so I could try you again. I didn't want you to see it on the TV news."

Sofia held her phone away for a second and saw she had missed several calls while the phone was muted in the exam room at the doctor's office.

"You have enough evidence?" She looked over at the bottles of pills spilling out of her handbag.

"He has an old case, an arrest. Sexual assault. Not a teen. A woman his age at the time—thirty-two. We didn't see it at first because it was in another state. Wisconsin. He was staying at the cabin or something. We took another look at him and what we found at his house. During the initial search, we'd found some shoes with mud that matched prints found at the scene. The mud is consistent, as well. That alone wasn't really enough at the time."

"Consistent?"

"With the mud they found at your daughter's ... at the scene. In addition, the SUV might be a good match. The one in the CCTV footage following your daughter."

"Might be?"

"We still haven't been able to pull up a clear picture of the plates. But we just picked him up and searched the cabin. Our initial search showed some child porn in an old shoe box. He's in custody on suspicion of murder."

Sofia started to see white.

"Are you there, Mrs. Kennedy?"

Her heart was pressing against her ribcage and she felt as if she were going to vomit.

"But what if it's not him? I think I know someone else who ... I need to come in and talk to you about it." She was so confused. Was her murderous desire for revenge so strong it was skewing her reality?

There were a few seconds of silence. The detective clearly hadn't expected that reaction.

"We're pretty confident in our arrest. We have ample evidence to charge him with murder."

"Pretty confident? That's enough? Pretty confident?"

"Let me rephrase that. We are certain we have our suspect."

"Please, please listen to me. I need you to hear what I have to say first. Before you charge him."

"Mrs. Kennedy, the press conference is starting. I need to hang up now. Rest assured, the man who killed your daughter is off the streets."

He hung up. Sofia stared at the phone.

He was wrong.

CHAPTER 54

SOFIA

October 2019
Minneapolis

"Was the letter to Kate?"

Sofia held her foot in the front door so Gretchen couldn't slam it. She held the piece of paper out in front of her. "This letter? Was it to Kate?"

Gretchen's mouth started working. Grimacing, clenching. She glanced down at the statue of The Thinker on a table by the front door. A stack of mail sat beside it.

"Look at me," Sofia yelled. "Was it? Answer me!"

Gretchen glared.

Sofia's arm lowered to her side. "You've known the entire time, haven't you? You've known that letter was to Kate?"

"No. I just figured it out." Gretchen pulled her shoulders back. "Besides, it doesn't mean anything."

"What?"

"It doesn't mean he killed her." Gretchen stood with her arms crossed over her chest, her lips pressed tightly together, her eyes like bullets, her chin held high in defiance. Her words hung in the silence.

Sofia had never said anything about Dan killing Kate. She stood there, balling her hands into fists, her rage boiling up from her middle. She could imagine, vividly see herself smashing the statue on the end table into Gretchen's smug face. Time slowed and the moment seemed to last an eternity as both women stood a few feet away from each other, chests heaving with emotions, words left unsaid.

Gretchen broke the silence. "I have to go now. I'm leaving for my mother's. You have to leave." She looked pointedly at Sofia's car in the driveway. "Besides, they arrested someone else. I saw it on TV just before you came."

Then oddly, Gretchen repeated her shocking words. "That letter doesn't mean he killed her."

"But it doesn't mean he didn't," Sofia said in a low voice, turned on her heel and left.

• • • •

IN HER CAR, HER HANDS clenching the steering wheel, she couldn't breathe. She clicked the ignition enough to roll down all four windows and gulped for air until her vision cleared. She was afraid to turn the key and start her vehicle. She was afraid that her foot would press down on the accelerator and that she would point her vehicle toward the garage and ram into the garage door and then through the wall into the house, through the living room, over Gretchen, through the kitchen and into Dan's office and wait there with Gretchen's body caught in her chassis until Dan came home and then she would take the statue and bludgeon his— "

The sound of her phone startled her. She glanced down.

Jason.

She couldn't talk to him right then.

A whiff of cigarette smoke trickled in through her open window. Again, a surge of desire swept over her. Staring out the windshield, she saw an elderly man in his side yard, examining some bushes with a cigarette hanging out the side of his mouth.

She started her car. Although she was still tempted to stomp on the gas, she slowly, carefully pulled away, so as to not draw attention to herself and her vehicle. She needed to avenge Kate's death. But she had to be smart.

She'd shown up uncertain, but the way Gretchen had reacted seemed like proof. As impossible as it seemed, Dan had been in love with Kate. And then killed her.

A keening sound came out of her mouth. Oh God, no. No. No. No.

Nearly blinded by her tears, she drove home. She was on autopilot, absorbed in her horrifying thoughts.

How could a man she considered one of her best friends even be capable of hurting her daughter? For the past seventeen years, he had treated Kate like his own child. His home had been like a second home to Kate. She had spent so many nights there, eaten hundreds of meals, swam in their pool on countless summer days. Sofia thought back to all the minutes, hours, days and nights Kate had spent around Dan.

Sofia screeched to the shoulder and opened her door in time to vomit onto the pavement. A car honked loudly and she pulled her door closed, not bothering to wipe her face.

Dan was sick. Disgusting. Had he killed her because Kate had fought back? As she drove home, Sofia felt like she was in a dream state. Nothing seemed real. She had thought the nightmare she was living could not possibly get worse.

She was wrong.

CHAPTER 55

KATE

July 2019
Dinkytown

There was another letter at the bookstore when I came in to work.

I looked at it like it was a grenade that could explode any second.

The manager pushed it over to me.

"This came for you."

I could tell he wanted me to explain why someone was writing me at work, but I shoved it in my bag and raced to the bathroom.

I locked the door and leaned against it, heart pounding.

Finally, when my breathing seemed normal again, I reached into my bag and took the letter out.

"I'll be there Thursday. What I have to tell you can only be said in person. DON'T TELL YOUR MOTHER ANYTHING. She will try to prevent me from seeing you. She has ruined my life and your grandfather's life and she will pay."

And that was it.

She was coming here? No. Instead of being excited about the chance to finally meet the grandmother I never knew I had, I was filled with fear. Who was this crazy woman? I should've never given her the bookstore address. She was going to make my mother pay? Good God. What would I do now?

• • • •

ON THURSDAY, AFTER making sure my mom and dad were safe—they were going to a movie and out to dinner—I called in sick to work.

But I lied to my mom and pretended I was going. Instead, I drove to the Witch Hat Tower, a water tower shaped like a witch's hat that overlooks the Minneapolis skyline. I sat on a bench at the base of the tower and texted Lily.

"Meet me at the Witch Hat Tower."

"Don't you work?"

"Long story. Meet me in ten."

"Can't," she replied. "On my way home soon. Come over."

"K."

It wasn't until I got in my car that I wondered where Lily had been. We used to know each other's every move. But lately she'd been acting a little secretive. I blamed it on her irritation with me seeing Ali. Oh well. She'd get over it. I wouldn't be able to see Ali once he returned to Somalia and I went away to college.

Thinking of him made me wonder if I should've called him instead of Lily.

But I felt stupid confiding my fears in him. We hadn't known each other very long. I didn't want to come across as needy or weak.

When I got to Lily's her car was in the driveway, but when Dan answered the door the first thing he said was Lily wasn't home.

"She and Gretchen went to a movie."

"I can just wait. She said they were on their way home."

Just then my phone dinged. It was Lily.

"God. I'm sorry. Gretchen wanted to stop to eat. Meet later?"

My face must have shown my disappointment because Dan said, "Come sit. How are you? How's everything ... with that situation you told me about."

He worded it so carefully and nicely that tears sprung to my eyes.

He guided me to the sofa and sat beside me, rubbing my back. I leaned into his shoulder letting the tears stream down my face.

"I don't know why I'm such a baby around you," I said, wiping my tears away. "I'm sorry."

He grabbed my chin and turned my face toward his. He stared at me and I was beginning to squirm when he leaned over and kissed me. I jumped back and off the couch, backing away. For a second I didn't understand what had just happened and then the shock of it hit me. DAN JUST KISSED ME. DAN JUST KISSED ME. DAN JUST KISSED ME.

He was beside me in an instant.

"Oh my God. I'm so sorry. That was totally inappropriate."

I was shaking.

"Yes." I didn't know what else to say. My blood was racing in my ear, a whooshing sound and my whole body was shaking.

He sighed and sat down while I stood frozen.

Then he ran a hand over his head and said, "I can't keep it in any longer. I'm in love with you, Kate."

"No!" I shouted the word.

He nodded sadly. "It's true. Believe me, I wish it wasn't."

"You can't ..." I stared. *You are my best friend's dad. You are my mother's good friend. You are an old man.*

"I was hoping I didn't have to tell you." He was wiping at his eyes now. "I was hoping you'd guess how I felt and that I was the one who left that note and flowers for you on your car."

"No." I didn't have anything else to say. I stood, hands hanging by my side eyeing my bag with my car keys on the couch beside him. I wasn't exactly afraid of him, but every single bit of me wanted to grab my bag and run and run and run and erase what he had just done and said.

Dan must've noticed what I was looking at because he stood and handed me my bag.

"I know this is a lot to digest," he said with a weird smile. "I'm going to give you some time to absorb it. And then we can talk again."

I yanked my bag away from him and turned toward the door. His voice stopped me dead.

"Kate, let's do each other a favor right now and keep this just between the two of us. Just like I'm keeping your secret about your grandmother."

I could feel the blood drain from my face. Was that a threat?

"I'm not saying anything." I gritted the words out.

"Good."

I raced out before he could say more, not even bothering to shut the front door behind me.

Once I had driven far enough away from his house, I pulled over on a side street and texted Ali.

"You around?"

"Yup."

"I'm coming over."

CHAPTER 56

SOFIA

October 2019

Minneapolis

Jason stood in the dark doorway of the bedroom.

"Sof?"

She mumbled an answer from beneath the covers.

"You sure it's okay if I go to work?" His voice was sincere, but as Sofia peeked her head out, she could see he was turned halfway toward the hallway. Good.

"Yes. Please go. I'll be fine. Just a touch of the flu. I think the news about the arrest was too much. I'll drink lots of fluids and sleep all day. You don't need to worry."

He paused by the window, drawing back the curtain. She peered at him over the covers.

"Are they still there?"

"Yes." He peered out and quickly let the curtain fall back again. "Well, a few of them."

When she had come home last night, her street had been filled with TV news trucks and reporters had run up to her as she got out of her car, thrusting microphones her way.

She had walked into the house in a daze.

"I'll call and check on you later." Jason had turned completely toward the hall now. He paused for a second. "It's going to be okay now, isn't it? Now that they made an arrest? We'll make it through the trial and then move on, right?"

He seemed so vulnerable and so in need of her reassurance. But at the same time his words pissed her off.

"Move on? There is no moving on. Not until the person who did this to our daughter is dead." *The person. Dan.*

Jason hadn't moved. "We can't keep living like this."

Narrowing her eyes, she glared at him. "When you say that, all I hear is that you don't give a fuck about our daughter."

Within a second, he was beside the bed, face red, fists balled at his sides. "No. You listen to me. Don't you ever, ever say that again. Don't you ever accuse me of not loving Katie as much as you do. Do you understand?"

Seeing his anger deflated Sofia's own. "Okay. I'm sorry."

Jason didn't answer. He stomped out of their room and she heard his footsteps pounding down the stairs.

Right then, she wanted to yell for him to come back so she could tell him everything. Tell him how Dan was the one who killed their daughter. But if she did, he would try to stop her plan. And she wasn't going to let anything stop her.

She was going to kill Dan. Jason need never know. And that meant that nobody but her would ever know the truth. It had to be that way if she were going to get away with it.

And she would have to live with that.

As soon as she heard the door downstairs slam shut, she pushed back the covers and stood up.

Throwing on some old yoga pants and a tank, Sofia headed downstairs. On the counter, she saw a stack of newspapers. She pulled the papers toward her.

With trembling fingers, she smoothed out the newspaper. Her vision grew blurry but she wasn't sure if she was crying or hallucinating. Staring at the black and white print before her, she slowly focused her eyes on the story about the arrest. There was a quote from Dan. Vaguely, she remembered telling Dan he could talk to the press if he wanted. Just so she and Jason didn't have to deal with it. He must be back in town. He must have come back not long after she left his house.

"We are all reeling in grief. Kate was a beautiful soul and her death is not only a loss to those who loved her, but to the whole world," Dan had told the newspaper reporter. "Thank God there's been an arrest. At least now the family can move on."

Bastard. Sick fucking lying murdering bastard.

She tossed the front section aside. On the local section, a different murder story was top of the fold: "Minneapolis mother cleared of charges she tried to drown her two children."

Sofia began to read. Before long, she had the paper up near her face, devouring every word of the article.

The mother had tried to kill her one-year-old and three-year-old sons by drowning. But after spending five months in jail, all the charges were dismissed. The district attorney's office said it was dropping charges because her temporary insanity was caused by "involuntary intoxication" due to prednisone prescribed for her asthma.

They'd evaluated the mother to see if she was mentally fit to stand trial. During the Rule 20 evaluation, they found the woman to be sane. Further testing showed that her murder attempt was simply a "bad reaction" to asthma meds.

Sofia held the paper long after she was done reading. Her old inhaler was gathering dust in the medicine cabinet. She reached for her laptop. Logging onto the clinic's website, she sent a message to Dr. Patel.

"I know I haven't had asthma for years, but something, maybe something in the air, has been making it hard for me to breathe. I don't know if it's a new allergy or if it's all the stress, but I'm wondering if you could refill my prescription for my inhaler and maybe prescribe some prednisone? I woke up in the night struggling to breath. And, I don't think it was a panic attack. Also, I think I am interested in that anxiety medication you mentioned."

She hit send and sat back with a smile. Rummaging in her bag, she got out the two pill bottles Dan had given her. She'd have to grind them into a powder. She'd spike the whiskey in his office with a lethal combination of ground up pills—the pills he had given her and top it off with the rest of the Rohypnol It would be perfect. The irony of killing Dan the way he had tried to kill her, with his own illegal drugs, was rich.

Even though Dan had suffered a heart attack, he was stubborn and refused to take heart medication. Because of his history, they might not even do an autopsy.

Everything had to be planned and executed perfectly. She'd have to actually be there. To make sure he was the only one who drank it so she wasn't killing off his patients as well. Who knew how many patients he drank with on a daily basis?

But he'd insist she have a drink as well. Spilling her drink would be suspicious. She'd have to figure out a way to fool him into thinking she was drinking right alongside him.

And she'd have to get into his office beforehand to spike the whiskey. Right beforehand.

She'd start using the asthma medication as a backup. Just in case she was caught, she would consider using that defense. But that was just a safeguard measure. She had no intention of getting caught.

She'd poison him. Then wipe her glass down and leave his on his desk. Or wear gloves. Other patients could verify that he occasionally had a drink during sessions.

It could be done.

And when he was dying, when he took his last breath, she would tell him what she had done and why.

Now, the hardest part was going to be acting normal and biding her time. She had to keep Jason in the dark and had to seem the same around Dan, even though she could feel her fists balling with rage. That's when she remembered. Gretchen might say something to Dan.

But right now, Gretchen was at her mother's house. Sofia was banking on the fact that Gretchen hadn't yet told Dan about their conversation. That meant Sofia had to act in the next few days.

Before Gretchen and Lily came home.

Thinking of Lily nearly made her gasp, but pushed the thought aside. She couldn't worry about Lily. Lily would still have Gretchen. Besides, what was worse? Knowing your own father lusted after and killed your best friend or knowing your father was dead? She would kill Dan and nobody would know why and that was okay. In a way, she was sparing Lily the hard-cold reality, the awful knowledge, that would scar her much deeper than a parent's death ever would. She knew that first hand. No one need know why Dan died.

Sofia knew she was sparing Lily her own fate. She already knew what life would be like for Lily if the girl knew her father was a murderer. It would be just like Sofia's secret life, always worried, always wondering. She was sparing Lily the torture she had gone through: spending her entire life wondering whether she had inherited the gene making her capable of murder.

For the first time since that night she'd woken to find Kate's bed empty, Sofia felt excited about something.

It would be over soon.

CHAPTER 57

SOFIA

October 2019
Minneapolis

When Jason walked in from work he took one look at Sofia and shook his head as if he were disgusted.

"I came home to check on you around lunchtime. Brought you some soup..." he gestured helplessly at the stove top.

"I'm sorry. I was feeling a little better so I went for a drive— "

She stopped talking when she saw his face.

"You left your computer on and open."

Sofia quickly glanced at the counter where her laptop was set up. "Oh." What had he seen?

"You set up fake social media accounts to try to find Kate's killer?"

"Jason, I'm sorry I didn't tell you," her voice was pleading. "But I had to find out who killed Kate. The police, they don't know what they are doing. They arrested the wrong guy."

"I thought this was over. I thought we were going to try to move on. But you posted something today. I saw it."

She didn't answer.

He leaned toward her. "You asked Katie's friends if anyone had ever seen her around an older bald man. Our neighbor isn't bald, Sofia."

Fear soared through Sofia. "The person they arrested, the neighbor, didn't do it. I am going to prove who really did it."

Dan's name was right there on the tip of her tongue. She could barely stop herself from blurting it out.

"You can't possibly do that on your own," his words were dismissive, short, and even seemed to hold a little disgust.

Which is why Sofia told him. She couldn't keep it in any longer.

"I did find out." She lifted her chin in triumph. "I know who killed Kate."

"What?" He turned back to look at her, a scowl on his face.

She sank into her chair. "It's even worse than I had imagined." She put her head in her hands. "I'm afraid to even say it, Jason."

Jason leaned down breathing in her face, fury distorting his mouth.

"Who killed Kate?" His head cocked, his eyes ablaze.

Sofia shook her head. Tears spurted out. "Dan. Our friend, Dan. He's been obsessed with her for years."

She cringed, waiting for Jason's outburst. But there was only silence. Sofia looked up. Jason was staring at her as if he'd never laid eyes on her before. Jason shook his head slowly never taking his eyes away from hers. Then he looked down at his feet. "I think you need to talk to someone. Professionally. Someone who can help you."

Sofia stood up. "I don't need anyone's help. What I need is Dan dead."

As soon as the word came out of her mouth, she knew she'd made a mistake. Jason's horrified expression made that clear.

"I didn't mean that," she said, covering her mouth. "I meant that he needs to be locked up. Forever. I'm just upset right now."

Jason sank into a kitchen chair. He bit his lip. He looked like he was going to cry. "I thought he was wrong. I thought he was confused."

Sofia's eyes grew wide. "What? Who?"

"Dan," Jason said. "Dan asked me to meet him this morning. He told me you'd come to him and seemed delusional, but I had no idea. He told me you had some far-fetched ideas."

"What?" It took Sofia a minute to process what he'd said.

"He was worried about you, Sofia. He thought you'd lost touch with reality."

Sofia realized her mouth was wide open. "He knows. He knows I'm on to him so he is trying to ruin my credibility. How could you for one second believe him?"

"Sofia, you haven't been yourself..."

"He's doing this to discredit me. You have to believe me. Don't you want to hear my evidence? What I found?"

He shook his head.

"You have to at least listen."

"Fine." Jason said. He looked deflated.

She told him all about the note Gretchen had found, the lethal combination of pills Dan had given her and about Gretchen being hot because she had the body of a sixteen-year-old.

When she was done, Jason looked up at her. "Listen, Dan told me about those pills and that he specifically warned you not to take them together."

Sofia felt the fury rise in her throat and tried to control her voice.

"That is not true." She bit out the words.

Jason bit his lip and shook his head. "He also told me that you'd talked about killing yourself." He looked sad.

"What? That's a lie. I never said that. Not once."

Jason blew out a big breath of air. "I don't know what is the truth anymore," he said. "But what I do know is you need to seek some professional help or ..."

"Or what? You'll leave?" Her voice was incredulous.

"I don't know. All I know is you need to get help. You need to get help or we may never get over Kate's death."

Sofia's anger flared. "See, that's the big fundamental difference between us, Jason. I will never get over her death."

He didn't answer, just shook his head again, slowly, pityingly.

CHAPTER 58

SOFIA

O*ctober 2019*
Minneapolis

Sofia slammed out of the house.

Dan had turned Jason against her.

Sofia had driven halfway to the police station before she realized that she couldn't hand over the evidence against Dan. Even if she wanted to do the right thing, play by the rules—have him legally arrested for murdering Kate—she didn't have enough to prove he'd done it and worse, Dan would tell them she was delusional. If her own husband believed Dan what was going to stop a detective who barely knew her from believing it?

No, she had to handle it herself. She couldn't count on the police. They wouldn't believe her. And taking her suspicions to the police would make her suspect number one if anything happened to Dan.

Because killing Dan was quickly becoming her only option.

Sure, if Dan died of a heart attack, Jason might suspect something, but not if Sofia made amends right now and told Jason he was right, she had made a huge mistake, that she was delusional and regretful that she'd ever thought anything bad against their friend.

Even though she was telling herself these things, steeling herself, trying to be strong, a small part of her wanted to curl up, give up, and die. She was going to lose everything she ever had. Maybe Jason would still love her. He'd stick by her, but there would always be that look. He would wonder if she was delusional.

Something had irrevocably changed.

But then again, when Kate died, Sofia's life had been forever altered.

Her propensity for violence, the one she'd tried to avoid all her life, had caught up with her. It had won. It seemed her fate was to kill Dan. Maybe her whole life had been leading to this moment. She would finally succumb to her violent nature. While it made her despise herself, she had to admit there was a small measure of relief. She could stop fighting—now she could finally give in.

It was out of her hands now.

She had to make it look like an accident. But first she had to make peace with Jason and make him believe she had given up on Dan as a suspect.

CHAPTER 59

SOFIA

October 2019
Minneapolis

When Sofia got home, Jason had moved into the guest bedroom off the kitchen downstairs. She could hear him snoring.

Fine.

Give him a night to get over his anger. They could make up later.

As soon as Sofia crawled into her bed, she was sleepy. Having a plan made it easy.

Tomorrow, Jason would be back beside her in bed.

When she woke the next morning, the guest bedroom was empty. Jason had gone to work.

There was no note, but that was okay. Jason sometimes needed time to get over his anger at her. She knew he would come around. In this instance, he might need a little extra prodding, but she was up to the task.

Time to put her plan into action.

The first thing Sofia did was schedule an appointment with a therapist across town—hopefully someone that had never met Dan.

When she told them it was an emergency—that she was worried about hurting herself—they said they had a cancellation and she could come that afternoon.

The therapist was nice—an older lady letting her gray roots grow out. She apologized and patted her hair as she explained she was sick of dyeing it.

Sofia told her, sincerely, she thought that was great.

They were off to a good start.

But for the next hour, Sofia lied. She talked about Kate and her murder, but then burst into tears saying she was worried that she was delusional, trying to blame friends. She didn't name Dan, but she waited to hear what the therapist would say.

"That is not a completely unusual reaction. We often try to blame others—or at least seek some source of blame—to help cope with tragedy."

The woman went on. Sofia barely listened, but nodded her head at appropriate moments. She was surreptitiously recording the session on her phone. She wanted to remember the therapist's jargon, clinical talk. She would repeat some of it back to Jason later today when she apologized.

She was tuning the therapist's words out when the woman said something that made Sofia sit up.

"I'm sorry can you repeat that?" She'd heard something about "parents" and "murdered children."

"It's a group that a few of my clients have found helpful. I know that unless you've had a child murdered, it is really hard to understand what that might be like. Even we therapists have a hard time wrapping our minds around the enormous depth of this tragedy."

"Wait, you have more than one client who has had a child murdered?"

"Sadly, yes." The therapist pressed her lips together.

"And parents get together to talk about it?"

"Yes," the therapist began rifling through a drawer. "It's called the National Organization of Parents of Murdered Children. Bear with me a second. Okay. Here is a pamphlet. Sorry it has a coffee stain on it, but you can see what it's about. Keep that one. I need to get more anyway." She leaned over and wrote herself a note on a small pink post it.

Sofia stared at the brochure in her hands as if she could see right through it. She smiled at the same time she tried to disguise her complete and utter repulsion. Sitting around with a bunch of other parents who were grieving, probably talking about "moving on?" It sounded like a nightmare.

"I guess we have a pretty active group here in the Twin Cities."

For some reason this made Sofia feel even more nauseous.

Was it selfish to believe that nobody could understand *her* particular grief ? Yes.

After the session, Sofia stopped at the market and picked up some rib-eye steaks, a batch of potato salad from the deli and some fresh shrimp cocktail. She also swung by the liquor store and bought a bottle of Jason's favorite red wine.

By the time Jason walked in the door from work, the entire house smelled like steak. The dining room table was set and candles were lit.

Sofia had changed into a dress and heels and applied dark eye makeup and red lipstick. That was their thing. When Kate was little they'd put her to bed early, Sofia would dress up, and they'd have a romantic candlelight dinner and afterward make love.

Jason paused in the doorway to the kitchen with a wary look on his face.

Acting demure, Sofia stood before him eyes down, "Jason, I'm so, so sorry. You're right. I was having a terrible morning. I went to see a therapist this afternoon in Edina and she helped me sort things out. It was horrible for me to ever suspect Dan of hurting our Kate."

"I've had the shittiest day," Jason finally said, "completely worried about you."

"I'm so sorry." She paused. Here was her trump card. "I guess we never know how losing a child will affect us." Every word was the truth, but it was also her way of getting him to forgive and forget.

"Something smells good," Jason peeked over her shoulder at the dining room.

She took his hand. "Come and sit. I figured we should have a nice dinner. I know we've felt guilty enjoying anything since Kate's ...

but I also think she would want us to still enjoy life, as much as that is possible."

Again, all true words.

That night Jason and Sofia made love like teenagers—uncertain at first and then completely abandoned and wild and desperately as if they could never get enough of each other's bodies.

At the end, they were both in tears. Jason sobbing and weeping, Sofia with a seemingly endless stream of tears dripping down.

CHAPTER 60

KATE

J*uly 2019*

Minneapolis

Ever since I read the letters from my so-called grandmother, I'd caught myself watching my mother for signs of deceit or betrayal. But no matter how much I scrutinized her, she seemed to be the same what-you-see-is-what-you-get person I'd always known.

But I found myself starting arguments with her for no reason. I mean, even I knew I was acting irrational and ridiculous. A small part of me wanted to get into a screaming match with her, to yell and shout and tell her that she was a liar and I knew it.

It was getting to be exhausting. I couldn't stop thinking about this woman who said she was my grandmother. Every time I showed up to work at the bookstore, I startled when an older woman walked in, waiting for her to confront me and introduce herself as my grandmother.

It had me on edge.

CHAPTER 61

SOFIA

O*ctober 2019*

Minneapolis

Sofia languidly stretched. She was tangled in her soft, warm down covers. She pushed back the fluffy white duvet as the sunrise outside the windows made the bedroom glow golden.

It had been good to have sex. Necessary even. She felt closer to Jason than ever.

And for the first time since Kate's death she didn't feel struck with horrific guilt when she noticed the beauty of the morning sunshine seeping into the room. It was a step. A small one, but still.

Everything would be okay. All right, maybe not okay, but they would survive.

But then Sofia rose from bed and walked by Kate's empty bedroom on her way to the bathroom. A large stone lodged in her gut, making her want to claw it out of her insides. But it wasn't something she could make go away. Who was she fooling? Life could never be good again. Never.

One thing she could do is vow not to destroy Jason's life even further. While killing Dan would give her some semblance of relief—or at least that's what she believed—it could destroy Jason if he ever found out what she had done. Making Jason happy, sparing him from more pain would give her a goal. Something to work toward that was constructive instead of destructive. Who knows, maybe it would even bring some tiny bit of peace. Or whatever sort of peace the mother of a murdered child could find.

Jason was already at work. But as soon as she poured a cup of coffee the phone rang.

"Hey." His voice was low and sexy.

"Hey." She felt like a blushing schoolgirl.

"You still got it, Sof."

"You, too." Sofia took a sip of coffee and realized her stomach was grumbling.

Jason cleared his throat. "So, something interesting came up today."

"Oh yeah," Sofia scrounged through the refrigerator looking for something to eat for breakfast. Another sign of normalcy—her appetite was slowly returning.

"They have an opening for a job in Oceanside. They've offered me the position."

"Oceanside? As in California? As in the beach town with the best climate ever?"

"Uh, yeah."

"Wow." Sofia shut the refrigerator door and sat down on the floor. "What did you say?"

"I told them I'd have to think about it, talk to you, of course."

"Right."

They both sat there in silence for a few seconds.

"So?" He said.

"What do you think?" She closed her eyes waiting for his answer, holding her breath, hoping.

"We should consider it."

"Okay." Relief flooded through her.

"Listen, just wanted to tell you that really quick. I've got to run, but let's talk about it more tonight. Love you."

She hung up the phone and sat there for a minute staring into space.

They'd visited Oceanside once when Kate was little. Jason was writing for GQ and had been assigned a cover story on Ryan Gosling. They'd rented an apartment near the beach for three weeks and while Jason visited the actor every day, Sofia and Kate spent long days at the beach, splashing in the waves, playing in the sand, lying in the sun. It had been heaven.

At night, they'd left Kate with a babysitter and hit the town, ordering fish tacos at a beachside restaurant, sipping beer as the sun set behind them.

A move. A brand-new start. It might be just what they needed.

Sofia felt a surge of excitement as she padded around her big empty house. She remembered that before Kate was murdered, she'd had plans. All summer she had planned ways to fill her days once Kate had gone away to college. She'd find a new job or do more freelance graphic design work from home. Something to keep her busy.

It was time to do that now. She couldn't sit around the house all day plotting murder. She had to stay busy. She could find a new job in California, have a fresh start. Maybe apply to do graphic design at a firm. It would be good to be around people every day. In a real office. Oceanside!

Such a big decision. For the first time since Kate's murder, Sofia felt a tiny bit grateful to still be alive.

Looking at the giant silver cross on her wall, Sofia reached for her keys.

• • • •

THE BASILICA WAS EMPTY. Father Genovese was out. Sofia stuffed five dollars in the offering box and lit a candle. She knelt before the Virgin Mary statue, praying to another mother who had lost her only child to violence, as well. For more than an hour she knelt there and tried to forgive Dan. She prayed—with tears dripping down her face—for the ability to forgive him. Finally, she realized she couldn't. At least not now. Maybe in the future. Right now, the decision to not kill him would have to be enough.

CHAPTER 62

KATE

July 2019

Dinkytown

When I got out of bed this afternoon, Ali propped himself up on one elbow and examined me. I pulled my clothes on as quickly as I could. I didn't like him looking at me naked.

"Is everything okay?" he said.

I shrugged. "I don't know." I was too embarrassed to tell him that his appraisal of me naked was disconcerting.

"You seem upset lately. As if there's something bothering you?"

"I'm fine." I didn't meet his eyes.

"And you've lost weight," he said. "And you don't really have much to lose."

"Maybe."

"No, maybe. Do I have to start force feeding you cookies?" He stood and stretched languidly. He definitely wasn't shy about being naked in front of me. I could feel the blush rise up my neck to my cheeks. He was really gorgeous.

"I'm not really hungry lately."

"You want to talk about it?" Damn. He knew I was lying.

I shook my head. More than anything I wanted to confide in him, but I didn't even know how to begin. I was also worried he would want me to tell someone about Dan. And I just couldn't do that. It would ruin too many things: My friendship with Lily, my parent's relationship with their good friends. It was a landmine that I wasn't willing to step on.

The only good news out of the whole thing, was that apparently, nobody had shown up at the bookstore asking about me on the day I called in sick. And no more letters had arrived.

Maybe she knew she had gone too far.

CHAPTER 63

SOFIA

October 2019

Minneapolis

The house was dark when she got home.

She was excited to see Jason. Her face felt flushed, her mood possibly the best it had been since the night of the empty nest party, before her life had shattered.

It was time for a fresh start. She'd fix things. She'd make things great with Jason. He was all she had. He was her whole life. She wouldn't jeopardize it all. Not anymore. She would fight her base, primal urges and learn to tamp down the murderous rage she felt toward Dan.

With this job offer, they could start a new life. They could move. They could move far away from Dan. Maybe then things could be different.

Juggling her grocery bags, she shoved open the door with her hip. Plopping the bags on the kitchen counter, she jumped when she realized Jason was sitting in the dark at the kitchen table.

"Jason? You scared me half to death."

She reached over and clicked on the tiny light above the stove.

Some of the light reached his face and what she saw there made her freeze.

"What have you done, Sofia?"

She sank into the chair across from him. An icy chill ran across her scalp.

"What?"

"I talked to Dan again."

Sofia braced herself. What new lies had Dan spouted?

"What have you done to us? All of this," he gestured broadly. "All of this, our entire life is a lie. Everything we have together. Lies.

You've made me live a lie. None of this is real. For the past thirty—Jesus Christ, thirty—years you've woken up every single day and lied to me."

She closed her eyes. She couldn't swallow. Her face felt numb. A buzzing had begun at the back of her skull. He knew everything.

"No, Jason. No. It's not a lie. It's real."

"Sofia Castellucci. You are not Sofia Castle. You are not an orphan." He held up a sheaf of papers with printing on them. "I found these online after I talked to Dan. Your dad is Marco Castellucci. You are the daughter of a mob hit man." Jason's voice kept growing louder.

Sofia threw her hand up to her mouth, her eyes wide in horror. "No. No. No."

Jason stood, his chair toppling behind him. "Yes."

That's when she noticed the empty bottle of rum and the glass beside it.

He stumbled toward her, waving the pieces of paper. "You ... you ..."

She stood, standing in front of him. For a second, in the dim light, their eyes met. His were red and full of pain and anger and confusion. "Why?" His voice was quiet now.

At that moment, she would have done anything to take it all back. To never have met Jason and caused him this hurt. But it was too late.

"Jason ..."

But then it got worse.

"You are sick, Sofia."

Her mouth opened. She was speechless.

"Dan said you are bi-polar, dissociative, even psychotic. You are directing all your hate, anger, pain at him. He didn't kill Kate. I can never believe anything you say ever again."

Sofia couldn't breathe. This was how it happened. This is how Dan went after her, discredited her, and got away with murder.

Even though she wanted to scream and break everything in sight, she needed to remain calm. To show Jason she was rational. To prove Dan wrong.

"Jason." She waited until he looked at her. "You know me. I'm not psychotic. You've lived with me all these years. Don't you think you would know if I were mentally ill? You *know* me. You know that's not true."

To her surprise, he burst into laughter. "Know? I don't *know* anything. I don't *know* you, Sofia *Castellucci*." He drew out her last name. "I don't *know* who you are. In fact, I think you need to be admitted somewhere. Dan said there was a good chance you inherited the same gene that made your father a murdering freak."

Sofia felt a cold fissure of shock run down her spine. She was stunned by Jason's words. Dan was a more dangerous enemy than she'd ever dreamed.

"Jason? Please listen. Dan is trying to turn you against me. He killed Kate and this is how he is going to get away with it." Her voice was shrill; she was starting to lose it. This could not be worse.

He brushed by her. "I'm leaving. I don't want to see you. I don't want to hear what you have to say. I don't want to be anywhere near you."

Sofia grabbed his arm. "You can't go anywhere. You're drunk."

"I don't care." He looked down at her hand and then jerked his arm away. "I'd rather be dead than feel this way."

"Well, I do care." Sofia's voice was steel. "If you want to kill yourself driving drunk, that's your decision, but I'm not going to let you kill someone else."

He jerked away from her. "Don't. Touch. Me." He lifted his chin and spit the words at her. "If I can't leave then you have to go."

"Okay. Okay. I can go. I'll come back in the morning and we can talk about this when you are sober— "

"Get out!" He shouted the word, his arm flung in front of him pointing toward the door. "Get out or I'll call the police and you will be admitted to the psych ward. Or arrested."

Sofia grabbed her bag and headed for the door. With her hand on the doorknob, she paused. Carefully, as quietly as she could, she opened the closet door and took down the plastic case that contained Jason's handgun. She didn't think he would do anything irrational, but she couldn't take a chance. He'd said he wanted to die.

Before the front door clicked closed behind her, she paused, listening, her hand on the doorknob.

Jason's sobs echoed throughout the house.

Quietly, she slipped out the door, making sure it locked behind her.

CHAPTER 64

SOFIA

O*ctober 2019*

Minneapolis

Before she checked into the motel, Sofia stopped by Super Target and bought some toiletries, some pajamas, and a change of clothes. Walking through the store with its Christmas music piping overhead seemed surreal. It wasn't even Halloween yet. She felt like a zombie.

She knew she was in shock that Jason knew everything.

All the deep dark secrets she'd hid from him their entire relationship was out in the open. He hated her. He'd kicked her out of their house. He'd wanted her admitted to a mental facility or arrested.

Sofia leaned against the shelf in the frozen aisle, pressing her forehead against the cool refrigerator door and closing her eyes. It had only been a matter of time. Who was she kidding? Of course, Jason had found out. She had been a fool to think she could hide from her past. It was a miracle she'd been able to for as long as she had.

Along with utter despair, Sofia also felt a surprising sliver of relief. She no longer had to hide who she was. She no longer had to suppress her nature. It seemed like years ago when, earlier in the day, she'd been willing to move on. To let Dan live.

Now all bets were off.

Jason hated her. Maybe it was a blessing in disguise. Now, she no longer had to protect him. Getting away with murdering Dan without Jason knowing was now out of the question, anyway.

When Dan ended up murdered, Jason would tell all.

He wouldn't be able to help himself. He had good morals, the highest ethics. He would do the right thing, even if it meant sending his wife to prison forever. That was the kind of man he was. He always did the right thing. That was the reason she married him.

Stopping at the liquor store, she grabbed a bottle of Bacardi 151 and then stepped next door to the convenience store and grabbed a pack of cigarettes.

For all of her adult life, she'd needed Jason to stop her from doing the wrong things, from embracing her base, darkest nature and impulses.

But she didn't need him for that anymore.

CHAPTER 65

SOFIA

October 2019
Minneapolis

From the time she was ten and found the finger in the basement, Sofia had despised her father. That hatred, combined with her fear that she was like her father, had motivated her to go into hiding, to change her name and lie to the man she loved for thirty years.

Now, Sofia wondered for the first time what her father felt when he had killed someone.

After a nearly sleepless night, she'd quickly showered at first light and had gone for a long walk around the lake near the motel, trying to make a plan. The days were already growing shorter and colder and darker. Winter would be here soon. Her least favorite time of the year.

Across the small lake, she watched an older man feeding the ducks. Something about the man reminded her of her father. He had to be in his seventies now. If he was still alive.

What had made her father turn into a killer? Did he inherit some violent gene from *his* father? Why did he kill? How did he feel when he was killing someone? How did he feel afterward? Somehow, she didn't think her father felt remorse. Nor did she think he killed out of rage.

Instead, she pictured him calmly and methodically strangling someone with piano wire. The same way he perfectly peeled an orange all in one piece or carefully cut his steak up into tiny pieces so he didn't have to open his mouth wide when he put the fork in. The way his clothes were always perfectly pressed and his shoes buffed to a high shine. Her father's nails were so well manicured they sometimes seemed womanly. He was meticulous, organized, and efficient.

He would kill with little or no emotion.

The FBI said he'd likely killed thirty people, but they could only prove the two from that night.

For a second, Sofia let herself remember her relationship with her father before that night she found the finger. He loved her. That was certain. Unlike her mother. Her father was the one she always turned to when she was upset. He'd pull her up onto his lap and hug her and stroke her hair and whisper in Italian that she was his "beautiful girl."

He told her nothing was more important than family. She was his angel, he said.

One day when she was seven and they were spending the day at Ocean Beach, some men came up to her father. Unlike her father, who was wearing swim trunks and a shirt, these men were in slacks and white shirts and ties. He told her to go play. Her mother was sleeping on a blanket. Sofia decided to get into the water and surf the waves like the older kids were doing. The surf was licking her feet. She turned around to see if her father was going to call her back, but he gave her a distracted wave.

Sofia stepped into the surf. The older kids were not far out and were laughing and bobbing in the waves. She waded out further. She turned. Her father was talking animatedly, his arms waving. Her mother was still face down on the beach blanket.

When she turned around, a big wave engulfed her. All she saw was white and blue as she was tossed and turned. Not knowing which way was up, she panicked. She opened her mouth and it filled with water.

The next thing she knew she was on the beach, coughing. Somebody was pounding on her back. Hard. She spit up and then threw up. She was lying on her side and a crowd of faces peered down at her.

She looked over at the teenage boy who was hitting her back. He smiled, but then was yanked to his feet by her father. Sofia sat up frightened of what her father was going to do to the teen for hitting her.

"That's my daughter!" her father said.

"Sir, I apologize for hitting her. I was just trying to clear her lungs of water."

"No, you misunderstand," her father said. "I am now indebted to you for one life." Her father handed the teen his business card. "Call me."

The teen took it, looking confused.

Her father took her in his arms, woke her mother, and they headed for the car without him saying a word. Sofia looked back over his shoulder and saw a group standing around the teen. Everyone was looking at her dad's card and then over at her dad. When they saw her looking, they looked away.

That night after she went to bed, she heard her parents talking in low voices at the kitchen table. She snuck out of her room and stood outside the kitchen, listening.

To her amazement, her father was crying. He held a glass of wine. Two empty wine bottles stuck out of the trash. Her mother looked on, seemingly unsympathetic.

"You don't understand. If we had lost her ... if something had happened to her."

"So, you are saying it is my fault? For relaxing on the beach taking a nap on my day off?" Sofia could tell her mother was irritated.

"No. No, it is nobody's fault. I thank the Virgin Mary and all the saints for that teenage boy."

Her mother sighed. Then stood and started doing dishes. Sofia stared as her father put his face in his hands and sobbed.

After she had crept back into her bed, Sofia fell asleep with a smile on her face, feeling more loved than she ever had before.

CHAPTER 66

SOFIA

October 2019

Minneapolis

Back at the motel, thinking about her father still, Sofia lit a cigarette and reached for her wallet. In a few seconds, she had found the phone number of the prison where her father was housed.

Slumping on the bed, she felt a wave of dizziness as her first cigarette in years hit her system. She dialed the number and exhaled when someone picked up.

"How do I go about speaking to an inmate?" She asked, not mincing words.

"Name?"

"Sofia."

"No, inmate's name."

Sofia froze.

"Ma'am, I need the inmate's name if I'm going to call him to the phone."

She took a big breath. "Marco Castellucci."

"Hold please."

A Verve song, well, a Verve song as Musak, blasted through the phone as she was put on hold. Sofia scooted back against the headboard. She'd said her father's name out loud and hadn't burst into flames. Closing her eyes for a second, she thought about what the woman had said, "Call him to the phone." What the hell kind of prison was this? You call a prisoner and they go get them out of jail for a phone call?

The Giovanni Family must have pulled some strings getting her father into that prison. She'd heard rumors about how posh and easy it was to live there. Like a fucking dormitory.

She grabbed an empty cup and used it to ash her cigarette. Finally, she threw the second half in the toilet. She felt sick. After about ten minutes, her father got on the line.

"Sofia." So many emotions in one word—hurt, hope, and, maybe, a little fear. It was the first time she'd heard his voice in thirty years.

"Daddy?"

"I am so sorry about little Katie. My heart is broken. In a million pieces."

Sofia stifled a sob. Of course, her father had been keeping tabs on her this whole time.

"Daddy." She could barely choke out the word.

"I've tried not to interfere in your life. But you say the word, I make her killer disappear. Just because he is behind bars does not mean he is untouchable," Her father's voice had lowered to a whisper.

"Daddy, they've got the wrong man in jail."

"*Dio mio*!"

He believed her. She hadn't even had to convince him. She said it and he believed her.

"I know who did it."

"His name." It was a demand.

"No, Daddy. I'll handle it."

"No. Give me his name, Sofia. Now." His voice was vehement.

"You've taught me well." She stared at the ugly bedspread in the motel room. While she was out walking, the maid had picked up the covers from the floor and made the bed. Absentmindedly Sofia used her shoe to push the bedspread back onto the floor in a wad. God knows what kind of body fluids were on that bedspread.

His voice was quiet again. "No. Sofia, you are not a killer."

"Yes, I am. Oh yes I am. I have your blood, Daddy. Your DNA. Your genes were passed down to me. I'm just like you. I finally know this now."

"That is nonsense," Her father said. "There's nothing with DNA or blood or genes or whatever fairy tales you've been telling yourself. I only did it to support our family. I never liked it. I never wanted it. But I was good at it. And I owed the Giovanni family. They saved us. Many years ago, your mother had some ... trouble with a neighbor. Someone died. She was looking at a life in prison. The family stepped in. That is the reason you had a mother all these years. Them. We owe them for the house we had when you were growing up, the clothes, your piano lessons. We owe them for it all."

Sofia closed her eyes, biting back tears. None of this made sense.

"Someone died? Who? I don't understand."

"They argued. She hit the woman. The woman fell, unfortunate, and hit her head. She was married to an important man. The Giovanni's convinced him to agree that it was an accident. Their convincing cost a lot of money."

Something hovered at the side of Sofia's memory. Something dark with fluttering wings, but every time she tried to grasp it, it dissipated. Her father's voice interrupted her thoughts.

"You are not a killer." His voice was low, full of pain.

"I am Daddy. I am a killer. Just like you. And I'm going to kill the person who took Kate away from me." She stared at the picture above the motel bed. It was of the ocean. She remembered that day long ago on Ocean Beach and how everybody was in awe, in fear, of her father.

He was silent for a few seconds.

"Sofia? This line is recorded, you know."

"Yes. I know."

They were both silent again.

Sofia waited him out. There was nothing he could say to change her mind now.

"Your mother ..."

She stayed silent. She pulled back the sheets on the motel bed, looking for small dots of blood to indicate bedbugs.

"I have to tell you this." He gave a big sigh as if it pained him to continue. "I made her go away. I made her leave you. And stay away."

"What?" Sofia scrunched her eyes closed tightly. What the hell was he talking about?

"I told her to leave and if she ever contacted you ..."

"I don't understand. You told her to abandon me?"

Sofia remembered the day her grandmother had died. When she had been eavesdropping on her mother and Aunt Rose they had talked about this. They had talked about her father wanting Sofia to go live with Aunt Rose.

"You were better with Rosie. She was a good mother to you, no? She loved you."

Sofia swallowed. What he had left unsaid was something she had always known deep inside. "Mama didn't love me, did she?"

"Sofia." His voice cracked.

That was her answer.

She shouldn't be surprised.

"My own mother didn't love me." Her voice was flat. Monotone.

"Sofia, you don't understand. Your mother, her childhood, I wouldn't wish that on my worst enemy. She could not help herself."

"Do you love her?"

Another long silence.

"I didn't want you to be raised without a mother. I thought, mistakenly, that a bad mother was worse than no mother. Please forgive me. I had no idea what she had done. I was wrong."

Sofia realized tears were spurting out of her eyes. She stared at the case containing Jason's gun. She had forgotten her jewelry box. High on a shelf next to Jason's gun and tucked under a box of emergency scarves and mittens was the small wooden jewelry box that she'd had as a child. It was locked. She didn't even know where the key was. The box only contained one item. Something she had never looked at since she locked it at Aunt Rose's house after she testified. It contained a picture of her mother and father on their wedding day, smiling and happy. When she was little she used to stare at that photo and wonder why her mother never smiled like that anymore. Then, one day she realized why. It was because of her.

Motherhood had wiped any smile off her face.

Sofia wasn't sure why she'd kept it over the years. Jason had asked her numerous times why she didn't have any photos of her family and she'd lied and told him that everything had been lost in the chaos after her parent's death.

In reality, all she had of her mother was a picture. A picture of the way her mother was before Sofia was born. Happy. Smiling. She realized her dad was still speaking.

She interrupted. "What do you mean *what she had done*?"

Her father was silent for a second before he answered.

"Angelo."

The one word was like a knife through her heart.

Her father kept speaking.

"She came here and told me she did it. The day you testified. To spite me. To ruin my life more." He was sobbing now. "Allowing this to happen—her to blame you—is something that can never be forgiven. Allowing this, believing this, more than anything I've ever done, is my greatest sin."

They were both weeping now. She was gasping for breath. All these years Sofia had thought that she'd killed the baby brother she loved more than life itself. Her mother had led her to believe this.

"She was supposed to disappear and never contact you again. I knew Rosie would raise you. But she didn't listen."

"What?" Sofia could feel her eyebrows scrunch. "Daddy, she never contacted me."

"She found a way around it."

Sofia was confused, but then her father's next words sent terror tripping through her.

"She wrote to Kate instead."

"No. No, she couldn't have."

"I found out. She wrote to Kate a few months before—"

"That can't be true," Sofia interrupted. "Kate would have told me. She doesn't always get the mail. Sometimes I get it first."

But she remembered that for the past year, Kate had always got the mail first, saying she was eager to see whether her college applications had been accepted.

"Sofia," her father's voice was sad again. "I have proof. They showed me. It is true."

Sofia closed her eyes. She didn't know what her mother had written to Kate, but she could be certain it was something evil and destructive and awful.

Where were the letters now? The detectives had thoroughly searched Kate's room, taking all correspondence as possible evidence. They'd even taken every birthday card Kate had received in her life.

"Sofia? Are you still there?"

"I have to go now, Daddy."

"Sofia, wait. I want you to know. I'll never forget this day 49 years ago. It was the best day of my life."

"What?"

"Happy birthday, my dear daughter."

Without saying goodbye, she hung up.

For a long time, the tears came. Angelo. Sweet baby. She hadn't hurt him. Of course, she hadn't hurt him. She loved that baby like he was her own child. Her tears turned to rage. Her mother had killed her own baby. And blamed her other child.

Her mother would pay for this. Sofia would make sure. She dialed Marley.

"Have you gone through all the papers you took out of Kate's room?"

He sounded as if he had just taken a bite of a sandwich. "Um, yeah. Long time ago."

Sofia decided to pretend that Castellucci was her mother's maiden name. Finding out that her mother had taken on her own alias, of Castle, gave her the perfect excuse.

"Did you find any letters from her grandmother? My mother? Her maiden name was Marie Therese Castellucci and her married name is Nina Castle."

As soon as she said the name, Castellucci, Sofia held her breath waiting. Would he know now who she was? But Marley didn't say anything except "stand by."

Sofia heard some clicking as he typed on his keyboard. "It's all logged on the computer now. Let me check. Actually, I'll call you back."

Frustrated she threw the phone on the motel bed. She was tempted to grab her keys and drive over to the police station, asking to see all the evidence they'd taken. Then she remembered, she had the sheet somewhere in her bag.

She extracted the wadded-up piece of paper. It listed journals but no letters.

Looking at the list, she saw they had categorized the journals, just like Kate had. Each journal had been dated for a three-month period.

The last three-month period was not listed. Her phone rang. Marley.

"I looked. Couldn't find anything from Castellucci or Castle. And no letters. Nothing from a grandma-type person. Nothing talking about family history."

"Thanks. I just realized that the last journal Kate had, from June through August, was not listed in your evidence sheet. I know she had one. She's kept a three-month journal since she started high school. The same black Moleskine ones. Are you sure you don't have that one and it just didn't make the evidence sheet?"

"Let me check."

Sofia's heart was racing as she waited.

Marley came back on the line.

"Last journal we have was dated March through May. Nothing after that. Sorry."

"Are you sure?"

"Yeah, our evidence techs are damn thorough."

"That means her most recent journal is missing."

There was a long pause before Marley spoke again.

"Hey, Sofia, you know we got our guy now so we should be able to return some of this stuff before too long. We only need to keep what we need to use as evidence in the case."

"Have you found out where he sent the pictures?"

"Not yet."

After hanging up, Sofia wondered where in the hell the other journal was. If the police didn't have the journal or the letters where were they? Kate could've destroyed them.

Sofia got in her car and headed over to buy some food at the market. She'd store some cheese and crackers and fruit in her tiny refrigerator and eat that while she figured out what to do next. As she pulled into the strip mall, she saw a man near the side of the liquor store taking apart and stacking boxes. Something about it made her pause, but she kept driving.

Later, as she left the store with her purchases, she drove past the back of the liquor store. The boxes were neatly flattened and stacked now.

Boxes.

She glanced at the time. Jason would be at work. Squeaking the tires, she did a U-turn and headed toward her house.

CHAPTER 67

KATE

J*uly 2019*
Dinkytown

When I got off work Tuesday, I found a love letter and bouquet of roses on my windshield.

For a second my heart leapt. Ali!

But then when I opened the note, my stomach flip-flopped.

It was from Dan.

"I hope one day you will feel the same way about me as I feel about you. —D."

I was grossed out and sad and mad at the same time.

It wasn't fair that he was doing this to me.

I felt sorry for him and despised him at the same time.

Of course, I didn't feel the same way. He's like a dad to me. Duh.

There's nobody I can talk to about it. Not Julia. She would just tell me to fuck him and then make him buy me expensive gifts. Not my parents—I mean how could I tell my mom and dad that their best friend is in love with me? And I can't talk to Lily. That would kill her. Hey, your dad is in love with me! Oh my god. The thought alone was mortifying.

I was starting to think that Ali was the only one I could talk to about it and I really needed to talk to someone. Otherwise, I would go crazy.

I was counting the days until I could go away to college. I thought I could just not think about Dan or my grandmother and enjoy these last precious days, but the truth is I'm so miserable. I just need to be far, far away from him. If I tell my parents it will break their hearts. Maybe one day I'll tell them, but right now I just want to get away. He'll get over it when I'm away at college. He's probably just having a midlife crisis or something.

But when I showed up at Ali's and he got in the car for us to go to dinner, he saw the flowers.

"What's that about?"

I could feel the heat rise to my cheeks.

"Long story."

He cleared his throat. "I know we're not exclusive," he said.

I turned at the stop light and raised an eyebrow. Did he want to talk about his ex?

"But you should know, I'm not sleeping with anyone but you."

"Well, that's a relief." My voice dripped sarcasm. We used condoms so I wasn't worried about STD's but the thought of him doing to others what he did to me was distasteful to say the least.

"It's not fair to ask you to be exclusive."

"Why? Because there's an expiration date on us?"

He grimaced. "Well, yes. But it's not my fault."

He was right. I was going away to college and he was going back home to Somalia. It was inevitable that we would have to stop seeing each other.

"I wish it could be different." His voice was so quiet.

I pulled over and put the car in park. "Me, too."

I reached for his hand.

"The flowers? I'm more upset about them than you. It's someone who would never have a chance in a million years."

I knew it was my chance to tell Ali about Dan and even my grandmother, to confide in him, but what he said next made it clear that would be a mistake.

"Kate, I have to tell you. Even though I have zero rights to you and no claim on you whatsoever, the thought of you with someone else? If I allowed myself to go there it would drive me insane. I can't go there. I'm not really a violent person. At least not anymore, but the thought of that? I would want to hurt that person. Badly. And I don't want to be that person anymore. I just feel like if I saw you with someone else ...."

He trailed off. Part of me was thrilled that he basically admitted he'd fallen for me, but the other half of what he said had struck terror through me. *I'm not really a violent person. At least not anymore, but the thought of that? I would want to hurt that person. Badly. And I don't want to be that person anymore.*

What the fuck was that about? *Not anymore?*

He didn't notice my silence.

I didn't know exactly how I felt about what he said, but I knew there was no way I could tell him about Dan.

CHAPTER 68

SOFIA

October 2019
Minneapolis

Sofia slipped in the back door of her house.

Barely glancing at the stack of boxes in the living room, Sofia headed for the junk drawer in the kitchen. Armed with the box cutter, she came back and started slicing the top box open. When it split, she began digging around and tossing items on the floor—clothing, pillows, blankets, towels. Most of the items were brand new: purchased just for Kate's dorm room and new life in college.

She dumped the first box. Nothing.

Then she began on the second, again, tossing items aside until at the bottom, she found it. A shoebox.

Heart pounding, she lifted the lid.

A stack of letters lay inside. But no journal. Glancing at the outside of the envelopes, her face grew icy. She recognized, after all those years, her mother's handwriting.

Her father had been right.

Sofia laid them all out in a row, staring at them. Something was stopping her from reading them. Her mother had been alive this whole time and known where Sofia was, known she had a daughter. And yet, she had never once written to Sofia. She had never once tried to get in touch with her. Last spring, she had begun writing Kate. Why? Sofia realized she was afraid of the answer. Terrified to read her mother's words.

She glanced at the clock on the mantle. It was noon. She scooped up the letters and hurried out of the house leaving her mess.

Before she could read the first letter back at the motel, Sofia lit another cigarette and poured four fingers of Bacardi 151, quickly choking it down between puffs. When she started to feel a little fuzzy, she propped the pillows against the wall and climbed into the bed, muting the infomercials playing on the TV.

With trembling fingers, she opened the first letter dated in April. It was only when she started to slip the letter out that she noticed the address on the envelope. The bookstore.

The last letter was dated in May.

"I'll be there Thursday, What I have to tell you can only be said in person. DON'T TELL YOUR MOTHER ANYTHING. She will try to prevent me from seeing you. She has ruined my life and your grandfather's life and she will pay."

And that was it. The last letter. She set it down on the pillow beside her, poured the rest of the Bacardi into her glass. After she downed it, she turned off the bedside light and closed her eyes.

Yes, she had paid. She had paid with the life of her daughter.

CHAPTER 69

SOFIA

O*ctober 2019*
Minneapolis

For a few seconds after waking, Sofia considered buying a plane ticket, wondering if she should confront her father in person so she could see his eyes and tell if he were lying. But then she decided she didn't have the patience to wait that long.

She needed answers now.

"I hope you did something nice for yourself on your birthday," her father said as soon as he got on the line.

"Where is my mother?"

"What?" He sounded surprised, which startled her.

"God damn it, you owe me this. You've destroyed my life. You owe me. Where is she? I traced her to New Mexico where she was Nina Castle. After that she disappeared. I need to know where she is."

Sofia waited, hardly daring to breath.

"She's dead, Sofia. Your mother is dead. She died in May."

Instead of feeling sad, Sofia was filled with blind rage. "I hope she rots in hell. She tried to turn my own daughter against me."

"But it didn't work, did it?" Her father's voice was calm.

Sofia shook her head knowing he couldn't see her. Then the tears came. She tried not to make a sound, but a few loud sobs escaped.

"Sofia, she can never hurt you again."

"It doesn't matter, Daddy. No one can ever hurt me again."

CHAPTER 70

KATE

A*ugust 2019*
Dinkytown

I was going to lie to my mom one last time and go out with Lily and Julia. Ali said he'd come by Lucky's to see me.

My mom was glued to her laptop like she always was when I came downstairs.

I watched her for a few seconds before she noticed I was there.

She was beautiful. She had little lines around her eyes and mouth and some dark spots on her hands, but she still looked mostly like she had in her wedding pictures. I was lucky to have such a loving, beautiful mom.

Once again, I felt bad thinking about the mother she had grown up with.

That woman was a piece of work.

My mom was the opposite of that. She was honest and loving and fun.

There had never been a second in my life when I'd ever doubted her love for me or ever questioned that she would do anything for me.

I felt a lump in my throat. I knew after next week, I wouldn't see her again until Thanksgiving. The reality of that suddenly made my stomach hurt. I was both excited and scared.

My mom loves to tell everyone how I was such a precious child. How when I was three, the night before I started preschool, she came to my bedroom and talked to me about starting school the next day.

"What do you think about all of that?" she asked after telling me about what it would be like.

"I'm both excited and scared."

Everyone thought the story was so delightful, that a three-year-old could name her emotions that exactly and pinpoint them so well. Now I realized I felt the exact same way fourteen years later except I would phrase it as excited and terrified as fuck.

I tried to keep my voice casual.

"Bye, mom."

She was distracted and didn't even look up.

"I love you. God bless you."

Her standard parting words.

I ran out.

An hour later I was on the side of the road with a flat tire.

I dialed my Dad.

He showed up with a grin.

I jumped out and wrapped him in a big hug.

"My hero!"

"Katie, what are you going to do when I'm not around? Tomorrow, I'm going to teach you how to change a flat. I've been a terrible father. You should've learned this before I let you get behind the wheel."

I laughed. "Such a terrible father!"

"But really, Katie," he grew serious. "You need to be able to take care of yourself. I don't want you to ever feel like you have to rely on someone else."

"Oh, Dad. You're so cute," I said. "I'd just call Triple A if you weren't around."

He grew red. "Oh yeah. That's right. I forget the times we live in. But it still wouldn't hurt to learn how to change your own tire."

I smiled. "Let's do it."

"It's a date," he said. "O five hundred hours. Tire changing in the driveway!"

"How about noon?"

He gave an exaggerated sigh as he turned the wrench. "Fine. I forget I am dealing with a teenager who has no concept of regular sleeping hours."

"True."

He sat up and brushed off his hands. "There you go Katie. Good to go."

I threw myself into his arms and hugged him tightly burying my face in his shirt. I was trying not to cry. I was going to miss my parents' way more than I had thought. I'd been so excited about going away to college I hadn't really thought about what it would mean—leaving my childhood and my loving parents behind.

"Thanks, Daddy." I said as I pulled away and jumped in my car.

"Love you, honey." He said in a low voice.

"I love you, too," I said as I pulled my sunglasses down over my eyes to hide their brightness.

"Get out of here!" He said and slapped the top of the Volvo before I drove off.

I watched him stand there on the side of the road through my rearview mirror.

How had I been so lucky? My dad was the best dad a girl could ever ask for. My heart broke thinking of Lily. I couldn't even imagine how awful it would be if my dad was in love with my best friend. I would want to die.

But luckily, I had the best dad in the world. My heart was full. I was happy, grateful, but also felt a bittersweet pang knowing I was going to leave home in a few short days.

I couldn't take my eyes off the rearview mirror and the image of my dad standing with his hands on his hips watching me drive away. I knew he wouldn't move until he couldn't see my car any longer.

I kept one eye on him, ignoring the tears streaming down my face, until the road curved and his small figure disappeared from the mirror.

CHAPTER 71

SOFIA

O*ctober 2019*
Minneapolis

In the end, it was simple.

After a night of sleeping on it, she'd made up her mind.

She would take Jason's gun. And she'd shoot Dan through the forehead. Cold and calculating. Just like her father. She'd do it today, while Lily was still at her grandmother's house.

What she had said to her father solidified that in her own mind: Nobody could ever hurt her again. Nothing could be worse than losing Kate. Nothing. Not a lifetime in prison. Not incurring hatred from the man she'd spent most of her life loving. Nothing.

The cold hard fact was that Dan had killed her daughter and now Dan must die.

The headlines would be sensational: "Daughter of mob hit man a killer too."

Sofia spent the rest of the day figuring out a plan. In between, she polished off a pack of cigarettes and drank several glasses of Bacardi 151. Around three, she downed four aspirin and a big glass of water and crawled between the sheets where she slipped into a restless sleep, sedated from the alcohol.

Waking close to sunset with a dry mouth but no headache, she downed another big glass of water and four shots and got dressed.

With trembling fingers, she loaded the gun like Jason had showed her so many years ago. Putting on the safety, she tucked the gun in her tote bag and looked around the motel room, wondering if she'd ever come back to it.

For a second she eyed the pad of paper on the desk, wondering if she should leave Jason a note. But then, gulping back her despair, she knew there was nothing she could say.

Maybe sorry, but the truth was she wasn't sorry. That would be one more lie.

At least she could be honest in her final act.

When she pulled up, all the lights were off inside the house, but Dan and Gretchen's cars were parked in the driveway.

Holding the gun in one hand, she loudly slammed the car door.

No use pretending she wasn't there.

Her only fear was that if Dan had a gun, he'd shoot her first.

Standing at the front door, she tried the doorknob. It was unlocked.

Carefully, she pushed the door open. It made a soft creaking noise.

Inside the house was dark. A few slats of light streamed in from the windows. The streetlights had already turned on.

Stepping inside, she eased the door shut behind her, sealing herself in the darkness of the room. She paused, her back against the door, holding her breath, listening.

She heard clicking noises coming from the kitchen. Her heart thumped double time. And then she heard the sound of a small whimper.

The dog. Sugar. It was walking around the tile floor in the kitchen. Then she heard the jingle of its collar as it ran toward her, a white blur. She knelt down, the gun at her side as Sugar came up wagging her tail so hard her entire body wiggled. She gave a tiny happy whine.

"Shhhh," Sofia said, not taking her eyes off the dark doorway to the kitchen.

Her eyes finally adjusted and she saw something white on the ground. It looked like a sock. On a foot. A gush of fear dribbled down her spine.

It seemed like all her senses were on overdrive. She could smell something foreign and metallic in the air and the slow drip of a faucet somewhere seemed earsplitting.

Heart pounding madly, Sofia crept toward the kitchen, holding the gun in front of her, hyper alert. Coming up to the doorway from the side, she ducked and slowly peeked her head around the frame at about waist level.

Stepping into the kitchen, she peered into the darkness.

Gretchen's body lay sprawled on the floor. Blood pooled around her. A single orange beam from the streetlight filtered in the window illuminating her face. Her eyes stared straight up. Sofia's stomach heaved. Clutching her middle with one side, her hand with the gun was shaking wildly now.

She froze, listening in the dark. The silence was broken by the soft humming of a familiar song that sent terror streaking through her. U2's "With or Without You."

Dan.

She jerked the gun toward the sound, slid the safety off, and abruptly stood, pressing her back tightly against the wall, inching toward the open doorway to the living room.

"Sofia. You came. Just like I knew you would. Are you going to shoot me?" His voice was calm. How did he know she had a gun? Could he see her? She looked down, her body was shrouded in darkness. She couldn't even see her feet. If she couldn't see him, he surely couldn't see her, right? A long patch of light from the window was between her and the doorway to the living room. She'd been so focused on the foot on the ground, she hadn't realized she'd stepped right through a patch of light to enter the kitchen. He must have seen her—and her gun—when she walked in.

Her mind was screaming to run, but she had to play it smart. Her eyes strained toward his voice but she could see nothing.

"Go ahead. You came here to kill me. What are you waiting for?"

She didn't respond. Her mind was racing. What kind of game was he playing?

"Before you kill me, let me explain. Then you can shoot me. I know you can barely control yourself. Just let your nature take over, Sophia. You are a killer. Just like your father. Why hide it anymore? Nobody will be surprised that you killed me. It will make perfect sense. You're crazy and thought I hurt Kate. You didn't know that Gretchen actually killed Kate. ... That's why I killed her. I confronted her, told her to come home and we'd have a romantic night with Lily still at her grandmother's. But I hate Gretchen. I've wanted her dead for years. When I found out she'd killed Kate it was the perfect excuse."

Sofia fought the urge to look over at Gretchen's body.

He was desperate. He was desperate and bluffing. But something about what he said made a strange sense ...no. It couldn't be. He was a liar.

"You killed Kate because you wanted her and she was disgusted by you." As she spoke, she moved quickly, taking cover beside a cabinet.

"You're wrong." His voice was so certain and matter of fact that Sofia froze. "I didn't kill her. I know that's what you think. Gretchen told me you were here asking questions. But it was Gretchen. When she found out about my feelings for Kate, she couldn't handle it. You know how jealous she is. She found out the night of the party. That's why she left early. She went to find Kate. I didn't know or I would've stopped her."

He sounded so sure. So confident.

Dan's voice seemed closer. Ducking, she moved toward the table in the middle of the kitchen, a large black lump in the dark. If she were really quiet, she could slip underneath it. For a second her body would have to cross over a patch of light streaming in from the window. She'd have to be fast. She'd do it in three. She began to count down. Three. Two.

The light flicked on. Whirling and partially blinded, she quickly focused on Dan by the back doorway. He was leaning against the doorframe, smiling. Small tufts of his balding pate stuck up and his hands and shirt were covered in blood. He was holding a framed photo.

Sofia raised the gun toward him and glanced at the photo.

It was a picture of Dan and his first wife, Carla. Sofia had seen it in Lily's room before. In the picture, the couple had been on their honeymoon. Carla was beautiful. Her long blonde hair was bleached white from the sun and was striking against her deep tan. She had bare feet and wore a thin white gauzy sundress and a silver cuff. Dan was looking at Carla like she was the sun, moon, and stars. There was something about the picture that sent a stab of pity through Sofia.

But she swallowed that emotion. She had a job to do.

Eyes flicking over at the gun, Dan raised his hands in surrender. "Show them what you really are, Sofia. You can't fight it. Your DNA. Your genetic predisposition. You were right. You are destined to kill. But first, you have to believe me. Gretchen killed Kate."

She frowned at his words. He looked over her shoulder. She almost instinctively glanced behind her. It was a trick. But her arm with the gun lowered slightly. Her mind was fuzzy, spinning. He was playing with her head. He was a shrink. He was toying with her.

"Why, Dan?"

He shook his head slightly.

She lifted the gun again and pointed it toward him. Her arm was shaking madly.

"Tell me why you killed Kate, Dan."

He clamped his lips together and shook his head.

"Tell me, Dan."

He shrugged. "It doesn't matter now, anyway."

She walked closer.

"It's all in Kate's journal," he said. "They took it that day. The morning after Kate's death when you sent Gretchen and Lily back to the house, Lily took Kate's journal. I saw it. I read about it. When I confronted Gretchen, she attacked me. Look." He lifted his arm. His chest had a small, gaping bloody wound. "Listen, I'm probably dying anyway. I've lost a lot of blood. Do me a favor for old time's sake and tell Lily I love her. Tell her the bracelet meant nothing. Tell her that I have always loved her more than anything or anyone in the world."

Sofia's head spun. Something wasn't right. It didn't make sense. Deep down inside, Sofia knew if she killed Dan it was over. Everything. She would have her revenge, but would have lost her soul by giving in to the deepest, darkest, most aberrant part of her. The part she now realized she had inherited—not from her father—but from her mother.

Sofia's finger itched toward the trigger. It would take a gentle squeeze. She knew how it felt from going to the gun range with Jason. It wouldn't take much. The trigger on this gun didn't take much strength.

"Dan, you are going to die for killing my daughter. You can decide if you want it to be easy or terrible. But first tell me why you killed her. I thought you loved her like your own daughter." Sofia's voice caught saying this, but she quickly swallowed her tears.

"I did love her. But I love Lily more." Dan closed his eyes. A few tears escaped.

"Then tell me how you could possibly have killed her. You killed her, Dan. My daughter is dead because of you. Tell me why."

"I can't."

"What does that mean?" Sofia's voice was steel, emotionless.

He looked up at her, his face filled with triumph, which confused Sofia.

It would only take the slightest pressure to pull the trigger. Just a small movement of her right index finger. Her arms were no longer shaking. Her aim was steady.

"Sofia, it's over. Your fingerprints are on the knife that killed Gretchen. I saved the knife. Do you remember the white-handled one you used to cut up the limes for our gin and tonics? I've saved it. Hid it away in case I needed it."

Sofia put her finger back up above the trigger, resting it on the cool metal. She needed time to think. She was confused. He'd planned this for a long time. He wanted out of the marriage but didn't want his business to take a hit or for his daughter to hate him. So, he killed Gretchen and was framing Sofia?

Sofia couldn't help but glance over at Gretchen's body. In the light, Sofia saw a knife with a white handle sticking out of Gretchen's abdomen. It was the knife she'd cut the limes with. Sugar now sat beside her owner's body, whining.

"I'll wipe my fingerprints off the knife after I kill you."

Sofia took another step closer. Dan was now openly weeping. "I hate you. You and Jason and your perfect god damn life. Your perfect daughter. She always made Lily feel inadequate. I never knew this until it was too late. I would've never stayed friends with you and your family if I would've known this. My poor Lily. She never felt good enough. I never knew. I never knew." His tearful voice was laced with fury.

A surge of rage zipped through Sofia. She could feel her face distort as if it were no longer under her control. A strange taste filled her mouth. Her vision turned white. Her mouth was moving and she couldn't control it. He saw it. He watched and smiled. She would have to kill him now. She had no choice, she couldn't control it any longer.

Sofia raised the gun one last time. She took another step closer. The gun was pointing at his forehead. There was no way she could miss. She was too close. She heard something behind her, some noise she couldn't quite figure out. Glancing over her shoulder, she didn't see anything.

Slowly, as slowly as she could, she squeezed the trigger. At the last second, she lifted the muzzle of the gun and the bullet lodged in the wallpaper a foot above Dan's head.

He was wrong. She wasn't a killer.

Her arm with the gun fell to her side just as chaos erupted.

"Freeze!"

"Drop the gun!"

"Put your hands up!"

CHAPTER 72

KATE

A*ugust 2019*
Dinkytown

Dan showed up at the bookstore right before I was supposed to meet Lily. I looked around outside frantically. I was supposed to meet Lily there in a few minutes.

"Lily is coming here. You have to leave. Now! Aren't you supposed to be at my parents' party anyway?"

We'd counted on them all being occupied while we drank at Lucky's tonight.

"This will only take a minute." He said. He looked like he'd been crying. "Put your arm out?"

I did, wary. He clasped a bracelet on my arm. I recoiled at his touch and was mad at myself for thinking it was beautiful.

"It's a goodbye present. You're right. We could never be together. Society would never accept it."

I stared at him. Society not accepting it had nothing to do with it.

He was gross and old and my fucking best friend's dad. But I tried to force a smile.

The fact was I didn't care what he thought as long as he left me the fuck alone. I'd smile and take his bracelet.

"This bracelet is a symbol of my promise to never make you feel uncomfortable around me again."

I was starting to feel better but he kept talking and made it worse.

"And it's a symbol of my never-ending love for you."

He had to go and ruin it. My flesh crawled with revulsion. I wanted to run away. Just then over his shoulder I saw Lily across the street. She was looking both ways for an opening in traffic to cross.

"There's Lily," I shouted. "Go! Now. Out the back. Before she sees you."

It seemed that the back door had only just closed when Lily came in the front door. I searched her face to see if she'd seen her dad but she gave me a bright smile.

"Hi! You ready to party?" But something about her words rang false. I was right. She was angry at me.

"Lily? Is something bothering you?" I asked.

She turned away so I couldn't see her face as she answered. "Nope."

"Are you sure?"

She shrugged. "What were you up to today?"

"Nothing." I held my breath. Had she seen her dad in here or not?

She whirled toward me so suddenly I jumped. "That's a really beautiful bracelet," she said. "Where did you get it? Maybe I can get one too for our matching birthday jewelry. We have to do that this week. Before we leave for school."

She was looking down at it smiling. I was glad for the distraction.

"Oh, it's my mom's. I'm just borrowing it. We'll find something better for our presents I bet."

"I don't know. That's really nice."

I nodded. It was. It was obviously an antique and looked quite valuable. I was irritated she'd seen the bracelet before I had a chance to take it off and throw it in the trash. Now I was stuck wearing it all night or she'd get suspicious.

"I was looking at these really beautiful jade chandelier earrings," I said. "I saw them on Kylie Jenner's Instagram. They would look really great with your eyes."

"Huh," she said. She seemed distracted as she turned toward the door. "You ready?"

"Yeah. Let's go."

I locked up the bookstore and we headed toward the bar.

CHAPTER 73

SOFIA

October 2019
Minneapolis

The police officer rolled Sofia's index finger in the black ink and then pressed it onto the white card. One by one he pressed the rest of her fingers into the inkpad. She stood, catatonic, not thinking, not feeling.

She stood expressionless as the camera clicked, taking her mug shot.

Although Sofia might have been imagining it, it seemed like the female guard shot her a sympathetic look after the body cavity search.

It was over.

Dan would get away with murder.

When the police arrived, they'd taken Sofia into custody. She'd fought and they'd tasered her and that was that.

From what she overheard stuffed in the back of the squad car, crunched over in pain from the tasering, Dan had called 911 right when she arrived, saying he was worried about her showing up to kill him and his wife. That's why he wasn't worried about her wiping her fingerprints off the gun or her shooting him. He knew the cops would walk in any second. They'd been delayed by a car accident blocking traffic on the way or they would've been there even sooner.

As they loaded Dan onto an ambulance gurney, he'd shoved a folder at the police, saying, "This documentation should go to the detectives investigating my wife's murder. I'm sorry to say that Sofia has been mentally unstable for years. I'm just sorry I couldn't stop her sooner."

She'd wasted her one phone call to Jason. He'd promptly hung up on her. She'd stared at the phone in disbelief. But then within the hour, the guards took her to a small windowless room. After a few minutes, a short, pudgy man dressed in a bad suit had come in toting a beat-up leather briefcase. The hair on one side of his head stuck straight up as if he'd just woken.

"I'm Carl Pierce. Your husband called me."

Sofia shook his hand. But the person she really needed was Cecile. Who was still in Paris celebrating her trial victory.

"You don't have a chance of getting sprung until Monday—when, if we're lucky—the judge will set bail."

Sofia shrugged. She'd figured as much. She eyed the attorney. He looked like a hack and talked like his law school training had involved watching *The Godfather*. What kind of attorney used the word "sprung?" She wasn't some fucking thug. She was a suburban mom who wore mom's jeans. But apparently, all criminals were the same to him.

He thrust a plastic Target bag at her. "Here are some clothes for court your husband gave me."

She took the bag and peered inside. Jason had picked out a black skirt, white silk blouse, a black sweater, and black pumps.

The attorney cleared his throat, but she interrupted.

"I didn't kill Gretchen. Dan set me up," she watched the attorney try to hide his annoyance. She could imagine what he was thinking: *That's what they all say*.

"Okay. We'll work on all that. I'm sure it was self-defense, right?"

Sofia pressed her lips together tightly and shook her head.

"I didn't kill anyone."

"You are also being held on attempted murder. That one's going to be a little tougher since one of the cops actually saw you shoot at the victim's head."

"I meant to miss."

He let out another long breath. "Okay."

There were a few seconds of silence. Where did Jason find this guy? 1-800-Defense-Attorney? As soon as she could, she was going to try to reach Cecile and get a real attorney.

"You had the unfortunate bad luck to get arrested on a Friday night," he said. "No arraignments until Monday, so you get an extra few days in jail. See you Monday."

He stood to leave. If Sofia got her way, she'd have a new attorney by Monday.

"By the way," he said, pausing at the door. "When the judge sets bail on Monday, you'll be happy to hear that if it's anything less than two mil, you're walking."

"What?" She and Jason didn't have that sort of money, or collateral. Maybe Cecile was already on the case.

"Our office got a call earlier. Your attorney fees are covered in full and someone has guaranteed up to $2 million bail for you."

Sofia wrinkled her nose. "Who?"

"Didn't say. The number had an East Coast area code."

Her father.

She'd rather sit in jail and use that money for a different attorney. She had no home to go to anyway. Not really.

The attorney turned, but she reached out to touch his arm. She'd better play nice in case she ended up being stuck with him after all.

"Do you think I have a chance?"

He stared at her for a long moment and then walked away without answering.

Despite her initial thoughts about using bail money for a new attorney, now that she was in jail, Sofia was desperate to be free. If this was her father's life, then maybe he *was* being adequately punished for his crimes.

It smelled like piss and vomit and it was bone-chillingly cold. She rummaged in the plastic bag and found the soft sweater Jason had thrown in there. Wrapping herself in it, she perched on the bed, unwilling to put her head down on the soiled mattress. It was probably full of lice and bed bugs and mites. That night, she slept on and off, sitting up. Each time, she startled awake because someone else in the jail screamed or laughed or cried.

As she drifted in and out of consciousness, she moaned and winced. In her dreams she was desperately trying to remember something. Something important was right on the edge of her consciousness. Something that she needed to know. But for the life of her, she couldn't grasp it.

However, when she woke, she knew.

Dan hadn't killed Kate.

It had been right before her the whole time.

CHAPTER 74

KATE

A*ugust 2019*
Dinkytown

I was wrong.

Lily is pissed off at me. She was lying in the bookstore when she said she wasn't.

But after two Mojitos, the truth came out.

We were sitting at the bar when Ali called to tell me he couldn't meet me at the bar because he was dealing with Jenna.

Lily had gone to the bathroom and returned just as I was ending the call.

"That was Ali. He's not coming."

"You are so dumb."

"What?" It took a few seconds for the words to register. "What are you talking about?"

"If you think Ali really likes you, you are dumber than I thought." Her words were slightly slurred but they still packed a punch. My stomach hurt.

I whipped my head around to hide my cheeks. I could feel they were growing red with both embarrassment and anger. The movement of my head made me realize I was buzzed. The alcohol had hit me hard.

She kept talking. "I saw him. With that girl."

Jenna.

"We aren't exclusive." I said. I tried to sound nonchalant. But it hurt. Was he seeing her again?

"They looked pretty cozy too."

I shrugged. But I wouldn't look at her. I didn't want her to know how much her words hurt.

"You don't care?" she said. Her voice growing shrill. "What happened to you this summer, Kate? Are you too cool now? Now that you aren't a virgin anymore, it's all fun and games for you?"

I looked around wildly. One boy at a nearby table met my eyes and winked. Shit. Had he heard Lily say I wasn't a virgin anymore?

I took a big slug of my drink and turned to her, feeling emboldened by the alcohol.

"What's your problem, Lily? Are you pissed at me because you're a virgin and I'm not?"

I arched my eyebrow. This time she looked around to see if anybody had heard.

But she quickly regained her composure.

"I'm pissed because you don't know how to keep your hands off what's not yours," she hissed the words.

My heart stopped for a minute. Was she still talking about her liking my old boyfriend first? Or did she know about her dad's sick crush on me?

But she kept talking. "If I remember correctly, Jenna and Ali were a thing when you met him, right? So, what do you expect? If he cheated on her with you, you really think he wasn't going to cheat on you, too?"

I glared at her. I knew she was right. "It's none of your business, Lily."

"I just feel bad for you," she said. "You gave your virginity to some player who couldn't give a shit about you. He's using you. He has a girlfriend. You're an idiot."

"Fuck you." I slammed down my drink, grabbed my bag, and raced for the bathroom before she could see my tears. How lame that I was crying. Totally lame! But once I was back there I found the door locked. Fuck. Fuck. Fuck. I wanted to hide. I saw Lily leaning over and talking to a boy laughing.

I hitched my bag on my shoulder and took off through the kitchen and out the back door.

Fuck her.

I'd go to Ali's. She was wrong. He cared about me. He hadn't been using me. He'd always been extremely honest with me. Almost to a fault.

I stormed down the alley and turned onto the street.

I'd go see him and have sex again if I could. Screw Lily.

But a small part of me wondered if when I showed up, he wouldn't be alone.

Lily's words echoed: "He's using you. He has a girlfriend. You are an idiot."

CHAPTER 75

SOFIA

October 2019

Minneapolis

It had come to her upon awakening.

At his house, Dan had told Sofia to tell Lily the bracelet had meant nothing. That he loved Lily more than anything or anyone in the world. And that while he loved Kate, he loved Lily more. At the time, Sofia had no idea what he was talking about. Now she realized.

He was talking about the cuff bracelet that she'd spotted on Lily's arm that day when the girls stopped by before going to college. The one she'd also seen on Kate's wrist in that photo taken the night she was last seen. At Lucky's.

The photo of Lily's dead mother that Dan was holding. In that photo, Dan and Carla were on the beach in Mexico. Lily's mother was wearing that same cuff bracelet. There weren't two matching cuff bracelets. There was one. And it had belonged to Lily's mother.

Sofia thought back to the short list of personal belongings that Marley had given her. The cuff bracelet was not on the list. It was not on Kate's body when they found her. Even though she had been wearing it earlier that night.

Dear God.

Lily had the bracelet that Kate was wearing when she was killed.

Dan had also said Lily had taken Kate's journal the morning after her death. She was hiding something. Covering up something. Hyperventilating, Sofia jumped up and paced the small space within her cell, shaking her head and muttering.

She went over every interaction she had with Lily after Kate's death.

And then she remembered something that had struck her as odd. When she had that boy, Jake Walker, in the motel room, he'd said something strange about Lily. At the time, it was so uncharacteristic of Lily that Sofia had dismissed it as nonsense. He'd said that Kate's friend, the one with the "spot on her face" had told him that Kate was a prude.

But then he had laughed and said, "Her friend sure wasn't a prude."

Sofia realized she did not know Lily at all.

And with a jolt, it all came together.

It was Lily.

Lily had killed Kate.

Deep down in her bones, she knew it as fact: Lily had murdered Kate.

That night, at the empty nest party, she'd thought Dan was drunk. But he had known right then. He had sobbed and apologized saying, *"Kate was such a good kid. I don't know what went wrong with Lily. I tried. I swear. I'm so sorry."*

She began pounding and yelling for the guard.

Nobody came.

One man down the hall said if she pleasured him in the transport van on the way to court Monday, he'd make sure she had protection in the holding cell.

Sofia was pulling at her hair when someone stopped in front of her jail cell. Detective Marley. Springing up from her mattress, she clutched the bars, staring bleary-eyed at him.

"Thanks for coming. I didn't kill Gretchen."

He didn't look convinced. "I'm actually not here to see you."

"What?"

"I've got another perp down the row I need to have a little chat with. I'm not investigating your case."

A voice echoed in the hall: "Yo, Marley, you Rasta motherfucker. What's taking you so long, man?" The inmate he was there to see, apparently.

He turned to walk away.

"Wait," Sofia said.

Marley paused.

"I didn't do it. And Dan didn't kill Kate."

Big sigh.

"Yes. We have Ronald Derry in custody for her murder, if you recall."

"He's innocent. It was Lily."

Marley looked pained.

"Really. I think I can prove it. I just need to get out of here."

"Not happening."

Sofia squeezed her eyes shut for a second. "Then I need you to prove it."

"I'm really sorry. But it's not my case." He started to turn toward the hall again.

Sofia blew out a big breath of air. "But you want the truth as much as I do."

He turned back toward her.

"If you find Kate's last journal, it might be evidence. It's somewhere in the house. Dan mentioned it. I think that's why he killed Gretchen, because she had Kate's journal. And plus, he said a long time ago he wanted out of the marriage but he couldn't divorce her. It would ruin his marriage counseling practice and it would make his daughter hate him. So, he got rid of her by killing her and blaming me. He did it. Listen, he planted my fingerprints on the knife. He *told* me he did."

Marley bit his lip, but remained silent.

"Arriving officers witnessed you shoot at Dan."

"I know. But I changed my mind at the last minute."

Marley sighed loudly.

"Please believe me. It was Lily. Everything Dan did ... it was because he was protecting her. I bet Gretchen found out and that's why Dan killed her."

Marley stared at her for a long moment and then walked away.

Sofia wanted to punch the bars, instead she sat back on the bunk and put her head in her hands.

She needed to find that journal. When it grew dark, she was still thinking about it. Tossing and turning, Sofia sat on the jail mattress and tried to think where it might be hidden. In the middle of the night, she jumped up. Dan's secret drawer in his desk where he'd hidden the meds from Cuba.

At first light, she asked to make a call. She was refused. Later, when a female guard came on duty, she asked again about procedure to make a call. The woman looked her up and down and then unlocked her cell.

"I seen you on the news. You lost your kid to violence. I don't know what you did or didn't do, but I'm a mother. I'll let you make that call. Two minutes only."

Sofia got Marley's voice mail. "Dan has a secret drawer in his desk. Look there."

Although she waited all day long, sitting up every time the main door to the cellblock opened, nobody ever came to see her.

Monday morning she tried to wash her face in the small sink and slick back her hair. She smelled and looked awful, but she dressed in the black skirt, white blouse and heels. She perched on the edge of her bed and waited, alternately cracking her knuckles and chewing her fingernails. She would scream her theory in court. She would make sure everybody knew.

She watched as one-by-one guards came in and led cuffed prisoners out toward a back doorway.

One inmate winked as he passed her cell. "Offer's still open."

The jail grew silent. She stood and tried to peer out the sides of her bars. She couldn't see far, but from what she could see the other cells were empty.

"What the fuck?" Then she sat back down.

Within a minute, a guard appeared and opened her door.

"Follow me."

Instead of leading her toward the back door, he turned left, toward the entry.

Sofia wordlessly followed, shuffling her feet. Maybe Jason had come to visit her. She dared to hope it was true. If she didn't ask where they were going, she could imagine that reality for a few more seconds. She had a feeling the rest of her life behind bars was going to involve imagining an alternate reality.

CHAPTER 76

KATE

August 2019
Dinkytown

It wasn't until I turned off the busy street and left Lucky's Bar behind that I was able to breathe in a normal manner and unclench my fists. This street was darker and I jumped when headlights flickered over me. An SUV had just turned onto the street behind me.

I glanced around. I could duck into a doorway and hide if it came closer.

But right now, I was fuming.

Lily was acting crazy.

Why was she so angry with me? Was she really that jealous that I had a boyfriend and she didn't?

I'd been tempted to tell her he was going back to Somalia soon, but she made me so mad, I didn't want to make her feel any better. Was there any chance she knew her dad was in love with me?

It seemed like she would have just said something.

I'd ask Ali about it. He could think I was weird, but I needed a friend. I needed to talk to someone about it or it would drive me crazy.

Meanwhile, I'd try to patch things up with Lily.

Hitting voice memo, I began to talk. Writing that unsent letter. Thanks, Dan.

"I'm so angry at you right now, Lily. Don't you know that no guy could ever replace you? Haven't you heard how boys come and go, but friends last forever?"

My footsteps echoed loudly on the dark street. For a second I thought about calling Ali and telling him to meet me halfway, but I wanted to surprise him. I wanted to see if he was telling the truth about a quiet night at home or if he had lied and had Jenna over one last time.

But at that point, I was almost there. I'd see for myself.

The night seemed to grow darker. I glanced behind me as I turned onto Ali's street. The SUV and its headlights had disappeared. The street lights weren't on, so the sidewalks were creepy and shadowy, but I felt better now that the SUV was no longer behind me.

"Listen, Lily," I said into my phone. "You are my best friend. Oh my God, don't tell Julia I said this, but you know it's true. You and I are more alike. Please don't be mad at me."

The wind kicked up sending a discarded paper cup skittering across the street and I startled. The hair on the back of my neck stood on end.

A twig cracked right behind me and my blood ran cold.

Suddenly, I realized I'd made a terrible mistake.

CHAPTER 77

SOFIA

October 2019
Minneapolis

The guard led her into a windowless room and shoved a bag of clothes at her. The same clothes she had on the night she was arrested. The bag also contained her purse and car keys.

"You're free to go."

Her mouth opened and she couldn't form words for a few seconds. "Wait. Why?"

The guard shrugged.

Jason and Detective Marley were waiting in the lobby.

Sofia searched Jason's face, but he looked down and walked outside. Marley followed.

Glancing around at the people in the jail waiting room—what looked like scruffy defense attorneys, dirty-faced kids and some babies' mamas—she saw why they wanted to leave before talking to her.

Mutely, she trailed behind them.

Outside, the two men waited for her near a low wall. Marley was lighting a cigarette. He offered the pack to Jason, but her husband shook his head. Jason swallowed but wouldn't look up at her. Instead he stared into the parking lot.

"Derry's been released. He finally gave up the ghost," Marley said and exhaled a plume of smoke straight up in the air.

"What?" Sofia squinted. "You bailed me out of jail to tell me that he didn't kill Kate? I knew *that*."

"When he realized he was going away for murder, he spilled it. Some woman had contacted him years ago about taking pictures of your family. Each month she paid him to take pictures and send them to her at a PO Box in New Mexico."

Sofia's heart clenched. "Let me guess. The woman's name was Nina Castle."

"Bingo. I remembered the name from when you called asking about it. That's one reason I started digging around in everything over the weekend. Boy, I'm glad I did."

"Me, too."

"There's more," Marley said. "Not only are you free, but we're holding Dan for Gretchen's murder and picking up Lily at her grandmother's house," Marley said. "She's going to be booked on suspicion of Kate's murder."

Sofia's knees buckled. She felt for the low wall and sat down.

"Want to talk about this somewhere more private?" Marley said. "My car? A café?"

Sofia shook her head. "No, I'm sorry. I just need to have air around me right now. Just for a little while."

Marley paced in front of her, smoking as he spoke.

The day Sofia had seen Marley in the jail he'd gone back to the station and reviewed all the camera footage. He'd found some images shot from the bank's ATM that showed Lily following Kate when she'd left the bar.

They searched Dan's office and found the secret compartment. Inside, they found Kate's journal and a SIM card in an envelope. It was to Kate's phone. She'd been recording while she was walking using her voice memo when Lily attacked her.

Marley took a long drag and then dropped the butt of his cigarette onto the ground, crunching it under his foot. He took his phone out of the holder on his belt loop and handed it to her with some earbuds.

Heart pounding, Sofia put the earbuds in and hit play.

CHAPTER 78

KATE

A*ugust 2019*
Dinkytown

I whirled in the dark ready to face whomever was following me.

It was Lily.

My entire body sagged in relief.

"Jesus! You scared the shit out of me." I lifted my phone. "I was just talking about how you are my best friend."

"To whom?" Her voice was emotionless.

"Lily, please don't be mad at me. I was going to tell you that Ali is moving. Out of the country—"

"Give me my mother's bracelet now."

I closed my eyes. She knew. She must know everything.

Lily was now crying. "My dad doesn't love you. He can't. That's wrong."

"It's not what you think," I said. My mind scrambled. I couldn't imagine how awful she must feel. I'd put myself in her place so many times. I would die if my father fell in love with my best friend. Lay down and die. I had to make it better. I would do anything to make it better. To wipe that ravaged look from her face. I wanted to hug her, but her entire body was tense.

"It was a goodbye present ..." I began to explain, but knew I'd said the wrong thing.

"Give me the fucking bracelet, Kate."

As fast as I could, I unlatched the bracelet and thrust it at her.

"Lily, you can have the bracelet. I'm so sorry. Your dad never said it was your mother's. I swear, Lily. I would've never accepted it. He gave it to me as a way to say goodbye. He wanted to apologize for ..."

She swatted my hand and the bracelet went flying.

Lily's voice was cold. "Apologize? For what? For having sex with you?"

"No. It was never like that. It was innocent, really." But she interrupted me.

"You've always thought you were better than me. You did this. You wanted my dad to love you more than he loves me."

My heart sank. The hurt was unbearable. I felt so bad for her. I tried to see her eyes in the dark but she was hard and cold and wouldn't look at me.

"No, Lily, no. I promise. No. It wasn't like that. I swear. Lily, please listen to me."

"Lying bitch." The words came at the same time she lunged at me. "I hate you! I hate you! I hate you!"

I fell backward, scrambling to regain my footing or stop my fall.

But it was too late.

The back of my head hit something hard and then the world exploded in shattering pain.

CHAPTER 79

SOFIA

October 2019
Dinkytown

In the dark outside the jail, Sofia listened to Lily's voice coming through the earbuds. She was screaming at Kate, full of vitriol and then there were the sounds of a scuffle and groaning and a loud thud of something hard hitting something hard.

Her hand flew up to her mouth as Sofia realized what she was hearing.

Even though Jason and Marley were nearby, Sofia was completely caught up in the world she was listening to.

She didn't hit pause. Lily was crying and mumbling. "I hate you." This time she was sobbing as she said it, all the anger seemed to have dissipated. "You can get up now. I didn't hit you that hard. I let go of your neck in time. I'm not that strong."

A few seconds later. "Kate? Kate? Kate? Oh my God. Oh my God. Where's my phone? Oh my God, where's my phone? Dad? Dad? Dad? You have to come right now. Please Daddy please. Something terrible has happened. I swear it was an accident. Okay. I'll hang up now."

Tears were streaming down Sofia's face as she took out the earbuds and handed Marley's phone back to him. Jason reached out a hand to touch her arm, but then drew back.

"We found some deleted texts on Lily's phone that seem to seal the deal," Marley said.

A breath Sofia hadn't realized she was holding whooshed out.

Jason took her arm. "They also found an unsent text on Kate's phone. It's to you."

"Me?" Sofia held back tears. "What did it say?"

Looking at Marley for permission Jason said that the text was about Dan and how Kate was going to confront Lily about it that night when they went out.

"Why didn't she send me the text? Why didn't she tell me? Why didn't she just tell us?" Sofia balled her hands into fists and shot a look at Jason. He shook his head.

"We were able to trace her calls," Marley said. "The second to last call she received was from Dan Williams. He called your daughter from your driveway. It looks like shortly after Lily called him. Then he called her about an hour later. We pinged it. He was calling from ten feet away from the murder scene. He called after he knew Kate was dead. He called her phone so in case we ever found it, it would look like he was the one who killed her and not Lily. He confessed to murdering Kate."

Sofia slumped onto the small wall. "Why? Why did he do that? Why did he confess? I mean, it sounds like..." she took a deep breath. "It sounds like it might have been an accident."

There. She said it.

Marley nodded. "We're looking at involuntary manslaughter."

"Why didn't they call an ambulance? Or the police?" Sofia shook her head. Why was Dan's first instinct to hide Kate's body. Why would he put her through that? Why had he let her believe for so long that an unknown murderer was out there who had targeted Kate?

The simple facts were horrific enough, but he had turned her daughter's death into an even more devastating nightmare if that was possible.

But then a thought, a terrible, horrible thought entered her mind.

She closed her eyes for a second before she spoke. When she opened them, she looked at Marley, willing him to tell the truth.

"What if Kate was still alive? What if they left her to die and she could've been saved?"

Marley's eyes widened slightly but not so much that he hadn't also considered this.

"How will we know? How will we know?" Her voice had grown shrill.

Marley just shook his head.

"Far as I could figure everything Dan did was to try to save his daughter. We also found texts from him to Gretchen he'd tried to delete that have been going on as long as Kate's been dead. He's been on a strident campaign to convince Gretchen she killed Kate out of jealousy because he was in love with Kate. We think he was trying to set up her murder to look like a suicide, but Gretchen fought back, stabbed him and then you showed up. He even wrote a suicide note from her saying she killed Kate, but it looks like she refused to sign it. It was all bloody and ripped, lying by her body."

It was horrific. But then again it was right up his alley. Dan had tried to make everyone take the blame for killing Kate except Lily. Sofia remembered her conversation with Dan at the lake. Gretchen was convinced she'd done things she hadn't done, he'd said. Violent things. Like killing a deer. She could see Dan try to convince Gretchen that she had killed Kate.

Marley continued. "And far as we figure it, based on the voice memo and deleted text messages, Lily called him after ... and asked for his help. He was the clean-up crew."

CHAPTER 80

SOFIA

October 2019
Minneapolis

"You sure you want to do this?" Marley looked worried as he walked into the small room at the police station.

Sofia stood. Her hands were shaking as she reached for the giant sheaf of papers Marley held toward her.

"These are yours," he said.

"What do I owe you for the photocopies?" Sofia reached for her purse.

"You don't owe me nothing."

"Thank you. Thank you for everything."

He looked down. "I shoulda listened to you a little quicker. You know, my wife told me something after all this."

"Oh yeah, what was that?"

"She told me, 'Don't ever doubt a mother's intuition.'"

"Smart woman."

"She also says I need sensitivity training."

Sofia looked up. "Hmm. Maybe a little bit."

"Damn straight. That woman is always right. I mean always."

"You're a lucky man."

"Yes, I am." He smiled and turned toward the door. "So, I'll leave you at it. You have my number. You can call anytime." He paused. "You can take those with you and read them at home, you know."

"Would it be all right if I sat and read them here. I'm not sure I can wait."

"Sure thing," he said.

"Detective Marley?"

"Yes?"

"You know how you were asking about my parents and my past—"

He cut her off. "That's your business. We can't help who we're born to."

The door closed behind him before she could respond.

He knew. He knew about her father and her last name and never said anything. She didn't know how long he had known, but he didn't seem to care. Her throat welled with emotion.

Sofia's hands were shaking as she undid the large rubber band across the top sheet.

Kate's handwriting was instantly recognizable and brought more tears to Sofia's eyes.

It took a few pages before Sofia found anything telling. The journal entry was dated in May.

"I told Dan about mom and my grandma. He hugged me. And then, like a big baby, I got snot and stuff all over his shirt. He was really sweet about it, though, telling me to shush and that it would all be okay. He said that no matter what my mom loved me."

Sofia had to stop reading, right then, heart pounding.

A page later: "Dan was right. My mom only looks out for me. She must have a good reason for lying. I feel so bad about being angry at her. I can't imagine how awful her life must have been for her to want to change her name and never talk to her parents again. She said my mom killed her brother. I will never in a million years believe that. There is no way."

The words broke what was left of Sofia's heart.

I will never in a million years believe that. There is no way.

Kate had believed in her even when Sofia hadn't believed in herself.

Sofia hungrily read every word in Kate's journals, looking for evidence that her daughter had hated her before she died. But what she read hurt more than Kate's hatred ever could.

"I feel so bad for my mama," Kate wrote. "She is so worried about something she can't control. I want to tell her that we can't pick our parents. Dan was right, it's not her fault."

And then, as she read more, Sofia sobbed.

"My grandmother is a horrible person," Kate wrote. "I can't believe my poor mom had to be raised by such an awful, awful woman. No wonder she told my dad her parents were dead. My poor mama. I don't know how she ever turned out as wonderful as she is. She's the best mama ever and there is no reason she should be after being raised by that awful woman."

Sofia cried as she read, her tears wetting the pages.

As she continued to read, Sofia realized that Kate had really fallen hard for that boy Ali. And, as far as Sofia could tell, it had stayed pretty innocent. Kate talked about not wanting to get too serious since she was leaving for college and he was leaving to go back to Somalia.

"But I think I love him. That's stupid, right? We are going to be living in different parts of the world. God, why is life so hard?"

Then, in June, with her new journal, the one Lily had taken and that Dan had found, the entries took a different tone.

"It's kind of weird. I woke up in the middle of the night at Lily's and Mr. Williams was standing in the doorway staring at me. When I sat up, he left without saying anything."

And a few pages later.

"Dan kissed me. I want to die."

Sofia sat back mouth open. She continued flipping pages, her legs falling asleep from sitting still. At one point, a uniformed officer peeked in but then quickly apologized and backed out. Marley must have explained her presence there.

Sofia continued to read. Kate wrote about finding love notes and flowers waiting for her at work and on her car windshield. From Dan.

"It's disgusting. At the same time, I feel sorry for him. How can I tell my mom and dad that their best friend is in love with me?"

Sofia's eyes blurred. But she turned to the next page and read on.

"Lily can never ever know. If I tell my mom and dad they'll confront Dan and then Lily's life will be destroyed. I can't do that to her."

That was it. The last page.

That was the last journal entry Kate ever wrote, the morning of her murder.

Sofia closed the journal.

It was truly over.

Sofia sat back. So much had happened in the past week.

Lily had pleaded guilty to involuntary manslaughter.

Sofia had been torn—trying to decide whether she should go visit Lily in jail and confront her.

Every day, a letter had come in the mail from Lily begging for forgiveness. The first day, Sofia had thrown the letter in the trash, but then late that night, got out of bed and read it by the light over the oven in the kitchen.

Lily had said she wanted to die. That she'd been wrong about everything. That killing Kate was an accident. She realized that the morning after Kate's death when Lily and Gretchen had gone back to the house in case Kate turned up. That's when she found Kate's journal and found out that Kate didn't love Dan. That Kate had been worried about Lily the whole time.

Lily realized as time passed that she'd been wrong about her Dad loving Kate more. He'd proven it when he raced over to help her hide Kate's body and then even more so over the last few months. She wasn't worthy of his love and devotion and wanted to die. She begged Sofia to come visit her. Sofia read every letter over and over. Lily never included details about that night in her letter, only saying Kate's death was a terrible accident.

But as far as Sofia was concerned it was cold-blooded murder.

Marley had provided details to convince her.

Lily had accidentally seen Dan and Kate meeting at the bookstore. She'd watched as Dan gave Kate the cuff bracelet.

Kate didn't know it was Lily's mother's bracelet. But Lily sure did. She'd never seen the bracelet in person, but she'd studied the photograph of her parents' honeymoon in Mexico.

This knowledge—that her Dad had given Kate a bracelet from her mother—sent Lily over the edge. She argued with Kate at the bar, saying she no longer wanted to be friends, but before she could bring up her dad, Kate left and headed toward Ali's.

Lily followed her.

Once Kate turned off the main drag onto Oak Street, Lily caught up and grabbed her, pushing her and confronting Kate about the bracelet. They fought, struggled. Kate fell and hit her head. Lily got on top of her and then took Kate's own scarf and wrapped it around her head, suffocating her.

After Lily murdered Kate, she called Dan, hysterical, asking for his help.

Investigators found minute traces of Kate's blood on a blanket in Dan's trunk. The theory is, Marley said, that he loaded Kate's body into the trunk, drove to the end of the street and tossed her over the small wall and down the steep hillside overlooking the Mississippi River.

Then he made a plan to protect Lily.

It was all there. It was a slam-dunk case, Marley said.

Sofia closed Kate's journals and decided she didn't need to see Lily in person.

She wanted the last word to be from Kate. Not Lily. It didn't matter how remorseful Lily was. Sofia wasn't interested in granting her forgiveness or absolution.

By reading Kate's journals, Kate would have the last word.

Besides, most likely, neither Dan nor Lily would ever be free again. And that would have to be good enough.

Sofia remembered Dan's taunting words the night he killed Gretchen: "I know you can barely control yourself. Just let your nature take over. You are a killer. Just like your father. Why hide it anymore?"

You are wrong, Dan Williams. I am not like my father. I am not like my mother. I am not a killer. What I do know, for certain, is that if I try very hard for the rest of my life and I'm very lucky, I might achieve a sliver of the goodness that was contained in my daughter. I might be able to spread the kindness and love and hope she had inside her. If I can do this even a little bit, then my life will have been worth living.

Scooping up the pages, she shoved them in her bag, then drove home and headed straight into the house. Inside, on the bookshelf, it only took her a second to find the book about being an empty nester from Dan. It was still facing out. Because of Kate's murder that night, she'd never opened it. Now, with trembling hands, she opened it. He had written an inscription on the title page.

"*To Sofia, the perfect parent with the perfect life.*"

Rage rippled through her.

Slamming the book closed, she swept out the French doors, grabbing a small bottle of lighter fluid from near the grill and a lighter and took the steps down into the side yard. Grabbing the recycling bin from the side of the house, she dumped papers and cardboard boxes into the fire pit and then tossed the book on top, dousing it all with gasoline. Right when she tossed in a lit match, Jason came outside. He'd been staying in the guest bedroom until he could move into his own apartment that weekend.

"Sofia? It's three in the morning." He spoke just as the flames sparked, shooting up six feet in the air. As the orange flames flickered between them, their eyes met and she simply nodded.

He turned and went back inside.

She sat there until dawn, until the last spark had died in the fire pit.

CHAPTER 81

SOFIA

D*ecember 2019*
Minneapolis

Deep wrinkles were etched in the woman's ebony face. Her eyes were so warm and welcoming Sofia wanted to hug her instead of just shake her hand.

"Welcome. Please come in and have a seat," the woman gestured to a wide empty room with a circle of chairs in the middle. "There's coffee and treats on the table. Please help yourself."

"Thank you," Jason said.

Sofia could tell he was nervous. He was biting his inner cheek like he did when he felt uncertain. They lingered at the table, pouring coffee and putting cookies on a plate until a few more people filed in and took seats.

Sofia found two chairs next to a small man in a red plaid coat.

Jason sat beside her. They still weren't living together. Jason had rented a small studio apartment downtown. But he'd only signed a six-month lease. They were working toward living together again someday. At least that's what they both told the marriage counselor.

Jason had passed on taking the new job. The thought of a move was too much to think about with what they'd gone through in the past year. And with the status of their marriage up in the air, it would've been the death knell for them.

Sofia was relieved. The idea of leaving behind the only home that Kate had ever known was now overwhelming. At first, the memories that filled the house had been too much, but now they comforted Sofia. She was confronted with Kate everywhere she looked. The bathroom filled with Kate singing pop songs in the shower, giggles from the first-time Kate laughed, lying in her crib, looking up at her mother making funny faces, even the echo of her shouts and slamming her bedroom door as a moody teenager. The house contained all of it and Sofia couldn't leave it behind. At least not right then.

A few people who had sat down spoke in low voices. It seemed like most people already knew one another.

Then the woman who greeted them at the front door cleared her throat.

"If she says something about 'moving on' I'm outta here," Sofia whispered to Jason.

It achieved the desired result: He cracked a tiny smile.

"I'm Glenda Hawkins. Thank you for coming to our meeting tonight. We are the Parents of Murdered Children group. If you accidentally wandered in here–God knows it won't be the first time—the Finding the Color of Your Aura class is down the hall."

A few people snickered.

"Our guest speaker today is Cristina Pippa from the Attorney General's Office." Hawkins gestured at a pretty woman with long blonde hair and bright blue eyes beside her. "She will speak about the legal rights of crime victims and will walk us through the criminal justice process."

The woman smiled.

"But first, let's do introductions," Glenda said. "As I said, I'm Glenda. My son was killed by his fiancé's ex-boyfriend."

One by one each person stood and told why they were there. Some people cried. Others recited details emotionlessly.

Jason and Sofia exchanged looks.

Sofia listened, but she also started to flip through the pamphlet she'd picked up near the coffee. It listed October Anniversaries. Names of children with the date of death underneath.

It also had a section called "Trial, Judicial, and Arrest Updates."

It listed details of the arrest of a mother who had killed her fourteen-year-old son. It also gave the trial date of a daycare provider who hung a baby.

The last few pages contained letters and essays written by parents to their deceased children. Sofia quickly closed the brochure, tears pricking her eyes.

Then, the man in the plaid coat beside Sofia stood. His son was involved in gangs in North Minneapolis. His son was killed in crossfire two years ago. The entire family was devastated. His wife left him and moved back to Mexico. His sixteen-year-old daughter tried to commit suicide. He got a DUI. He lost his job. They lost their house. But he has been clean and sober for three months. He has a new job at Home Depot. They rent an apartment in a safer neighborhood. His daughter is doing well, getting straight A's at her new high school.

Sofia stood. It was her turn.

"My name is Sofia Castellucci Kennedy. My seventeen-year-old daughter Kate was murdered by her best friend."

Jason reached out and squeezed her hand.

She took a deep breath and told her story.

• • • •

FROM THE AUTHOR: HERE is a sneak peek at another standalone novel I wrote. Please continue scrolling to my bookshelf for all my books including my two different crime thriller series.

SANCTUARY CITY[1]

By Kristi Belcamino

1. https://geni.us/SanctuaryCity

PROLOGUE

A*pril 20, 2019*

At first, Timothy McDonald thought he was seeing things. His truck jerked over the potholes, making his headlights bounce erratically, distorting once familiar shapes and shadows. A thick line of trees bordered the old logging road, blocking out the sunrise to the east.

He swiped a beefy hand across his eyes and turned down the thrashing guitar riffs blaring from his speakers as if that'd help him see more clearly. It'd been a long night what with Sandra showing up sloshed, hauling him out of bed for another round of Jack Daniels. He'd offered a feeble protest, but her dimples won him over the same way they did twenty years ago at Sanctuary High School.

As his rusted-out 1986 Ford Ranger slowed, Timothy knew it wasn't lack of sleep causing hallucinations—there *was* something crawling on the side of the road, dragging across the pine needles.

Something bloody.

He slammed on the brakes, skidding to a stop.

A pale arm rose from the pile of flesh.

Timothy leapt out of his Ford and was nearly on top of the small form when he drew up short. He yanked off his John Deere tractor hat, tore at his hair, and bellowed into the dark. "Jesus Christ. It's a goddamn little kid."

He knelt down. It was a girl, maybe his niece Jeannie's age, stuck somewhere between a child and a teenager. Other than that, he couldn't tell anything about her except she had long hair matted with blood. Her head was turned toward him, resting on her arm. His fingers trembled as he lifted a sticky clump of bloody hair away from her face, revealing a large brown eye. His body heaved with relief when a small sound, barely a sigh, emerged from her tiny mouth.

He fumbled for his cell phone before he realized he'd left it in the truck.

"Hang in there. I'm gonna get help."

Panic flashed across the brown eye and a small sound bubbled out of her mouth. He squeezed her hand softly.

"I won't leave you. I promise. I'll be right back." He tried to sound reassuring.

He raced to the truck. It took three tries for his fingers to stab the right numbers.

"Holy Christ, this is so bad," he said when 911 answered. "Got a little girl up here on Old Courtemanche Road by Whiskey Flats, just come crawling out of the woods and she's hurt bad, real bad."

"What's the nature of her injuries?" The dispatcher sounded bored.

Timothy glanced over at the girl lit up in the halo of his headlights. She hadn't moved.

"She's bleeding something fierce. Everywhere. Like a goddamned horror movie. Get someone up here fast. Please. Goddammit, quit asking me questions and get someone up here now."

CHAPTER ONE

March 10, 2019

Roll call tonight was excruciating. Officer Maggie Bychowski felt the glares like small pinpricks piercing her back.

Based on the mumbled insults drifting her way, she wondered if a Sanctuary Police Officer had ever been more despised. *Rookie. Boot. Newbie. Lesbian. Cunt.*

The words, combined with the overpowering smell of cigarettes and aftershave from the next guy over, sent a wave of revulsion through her.

Maggie shut her eyes for a second. If she could only take a little nap. Just a tiny one. A catnap. Like Yoko Ono and John Lennon used to take. For fifteen minutes. If she did that, she could make it through the rest of the day on the three hours of sleep under her belt. She could park her squad on some shady abandoned street, put her sunglasses on and nap for a few minutes.

Somebody nudged her and her eyes flew open. It was Hendricks, the closest thing to a friend she had in this town. He didn't look her way, keeping his eyes trained on the lieutenant, but he gave a slow wink. Those eyelashes were such a waste on a man. But Hendricks knew how to work them like nobody's business.

She thrust her bony shoulders back and stood ramrod straight, pulling herself up to her full five-foot-eight inches. If she showed even a sliver of weakness, she was done for.

Thinking of the stack of overdue bills on her kitchen table, Maggie squeezed her hands into tight fists at her side and pressed her lips together. They could call her all the names they wanted. She'd put up with it all so her daughter could live in the clean, cozy—and safe—care home down the ridge in Apple Valley. Physically, Melody couldn't walk, couldn't talk, and didn't seem to notice whether her mother came to the care home every other day or once a month.

But she was safe there. And Maggie would do anything to keep her daughter safe. Even if it meant eating Ramen every night to pay the bills.

Six months ago, finding this job so close to the care home had seemed like a Godsend. Too bad nobody warned her when she joined the force that she'd be dealing with backward hick bigot cops who got away with the kind of immoral, unprofessional— hell, probably *illegal*—shit she'd already seen in her few short months with the department.

The lieutenant in the front of the room droned on: another string of car burglaries along Vista Drive; an abandoned meth lab found in the canyon down by Little Falls; and St. Mary's annual spaghetti dinner was tonight so officers should try to stop in and say hello.

Maggie had taken a spot in the back of the room—to be near Hendricks, but also a strategic move to make a quick exit. It was only when roll call was nearly over that she remembered rookies were supposed to be in the front row. Tomorrow she'd stand front and center.

As soon as the lieutenant finished reading the reports, Maggie was out the door toward the parking lot. Her squad, number 320, was the oldest car in the fleet. And for some reason—surprise, surprise—she was assigned this vehicle every shift. She'd bought half a dozen coconut tree deodorizers, but still occasionally caught a whiff of the sweat and vomit that had permanently seeped into the holding pen of a backseat. She suspected the squad sat empty on the days she didn't work.

By the time she checked the headlights, siren, emergency lights, and computer, several other officers had trickled into the parking lot. Most officers skipped the required vehicle safety checks and took off, probably heading toward the nearest donut drive-through.

But today three of them remained, clustered by a red mustang, talking in low voices, one guy spitting an ugly stream of chewing tobacco her way every once in a while. Although she was pretending not to pay attention, Maggie slid her eyes their way. They were all in plain clothes. Off duty.

After she couldn't put it off any longer, she popped the squad's trunk, reluctantly turning her back to the men's sneers. Even though she'd worked yesterday and been assigned this same squad, somehow the first aid kit, crime scene tape, fire extinguisher, and road flares that were supposed to be in the trunk were gone.

It meant she had to walk past the group and back into the station to stock her vehicle. She slipped on her sunglasses before heading their way.

To her dismay, as she grew closer to the men, her heart hammered and her palms grew slick. So far, they'd never said anything to her directly. It had always been the same passive-aggressive bullshit whispers she'd heard during roll call. But she had a feeling that was all going to end now.

CHAPTER TWO

One of the cops, a young baby-faced guy named Johnson, flexed the muscles bulging out of his short sleeves and side-stepped so he stood spread eagled in front of Maggie, his bulk blocking her way. His cropped hair stood up, still wet from a shower. A breeze rustled the leaves in nearby trees and brought with it the smell of his aftershave or deodorant or man perfume—whatever it was.

Maggie froze. But only for a second. There was a narrow slip of space between him and a car. She'd shoulder her way past. The last thing she wanted was physical confrontation—or any type of confrontation at all—but it didn't look like she had a choice. If she backed down, she was marked. Weak. A push over. A target and a victim. Steeling herself, she stepped forward.

The crackle of her radio stopped her. Dispatch was calling a code three—emergency response—lights and sirens. She dipped her head to listen to the small radio clipped to her shoulder.

An intruder on Skyline Drive. Called in by a child hiding in the house.

Maggie turned in mid stride and within seconds was in her squad, turning over the ignition. The address was only a few blocks away.

Maggie squealed out of the parking lot, reassuring herself by patting her gun in its holster as she peeled onto the main road. Blood racing, Maggie hit her lights and siren and huffed into her mike, "320 in service. En route."

"Good morning, 320. In service. En route Skyline Drive."

The dispatcher repeated the call information: a twelve-year-old girl had called 911, saying a man was in her house and was going to kill her.

Melody was twelve.

"Where's the girl now?"

"Stand by," the dispatcher said. A few seconds later: "Hiding in the closet, first door on right, top of stairs. Complainant says front door to house is unlocked."

Maggie pressed hard on the accelerator and skidded around a turn, feeling alive for the first time in months. Fact was, Maggie was an adrenaline junkie. She liked action. It was one reason the Navy commercials appealed to her and compelled her to sign up for a four-year tour.

Nowadays, the only rush Maggie got was when she ordered a triple espresso at the small-town coffee shop during her shift. And she only allowed herself that luxury on payday once every two weeks.

When she reached the address, Maggie jerked the steering wheel and squealed to a stop in the circular driveway lined with hedges. In front of her lay a sprawling two-story home perched on the edge of a canyon overlooking the college town of Apple Valley below. Even from the driveway, Maggie could tell the back of the house offered stunning views of the California coastal mountain range in the hazy distance. She grabbed her mic.

"On scene ... I mean 10-23."

"Unit 320 is 10-23," the dispatcher repeated back. "Units 370 and 420 en route."

Her fellow officer's sirens grew closer as she headed toward the front door with her service weapon drawn, the gun feeling solid and cold under her grip. Maggie didn't even consider waiting for back-up. If there was someone inside trying to hurt the girl, any hesitation could mean the difference between life and death.

Maggie turned the knob and then kicked the door open with her foot, swinging her gun in a wide arc before stepping inside. Nothing moved. To the left was a large living room filled with flowers. They were droopy, turning brown, filling the house with the faint whiff of decay. The staircase lay a few feet to her right. Scrambling, she scaled the stairs, her back to the wall, head pivoting, scanning from the bottom to the top of the stairs and out into the room beyond. Along with the sound of her breathing and the distant hum of a refrigerator, a rhythmic clicking noise she couldn't identify sent her heart skittering into her throat.

When she reached the top of the stairs, she paused, listened, and peered around the wall, arching her neck to see, her finger involuntarily snaking toward the trigger on her gun. The carpeted hall at the top of the stairs was empty. Keeping her back to the wall and her eyes on the doorways lining the hall, she leaned over and turned the doorknob of the closet and was greeted with a piercing scream. Maggie felt sweat drip down her temple but there was no movement down the hall. She slid her eyes down to the open door of the closet.

A dark-haired girl cowered in a corner, partially hidden behind some coats.

Maggie crouched and patted the girl's knee, keeping her eyes trained down the hallway.

"Shhhhh. It's okay. I'm a police officer," she said in a low voice. "What's your name, honey?"

"Ellie."

She shot another quick glance at the girl. The girl's eyes were wild, frantic. Even though her shoulders were already pressed against the wall, the girl tried to scoot further back into the closet. She wore garish lipstick and thick eye makeup. She looked older than twelve.

But then again, Maggie didn't know what twelve-year-olds looked like nowadays. Melody's mind was that of a two-year-old trapped in a twelve-year-olds changing body.

"It's okay, Ellie. You're safe now." Maggie leaned toward her shoulder mic. "I'm with the girl. Tell the other units to proceed with caution. No suspect in sight."

Maggie's radio crackled. She quickly lowered the volume. "Unit 320 is code 4 with the girl," the dispatcher reported back.

"Not code 4 yet. Still need back up. Keep 'em coming," Maggie said. She was on one knee, half in and half out of the closet, gun pointed down the hallway. She glanced at the girl and held her finger to her lips. The girl nodded solemnly.

"Copy. Back up en route."

The sound of the sirens grew closer until they were right outside.

"Units 370 and 420 are 10-23." *On scene*. The dispatcher's voice sounded far away.

From downstairs, the front door slammed open followed by a volley of shouts and stomping feet. Maggie's limbs flooded with relief, but she kept alert, eyes focused on the hallway, every cell in her body was on high alert, ready to pounce. Or flee. She reached back and tried to give the girl's hand a squeeze. The girl jerked her hand away.

"I want my dad. Get my dad. Why isn't he here yet? I want my dad."

Maggie leaned into her mic and whispered. "Has the homeowner been notified?"

"Stand by," the dispatcher said.

Meanwhile Maggie heard shouting downstairs. "Clear."

Still, she kept her eye on the doorways lining the hall, imagining a dark figure darting out any second. Her radio crackled. "Unit 320? Judge Hatton is on way."

Judge Hatton?

"Your dad's on his way, honey," she whispered back into the closet. She couldn't search the rest of the upstairs until she got the girl out of here. Right now, her job was to keep the kid safe.

A face appeared at the top of the stairs. Hendricks. His black eyes flashed with intensity. His gun was drawn, both arms extended in front of him as he rounded the corner. He gestured with his chin down the hall. Maggie shook her head.

"Downstairs is clear," he said in a low voice. "Let's get the girl out of here."

Officer Johnson's baby face appeared behind Hendricks. He was still in his plainclothes, but had thrown his bulletproof vest over them, apparently not off duty anymore. Maggie looked away. The girl scrambled out of the closet and threw herself at Hendricks. To Maggie's surprise, Hendricks led her down the stairs. She'd assumed he'd have handed the kid off to her so he could search the upstairs with Johnson.

Maggie stood, holding her gun in front of her with both hands. She glanced over at Johnson and nodded.

"Let's go," she said in a barely audible voice and jutted her chin. He went left. She went right.

Filled with a surreal sense of hyper-alertness, Maggie peered inside the first door, pushing it all the way open with her gun. An office. She could see everything with one glance. Except inside the closet. Creeping over to it, with her pulse pounding in her ears, she kicked open the partly ajar door, gun extended in front of her. She let out her breath. Empty.

She exchanged a look in the hall with Johnson and they moved onto the next set of doors.

A few minutes later there was only one doorway left for her to clear. The door was open. The girl's bedroom. It smelled like the peach scented candles that were scattered on nearly every surface. First, Maggie checked the closet and then kneeled down to check under the bed. When she stood, she realized she was hyperventilating.

The room had cast a spell on her. The second she walked in, her mouth had grown dry. She was both attracted and repelled by what this room offered up to her—a sobering snapshot of a normal twelve-year-old girl's life.

Even thinking the word *normal* made Maggie cringe, but it was true.

The room was everything her daughter would never have.

The walls were plastered with framed posters of movies and pop stars, such as Adele and Taylor Swift. A multi-tiered lavender shoe rack was piled with fancy sneakers and ballet flats and sparkly sandals with small heels. Across from the bed a small white desk with a ceramic mug full of pencils and pens next to a laptop with a purple case. Maggie absentmindedly trailed her fingers over the keyboard. As she did, the laptop flickered. The page was all dark greens and black. In the middle of the screen was the silhouette of a tall figure in the middle of a woodsy area. Above his head dripping green letters said "Shadow Man."

Feeling as if she were snooping, Maggie gave one last glance at the computer screen and moved over to the dresser. The mirror above the dresser was lined with photos of the girl and her friends ... one girl in the picture had curly hair like Melody.

Maggie leaned in to see the picture better. As she did, she felt another presence in the room. Whirling, she reached for her gun. Johnson stood in the doorway, an ugly smirk marring his baby face.

"Clear," she said and brushed by him, feeling her cheeks warm as she hurried out of the room.

• • • •

AFTER A THOROUGH SEARCH, no signs of an intruder had been found. She was about to go talk to the girl when Hendricks called to her. He was in a giant finished basement lined with at least ten French doors opening up onto a small deck. The deck was ground level on the steep hillside and several trails led away from it into the canyon. Maggie tried all the doors.

"You found them like this?" she said.

"Yup. Not one of them locked."

Maggie eyed the wilderness beyond with its thick trees and steep drop. If someone had been in the house they were long gone.

Out in the driveway, a community service officer sat in a squad with the girl. Hendricks and Maggie paused on the front porch. The girl's father was expected at any minute.

"I already talked to the kid," he said, lighting a cigarette.

"Heard her dad was a judge."

"Yup. Judge Hatton. He's buddies with Sgt. Earl. They play poker together. With Earl's cousin the D.A., brother the mayor, and uncle the chief." Hendricks turned and blew his cigarette smoke away from Maggie.

"Good grief. Is nepotism this common everywhere in Northern California?"

"Total incest."

"What'd you get from the kid?"

The girl had told Hendricks she was about to leave when she heard the front door open. When she looked down the stairs, she saw a man with a knife standing there. She hid in the closet and called 911.

"She say what he looked like?"

"Doesn't remember," Hendricks said, exhaling a plume of smoke above Maggie's head.

"Doesn't remember?"

"Yup."

"But saw a knife?"

"Yup."

Maggie thought about it. The girl had run and hid in the closet, which had no lock. Most people would automatically run to a bathroom or their bedroom and lock the door. She'd seen locks on every upstairs door. Except the closet. The closet was the first room you came to upstairs and also the closest room to the intruder at the bottom of the stairs. It didn't jibe. But then again, who knew how people acted when they were frightened beyond belief, panicking.

As she stood on the front porch with Hendricks, Maggie crouched down and took a look at the front door. Didn't have a scratch on it. No sign of forced entry.

"Why the knife?" Maggie said, squinting her eyes looking off into the distance. She could figure the luxury home would attract a burglar, but most burglars didn't carry knives. "Think he was after the girl?"

"Nah. Think that's why he bailed—cause she was there," Hendricks said. "The last thing a burg wants is to find someone home. They just want to get in and get out with the loot."

He smiled widely, his white teeth unnervingly attractive against his dark skin. He stubbed out his cigarette on the bottom of his boot and then put the butt in a small plastic bag. Maggie wondered why he was so nice to her when everyone else either ignored her or harassed her.

Maggie thought about what he said. "Yeah. But it doesn't sync. I'm hung up on the knife."

"Maybe it wasn't a knife. The kid's imagination might have turned anything silver into a knife. Maybe a crow bar or some burglar tool." Hendricks scrunched up his face. "But damn if there isn't a single sign he forced his way in. *Nada*."

Maggie backed up off the porch and looked around. The nearest house was over a row of hedges. "If she hadn't seen him come in the front door, he could have easily come up from the canyon and walked right in to the basement."

"She said she saw him open the front door. Could've brought the tools and then tried the door handle and boom—easy peasy, unlocked. Like Occam's Razor—the simplest explanation is often the correct one."

Maggie nodded. But still. It was odd.

"Why don't you wait for the dad? I'll head back and file a report," she said, heading to her car.

Then she turned. "By the way, Hendricks, I figured something out."

"Oh yeah, what's that?" He loped down the steps toward her.

"I figured out why you're still single."

He tilted his head back and laughed. They both knew his dating life was out-of-control crazy, with him sometimes dating five women at one time and then dumping them all because they wanted to get married and have his babies. He wasn't interested in getting married until he was at least forty, he said.

"Oh yeah, why's that?" he said, putting his hands on his hips with a cocky grin. "Why, pray tell, am I still single?"

"Because you smell like an ashtray." She turned and walked away without waiting for his answer, but heard his guffaw behind her.

"Fair enough," he hollered after her. "But what's your excuse?"

Ten years ago, that would've felt like a punch to the gut. Five years ago, it would've still stung. Today, Maggie smiled and flipped him off as she walked away.

At that moment, a black Hummer skidded to a stop in the driveway. The girl burst out of the community service officer's car and raced toward the car, her long dark hair streaming behind her. The man behind the wheel leapt out and swooped down to hug her. It must be the judge. He didn't look like judges Maggie had seen before. He looked more like an actor who would play a judge in a porno. His fit body was encased in tight black jeans, black cowboy boots, and a crisp royal blue shirt under a black blazer. His hair was respectably short except for a hunk of dark bangs that hung in his eyes a little. Maggie would bet money his shirt matched his eyes. He didn't look like the sort of man who wore—or did—anything without careful calculation.

The girl stood on tiptoe and pressed her face into her father's jacket for a few seconds, her cropped top riding up and revealing a slight belly. When she pulled back, the girl swiped at the tears streaming down her face.

"I thought he was dead." The girl's voice was stuffed up.

The man grabbed his daughter with a fierce look. "He's dead. I made sure of that. I saw his cold dead body. He can never hurt you again."

Maggie paused with her squad door open wide, unable to not eavesdrop. Did they know the suspect?

"I'll drive you to school, sweetheart," the man said and ruffled the girl's hair.

"I thought you had a breakfast date with Janet? I thought you didn't have time to take me to school today."

"All that can wait," the man said. "This is more important."

"So, can we stop at Starbucks?"

"Sure."

The girl glanced around. Her eyes met Maggie's. The girl's face held a strange look of triumph.

Maggie walked over. "Sir, I was wondering if your daughter recognized the intruder?"

He shot a glance at the girl who was glaring at Maggie.

Then he looked up and shook his head slowly. "No. No, I'm afraid not."

"My colleague has a few questions for you," she gestured toward Hendricks who was walking over. "But before that, I'm wondering if you always keep the French doors in your basement unlocked."

The judge ran his fingers through his hair and made a face. "Yeah. I do. It's just way easier that way. I always keep the door down to the basement locked, though, at night and when we're not home."

"Do you think it was locked today?"

The judge thought for a second and said, "Yes, I think so. But if someone came in the front door, they could just open the basement door from the main level. It opens on that side even if it is locked."

Maggie nodded. She watched the girl twirl her hands around her father's arm, burying her face in his shirtsleeve.

"You think that's how they got away."

"Maybe." Hendricks was at her side. "I'll let Officer Hendricks take over. Thank you for your time."

Maggie slipped into the driver's seat of her squad. Before she pulled away, she caught another glimpse of the man with his daughter. She shook off the melancholy feeling it gave her. It was tough to see the interaction between a father and daughter knowing it was yet another moment Melody would never have.

READ MORE HERE[1]: https://geni.us/SanctuaryCity

• • • •

1. https://geni.us/SanctuaryCity

AUTHOR'S NOTE

Getting to know my readers and building strong relationships with them is one of the best parts of being a writer. I'd love to know more about you and more about what you thought about this book. What did you like about it? Who was your favorite character? What do you want to see, or think will happen next?

Please reach out to me and let me know. I want to hear from you. Because while I'm a writer, I'm always a reader first. I know that when it comes to the books I read, I love connecting with the author. Often, when I interact with authors I love I get downright giddy!

Ask my family how I act each and every time S.E. Hinton responds to my tweets. (HINT: I am a ridiculously starstruck fangirl! Every. Single. Time.)

Or what about the time I got to interview Jackie Collins on Huffington Post's live video. (Still one of the greatest moments of my writer life!) (Only thing that tops that is when I opened up an email from Lisa Unger telling me that she read and liked my book and would be happy to support it with a quote we could use on the book cover! A dream come true right then and there!

Or years and years ago when I was a new, sleep-deprived mother who looked forward to my monthly book club for every second of the days leading up to it and having the New York Times bestselling author Adriana Trigiani call into our bookclub. (I had her on speakerphone and when I said hello, she said, "Hey, baby, how's it going?" and proceeded to chat with us and talk to us about what we thought would happen in her next book.

I told myself right then and there that if I were ever a published author I would interact with readers the way she did. And sometimes dreams come true! I'm a published writer who has readers who enjoy my books. Even writing that still seems surreal.

So, all of this leads me to tell you about my two favorite ways to interact with my readers:

My newsletter. My private Facebook group. Hopefully you will consider joining both.

I send out a newsletter with details of new releases, special offers, giveaways and other bits of news about my books.

When you sign up for my no-spam mailing list, I'll send you all of this free stuff:

1. A copy of GIA, the introductory novella for my Gia Santella Crime Thriller series.
2. A copy of THE SAINT, the introductory novella for my Gabriella Giovanni Mystery series.
3. A copy of EVA, the introductory novella for the Queen of Spades Thrillers.

You can get the three novellas by signing up at https://www.subscribepage.com/KristiBelcamino

You can join my private Facebook group, Crime, Coffee & Cannoli here: https://www.facebook.com/groups/CrimeCoffeeCannoli/

• • • •

• • • •

Kristi Belcamino Bookshelf

#

Gia Santella Crime Thriller Series

Gia

City of the Dead[1]

Forgotten Island[2]

Dark Night of the Soul[3]

Lone Raven[4]

Black Widow[5]

Taste of Vengeance[6]

Day of the Dead[7]

Border Line[8] (Out March 26)

• • • •

Gabriella Giovanni Mystery Series

The Saint[9]

1. https://www.amazon.com/City-Dead-Santella-Crime-Thriller-ebook/dp/B0751LCQLQ
2. https://www.amazon.com/Forgotten-Island-Santella-Crime-Thrillers-ebook/dp/B07562K7HZ/
3. https://www.amazon.com/gp/product/B0767MXG14/ref=series_rw_dp_sw
4. https://www.amazon.com/Lone-Raven-Santella-Crime-Thrillers-ebook/dp/B0774H5WBR/
5. https://www.amazon.com/Black-Widow-Santella-Crime-Thrillers-ebook/dp/B07B6RG8GY/
6. https://www.amazon.com/Taste-Vengeance-Santella-Thriller-Thrillers-ebook/dp/B07FPMWQKS/
7. https://www.amazon.com/Dead-Santella-Crime-Thrillers-Book-ebook/dp/B07G65ZJXM/
8. https://geni.us/Gia8Amazon
9. https://www.amazon.com/Saint-prequel-enovella-Gabriella-Giovanni-ebook/dp/B074D4DLBN

Blessed are the Dead[10]
Blessed are the Meek[11]
Blessed are Those Who Weep[12]
Blessed are Those Who Mourn[13]
Blessed are the Peacemakers[14]
Blessed are the Merciful[15]

• • • •

Queen of Spades Thrillers
Eva
Queen of Spades[16] (May 2019)

• • • •

Standalones
Coming For You[17]
Sanctuary City[18]

• • • •

10. https://www.amazon.com/Blessed-are-Dead-Gabriella-Mysteries-ebook/dp/B00GLS4VR8/

11. https://www.amazon.com/gp/product/B00GLS4VS2/ref=series_rw_dp_sw

12. https://www.amazon.com/gp/product/B00MMG1AUY/ref=series_rw_dp_sw

13. https://www.amazon.com/Blessed-are-Those-Who-Mourn-ebook/dp/B00SG1ELNW/

14. https://www.amazon.com/Blessed-Peacemakers-Gabriella-Giovanni-Mysteries-ebook/dp/B074RJYMP6/

15. https://www.amazon.com/Blessed-Merciful-Gabriella-Giovanni-Mystery-ebook/dp/B07992159X/

16. https://geni.us/QueenofSpades

17. https://geni.us/ComingForYou

18. https://geni.us/SanctuaryCity

DID YOU LIKE THIS BOOK?

Reviews are the lifeblood of this author business. Reviews, honest reviews, mean the world to me. They don't have to be fancy, either. Nobody is critiquing you on your review. And they don't always have to be five-star, either. What matters is that people are reading and have opinions on my books. I am a fairly new writer and don't have the marketing push that many other writers do that gets their books out in front of other readers.

What I do have is you.

I am unbelievably lucky to have very passionate and loyal readers who take the time to let me know what they think of my books (and sometimes even where they think I could improve).

If you liked this book, I would be extremely grateful if you could take a few minutes out of your day to leave a review HERE[1]. As I said, it doesn't need to be long or involved, anything will help. Thank you!

••••

1. https://geni.us/ComingForYou

ABOUT THE AUTHOR

KRISTI BELCAMINO IS a Macavity, Barry, and Anthony Award-nominated author, a newspaper cops reporter, and an Italian mama who makes a tasty biscotti. As an award-winning crime reporter at newspapers in California, she flew over Big Sur in an FA-18 jet with the Blue Angels, raced a Dodge Viper at Laguna Seca and watched autopsies.

Her books feature strong, kickass, independent women facing unspeakable evil in order to seek justice for those unable to do so themselves.

Belcamino has written and reported about many high-profile cases including the Laci Peterson murder and Chandra Levy's disappearance. She has appeared on Inside Edition and her work has appeared in the New York Times, Writer's Digest, Miami Herald, San Jose Mercury News, and Chicago Tribune. Kristi now works part-time as a police reporter at the St. Paul Pioneer Press. She lives in Minneapolis with her husband and her two fierce daughters.

Find out more at http://www.kristibelcamino.com[1]. Find her on YouTube[2] here (https://www.youtube.com/kristibelcamino), Insta-

1. http://www.kristibelcamino.com/

gram here[3] (https://www.instagram.com/kristi_belcamino/), Facebook at https://www.facebook.com/kristibelcaminowriter/ or on Twitter @KristiBelcamino.

• • • •

@Cover design by SwoonWorthy Book Covers

2. https://www.youtube.com/kristibelcamino

3. https://www.instagram.com/kristi_belcamino/

Made in United States
Troutdale, OR
01/20/2024

17013428R00224